CROOKED MOON

A NOVEL

by

LISETTE BRODEY

SABERLEE
BOOKS

Published by:

Saberlee Books
Los Angeles, CA
United States of America

lisettebrodey.com
twitter.com/lisettebrodey
facebook.com/BrodeyAuthor

Cover design & Illustration by Charles Roth
Author photo by Robert Antal
Book set in Minion Pro 11.5pt. type

lisettebrodey.com
twitter.com/lisettebrodey
facebook.com/BrodeyAuthor

ISBN-13: 978-0-9815836-6-2
Printed in the United States of America

To Charles,
my friend beyond measure

Wisdom entails years of sleep,
And waking to find the river is deep,
Falling closely avoiding the rocks,
Knowing the time in a world without clocks.
—Lisette Brodey

*With very special thanks
to Laura Daly, for her expert editing;
to Kenneth Brodey, for his preliminary editing;
to Talatha Allen, for her amazing inspiration;
to PattiAnn Cutter, for her unwavering support;
to Diana Bayer, for her gracious assistance;
to Kim Reiter, for her extraordinary thoughtfulness;
to Michael Putini, for giving me enough material to write
another 50 books;
to Charles Roth, for his tireless efforts on behalf of this book,
to Dara Brodey, my niece extraordinaire,
and
to my mother, Jean L. Brodey*

SABERLEE BOOKS BY LISETTE BRODEY

Crooked Moon
Squalor, New Mexico
Molly Hacker Is Too Picky!
Mystical High
Desert Star
Drawn Apart

CROOKED MOON

CHAPTER 1

Surreal. Like the odd light of day when the sun is eclipsed, or the melting of time and reality in a Dali painting; that is how the physical act of returning to Rainytown felt to Callie Hethers. Parallel parked in her green BMW and neatly pressed in her country club whites, she quietly surveyed the blue-collar universe she had just reentered. Looking across the street at the modest row home in which she grew up, she saw Callie Mason, dirty kneed and pigtailed, swinging Barbie by a tuft of platinum vinyl hair as she played jump rope with the neighborhood children.

Aunt Emily's voice was loud and cheerful as she called her niece to supper, reminding her to perform the necessary preprandial ablutions, then announcing that evening's fare as if to coax her into obeying.

"Don't forget to wash up! Then we'll have spaghetti!" came the familiar cry. Once, Callie Mason wanted to know what would be served if she didn't wash up.

"The palm of my hand on your rear end," her aunt teased. "And just for that, I want you to wash behind the ears…twice!"

Callie giggled and scampered off to the powder room, returning ten minutes later with the rest of the family in tow: Barbie, Ken, Smokey the Bear, and Bailey the cat. The animate family members, Aunt Emily, Callie, and Bailey, were all privileged to have chairs of their own at the dinner table, while the rest of the brood had to share the one remaining chair and to eat pretend food.

Callie Mason had been only six when she came to live with her aunt, Emily Phillips. Her mother, Anisa, who had been quite a beauty, married a wealthy older widower from Philadelphia's Main Line at the age of twenty-three, deluding herself into believing that the procurement of a fortune was all one required for a happy life. Love, companionship, a sense of purpose, a career, and family were all extraneous concepts not worthy of prenuptial consideration. Anisa's name had barely been added to her husband's credit card accounts when the stork handed her an I.O.U. — just moments before her first New York shopping spree had come to pass. Nausea en route to Bloomingdale's! What had she done (as if she didn't know) to bring on such a cruel cosmic joke? She certainly had no desire to shop for "fat clothes" and "baby things" — just to prepare for a child she hadn't even ordered. Perhaps if the young Mrs. Mason had matching friends with whom a new baby would've been a social asset, a pregnancy might have been advantageous to her. But as things stood, it was not.

When Callie was born, however, Anisa did her best to make sure that the nannies and servants took good care of the infant, while she attended to more pressing matters, like reclaiming her figure and acquiring her long-overdue wardrobe. Once accomplished, she actually had time to develop a fondness for the little one, but it was a fondness one develops for a friend's or a neighbor's child — not for one's own.

Samuel Mason, Callie's father, who had been childless on his first go-around, doted on his little girl to the best of his ability. Most of his efforts, however, were wasted trying to please the child he had married, not the one he had sired. With great patience, he endeavored to slowly ease Anisa into his circle of friends, but she was not interested in "those old codgers, coots, and curmudgeons, who played something called bridge instead of jumping off of one." Exasperated by the sheer futility of his efforts, and realizing that the various "C words" also described him, Samuel left town to oversee his European business concerns. Anisa stayed happily behind, taking up with a string of naughty young men, mostly opportunists like herself, who, when she had finished with them, called her some "C words" of their own.

Sinking quickly into her own quagmire, Anisa planned a foray into the society she had previously snubbed, a tight clique comprised mainly of the offspring of her husband's friends. Realizing that her reputation had long since preceded her, and that she was neither wanted nor welcome, she tried contacting the friends she had known before marrying. But they had no interest in reuniting with someone who had clearly discarded them long ago. And so, with nowhere to go, Anisa dove headfirst into the bottle, where she splashed around recklessly for the next several years. At the age of thirty, she came close to "drowning," and on the day following her suicide attempt, Callie was sent to live with Anisa's older sister, Emily, while Anisa was discreetly carried off to a "resting hospital," one with pastoral grounds and a pleasant-sounding name.

Emily, whom the times considered a maiden aunt and not a single woman, was delighted to raise Callie. At forty-five, she had long since given up hope of getting married and had resigned herself to being a temporary mother to the many fourth-graders who passed through her classroom. Meantime, Samuel Mason had taken up permanent residence in London, seeing his little girl only on occasional visits home, though he made a point to call her at least twice a month. Callie adored her elusive father, who had promised his daughter and her aunt a trip to England for Callie's twelfth birthday. Sadly, he died of a heart attack just two months short of fulfilling his promise.

Feeling bereft of parental ties, Callie informed her aunt that she wanted to visit her mother in the "resting hospital." Emily agreed to make the necessary inquiries, only to learn that Anisa had "unofficially released" herself years ago, leaving no forwarding address. The doctor whom Emily spoke with was quite surprised to hear that her former patient had never arrived in Rainytown. Anisa, it seems, had loudly proclaimed to the attending staff that she had every intention of reclaiming her daughter upon release, official or otherwise. But she was never heard from again and that was just fine with Emily. And so, Callie continued to live a life without biological parents, though Emily made a finer mother than biology could ever have provided. And, although he was no longer able to offer paternal affection, Samuel left behind a very large trust fund to pay for Callie's college and living expenses and to help her live subsequently in the manner to which she would become accustomed.

Callie's greatest happiness in those years, without a doubt, came from her best friend, Mary Frances "Frankie" Cavalese, a young girl of the same age who resided just on the other side of Callie's bedroom wall. When the girls were ten, they joined forces to develop their own "horse code," a series of long and short knocks that conveyed secret messages. It was actually the brainstorm of Frankie's younger brother, Paulie, who had seen it in a war movie on TV, although he was never rewarded for his suggestion by being made privy to the code once it had been devised.

During Callie's first four years in Rainytown, as much as she adored Emily, she was often envious of Frankie for having "a real family," one that included a brother, a mother, and a father. But there was nothing utopian about the Cavalese family. With each passing year came more fights, more slamming of doors, and more ugly words that rang loudly through the shared walls.

Late one night, when the girls were twelve, with no previous notice, Louie Cavalese left for good. While his girlfriend sat outside in the car, with the engine purring, Louie said good-bye to his children and told his wife, Ruby, he was calling it quits. Then, looking right through her, he grabbed the suitcases he had packed in secret the previous morning and fled into the night. Ruby, who had followed him as far as the porch, canceled her pursuit when she saw him jump into the waiting car of another woman.

Now, as Callie Hethers sat in her BMW, waiting only for the courage to cross the street, she remembered Ruby Cavalese's tortured howl upon realizing that her husband had left her for someone else. She recalled how Callie Mason and Emily, awakened from their sleep, had rushed next door to investigate, just as the neighbors up and down the street had stepped onto their own porches to witness the fireworks. Frankie, she remembered, had cried, while a devastated Paulie reacted with frightening nonchalance. Emily, after realizing what had happened, put her arms around Ruby with sweet comfort, then quickly ushered Callie, who had recently lost her own father, back to bed.

Mindlessly, Callie Hethers picked up the chamois cloth that lay on her dashboard and began polishing the area in front of her. As she wiped down the leather steering wheel, she thought about Frankie. Going around for the second time, she wondered what became of her, and on the third revolution, it struck her just how much she really cared. Discomforted by this revelation, she looked desperately around the front seat for something else to focus on, but there was nothing else to distract her but well-paid-for elegance, reflective of the life she had been fortunate to lead in the twenty-three years since leaving…and a road map.

On the day that Callie left for college, both Frankie and Callie had silently feared the inevitable: that despite the best of intentions, their friendship would never survive the impending changes. Frankie, who dreamed of going to art school to become a teacher, took a job as a waitress at the Rainytown Diner. Louie's checks were not enough to afford her the luxury of a further education, and Ruby's salary as a supermarket cashier was just enough to keep the family going. With the hope of a brighter tomorrow, Frankie, saddened but not complaining, put her blue-and-white uniform on and went to work.

Just seventy-five miles away, in an idyllic Pennsylvania town, Callie was also putting on her blues and whites. Everyone agreed: it was important to have a proper wardrobe in the school colors, especially during football season. And while Callie learned the football cheers, Frankie learned diner lingo: "put out the lights and cry" meant an order of liver and onions, and "throwing it in the mud" meant adding chocolate syrup — but none of it meant anything at all.

When Callie came home that Christmas, the girls tried to pretend that circumstances had not divided them, knowing full well that their bond, at best, was strained. They exchanged gifts and made plans for the summer, but Callie never came home again, at least not to stay. That summer, she and a college friend headed for Nantucket and learned to sail, while Frankie learned that "wrecked hen fruit" means scrambled eggs and that life is never fair.

In her junior year, Callie met a Swarthmore senior named Jackson Hethers, whom she married two years later. She was drawn to his sense of humor, his appreciation of the absurd, and his sensitivity; they were qualities that she and Frankie both sought in a man (they'd discussed it so many times), and she knew Frankie would approve of her choice. But Callie never found the opportunity to introduce the two. Frankie, who heard about the wedding through Emily, pressed her for all the details, despite the fact that she was shattered by the snub. But when Emily brought word that Callie's twins, Stephen and Molly, had been born, Frankie was no longer interested in any elaboration. She just went to her room and cried, then swore never to think of Callie Mason Hethers again.

Over the years, Callie had made a diligent effort not to think about how her swift emigration from Rainytown might have affected her former best friend, despite the fact she had valid reasons, she believed, for having done so. But she had her own issues with abandonment, having been tossed aside by her parents, and didn't need or want the guilt of having done the same to someone else, especially someone whom she loved so much and who had loved her so much in return. But that didn't make her any less aware that she had most likely caused Frankie grievous pain; she merely relegated those feelings to a latent corner of her mind.

Callie unbuckled her seat belt, flipped down the sun visor, and checked her makeup in the small mirror, removing a tiny black ball of dried eyeliner from the corner of her left eye. No more stalling: she had a tough job ahead of her, and it was time to get started. Emily, who had been living in a nursing home for the past ten years, had recently died and the old lady who had been renting her house had gone to live with her granddaughter. Now the house was empty, and it was Callie's job to remove Emily's possessions, to make arrangements for the distribution of her personal effects, and to have the house cleaned out for the new owners. To Callie, it seemed as if everyone she cherished had left her in one mass exodus. Emily, the only mother she had ever known, was dead; Jackson was working ridiculous hours; the twins (with lives of their own) were leaving soon for college; and the closest friend Callie had, Patty, had just relocated to Houston with her husband. There were few people left who could offer Callie more than just a peripheral relationship, and she was in desperate need of a friend, especially the kind she had once known in Frankie Cavalese.

Callie clutched two fingers around the door handle and braced herself for the journey across the street. But just as she was about to open the door, she noticed some movement on the Cavalese porch…and stopped.

She was amazed. How could almost a quarter of a century have passed with so little having changed? There she was, Ruby Cavalese, just the way Callie Mason had last seen her: wearing a print house dress that hid her figure, her hair untrimmed and nondescript, with old sneakers and short white socks, tenderly and purposely watering her plants.

She hadn't always look so withered, Callie remembered. Before Louie left her for someone else, Ruby had been a striking woman, who almost always took fastidious care of her appearance. It was as if Ruby's self-esteem and reason for living had walked out of the house with him, permanently nullifying her faith in her own value. Callie thought of Louie's girlfriend, the one who had waited outside in the car that night. What a callous and unfeeling bitch, to lie in wait with her motor running while a family was being destroyed.

Callie, mesmerized, drifted back to the present as she watched Ruby, with her back to the street, pulling dead leaves from the plants and discarding them. The Cavalese house had always been filled with plants. Ruby loved them; it was one joy that Louie's departure did not destroy. She took better care of the plants than she did of herself. Next to beer and cigarettes, and her children, Ruby loved her plants and flowers.

And now, from what Callie could surmise, little had changed. Ruby's no-maintenance look had stayed in Rainytown vogue, at least for her. It was amazing, Callie thought, that Ruby's hair had not turned grayer in all these years. Surely a woman who ceased styling her hair some thirty years ago would not think to color what she rarely combed. Such action defied the laws of nature; it was an enigma, and certainly one worth pondering. It was also a good excuse to remain in the car, at least a few moments longer.

Suddenly, there was no mystery; it had been revealed with a turn of a head. Ruby's hair was not gray because the woman on the porch was not Ruby.

She was Frankie.

CHAPTER 2

Callie felt her breath leave her body as she stared in disbelief at the figure across the street. Callie Mason wanted to jump out of the car and run to her long-lost friend; Callie Hethers wanted to start the car and leave Rainytown as fast as her BMW could take her. Callie Mason felt joy at seeing her old friend; Callie Hethers felt guilt and shame. But Callie didn't know what to feel, and certainly had no idea what to do.

Finally, a compromise was reached. Callie Mason agreed to approach her old friend (after all, a meeting was inevitable), but Callie Hethers insisted on doing so cautiously. There would be no outstretched arms seeking an embrace (rejection would be too devastating), and any hint of affection would have to be initiated by the other party.

Callie opened the car door. Having a plan of action, it was relatively safe to advance. But the moment she stepped out of her BMW, the surrealistic veil of protection she had worn escaped her, and the Rainytown summer of her youth, with its frayed edges and prying eyes, enveloped her. Oh, so little had changed. There they were, the catty, well-intentioned souls who loitered on their own stoops and porches, their ears trained on each other, their eyes, always watching the neighborhood, making mental notes of each other's comings and goings, sending out red alerts any time a stranger, especially one as incongruous as Callie Hethers, came to call.

As the hot sun beat down on her, Callie crossed the street, shrugging off the glances and feigning oblivion to the world around her. She pretended not to see the beer cans that sat, one after another, on the porch railings, like ducks in a row. She pretended not to hear the music that came from multiple radios—each one vying loudly for center ring, as the voices of children and the songs of traffic intensified the discord. She pretended not to feel the scrutinizing glances searing like the sun on her tanned brow. But most of all, she pretended not to notice that Frankie, who had finished her watering, had finally noticed her.

And now it was Frankie's turn to experience the surreal, as the day she had long imagined and feared was upon her. There was no time to prepare, no time to smooth over the rough patches of indignation and indigence that ignored her pleas to play dead. No time to paint the house, to move away, or to jump into a new persona. No time for anything, except to be Frankie Cavalese.

Frankie had assumed that someone would be coming to clean out Emily's home; she just never imagined it would be Callie. She had been expecting a hired hand, someone whom Callie had paid to collect the past and pack it into boxes.

Holding tightly onto her watering can, Frankie walked two feet forward on the tiny porch until she reached the railing. She looked, without expression, into the eyes of the woman approaching. The woman looked back and smiled reluctantly, stopping right in front of the Cavalese stoop.

"You look familiar," Callie said, looking up at her, trying to ease the tension with a weak attempt at humor. "Do I know you?"

Frankie hesitated, then spoke. "No, I don't think you do, Callie."

Callie cast her eyes downward. "I'm sorry, I shouldn't have…that was stupid."

"Don't worry about it. "How have you been? You look well."

"Thank you," Callie replied, feeling the awkwardness of not being able to return the compliment.

"I was very sorry to hear about Emily. You stayed close to her over the years?"

"Very. I miss her terribly."

"She was the best," Frankie offered.

"Yes, she was."

Both women were in deep pain. It was an awful, torturous moment that should have been joyous but didn't know how to be. Callie, standing on the sidewalk with the eyes of Rainytown upon her, felt naked and demeaned. Frankie, standing a few feet above her clutching an old green can for comfort, felt worthless and ugly.

"Guess, in every way that counts, Emily was your mother."

"Yes, she was."

"Did you ever…"

"Did I ever what?" Callie asked. "Find my mother, Anisa?"

"Yeah, I guess that's what…never mind. It's none of my business."

"No, it's all right. I never found her. Nor she me."

"Sorry."

"It's okay. Besides, I never really looked. It's like you just said: Emily was my mother." Callie turned her head to see if the neighbors were still watching.

"They're worse than ever," Frankie said. "You wanna come in?"

"Oh, yes. I would love to," Callie said, feeling greatly relieved. "Thank you."

Frankie laid the watering can down on a small glass top table, turned, and pulled open the old screen door with a quick tug on the rusted knob. Callie climbed the stoop quickly and followed her inside.

"Sorry it's so hot in here," Frankie said. "I'll put on the fan, but it don't really help all that much."

Callie recoiled with grammatical umbrage but tried not to let it show.

"Sit down, please," Frankie said, indicating the couch with her left hand as she turned on the fan. "The sofa don't bite."

Callie smiled and took a seat. "Thank you."

"What can I get you? Ice tea? Water? Soda?"

"Iced tea sounds great."

"Ice tea it is," Frankie said, heading back toward the kitchen. "Oh, by the way, if it's too dark in there for you, switch on a light. I just keep 'em off in the day 'cause the lights make this place even hotter."

Frankie was right. The room was dark, and the fan did little to quell the intense heat. Unfortunately, the slight relief it did provide was not worth the swell of dust it stirred in the process. But Callie didn't want to turn the fan off or the lights on. And so darkness prevailed in the small row house, where there were no side windows to provide illumination. The only natural light appeared through the slats of the yellowed blinds in the front window. Callie watched as the particles of dust danced in the long streams of light, ironically the sole activity in the still, gray room. She looked to her left at the old leather recliner and remembered Louie Cavalese as he watched the Phillies on his Motorola console. He had saved long and hard for that television and was none too pleased when Ruby refused to let him take it with him after he had abandoned the family. The console set had most likely died years ago but had been too cumbersome to remove. So there it sat, just where Callie had last seen it. Only now there was an old color portable resting on top of it, one with a twisted wire coat hanger where the aerial should be.

The hypnotic darkness pulled Callie even further back in time. For a brief moment, she could hear the laughter of two seven-year olds, Callie Mason and Frankie Cavalese, as they smeared each other with the copious drool of Louie's old basset hound, Snoogie, screaming "Gross out!" as Ruby Cavalese screamed at them to stop.

"Sorry, I don't have no lemon. Can you drink this plain?"

Callie was momentarily startled by Frankie's reappearance in the current decade.

"Thank you," she said, taking the glass from her. "This will be fine. Aren't you going to join me?"

"I just finished a can of soda before you came," Frankie said, taking a seat on the nearby armchair.

"Oh," Callie said, wondering what to say next.

It was a clumsy, fantastic moment, pregnant with apprehension, uneasiness, and unrequited joy. Neither Frankie nor Callie wanted to make herself vulnerable by showing affection for the other, or by admitting that, despite the past twenty-three years, seeing each other again meant everything.

"You know who I was thinking about when you came back in the room?" Callie asked.

"No. Should I?"

"Snoogie."

"Oh. The droolmeister."

"Right," Callie said, feeling ridiculous that she could think of nothing else besides the saliva of a long-deceased, droopy-eared dog to open the lines of communication.

"When I was twenty, we got another hound, Figaro. He didn't drool like the Snooge did. Thank the Lord."

"You got lucky," Callie said, having no idea where to take the inane conversation she had initiated. "Wow. This is pretty difficult, isn't it?"

"Yeah, I'd say so," Frankie said, looking directly at her. "Pretty damned difficult."

"We could talk about the weather," Callie said, "and about how hot it is. And we could talk about the neighbors and their problems, or even the man in the moon…but inevitably we'd end up back here, with you and me. So we might as well skip all of that and…"

"What, cut to the chase?"

"I suppose so," Callie said. "That's what you always used to tell me."

"The chase don't matter now. Nothing does," Frankie said, tightening her defenses. "Look at us. We're so different now. Worlds apart."

"Don't be silly…"

"Look around this room," Frankie challenged her. "Look around this room and tell me that you can relate to me. I dare you. Tell me you ain't thinkin' 'Thank God it ain't me in this hell hole.' Just don't insult me by pretending you don't know what I'm talkin' about."

"I'm sorry. Frankie, I hope you're not feeling bad that I've been fortunate…"

"Damn it, Mason, it ain't about you. I don't even think about you. You're just some doll I used to play with when I was a kid."

Ouch. Callie felt that one. Frankie's words had stung and were certainly worthy of painful contemplation and some hurt feelings. But before she could feel the full impact of it, she was distracted by a faint medicinal odor in the house, one that clashed with the smell of her iced tea. She put her glass down on the cluttered coffee table and turned to Frankie, then tried to hide her uneasiness and pretend that she wasn't hurt by what Frankie had just said.

"Maybe you'd like to talk about things?"

"I got other shit on my mind."

"I really think it can be helpful to talk about things."

"Then talk to yourself," Frankie said. "You seem willing to listen."

Now Callie was amused but kept her smile hidden. That was the Frankie she remembered — the smart-mouthed little girl with the big heart who called 'em like she saw 'em.

"No, seriously, Frankie…"

"I'll tell you seriously," Frankie said, looking directly into Callie's eyes. "Seriously, you don't really wanna talk. Seriously, you just wanna unload the sack of guilt you've been carrying around since the day you left this town and swore never to come back. Seriously, you wanna dump your damn guilt right here in the room…on me. Only I don't wanna hear your excuses. I don't wanna hear how your momma never came home, and how your rich friends wouldn't have understood me. Or how you were young and stupid and wish you could take it all back. Save that crap. As you can see, I got more garbage in this house than I can deal with. I don't need yours."

"I'm really sorry," Callie said. "I didn't mean to upset you."

"Look, Mason," Frankie softened, "I get no thrill comin' down on you like this. And I'll be glad to help you with whatever you need while you're cleanin' out Emily's house. I loved her too, you know. Only I got my own problems right now."

"Maybe I can help."

Frankie rolled her eyes. "Woman, don't you know when to shut up?"

Before Callie could mumble another hopeless apology, she was blasted out of her seat by the sound of a ringing bell.

"What the hell is that?" Callie said, panicked, as she quickly rose to her feet.

"Time to evacuate," Frankie said. "It's the Martian bell. An official government warning that alien spacecraft is about to land."

"Seriously," Callie said. "Where'd the bell come from?"

"It came from my mother. She's upstairs, dying. And she's ringing the damn bell because she wants something. Hell, you can't get any more serious than that, can you?"

Callie fell back onto the couch cushion, as if an invisible vacuum had sucked her back into place. "Oh God, I'm so sorry."

The bell sounded again. Only louder and for longer.

"I gotta go see what she wants," Frankie said, as she got up from her chair and headed toward the stairs. "She ain't gonna stop if I don't."

And in an instant, she was gone. Callie looked up at the empty staircase Frankie had just climbed. She could hear her old friend talking faintly in the distance, but the soft whir of the living room fan made it impossible to decipher her words.

Frankie was right. Callie did consider herself lucky as she surveyed the life that wasn't hers but that easily could have been. There was something deathlike about the room; even the plants looked gray. Callie listened as Frankie's voice got louder. She wondered what she was saying. Suddenly, Frankie came clumping down the stairs with a plastic pitcher in her hand.

"She wants juice."

Frankie hurried into the kitchen without waiting for Callie to respond. Callie listened to the sound of the refrigerator door open, the pouring of juice, and the closing of the door. She watched as Frankie emerged from the kitchen, as if it were all part of some morbid ritual.

"What's wrong with you, Mason? You got the strangest look on your face."

"It's nothing. I'm just thinking about your mother. I'm still processing the fact that she's upstairs…and that…I was so sure you were alone here."

"Oh, I am," Frankie said. "I'm Norman Bates, and I'm delivering this juice to the skeletal remains of my dead mother. Sometimes I talk for her, and we have long conversations. But not when I have company. Wouldn't want anyone to think I'm crazy."

At that moment, the bell rang again.

Frankie looked at Callie. "That…I do by remote control. Sounds pretty real, don't it?"

"Oh God, Frankie. Please. Stop it," Callie said, as Frankie raced up the stairs without paying attention to her.

The bell rang again, and Callie could hear Frankie mutter some words of annoyance. Then all was quiet. Callie rose from the couch and walked over to the long table by the foot of the stairs. There were all the Cavalese family photos, still in the same place. She turned on the little Tiffany lamp and for the first time saw color, albeit faded, in the smiling faces.

Ruby had been a real knockout in her twenties, with her long, dark hair swept up on top of her head, her dark lipstick perfectly in place. Callie picked up the frame and shook off the dust. She hadn't remembered Louie Cavalese being so handsome; she had only remembered him leaving.

Callie never knew the Cavaleses when they were so much in love. She looked first at Louie, tightly clutching Ruby's waist as he posed for the camera, then at Ruby, bursting with love for the man beside her. What the camera had captured would outlive their love by many years. Perhaps, Callie thought, the photo had been a portent of things to come. Louie, seemingly more impressed with his own good looks than with Ruby's, was flirting madly with the camera…or perhaps it was the photographer. Ruby, on the other hand, unaware of her lover's self-absorption and roving eyes, had most likely been the kind of woman who catered so heavily to his needs in the beginning of their relationship that she inevitably disappointed him in the end. It was foolish, Callie decided, to assume so much from a photo that represented only seconds in time, even if everything else indicated that her assumptions must be correct.

In a small blue frame with painted daisies, Callie saw her friend Frankie laughing at, not smiling for, the school camera. Frankie never primped for pictures the way the other little girls had. Though she couldn't quite articulate it, she thought tomboys who smiled in photos looked silly. And so Frankie dismissed the annual process of freezing one's image for posterity as a minor inconvenience, passing off her insecurities with a great big laugh — leaving absolutely no one the wiser.

Paulie's school photos, however, which Callie noticed next, implied a proclivity toward narcissism not unlike his father's. Even at twelve, Paulie's slicked back crop of dark brown hair and smoldering brown eyes revealed a young man bent on capturing the attention of anyone he chose.

Partially hidden behind a larger photo of Ruby's older sister, Belle, Callie discovered another photo of Paulie that had been taken years after she had last seen him. Callie quickly did the math: Paulie, three years her junior, had been only fifteen when she last saw him, and most likely, had been approximately thirty when this photo was taken. Callie picked up the framed photo for closer inspection. Wearing a saxophone around his neck, Paulie was smiling, standing with two other men who also wore musical instruments. Logic concluded that Paulie must have followed his musical aspirations and joined a group. Whether music was Paulie's vocation or avocation, Callie had no idea, but he was amazingly handsome, she thought. Even more so than his father.

"If you put that picture down, you can have the real thing," a voice said.

Callie was so startled that she lay the frame down with a thud, then turned to find Paulie, grinning coyly at her, standing by the front door.

"Oh God. Paulie. I didn't realize you still lived here."

"I don't, babe. Just came to see Ma. Heard you were here…Murph, you remember him, don't you? Just had to chase me down to tell me you were here. Well, well…my little Miss Callie-fornia."

Callie blushed. She had completely forgotten about the nickname Paulie had for her when they were children.

"You're looking even sexier than I remember you," Paulie said.

"Thank you," Callie choked. He was even more breathtaking than his photograph, and he knew it. His tight jeans and painted-on black T-shirt were a clear indication that he had made a full inventory of his assets.

"How do I look?" Paulie asked, as if he could read her mind.

"Uh, you look…"

"I look pretty good. Huh, babe?" Paulie said, as his eyes danced dangerously around Callie. "In fact, if you look around this room, I'll bet I'm the only thing that looks better than you remember it."

Paulie laughed. He knew he was right.

But Callie wasn't giving in so easily. She looked around the gray room. "It's not like you've got a lot of competition."

"Touché, babe. A woman who can think on her feet as well really turns me on."

"I don't really think I really needed to know that," Callie said, determined not to let him get the better of her.

Paulie leaned against the front wall and folded his arms. He grinned at Callie, then said, "I'm getting to you, aren't I, babe?"

"Like a mosquito…or a gnat."

Paulie laughed. "Ooooh, squash me, babe. Like a bug. I'm ready. Squeeze me till I'm dry. C'mon, baby. Squash!"

"Oh, go squash yourself!" Callie said, feeling strangely stimulated by the repartee. "Are you always this obnoxious?"

Paulie looked right through her, his grin on temporary hiatus. "I can be anything you want me to be."

"How about quiet?"

Paulie's mouth turned slightly upward; he continued to gaze at her as if he could see her undressed. "If that's what you'd like."

Callie, despite her efforts, was feeling intimidated. "Where did you come from? The cover of some cheap romance novel?"

Paulie challenged her with his eyes. After a long pause, he spoke: "I think you know better than that."

Callie couldn't believe what this man was doing to her. She turned to look at his photo. "You play sax?"

"Tenor sax. Yeah. I play. I'm good."

"I'm sure you are," Callie said, swallowing the lump in her throat.

"She's been asking for you," Frankie said from the top of the stairs. "She thought you were coming yesterday."

Callie looked up to see Frankie glaring angrily at her brother. For a moment, she felt angry at Frankie for interrupting her verbal ping pong game with Paulie, then quickly chastised herself for such ludicrousness.

"Sorry, Sis. I got tied up."

Frankie began her descent down the stairs. When she got close to the landing, she said, "Hope Ma don't die on a day that you're 'tied up.'"

"It couldn't be helped, Mary Frances. Whattya want? A note from my teacher?"

Frankie's look of anger suddenly dissipated, as if she couldn't bear to be at odds with him anymore. She looked at Callie, then at Paulie.

"Just go see your mother," Frankie told him. "Like I said, she's waiting for you."

"I think I'll head next door, now!" Callie said brightly, trying to swim quickly out of awkward waters. "I'm sure I'll see you both at another time. Please, send my love to your mother."

"Later, Mason," Frankie said, barely looking at her.

"See ya, Callie-fornia," Paulie said, as his eyes followed Callie out the door. "Real soon."

Paulie was too entranced by Callie's backside to feel the eyes of his sister beading down on him. Finally, he turned to Frankie.

"I'll go see Ma now. Hey, your old buddy…she's a knockout."

"Yeah, right," Frankie said, and with an angry push on the old screen door, she walked quickly outside.

CHAPTER 3

As Paulie climbed the stairs, he paid no attention to the screams of anger and despair coming from his mother's bedroom. When he reached the top landing, he stopped in the bathroom to pay a visit, then splashed some cold water on his face and proceeded to Ruby's room, where the screaming had intensified.

"What's the topic today, Ma?" Paulie asked as he entered the room, "Pissed-off broads get even with their cross-dressing, cheating husbands?"

"Get real," Ruby said, staring straight ahead at the television. "I thought you were comin' yesterday. You think because I got nothin' to do but die, that I don't mind waiting for you?"

"Sorry, Ma," Paulie said, reaching for the power button on the television.

"Don't touch my television," Ruby said loudly, as one woman on the screen stood up and began physically attacking the other. "I'm watchin'."

"What are you watching? One broad kill another?"

"If I could've gotten my hands on the bitch who stole your father, I would've done just like her on the TV."

"No, you wouldn't, Ma," Paulie said turning off the television. "And you know that Pop wasn't stolen; he left. A million fucking years ago."

"Ah…whattya you know," Ruby said, defeated. "Damn it, Paulie, I told you to leave the set on."

"I know, Ma," Paulie said, sitting on the bed beside her. "I know."

"Did you bring me a cigarette?"

Paulie looked at the cluster of medicine bottles on Ruby's nightstand. "Did you take your pills?"

"I asked did you bring me a cigarette?"

"No, Ma, not today."

"Shit, what are you good for? And yeah, I took my pills. For what it's worth." Ruby picked up the remote control and pointed it at the television.

"Later for that," Paulie said, taking the device from her and laying it on his father's old dresser, to the left of Ruby's bed.

"I just wanted to see the end of the show," Ruby lamented.

"How about a hug, Ma?" Paulie smiled warmly at his mother, and for a moment, her sallow face became bright with joy.

"Okay," she said, then slowly raised her frail bruised arms, as he delicately pulled her toward him. Paulie was too fine an actor to let his own pain show, but when Ruby's head fell onto his shoulder and she could no longer see his face, he winced with grief at the bundle of bones who had given him life and was soon to lose hers.

"I love you, Ma," Paulie said, holding on to her. "I'm sorry I didn't make it yesterday. There was no one to cover for me. I really tried."

"You're here now," she said, holding him as tightly as her strength allowed. "Yesterday's all forgotten."

"That's good, Ma," Paulie said, releasing his hold and easing her slowly back into bed. "Tell me how you're feeling. Are you eating?"

"I've been feasting on mashed potatoes. Putrid, gooey slop they are…with gravy. And milkshakes: slimy, milky, tasteless goop. Hard to believe I used to eat that crap for pleasure. Hard to believe I'm trying to gain weight. Not with the hips I used to have."

"Ma, please…"

"Am I making you uncomfortable?"

"Why should I be uncomfortable?" Paulie lied.

"You don't fool no one," Ruby said. "But you better quit smoking if you don't wanna end up like me…with lung cancer. I was gonna quit once, then that bitch stole your father."

"Yeah, Ma, I know."

"As long as you're still smoking, give me one of your cigarettes."

"I don't have 'em with me."

"Yeah…Seen your old man lately?"

"I see him all the time. We work together. You know that."

"Does he ask about me?"

"Sure, Ma. Sure he does."

"Ever talk about comin' to see me?"

"You said you didn't want him to ever set foot in this house again. You want me to ask him to come see you?"

"Is he still with that bitch?"

"You know he is, Ma. They're married."

"Then screw him."

"Okay, Ma. Can I get you anything before I go?"

"Damn it, Paulie, you gotta leave already?"

"Yeah," Frankie said, entering the bedroom with a small vase of flowers. "Where are you going? You just got here."

"Sorry. Gotta work. I got a late start today. I meant to come by earlier."

Frankie looked disgusted. "Here, Ma, Arlene Humphries brought these by. Where would you like them?"

"Over there," Ruby said, indicating her dresser, filled with half-empty perfume bottles, old lipsticks, and an assortment of hair products. "Just don't mess anything up. I can't stand it when you move my stuff around and I can't find nothin' afterwards. Just 'cause I ain't go no hair now, don't mean this wig don't need brushin'. You hear me, Frankie?"

Frankie looked beaten. She put the vase down on the dresser, and walked over to the foot of the bed. "What can I get you to eat?"

"I ain't hungry."

"I'll bet you were hungry until he had to go," Frankie said bitterly.

"I said I got no appetite, Frankie. Now, leave me be."

"Ma," Frankie insisted, "the doctor said I gotta get you to eat. If you don't keep your weight up…"

"What?" Ruby snapped. "I'll die?"

Paulie kissed his mother and stood up. "I've gotta run, ladies. See you tomorrow."

"Good-bye, son," Ruby said. "Thanks for comin' by."

Frankie grabbed Paulie's arm as he hurried out the door. "Can't you ever do any of this for me?" she implored. "I'm dyin' right along with her. I can't take it. She's driving me fucking crazy."

"Sorry, Mary F. You know I gotta work the night shift, and I've got to go borrow Pop's truck and pick up supplies today. We're way low. I really do have to leave. Could you let go of my arm now?"

Frankie looked hurt and angry as she released her grip. "So sorry to have detained you."

"See you tomorrow," Paulie said, as he rushed out the door.

"Don't hurry back!" Frankie screamed after him. "You're useless!"

"Don't yell at your brother," Ruby scolded. "He ain't done nothin' to you. You're lucky to have him. Would you hand me my remote control?"

"As soon as you tell me what you want for dinner," Frankie bargained. "Then I'll give it to you."

"I told you, I'm not hungry!" Ruby screamed. "Why the hell can't you leave me be?"

"Fine!" Frankie said, picking up the remote control from Louie's dresser and tossing it onto Ruby's bed. "Eat this for dinner! I hear the channel selector is real tasty!"

Frankie turned on her heels and slammed out of the room. Ruby, about to zap the power button on, stopped and stared at her bedroom door, which was still rattled by the violent close. Alone in her world, she felt anger with herself for allowing her daughter, so loyal and so loving, to be hurt again — hurt by the pain that she couldn't seem to stop inflicting. And so, the question goes: If a dying mother shows compassion for the daughter that she continues to maltreat, and there is no one to notice, does it make a difference?

Frankie kicked open the old screen door and felt the sun on her face. She wanted to take a good, long walk around the block to "cool off," but she knew that was not possible. The inquiring minds were out in full force, and they would have questions for her: questions in the form of good wishes, questions in the form of invitations, and questions in the form of questions. Even staying on the porch for too long could be dangerous; but Frankie hoped the hot weather would render them too lazy to move.

Sitting down on the old wooden rocker, Frankie tried to calm her nerves. She noticed that Callie's BMW was still across the street. For a moment, with Ruby and Paulie at the top of her angry list and Callie running a distant third, Frankie considered going next door to talk to her old friend; after all, Callie had already offered her services. But Frankie still couldn't get past the betrayal, nor was she in the mood for any more disappointment.

So Frankie rocked slowly on the old chair, hoping instead that Callie would see her sitting there and come outside to talk. But Edna Murphy down the street had seen her first, and just as Frankie was beginning to calm down, she saw "Fat Edna" tramping her way toward the Cavalese home, intent as she always was on collecting whatever information necessary to maintain her status as the resident town crier.

Not today you don't, Frankie thought, as she jumped up abruptly. Not today. And while the rocking chair swayed back and forth, as if it were still occupied, Frankie pulled open the weary screen door, walked inside, and immediately shut the front door behind her. She had barely reached the kitchen, trying to think of something her mother might eat, when she heard Edna Murphy leaning on the bell. Without a thought, Frankie flipped on the radio, closed the kitchen door, and for a splendid moment or two, blocked everyone out of her mind.

For Callie, her world again was cloaked in surrealism. Emily's living room seemed distorted and impaired, as if the mere touch of a human hand would crumble it. Like a body in an open coffin, it was dead. Just a shell, a real and sometimes chilling reminder of what used to have life and purpose.

As Callie sat rigidly in her aunt's old easy chair, unsettled by its touch, she wondered: why do things have to feel this way? Why couldn't the room be alive with color and memories, perhaps like the homes that have become museums and have thick cords of velvet rope blocking their rooms from public access?

It was strange, Callie thought. Mrs. Balducci had resided in Emily's house for over ten years, yet everything was exactly as Emily had left it. This old woman faithfully paid her monthly rent, yet lived for over a decade steeped in someone else's memories, someone else's tastes.

Certainly, age changes everyone's priorities, Callie thought, but does it change one's need to be surrounded by the things that are one's own?

Possessions don't matter, she heard Emily say. Loved ones matter; memories matter. Don't dwell on the unimportant.

Callie, momentarily stunned by the clarification from her dead aunt, shook off her spirit like a chill, not quite prepared for any further conversation. She smiled, as she noticed Emily's lace doilies and silly knickknacks that graced the room. But when she thought about their fate, she felt sad. There was nothing here that she could use; there were few things she wanted. Why couldn't she just leave everything as it was and walk away? Why did she have to dismantle her childhood, piece by piece, just to have its fragments end up God knows where?

Life goes on, Emily told her. These are mere objects; their spirit is with me, and within you. Do what has to be done. Stop your worrying.

Callie could not get a grip on what she was feeling or hearing. But she knew Frankie would understand. In fact, she was sure of it. But Frankie had made herself clear: heart-to-hearts were out.

Callie rose from the chair and headed for the front door. The packing could wait until tomorrow. Jackson's loving touch and a glass of red wine were just about all she could handle right now.

CHAPTER 4

Although she had lived there for seventeen years, Callie was momentarily daunted by the opulence of her own home as she drove up the twisty brick drive that led to its majestic front doors. As she parked her car alongside Jackson's burgundy-colored Jaguar, she noticed Eduardo, the gardener, still tending to the exotic plants and flowers that had been imported earlier that year from East Asia.

At seven o'clock, there was still quite a bit of light left in the sky, and Callie considered, then rejected, a quick swim to neutralize the effects of the heat. As she got out of her car, she waved hello to Eduardo, then hurried inside to seek some solace from her loving husband.

When she found him, he was in the den, sprawled out on the couch, his feet on the coffee table and his eyes closed, listening to Chopin, a favorite musical tranquilizer. As his right hand conducted the invisible orchestra, his left hand grasped his two-olive martini in the long-stemmed crystal glass.

"You started without me," Callie said.

As Jackson's blue eyes opened, his right hand brushed a wisp of thick blond hair from his eyes. "It's been one hell of a day."

"For me too. I went back to Rainytown."

"I know," Jackson said, looking to his left. "That's why I brought you those."

Callie glanced to her right and saw a vase filled with a dozen white roses, resting on the desk. She smiled and walked over to them.

"Thanks, honey, that was very sweet. They're gorgeous."

"So are you. Sit down. Let me get you a glass of wine. Did you get a lot done?"

Callie walked over to the couch, gave her husband a kiss, then sat down next to him. "Never even got the boxes out of the trunk. There was a lot to distract me."

Jackson carefully placed his martini on the table, then walked over to the bar and poured his wife a glass of Zinfandel.

"Here you go," he said, handing her the glass. "Now, just relax and listen to Fred."

"How can you call him Fred?" Callie asked, semi-amused. "You change the music when you call him Fred. I almost expect to hear a marching band or something."

Jackson resumed his seat and took a sip of his martini. He laughed. "I have every respect for the dearly departed March King, but John Philip could never bring me this close to nirvana."

Callie looked at him oddly. "Well, nobody called Fred could've written music like this," she insisted playfully.

"Then have it your way," Jackson said. "And have a listen to Frédéric."

Jackson closed his eyes and began conducting again. Callie was frustrated. She wanted his full attention.

"I saw my friend Frankie today," Callie said. "For the first time in twenty-three years."

"Really? How did it go?" Jackson asked, his eyes still closed.

"Awkward, heart wrenching, awful, wonderful."

Jackson opened his eyes and smiled. "Well, when you make up your mind, be sure to share it with me."

Callie was no longer amused, but before she could visibly display her lack of sport, his eyelids were fluttering again. "It was all of those things," she said. "An emotional garbage dump. There it was, my former life, like a heap of junk that used to have value, waiting to be snatched for pennies at someone's yard sale. And seeing Aunt Emily's home again…that was too much. And Frankie, poor Frankie, her life is a mess. You should hear--—"

"Let Frédéric soothe your tired brow."

Callie, wanting to suggest a more appropriate activity for Chopin, resisted the temptation. But just as she reconsidered, Cobbles, her Persian cat, sauntered in to say hello.

"Come to Momma, baby," Callie said, patting her lap to entice the cat. "I've missed you."

As Cobbles considered his options, Hungry, the alley cat Callie had found as a kitten, walked into the room, hot on Cobbles' trail. Hungry, out for a good time, hid underneath the chair to the left of the door. Callie watched with amusement as Hungry's back end began to twitch, a sure sign she was about to pounce on her unsuspecting brother. And just as Cobbles had decided to grace Callie with his presence, making strides in her direction, Hungry bounded out of hiding, smacked Cobbles on the rear end, and Callie's furry comfort went scurrying out of the room.

"That was very funny," Callie told Jackson. "Too bad your eyes were closed."

"Cats at it again?"

"You miss things when your eyes are closed," Callie said.

"I'm deliriously happy," Jackson said, feeling the swell of the music. "I've been looking forward to this all day. Trust me, I'm not missing a thing."

Callie stood up abruptly. "Forget it. I'm going for a swim. I'll see you later."

Jackson opened his eyes. "Aren't you going to finish your wine?"

"Give it to Fred," Callie told him, annoyed. "I've lost my taste for it."

Jackson, bewildered by the rebuttal, shrugged and closed his eyes again. He was too immersed in his comfort zone to ask any questions. He figured that Callie wanted to talk, as she often did in days of late, but he'd had a very stressful day and had no desire to relinquish the quiet time he'd so painstakingly earned.

"We'll talk later, honey," Jackson said, but Callie was long gone.

Normally, Callie loved the hard pounding of rain, but not on the days when she had to go out. She liked it on the days when she could sleep late and didn't have much to do but curl up with a good book or spend some time on her treadmill. But this was not one of those days. Today, in another part of town, Callie's life was waiting for her, tapping its fingers with cool insistence. Hurry up, Callie. Get over here. You've got work to do.

Half asleep, curled up on her left side, she wondered why the rain sounded so much louder than usual, as if it were raining right there in the bedroom. But being in a quasi state of slumber, it took her some moments before she could laugh at her own confusion, Jackson is taking a shower, dummy! Wake up.

Wake, however, was not what she wanted to do. With her right hand, Callie punched her down pillow for renewed comfort, then adjusted her body in preparation for an extended snooze. Still not comfortable, Callie punched the pillow again, this time with increased effort.

"Get up, my little pugilist!" Jackson said, walking into the bedroom with a towel wrapped around his waist.

Callie's eyes opened halfway, then closed again. "What are you talking about?" she mumbled.

"I'm talking about the right hook you just gave that pillow," Jackson told her. "Pillows are sensitive little creatures. They don't like to be punched. Especially so early in the morning."

"Oh, be quiet," Callie said, burying her head in the pillow. "Before I punch you."

"Waaa di you saaay?" Jackson said, speaking in mock muffled tones. "I caaan heh you."

Callie turned her head around and opened her eyes all the way. "I said, be quiet before I punch you too!"

Jackson smiled. "Good morning, love."

"Good morning is an oxymoron," Callie said groggily. "How can anything that happens in the morning be good?"

Jackson looked at her knowingly, then broke into a broad grin. "We've had lots of good things happen in the morning."

Callie gave him a dirty look.

"You're still angry with me, aren't you? Jackson said. "You disappeared last night, and you didn't even eat dinner with me."

"I was out by the pool," Callie said. "You knew where to find me."

"I figured you needed some time alone. I thought, and wrongly so, that you would want to have dinner later on."

"I did have dinner. By myself. Leftover fettuccine Alfredo and salad."

"So that's where that went to," Jackson said. "That's what I was going to have…once I realized I would be dining alone. C'mon, Callie. All I wanted was to relax after a rough day at work. That was no reason for you to take a hike; we could've talked over dinner. And for whatever reason, you saw fit to wait until I was sound asleep to come to bed. No wonder you're so tired this morning. How long are you going to hold this grudge against me, anyway?"

"I'm not holding any grudges," Callie relented. "I just needed to talk. I really did. But you weren't—"

Jackson smiled. "You want to talk? Good. Because there's someone here who wants to talk to you. Wait, I'll go get him."

"Who's out there? Don't you dare bring anyone into this bedroom," Callie shouted. "Are you crazy?"

"Just a little bit," Jackson said devilishly. "Hold on."

Jackson ran back to the bathroom, only to return seconds later with his wet blond hair slicked back, and the towel he had been wearing around his waist draped around his shoulders like a cape.

"Oh, no!" Callie said, covering her eyes. "Not him!"

"That's right!" Jackson said, "It's your friend and mine. Come to call!"

"No," Callie pleaded mirthfully, "Not Naked Matador! Not so early in the morning!"

"It's never too early for Naked Matador," Jackson said, grabbing his "cape" and coming toward Callie as if she were a bull. "I ees going to get you! And we can have zee nice long chat. You've heard of zee pillow talk, si?"

Callie couldn't help but laugh as she observed Jackson's antics. There he was, the dignified and respected CEO of his own construction company, prancing farcically about the room with his manhood swinging back and forth like a pendulum gone awry.

"I've got you!" Jackson shouted, as he threw himself on top of her. "You, Señora, are mine to ravish! Mmmm. You taste so good!"

And as the rain continued to pound outside, Callie silently agreed that Jackson had been right. Maybe there were some good things about morning.

❖ ❖ ❖

"What a rotten morning!" Ruby said, glancing toward the window as Frankie entered with a tray. "Look at it. It's raining cats and dogs."

"It shouldn't bother you," Frankie said, putting the tray down on the folding stand by Ruby's bed. "It's not like you're going anywhere today."

"It's depressing," Ruby told her. "Besides, Paulie might not show. He hates rain."

Frankie was unsympathetic. "Yeah, I know. It messes up his hair, poor boy. Well, I for one like rain. We need it. Cool things down a bit."

"What's that slop you brought me?" Ruby said, looking at the tray.

"Oatmeal, Ma. You know what it is."

"I hate goddamned oatmeal. Putrid slop. Just like all the food you bring me."

"I'm doing everything I can for you, Ma. Can't you give me a break? Can't you just eat a little?"

"I called Arlene Humphries last night," Ruby said. "To thank her for the flowers."

"Good, I'm glad."

"And she told me that Callie Mason had been by. That she's the one's gonna be cleanin' out Emily's place. Never would have thought—"

"That's right. Paulie and I saw her yesterday."

"How come none of yous told me about it?"

"We're not hiding anything from you, Ma, just didn't get a chance to tell you yet."

"Arlene says she's a fancy society lady now. Got a BMW and everything."

"Eat your oatmeal, Ma," Frankie said, placing the tray on Ruby's lap. "Or it'll get cold."

"Too bad you didn't marry rich like that," Ruby said.

"Callie had lots of her own money anyway," Frankie clarified. "You knew that."

"Too bad you didn't marry rich like she did," Ruby repeated, impervious to Frankie's explanation. "Then you could hire some fancy doc to fix me and some fancy nurses to take care of me. And a damn chef."

"It's not about money, Ma. Rich people die from cancer too. Your doctors are doing all they can for you."

Ruby looked down at the bowl of oatmeal on her lap. "This is what it comes down to, don't it? To hell with my nursing career. Lost any chance of that when I married your father. Gave up every damn thing to become Mrs. Louie Cavalese. And what did it get me: dumped for some trashy, home-wrecking bitch. And what did I end up with: a million years behind the register at the Save-Your-Goddamned-Money supermarket with two kids to raise. So what do I got to show for my life now: a bowl of putrid slop and a body filled with cancer. That's it, Frankie. That's all I got."

"What about me? Don't I matter to you?"

"Gave up nursing school to raise you, didn't I?"

"How about Paulie? Didn't you make sacrifices for him, too?"

"Yeah...whatever," Ruby said. "My life was one big, goddamn sacrifice."

"How about mine?" Frankie asked bitterly. "I'm forty-one years old, and I've never lived anywhere but here with you. You wanted to be a nurse? I wanted to teach art to little kids. But instead, I worked for fifteen years at the damn diner. And now, I'm on a leave of absence from the same miserable supermarket so I can take care of you."

"I told ya, Frankie. You shoulda married well, like that Mason kid."

Frankie began pacing the room. "Oh, come on! How can you say that? You never wanted me to get married. Why won't you admit it? You piled as much guilt on me as you could to make me stay here in this dump with you. Tellin' me only an ingrate would abandon you and shit. Like I owed you everything for raising me up or something."

"Least I did that!" Ruby snapped. "Your old man didn't do no raisin' up. Yeah, he talked a good line 'bout how much he loved you, but I'm the one who stayed with you...took care of you, wiped the food from your mouth, the snot from your nose, and the crap from your behind. What a damn hypocrite that man is with his sweet-talkin' garbage. Know what he used to tell me all the time? That his little girl was so perfect, she must've hung the moon."

"He did?"

"Don't go gettin' cocky 'bout it, Frankie. Just look outside tonight, after it gets dark. You'll see what I see: a damned crooked moon in the sky. I wouldn't go braggin' to no one 'bout this."

"Oh right! I brag about my wonderful life all the time."

"Least you've got a life!" Ruby said. "Mine's almost gone."

"And what kind of life do you think I have?" Frankie raged.

"A better one than I got," Ruby shot back. "Now, take this putrid slop and leave my room."

"I'll be back later," Frankie said, fighting the taboo urge to cry. "Just eat something. Please!"

"I said, take this now!" Ruby insisted.

"Later," Frankie countered angrily.

And with that, Ruby's weak arms picked up the bowl and hurled it toward Frankie, her meager toss splattering the oatmeal at the foot of the bed, drenching the cherished afghan that her late mother had made.

Frankie, stunned, stopped in her tracks to assess the damage, then looked at Ruby.

Ruby, suddenly quiet, turned away.

Frankie blotted a dab of water from her left eye, then glanced at what should have been her mother's breakfast. Ruby, covered with anguish and wrapped in disgrace, could not even glance in her daughter's direction. But Frankie, needing so to believe in her mother's remorse, looked kindly at the withered woman who had just been silenced by her own shame.

"You take it easy, Ma," Frankie said lovingly. "I'll be back soon to clean this up."

There was no response. Just a cold, hard stare in another direction.

"Okay then, Ma," Frankie said quietly, taking the soiled afghan in her hands. "Hang in there. I'll hurry as fast as I can."

Numbed by her perceived inadequacy as a daughter and caregiver, Frankie let the afghan drop once she reached the hallway. The enormity of her tribulation was too much to shoulder. She looked down at the small, faded blanket that now cradled her feet, then at the oatmeal that ironically had fallen in such a way as to cover an old stain on the hallway runner.

The once-tomboy, so afraid of tears, was no longer tempted to cry. Instead, she rested against the wall and prayed for the strength to continue. But her burden had rendered her temporarily unable to bear even the weight of her own body, and she slid helplessly to the floor, her limp and weary arms flopping to either side of her.

Callie, weary from a diminished sleep and an unscheduled morning exercise session, stirred in her bed, soundlessly cursing the digital display that reminded her of the hour, as her weary arms clutched the soft down of her pillow.

For years, Callie had barely been able to make peace with her privileged lifestyle, yet she was scared to death of losing it. Every day, she wondered what purpose she had in the world, what she had done to deserve the pretty toys she had been given, and who and what she would become should they suddenly disappear. Often, she felt covetous of her household staff for their daily sense of pride in a job well done. They knew the value of a hard day's work, something Callie believed she had rarely encountered. She gave herself no credit for raising two wonderful children and for providing her family with a happy home. She believed that the aid of household help negated such worthy accomplishments, just as Anisa's former misuse of domestics had negated her maternal value in Callie Mason's eyes. Sometimes, Callie sought self-praise for the many charitable efforts she had made over the years but inevitably concluded that volunteer work was simply a merit badge of the idle rich and deserving of little reward. But on this particular day, when Callie actually had something of vital importance to do, in loving tribute to the woman who raised her, she did not want to do it. And as she lay on her back and stared at the ceiling fixture, she felt the guilt chip away at her soul.

Frankie stared at the dust on the baseboard and listened for her mother's cries. There were none. The distant sound of rain transfixed her as the crying sky wept in her place. She wondered what time Callie would arrive and how she could arrange to run into her. Then, she banished the thought and ran her forefinger through the dust, staring with empty eyes at the streak that it made.

Callie, who had finally made her way to the shower, scrubbed her body with Jackson's oatmeal soap, as she wondered what to wear to

Rainytown and if Frankie would be any happier to see her today. Oatmeal made good soap and good cookies, Callie thought, but she hated it for breakfast.

It *was* putrid slop. Frankie agreed with her mother. How could she expect Ruby to eat it when she could not even bear to clean it off the floor? But the job had to be done, in loving tribute to the woman who raised her. And so, Frankie took the afghan, and with one fell swoop, wiped the floor and baseboard clean, then hurried downstairs to do the laundry.

Well over an hour had passed before Frankie returned to her mother's room with the cleaned afghan and a wet cloth. Ruby, curled up in a fetal position, was sound asleep. Frankie prayed it would be a long, dreamless sleep. No distractions. Just rest. Rest for her dying mother and for herself.

She placed the afghan down on a nearby chair and walked to the foot of the bed to inspect for any oatmeal fragments left by the cereal grenade. Finding three small patches on the sheets, she wiped them clean, then bent down to pick up the plastic bowl that had landed on the floor.

Slowly, as if with a newfound calm, she walked out to the bathroom to discard the bowl and the cloth, then went back to the bedroom, where she returned the afghan to its rightful place at the foot of the bed.

As she stood looking over her mother, she asked God to show mercy on them all and to find a small piece of joy for Ruby's dying heart. Then she walked over to the front window to watch the rain and to look up into the skies and pray some more.

Another day, Frankie might have laughed out loud to see Callie fumble so comically as she attempted to remove a stack of flattened boxes from her trunk. Today, Callie had managed to find a parking space right outside, but that didn't really help matters. The boxes were far too large to be held with ease, and even from Frankie's second-floor vantage point, she could see Callie's increasing agitation as the heavy rain threatened to destroy the boxes' utility with each additional second that she faltered.

Frankie smiled, looked up beyond the dark gray rain clouds, and said a small thank you. Then, like a kid on Christmas morning, she hurried downstairs to unwrap her gifts.

CHAPTER 5

Frankie stepped onto the porch, pleased with the rainy-day alibi she had just devised. Should Callie ask what had brought her outdoors, Frankie would explain that her hanging plants, endangered by the storm's menacing winds, required immediate rescue. Frankie chuckled as she thought of the perfect response: "The answer, my friend, is blowing in the wind, the answer is blowing in the wind."

As an obliging gust of air blew past her, validating what would never be questioned, Frankie pulled her "watering box" (an old crate) into position. She had just unlatched the last plant from the awning frame, when she heard Callie frantically calling her name. Feigning surprise and grateful for the timely response, Frankie stepped off the box, laid down the plant, and went rushing street side to help her friend.

As she grabbed one end of the stacked boxes, Frankie prompted Callie to take the other end with her left hand, then to close the trunk of her car with her right. With the cargo securely in hand, the two went rushing up Emily's steps, just as they had done so many times before.

"Thank God you came outside when you did!" Callie said, under shelter of Emily's porch. "Is this weather awful or what?"

"Least it ain't as hot today," Frankie said, shaking off the rain. "You should be glad about that."

"I am," Callie said. "But look at me, I look like a drowned rat!"

"When have you ever seen a drowned rat?" Frankie asked. "Didn't know they had them in your neighborhood."

Callie looked at her, as if to say "That wasn't fair," but didn't have the nerve to articulate it.

"That was rotten," Frankie apologized. "Sorry. Why don't you stick those boxes inside and come next door for lunch?"

"Oh, I'd love to!" Callie said. "Thanks, Frankie. I'll be right there."

Frankie, as she had done as a child, hopped over the railing that separated the two porches, then hurried inside her own house. Callie laughed with sweet remembrance, then opened Emily's door to deliver the boxes. When she had finished, she closed the door, then, aping her buddy's antics for old times' sake, hopped the railing in hot pursuit of friendship.

The Cavalese kitchen was eerily unchanged. The same table, with round, hollow chrome legs and a Formica top, rested against the back wall. Surrounding it were three chrome chairs with faded vinyl padding that had been patched in spots with gray duct tape. A fourth chair rested against the right wall, under the phone, piled high with magazines and phone books. The only new addition was a tacky display of plastic fruit in a yellow Tupperware bowl. Callie looked at it curiously.

"It's ugly as sin, ain't it?" Frankie said. "Edna Murphy gave it to Ma when she took sick. Hell of a lot of good a gift like this does. I told Ma, 'Looking at this goddamn thing's gonna *make* someone sick, let's get rid of this shit.' Ma said she'd seen nicer lookin' fruit in the garbage can, but for some reason, she didn't wanna hurt the old cow's feelings by tossing it. And she don't even really like Edna! Me, I'd like to take this plastic banana and use it to plug up that old bitty's—"

Callie laughed, cutting Frankie off before she could identify the designated orifice. "Maybe you could just bring the fruit out when Edna comes to visit."

"Nosy old cow shows up all the time. Pops in whenever she damn well feels like it. Only I'm sick of it. From here on in, she's ain't stepping foot in this house again. I'm gonna stop answering the door. Like I did yesterday."

"I know Aunt Emily didn't like her very much, " Callie said. "She was always offering unsolicited advice on how to raise me. She thought my aunt needed guidance because she was a single woman."

"Sounds like Murphy's old cow...sit down," Frankie said. "I'll make us lunch. I have some tuna salad from that deli 'round the corner. That okay with you?"

"Fine," Callie said, taking a seat. "How's your mother today?"

"Don't ask," Frankie said, as she opened the refrigerator door to retrieve a plastic container of tuna salad. "She's not doing well at all."

"Is her condition worse?"

"I don't know. Doctor'll determine that when she goes in tomorrow. But she won't eat what I give her, can't eat anything else, and rags on me constantly." Frankie put the tuna salad on the counter and turned to Callie despairingly. "I'm doin' all I can for her, I swear. I don't know how much more I can take. I'm losin' my patience. God help me, but it's true."

Now, it was not only Callie Mason who wanted to jump up and hug her friend, but Callie Hethers did too. But Callie didn't want to push things, and so she offered as much empathy as she thought Frankie would accept.

"I'm so sorry. This must be hell for you."

"It is," Frankie said, turning around to pull a loaf of rye from the bread box. "It's a living hell. My mother's a very unhappy woman. Has been since the day my old man walked out. I know it sounds ridiculous, but I swear she's waiting for him to come back."

"It sounds as if she's never been able to resolve the situation," Callie said. "I mean, it happened so suddenly…that one awful night when your father walked out. Didn't he move in with that other woman almost immediately?"

"You could say that," Frankie said, as she reached into the cupboard for two plates. "And if you remember, two years later, he married her, a week after the divorce came through."

Callie picked up a plastic apple and held it in her hands. "I remember now. Guess it's understandable why your mother never had any closure with all of this. The decision to end her marriage was made *for* her — by two other people. She had no say in it whatsoever. No chance to change her luck. Not to mention the suddenness of it all."

"Yeah, I suppose that's true," Frankie said, spreading the tuna onto the bread. "Believe me, Mason, she was dealt a rotten hand. Only I'm the one's had to play it."

Callie put the apple back in the bowl. "That sucks, Frankie. I'm really sorry to hear all of this. You've been cheated terribly. It's so unfair."

"Unfair's my middle name," Frankie said, placing two tuna sandwiches on the table. "How 'bout some chips?"

Before Callie could answer, Frankie grabbed a bag of potato chips off the counter and put them on the table. "What will you have to drink?"

"Whatever you're having," Callie said.

Frankie opened the refrigerator and took out a carton of two percent milk. "Milk okay?"

"Fine," Callie said. "My bones thank you."

"You're still an oddball," Frankie said, pouring a glass of milk, then handing it to her. "Here, tell your bones to enjoy."

"I was referring to the calcium," Callie explained.

Frankie poured another glass, then returned the milk to the refrigerator. "I'm just poor, Mason. Not stupid."

"Frankie..."

"Yeah, yeah. I know," Frankie said, taking a seat at the table. "Look at me. Here I am complaining about my mother raggin' on me, then I go raggin' on you. Sorry."

Callie smiled. "It's all right. You ragged on me when we were kids. It didn't scare me off."

"Something did..." Frankie blurted out. "Whoops. Sorry, Mason, there I go again."

"You're entitled," Callie said, taking a bite of her sandwich. "But try not to take advantage of that fact, okay?"

Frankie looked embarrassed. "Tell me about your kids. You got two of them, right? Twins?"

"Stephen and Molly. They just graduated from high school. They're spending the summer in Bar Harbor, Maine. My brother-in-law owns a resort there, near Acadia National Park. It's an incredibly beautiful area. Anyway, they're working for him...you know...running the front desk, working the dining room...things like that. This is their third summer there; they really love it."

"Sounds like the life."

"I guess," Callie said, feeling guilty. "But their uncle Cole does work them hard. Really."

"Kids coming back at the end of the summer?"

"Only long enough to pack for college. Then they're moving out. Stephen's going to major in business, so he can work for his dad, and Molls, well, she hasn't decided yet. She has wonderful artistic talent. Maybe she'll choose to do something in that area, who knows?"

Frankie flinched at the allusion to art school, but too subtly for

Callie to pick up on.

"All I can really think about now is the fact that they'll be leaving for good and how much I miss them already."

"This makes you an empty nester or something," Frankie said.

"Right," Callie said sadly. "I suppose so. I just hate that expression. Makes me sound like an old bird or something."

"Here, have some chips," Frankie said, pushing the open bag toward Callie. "A few calories won't ruffle your feathers none."

"It's not a few calories I'm worried about," Callie said. "Once I start eating these things, I can't stop. Unfortunately, I don't have a birdlike appetite."

Frankie jumped up from the table and grabbed Ruby's old kitchen timer, then set it for five minutes. "Here you go, Mason. Let's pig out for five minutes. Okay? We'll stop when the timer goes off."

Callie laughed and grabbed a handful of chips. "Sounds like a plan! Let's go."

When the timer rang five minutes later, it was Callie who reset it for ten, and for fifteen minutes, two women, whose bond of friendship had appeared irrevocably broken, found renewed joy in the simple pleasure of sharing a bag of chips. Resentment, strong and unwavering, hid behind dusty cans in the cupboard, and guilt, so intense it could not stand its own reflection, fidgeted nervously on the countertop, hoping not to see its image in the shiny Formica. For a brief moment, two friends, who for so long could see only differences, now saw similarities and discovered that their collective foundation, though precariously standing, had not yet crumbled. There was no worry over cancer and children, no talk of husbands and brothers, and no comparing of financial situations: only memories of a time when circumstance and change did not divide love, but strengthened it.

When Callie turned to see the sloppy, wet pregnant woman who was standing intrusively in the Cavalese kitchen, she wanted to blink her away. She wanted to dismiss her with a thought and to pretend she was nothing more than the onset of a small headache that could be easily banished with two ibuprofen.

But she was a big headache and had the mouth to prove it.

"I heard you had company," the thirty-something woman said, wringing out her extra-large Eagles T-shirt on the kitchen floor.

"You can see that I do," Frankie said, wishing she could hustle her out. "Callie, this is my neighbor—"

"Her friend—" the woman interjected proudly.

"—my friend and neighbor, Regina Cunningham. "Reggie, this is Callie Mason, uh…"

"Hethers," Callie finished for her.

"Mason, huh?" Regina said, pulling out the third chair and making herself comfortable. "You must've laid a lot of bricks to get a rock like that!"

Frankie looked appalled. Callie, hiding her disgust, looked at her ring, then at Regina. "My husband gave this to me. On our fifteenth anniversary."

Regina turned sharply to Frankie. "I keep tellin' ya, Frankie, you gotta get yourself hitched. And to someone'll give you doodads like that! What does that commercial say? Oh yeah…own a piece of the rock. Hey, maybe this is what they meant."

Frankie remained silent, burning at the irony of yet another person who condemned her single status, yet would be dismayed should she marry and no longer be available to fulfill her ongoing role as caregiver of the forlorn.

Regina turned to Callie. "Can you fix her up with one of your rich friends? Hell, never mind that. Can you fix *me* up?"

Regina roared with laughter, then screeched to a halt. "Just playing. I'm an old married woman with number four on the way. Due in August. Can't wait either. Being pregnant in the summer kills me. Next time, I'm carrying in winter. So how do ya like this rain we're having? Say it's supposed to keep up for a few days. Hell, I love it. Means that iguana-skinned bitch next door to me can't lay outside and bake her perfect little butt in the sun."

"Regina and her neighbor Susie don't get along," Frankie explained flatly to Callie, making it clear that she couldn't care less.

"We sure don't!" Regina punctuated. "I got no time for hussies who make a play for other women's husbands. Forgets she has one of her own, that woman does."

"Reg," Frankie said, bored with the dialogue. "I told you. Hal may look at her, but she ain't lookin' at him. His big ole beer gut may ring your chimes, but trust me, it ain't ringing hers. No one's that tone deaf. No one but you."

Callie bit her lip to keep from laughing, then turned so that she wouldn't make eye contact with Frankie and lose her composure.

"Maybe you're right," Regina said, ignoring the slight. "Come to think of it, the hussy'd rather mix it up with that brother of yours. Hell, what woman with two eyes in her head wouldn't!"

"Be quiet, Reg," Frankie warned. "Leave Paulie out of this."

"What are you gettin' so hot over?" Regina said, "Paulie ain't your husband, Frankie, he's your brother. Sometimes I wonder—"

"Drop it!" Frankie said angrily. "I mean it! Now!"

"So, Callie, you got kids?" Regina asked, unscathed by the public admonition.

"I have two," Callie said.

"Don't they say the damnedest things?"

"I suppose so," Callie said, wondering what road Regina was going to travel down next as she continued to exceed the verbal speed limit.

"Let me tell you what Harold Jr. came up with last night. Got back from his grandmother's house all upset. Seems she was eatin' something he'd never seen before, and when he asks her what it is, she tells him it's horseradish. Well, Hal Jr. don't say nothin', but when he comes home, he's actin' real funny…you know, in a quiet kind of way. I ask him what's wrong, an' he tells me Nana had chopped-up ponies on crackers with her clam chowder. Took me ten minutes to figure out what the hell the kid was talkin' about. So, I explain to him horseradish ain't made of ponies, and that it's just somethin' Nana likes to eat with oyster crackers. So then he wants to know why they make crackers outta oysters, and if all crackers had oysters in them, or just Nana's. Kid had me in stitches! Hadda come over and tell you. Is that a scream or what?"

"Yeah, makes me wanna scream, all right," Frankie said. "Hope you straightened him out."

"How old is your son?" Callie asked.

"Seven and a half. Now, let me tell you about my Steffie. Four years old. Brought her brother's GI Joe doll to me last night. Says, 'Mommy, why don't Joe have a pee pee like Daddy, Hal, and Billy?' Well, my Hal, he turned redder 'en blood and tells Stef not to play with boy dolls if she's gonna ask questions like that. Then my Billy, ten and a smart ass to boot, he tells Steffie the doll's pee pee got shot off in the war. So she starts cryin' and asks how the doll goes to the—"

Callie looked at Frankie with astonishment.

"Okay, Reg," Frankie said adamantly. "Listen, that's real funny and all, but we're kinda busy here."

"—then my Hal chimes in and says, 'Steffie, dolls don't—"

"Reg!" Frankie said sternly. "Enough! Okay?"

"Oh, all right," Regina said, pushing her chair back from the table. "Guess I can take a hint."

"Oh, Reg…"

"No big deal," Regina said, rubbing her stomach. "My feelings don't get all bent outta shape like yours do. I gotta rest anyway. Tired out from carrying this one. Just found out…gonna be another boy. Oh, by the way, Frankie, I put your gas bill out there on the coffee table. That new part-time mailman delivered to us by mistake. That guy ain't too swift. This is the third time he's fucked up, even after my Hal tried to set him straight last Saturday. Well, nice to meet you, Callie. Nice ring you got there."

Regina got up from the table and walked out, rudely leaving her chair in the middle of the floor and destroying the transient paradise that had just united two old friends.

"Are you and Regina very close?" Callie asked.

"She's nobody I'd seek out if I didn't live here," Frankie said. "But most of the people on this street are Ma's age, and my life ain't such that I got time to go lookin' for new friends, if you know what I mean."

"I understand," Callie said. "It's just that she's so…well, you know what…"

"I know what she is, Mason," Frankie said evenly. "And I know what she ain't. You take what you can get in this life. Aside from Paulie and Ma, and my occasional father, my friends from work and Reg are really all I got. Least she's been loyal…sticks around…what more can I say?"

And with that, the guilt, which had been waiting and wondering where to go, hurried back to Callie, bruised by the sharp edge of truth that had decided its fate.

"I'm sorry, I-I didn't mean…" Callie stammered. "Listen, thanks so much for lunch, Frankie. It's been wonderful. I really had a…well, I guess I'd better start packing. Haven't even put my first box together. I've got a huge job ahead of me. I've still got stacks of newspaper sitting in the car. You know, to wrap things in and…"

Callie faded out as the futility of her words grew evident. Frankie looked at her but did not speak.

"Again, I'm really sorry. I didn't mean anything. Thanks for lunch."

"You're welcome," Frankie said, rising slowly as she gathered the plates from the table. "You take care."

Callie swallowed the lump in her throat, then stood up as she prepared to leave. "You too, Frankie. You too."

With Callie gone and the front door shut behind her, Frankie put the dishes in the sink, then closed the kitchen door to wallow in her aloneness. After turning on the radio full blast, she resumed her seat at the kitchen table, picked up a plastic banana, then hurled it across the room. While the music blared in the tiny room and fruit flew in an airborne rage, Frankie prayed that any audible trace of her unfaltering despair would be hopelessly muffled beyond recognition.

Her bedroom was just as she'd left it; that was something Callie hadn't counted on. She didn't expect to see her dolls, still lined up neatly on a shelf, smiling and happy to see her, even after years of abandonment. Souvenirs of the countries her father had visited, her favorite had been the little Chinese doll because she loved its shiny black hair and silky red dragon kimono. The little Dutch girl had been a favorite too, because she wore real wooden shoes and a funny hat.

Callie, still reeling from the abrupt end of her lunch with Frankie, took the Chinese doll and sat down with her on the bed. She stroked the doll's hair and lamented not having had her to give to Molly, but amended her regret when she realized that Emily had probably received more pleasure from keeping the doll than Molly ever could have by receiving it. There would be no debate; Callie would not be giving these dolls to the Goodwill or anyone else. They were coming home with her. Callie took her right index finger and gently brushed the dust from the doll's faded kimono. Mei Linn, Callie remembered, that was her name.

Seeing Mei Linn again hadn't been Callie's only surprise; her feelings for Frankie were: the two had not grown apart, as Callie had conveniently resolved; she had pushed them apart and for years had been too deep in denial to truly acknowledge the wrong and to feel the absence of Frankie in her life.

Frankie made her laugh, the way Jackson did. How could she have forgotten that? Her other friends: they were nice people, but they didn't challenge her the way Frankie did. They didn't force her to be honest or to confront the truth head on. They didn't love her at her silliest or encourage her to look beyond the trappings. Callie fit well in polite society but was never really sure she belonged there. Emily had always told her that we most love the people with whom we can be ourselves: because loving and accepting oneself is essential for healthy living, and no one can truly love a person with whom he or she feels the need to always pretend. Callie had never totally understood what her aunt was trying to say, but on this day, as she sat holding Mei Linn, it became clear.

What had Callie been thinking as she questioned Frankie's friendship with Regina? It seemed clear that Regina wasn't able to fulfill Frankie's needs, but what right did Callie have to even hint at the woman's deficiencies? What about her own? Who was she to criticize Regina after what she had done? Was she jealous of her friendship with Frankie, now, at this late date? That was too outrageous to even consider.

Callie laid Mei Linn down and looked around the room. It seemed smaller than she remembered, but just as pretty. Was she being too hard on herself? Could she really blame the young woman with the big trust fund who didn't know how to juggle two different worlds, who felt as if she had no choice? She didn't know anymore; she just knew that she didn't want to make another horrendous mistake. But enough introspection: it was time to start packing.

Well over an hour had passed, when Callie heard someone pounding on the front door. Overwhelmingly grateful that Frankie had come to see her, and to work things out, she rushed out of the room and down the stairs.

"Hello, Callie-fornia," Paulie said, as Callie opened the door.

"Paulie—"

"May I come in?"

"Sure," Callie said, trying to catch her breath. "Please excuse the heavy breathing; I just raced down the stairs."

"Don't sweat it. I'm used to it," Paulie said. "I seem to have that effect on women. Pant like thirsty puppies when they see me coming."

"In your dreams," Callie said.

"There, too," Paulie said confidently with a grin on his face.

"Why don't you sit down?" Callie said, ignoring his comeback.

Paulie took a seat on the couch, patting the empty space beside him. "Sit next to me."

"I'll be fine here," Callie said, hunkering down into her aunt's easy chair.

"You'd be fine anywhere," Paulie said, eyeing her deliciously.

"Is that why you came over here?" Callie asked, "To indulge me in more of your narcissistic swagger?"

Paulie laughed. "C'mon, babe. That's not nice. At least I don't think it is. Narci-what? No, I just saw your car outside and figured you might need some help. I imagine it's gonna take several days for you to pack all the stuff in this place up."

"Most likely," Callie said. "When I'm all finished, I'll have a truck come to remove the furniture. Thanks for the offer of help, but this is something I have to do myself."

Paulie looked around the room. "Doesn't look like you've gotten much done."

"Well, no, I haven't." Callie said. "This is really my first day on the job. I thought I'd start in the bedrooms, then work my way downstairs."

Paulie grinned. "I find the opposite approach usually works best for me."

Callie repeated the line in her head before she realized what he was saying.

"Am I supposed to be amused by that?"

"You can be whatever you wanna be," Paulie said. "I thought about you last night, you know."

Callie looked uncomfortable and focused her eyes on her aunt's Royal Doulton Balloon Lady that sat on the bookshelf to her right.

"Don't you wanna know what I was thinking?"

Callie turned to face him. "Not really, but I suppose you feel the need to tell me."

"I thought about your superb beauty," Paulie said. "You really are an incredible female specimen. You work out, don't you, babe? It shows."

Callie blushed.

"Tell me, Callie-fornia. Are you satisfied?"

"What do you mean by that? Satisfied with what? My life? My husband?"

"I just asked if you were satisfied. Because if you're not, well, maybe I can help you out."

"I don't think I like where this is going," Callie said. "Nor do I think this is appropriate conversation. And if I did need satisfying, it would take more than some clown in tight pants—"

"Oh, Callie-fornia..." Paulie said, delighted that she had noticed.

"If the truth fits...or doesn't, in your case..."

Paulie laughed. "C'mon, let me help you out. What can I do?"

"Listen, Paulie, I don't mean to stick my nose where it doesn't belong, but don't you think you could be more useful to your own family than to me? Your sister is exhausted; taking care of your mother day in and day out has been a tremendous burden on her. Can't you lift it a little bit? And how about your mother? Don't you think she needs your help just a little more than I do?"

Paulie's smile disappeared but he continued to stare at Callie. "How about what I need? It's not easy going over there, you know. The damn house reeks of sickness...and it's so dark in there all the time...I can't deal with it...don't like emotional shit. Mary Frances handles those things better than I do. She's the strong one. Me, I never really know what to do or say. I just fuck it all up."

Callie looked disgusted. "What a sorry excuse. You and your sharp wit can do much better. And I don't care if Frankie is 'the strong one,' she's a lot more fragile than she looks."

"It's hard…I'm tellin' you. Watching my mother fade away is the pits. It's killin' me! Have you seen her? She's nothing but bones."

"Bones that still need you," Callie told him. "Sometimes we have a responsibility to take care of others. We can't just sit around licking our own wounds."

Paulie twisted restlessly on the couch. "Yeah, whatever. Well, I plan to see my mother today. Of course I do. I just stopped here first. And tomorrow morning I'm taking her to the hospital to meet with her oncologist, so Mary Frances can have a rest. It's not like I don't do things for Ma. But I can't be there for her the way my sister is—for one, I don't live there. And two, I work—managing my old man's club. It's a full-time gig, Callie-fornia. There are so many hours in a day…and that hospital, man, is that place depressing."

"I'm sure it is," Callie said, "But with you by Ruby's side, I'm sure that makes the whole ordeal much easier for her."

Smart broad, Paulie thought, realizing that Callie was quite aware he had been referring to his own depression, not Ruby's.

"And while you're there," Callie said, "maybe you can get the doctor to give you a testosterone reduction. Your needle is dangerously in the red zone."

Paulie smiled, taking Callie's gentle poking as a clear indication of her attraction for him. "My 'needle' is just fine. You're welcome to inspect it."

"Spare me," Callie said.

"Listen, you sure I can't help you? Carry a few boxes to the car?"

"On second thought, maybe that would be helpful," Callie said, eager to abandon the can of worms she had inadvertently opened. "Come on, I'll show you where the boxes are that I've packed so far."

As Callie led Paulie up the stairs, she could feel his eyes sticking to the back of her clothes. When they reached her old bedroom, she turned quickly to face him, as if doing so would dissolve the invisible adhesion.

"It took me twenty-five years," Paulie said, "but I finally made it to your bedroom."

"Are you going to help me with these boxes?" Callie asked, shrugging off his comment with a show of mild irritation.

Paulie moved closer to her. "Of course I am. Did you know how much I wanted you when I was in my teens? Hell, I fell in love with you when I was eleven."

"Paulie…"

"I wanted you real bad, Callie-fornia. Real bad. Changed a lot of sheets because of you."

"You're disgusting…"

"And here you are, after all this time, looking as fine as ever. You are one exquisite woman."

Callie was frightened, not so much by what he was saying, but by the way he made her feel inside. She hoped he wouldn't notice her vulnerability, or the fact her mild repugnance was at odds with her inexplicable attraction to him.

"The boxes?" Callie said, indicating three of them with a nod to her right. "Are you going to help me take them to my car?"

Paulie looked into her eyes and smiled knowingly. "Sure I am." As he knelt down to pick up two of the boxes, piling one on top of the other, Callie let out a small sigh of relief. Then, her eyes inexorably fixed on *him*, she picked up the third box and followed him downstairs to the front door.

"So here you are, asshole," Frankie said as Paulie opened the front door. "Thanks for comin' by."

Callie felt her heart drop. She knew how bad this looked…for so many reasons.

"Lighten up, Mary Frances. I was just helping Callie out."

Frankie glared at him, too angry to make the obvious protest.

"He was just on his way over to you," Callie said helplessly.

"Yeah, I was," Paulie said, putting the boxes down. "Just as soon as I put these in Callie's car."

Frankie shook her head in disgust. "I saw your car outside. I was wondering when you were comin' over. Didn't take much to figure I'd find you here."

"Mary F., how many times do I have to tell you—"

"No times," Frankie said harshly. "Zero. I don't want to hear it."

"Frankie," Callie pleaded, "I told him to—"

"Save it, Mason!" Frankie said, hopping the railing to her side of the porch.

Paulie and Callie shared a look as they watched Frankie rush inside.

"Go after her," Callie said softly. "She needs you. I'll take care of the boxes."

Paulie nodded reluctantly and turned toward the front steps. "See ya, Callie-fornia."

Callie said nothing and shut the door behind him. Was it possible? Could Frankie harbor more resentment toward her than she did a mere twenty-four hours ago? Would her bitterness continue to escalate? What could she do to make things better, without falling deeper into abysmal failure?

Dragging her heels, as if her sneakers were made of lead, Callie climbed the stairs to her childhood bedroom, hoping that it would provide some sort of sanctuary. She lay down on the bed and held Mei Linn to her chest. The rain was falling softer now, in a more tranquil, intoxicating kind of rhythm that quieted her soul. She closed her eyes and imagined Aunt Emily sitting next to her on the bed, telling her not to worry as her right hand brushed the hair from Callie's eyes. Never had a wish or a daydream felt so real, and as Emily spun her magic, Callie drifted painlessly off to sleep.

CHAPTER 6

"She just woke up," Frankie told Paulie as he came through the door. "And she's asking for her precious boy."

Paulie walked over to the floor lamp by his father's old lounge chair and turned it on. "Damn it, Mary Frances, it's like a crypt in here. I don't even know how you can see where you're going. Why the hell don't you turn on some lights? You got vampires living here or what?"

Frankie, who was sitting on the couch, picked up an old velvet throw pillow and began fiddling with the fringe. "Maybe there ain't nothing in this house that I need to see."

Paulie collapsed into the chair. "I didn't appreciate you calling me an asshole in front of Callie, thank you very much."

"She's not here now," Frankie said matter-of-factly. "Can I finish the thought?"

Paulie looked annoyed. "I really don't get why you're so pissed at me. So I stopped to say hello to Callie...asked if she needed a hand. Isn't that the neighborly thing to do?"

"I wonder how damn neighborly you'd be if she looked like Regina, or Fat Edna, or *me*, for that matter?"

"Damn it, Mary F., don't put yourself down like that. You know I can't stand it when you do that."

Paulie, the guilt-ridden hedonist, didn't even realize how honest he was being. It was true: he couldn't bear to hear his sister's words of self-deprecation or to watch her grapple with low self-esteem, because doing so reminded him of the ongoing sacrifices that she had been making for the past two decades — sacrifices that considerably relieved him from having to do the same. While in theory, it was neither child's responsibility to mend their mother's broken heart, Paulie's intervention in later years would have helped (at the very least) to assuage Frankie's burden. But instead, he became a master at rationalization: there was always a good reason not to get too involved, a good reason to make his visits short (or stay away altogether), and a good reason to watch his sister bobble back and forth while Ruby threw her best jabs at her. And so, whenever Frankie put herself down, or lamented her station in life, it was torture to Paulie's ears, for it is never easy coming to grips with pangs of contrition when one has so ingeniously denied all feelings of culpability.

For years, Frankie had done a respectable job of accepting her brother's limitations. But when Ruby fell ill, her responsibilities increased so substantially that she began to demand more of him. She wanted validation for all that she did and for what she had lost in the process. But most of all, she needed someone to share the burden. Paulie, true to form, rationalized the situation until his own selfish spin made sense, and Frankie's requests were rarely obliged in a manner she saw fit.

"What do you care how I talk about myself, anyway?" Frankie said.

"It bothers me, is all," Paulie said. "And you're *not* a bad-looking woman; it's just that you—"

"What?" Frankie snapped. "It's just that I haven't had my hair done in two years, I don't wear makeup, and I run around this house in nothing but old rags?"

"Well…yeah, to be perfectly honest. That's right. You've got nicer clothes than what you're wearing."

"Damn it! You think I don't know how bad I look? So who should I dress up for? Who's gonna notice? Who's gonna care? You? Pop…much as I see *him*…Hal Cunningham? Bud Murphy? Why bother?"

"You could do it for yourself, Mary Frances."

"Oh, go jump in the mirror," Frankie said angrily.

"C'mon, Mary—"

"Just go upstairs and see Ma, will ya?"

"Sure. But before I do, I've gotta go to the pharmacy and pick up that refill she needs. She wants some of those trashy newspapers, too. And a *TV Guide*. I'll be back as soon as I can, okay?"

"Don't know why you didn't do all that in the first place," Frankie mumbled.

"Do what?"

Frankie turned away from him. "Never mind. Just go. And turn that lamp off on your way out."

Paulie obliged, then left the house. Letting better judgment reign victorious, he decided against a return visit next door, then made a mad dash through the rain to his car.

Frankie, seeking only a brief respite from the stress and storm of another day, was instantly summoned upstairs by the ringing of Ruby's brass bell.

"I'm here, Ma," Frankie said wearily, as she entered the room.

Ruby's gaunt face and sunken eyes returned the greeting with a blank stare, and her wig, which she rarely took off, lay forgotten in a pile of old newspapers on the floor by the bed.

"Ma, you okay?"

"Where's your brother?" Ruby asked. "I thought he was here."

"He was. Said he needed to get some things for you at the drug store," Frankie explained. "Why'd you take the wig off?"

"I just don't care no more," Ruby said. "And it's uncomfortable."

Frankie walked over to the wig and picked it up. "I'll put it here on the dresser, case you change your mind. Okay?"

"Do whatever you want," Ruby said. "When's Paulie coming back?"

"Soon, Ma. Least that's what he said. Who knows? Might meet a babe or two on the way and stop to work his charms."

"You could use some charm, Frankie. You ain't got none that I can see."

Frankie immediately tensed up. "What if *I* only came to see you for five minutes every day, and what if *I* had someone else take care of you? Would you find *that* charming?"

"Your brother's got other obligations," Ruby said.

"I would too," Frankie said, "if I hadn't put them aside to take care of you."

"And I didn't take care of you?" Ruby said defensively. "All them years you was growing up?"

Frankie shook her head. "Isn't that what mothers are supposed to do? Take care of their kids? How many times do I gotta thank you? If you didn't want me, you shouldn't have had me. That's all."

Ruby turned and looked toward the window. She looked as if she had wanted to respond but thought better of it.

"Come on, Ma," Frankie pleaded. "Let's not fight."

"Ahhh…" Ruby muttered, still looking away.

"Can't you even look at me, Ma?"

Ruby turned to face her. "Just send your brother upstairs when he gets here."

Frankie's eyes welled up with tears, but she fought them off before Ruby could notice. "Remember what you told me this morning, Ma? About how you're the one who took care of me, and how Pop's sweet words didn't really matter none, 'cause he wasn't here?"

"What of it?"

"Well, your little boy apple didn't fall far from his father's tree. Lays on the charm, then takes a hike. Me, I'm here day after day taking care of you, but you don't appreciate that at all."

"I never said I didn't appreciate you, Frankie. You tell me when I said that."

"I guess you didn't," Frankie said dejectedly. "Not in so many words. But you never say that you do."

Ruby turned away and muttered something to herself.

"Why'd you ring for me, Ma? You hungry? Want some soup?"

"I just wanted to know where Paulie was. That's all."

"Well, now you know," Frankie said walking out of the room. "Now you know."

And like she always did, under cover of solitude, Ruby winced and shuddered as she proceeded further down the path of her own destruction, a victim of her own misery, as she lay frightened by the impermanence of life and loved ones, trying to understand what compelled her to destroy the very thing she was afraid of losing.

"Is everything okay, Mrs. Hethers? Mr. Hethers and I were worried about you. We expected you home by six o'clock."

"I'm fine," Callie told Rosa, the Hethers' longtime housekeeper, as she handed her a wet umbrella. "Just a little soaked, that's all. What time is it, anyway?"

"Almost eight thirty," Rosa said, graciously taking the umbrella. "Mr. Hethers just got home a half hour ago. He seemed awful worried when I told him you hadn't come home yet."

"Where is he?"

Rosa moved closer to Callie, a clear indication that she had a confidence to share. "He's in the exercise room. But I must warn you: he's not in a real happy mood. Must've had a bad day at the office."

Callie rolled her eyes. "Oh, he has lots of those. Well, thanks for letting me know, Rosa. Forewarned is forearmed, isn't that what they say?"

"Good luck, Mrs. Hethers," Rosa said, as she headed toward the pantry with the umbrella.

Callie rushed up the grand staircase, then hurried down the left hall to the exercise room, where Jackson was giving his deltoid muscles a hearty workout.

"Hi, honey," Callie said. "Are you sure you should be doing that? Wasn't your left shoulder bothering you the other day?"

"I'm fine," Jackson said, lifting two twenty-pound weights over his head. "Where have you been? I thought you would've been home hours ago."

"I fell asleep," Callie said. "In my old bed at Aunt Emily's house."

"You fell asleep?" Jackson said, as sweat poured down his face. "Rosa said you slept in late this morning. What gives?"

"I was tired," Callie said, annoyed at having her activities reported by the housekeeper. "It was a rough day. Very emotional."

Jackson, visibly tiring as he completed his final reps, put the weights down and wiped his forehead with a towel. "Spend a day at the office with me. You'll see rough."

"It's not a contest," Callie said, taking a seat on an empty workout bench. "Can't we both have rough days without comparing them to see whose was worst?"

Jackson picked up a lighter weight and began working the triceps on his right arm. "Just as soon as I can find a replacement, that bimbo I hired last March is history!"

"Joely giving you problems again?"

"What an abominable excuse for a secretary," Jackson said,

extending the arm. "You know the Seattle project we've been working on?"

"Of course, it's all you've been talking about."

"Well, it seems that the little twit hasn't been backing her work up on a regular basis. Her computer crashed today, corrupting the file, and when I asked her to take one of the backup disks and to finish the proposal on Rochelle's computer, it turns out she hadn't backed up *any* of last week's revisions. Says she forgot in all the confusion. The only confusion is in that tiny orb that loiters between her shoulders. Do you know what a goddamned idiot I looked like when Sterling called me from Seattle? Now I've got to waste precious time putting all those numbers together again, and to make matters worse, looks like I'll be heading out west sooner than later."

"Oh, Jackson," Callie said. "You just got back from Denver."

Jackson put the weight down with his right hand and picked it up with the left. "I'm not happy about it, Callie. Do I look happy?"

"No…"

"Well, I'm not, goddamn it. I'm not happy at all.…goddamn twit. I swear I'm going to fire her just as soon as I have time to interview for a competent replacement. If she spent more time at her desk and less time in the ladies' room…Oh, that's another thing. Every time I turn around, she's running down the hall. 'Mr. Hethers, I have to go the bathroom.' Have to go *the* bathroom? That's how Molly and Stephen spoke when they were five. Doesn't she know how to say, 'I have to go *to* the bathroom?' It drives me crazy. Why can't she say the word 'to'? Too many letters in it for her? Jesus, what a twit!"

"I doubt if adding a preposition would help her bladder any."

Jackson put the weight down and took a sip from his water bottle. "Don't make jokes, Callie. And besides, I'm sure half the damn trips are to fix her face paint or to tease the fibrous glob that sprouts from that useless orb. It's no secret that she's hot for Jerry what's-his-name in the sales department. I know what cats look like when they're in heat. Oh, and speaking of which, your little alley monster, Hungry, hissed at me tonight. Ungrateful little fuzz ball: I only tried to pet her. Cobbles never hisses at me. He knows who puts food in his bowl."

Callie laughed. "We all have our moments, dear."

Jackson picked up his heaviest weights from the rack and began working his biceps. "So tell me, what was so awful about your day?"

"Is this a challenge?" inquired Callie. "Or are you genuinely interested?"

"I asked you, didn't I?" Jackson replied, watching the way his muscles flexed.

"Then I'll tell you: it was pretty awful. And what made it awful, was that it started out really great. Frankie invited me over for lunch. Believe me, it was an unexpected but welcome surprise, and for a short but wonderful time, she let her guard down and it felt like old times again. Then this neighbor of hers, some chatty pregnant woman named Regina, bursts in on us without so much as ringing the doorbell. Unfortunately, everything went sour after that. Once this woman left, I made a remark that I shouldn't have, which Frankie resented, and her guard went back up faster than it had come down."

Jackson continued to focus on his muscles, alternating arms as he worked. "That's too bad."

"Well, I can see you're not interested in a blow-by-blow, but suffice it to say that the tension only escalated as the day wore on."

"So that's why you slept all those hours? Because your lunch didn't work out?"

Callie stood up abruptly and began circling the weight area. "Damn it, are you so engrossed in your own problems that you haven't heard a word I've said? Do you have any idea what that woman's friendship meant to me?" Callie stopped and looked at him angrily. "I'm not talking about a mere lunch here, Jackson. She was the very best friend that I ever had."

Jackson put down the weights and turned to face her. "I know that. Then why did you cut her loose, Callie? Why haven't I ever met her in all these years?"

Callie bit her lip, then walked over to the bench and sat down again. "I don't know. That's what I'm trying to deal with. That's why she resents me so much."

"Well, once you get Emily's place packed up, this will all be behind you."

"Are you crazy?" Callie said. "Aren't you listening? Do you think I can just walk away from this?"

"You did once…"

"God, you sound just like Frankie. Don't you know how tough it's been for me going back there?"

"Why do you think I bought you flowers yesterday? Geez, Callie, I'm not the insensitive lug you make me out to be."

"I never said that. I just inferred from what you said a moment ago that you didn't think any of this really mattered."

"I never realized how important this woman still was to you. Quite frankly, I had no idea that you wanted to revive this relationship. You certainly didn't indicate that to me yesterday when you set out for Rainytown."

"I didn't know myself," Callie said, exasperated. "Too much time had passed. I hadn't the foggiest notion what to expect, nor did I know how I would feel or what I would want. I didn't—"

"Well, do you know now?" Jackson asked, as he lay down on the mat, preparing to work his abdominal muscles. "Because my advice to you is to figure out exactly what you want before you go any further with this. Otherwise, you'll just spin your pretty little wheels for nothing." Jackson put his hands behind his head, bent his knees, and began doing his abdominal crunches.

"Is that all you have to say?"

"I think I've about covered it," Jackson said, as he curled up toward her.

"Okay," Callie said. "Fine. I'll go see about dinner."

"I grabbed something at the office around six," Jackson said, continuing his reps. "I wasn't sure what time I was going to get out of there, so I decided to refuel when I had the chance. Sorry, sweetie, but you'll have to masticate alone, just like I did."

Callie gave Jackson a dirty look as she prepared to leave. "You *masticated*? Don't you know you can go blind doing that? Didn't your mother ever warn you about—"

"Ha ha. Very funny," Jackson said, lowering his torso to the ground. "Let me rephrase then: you'll have to dine without me, my dear.

I've already eaten."

"Well, it wouldn't be the first time," Callie said, too proud to show her disappointment. "Enjoy your crunches; I'll see you later."

Frankie had no trouble remembering the sequence: a knock, followed by three short taps. That was horse code for "It's urgent. I must talk to you right away." As she lay on her bed, curled on her left side and facing the wall, she tapped her message on the faded floral paper, a silent admission of hope that Callie Mason Hethers, wherever she was, could somehow hear the words she could never say out loud: I need you. I'm sorry I was so rough on you. When can we talk?

The rain had stopped, silencing the nocturnal lullaby that Frankie had relied on to lull herself to sleep. Only quiet, broken by an occasional passing car or creaking of the house, surrounded her.

Paulie was long gone. He had returned from the pharmacy hours ago, staying only long enough to deliver Ruby's packages and to apologize for "pressing obligations" that required his presence elsewhere. Tuesday was Paulie's night off, so Frankie surmised that any obligation pressing Paulie was most likely to have two legs and a curvy figure. Asking Paulie to change his plans was futile; besides, Frankie's battered pride couldn't handle the rejection. His worn protestations wounded her; his frequent absences unnerved her. And so, as if to punish him, she avoided him altogether that evening, closeting herself in her bedroom and pretending not to feel his undeniable presence as he rushed up the stairs to their mother's room, pretending it didn't matter if she saw him or not.

It had been a long day, deserving of rest, but Callie could not close her eyes: not after sleeping late, then napping the afternoon away at Emily's. Her mind was overrun with conflict, and there was no one to help sort it out. Jackson, after completing his workout, had spent the remainder of the evening in his study reconstructing the Seattle proposal. Callie, occupying her time with odds and ends, had patiently waited for a bedtime talk, hoping to pick up where they'd left off in the exercise room. But only a few words, exchanged between segments of the eleven o'clock news, resembled the conversation she'd so desired.

In Callie's mind, there was no time for superfluous or idle chatter. Pleasantries about the weather, political opinions, and snide comments about the anchorman's grammar did nothing but irritate her. They were stumbling blocks, standing in the way of what she needed, restricting the channels of real communication, and making a mockery of the honest relationship she had cherished for years. Ironically, sharing the evening news had always been a gentle reassurance of love enduring; now, to Callie, it was merely Jackson's way of shutting her down.

CHAPTER 7

By late Wednesday morning, the storm had picked up momentum again, and with uncharacteristic fervor, Callie prepared herself to do battle with the elements. This was one rainy day that she had no desire to loll in bed or to pad about the house in her slippered feet.

As she drove through the blinding downpour to Emily's, she admitted to herself that it was not the empty boxes and household relics that beckoned her to Rainytown: it was Frankie. The packing could wait; the apology could not.

"Callie Mason! Come on in!" Regina chortled like a game show host as she opened the Cavalese's front door. "Frankie's on the phone. In the kitchen. Talkin' to her mom's doctor."

"Oh," Callie said, frustrated by Regina's presence. "If that's the case, why don't I go next door and get some work done? I can see Frankie later — when she's not so busy."

"Nonsense," Regina said, grabbing hold of Callie's left arm and pulling her inside. "I just came by to see if she needed anything at the market. I'll be gone in ten, and she'll be off the phone in five. Why rush off? Sit down. Take a load off."

"Thank you," Callie said, reluctantly taking a seat on the couch.

"Sure is some nasty day!" Regina said emphatically, as she sat down next to Callie. "It's a wonder you even bothered to come out. Just heard on the TV, there's been accidents all over town. I wouldn't be goin' out now if I didn't need to."

"You should be very careful," Callie said, referring to Regina's pregnancy.

"Oh, don't worry 'bout me. I ain't drivin' nowhere. Believe it or not, I'm just going 'round the corner to the grocery store. Need some stuff for my Hal. He's home from work today. Had an accident last night."

"Oh no. I'm sorry to hear that," Callie said, gently touching Regina's left arm with concern. "Is he all right? I hope he wasn't badly hurt."

Regina laughed. "Ah, he'll be just fine. Got punched in the jaw, is all. Pride's hurt more n' anything else."

"I see," Callie said, quickly retracting her right hand.

"I'm much more worried 'bout Frankie," Regina said, lowering her voice. "Paulie just brought Mrs. Cavalese back from the hospital. Carried her upstairs and left soon after that. Said a few words to Frankie, then split. Mrs. C. is sleeping now and Frankie's gettin' the lowdown from her doctor."

"Poor Frankie," Callie said. "She's really got a lot to deal with, doesn't she?"

"I'll tell ya," Regina said, inching closer. "That good-looking brother of hers don't help matters much. Maybe, if Frankie felt differently…well, maybe she wouldn't get so hurt all the time."

"I'm not following you," Callie said curiously. "What do you mean 'if Frankie felt differently'?"

Regina looked toward the kitchen, to make sure Frankie was still there, then looked at Callie. "I don't like to say nothin', 'cause she's my friend and all, but sometimes you gotta say something in order to help someone. You know what I mean?"

"Sort of," Callie said confusedly.

"Well," Regina said cautiously, "I think Frankie's got funny feelings about her brother, if you catch my drift. Mind you, that's only my opinion, but—"

"Mason!" Frankie said, walking into the living room. "I'm surprised to see you today. Thought the weather might keep you home."

"That's what I told her," Regina said, turning around. "I was just saying—"

"How's your mother?" Callie interrupted.

"Not so great," Frankie said, entering into the living room. "She won't be taking her last scheduled round of chemo like she'd planned. It just…it just ain't working anymore. Ma…she's not doing well at all."

"Oh, Frankie," Callie said. "I'm so very sorry. How is she—"

"Thank you, but I'd rather not talk about it right now. I just can't."

"I understand. Just know that I'm here if you need me."

"I know, Mason," Frankie said, slipping into her favorite armchair.

"Thanks."

"I'm here, too," Regina added. "Right across the street, day and night. Any time at all. Just pick up the phone and call or give a knock at the door."

Callie winced, feeling a twinge of something that felt like a cross between anger and jealousy.

"Thanks, Reg. I appreciate it," Frankie said, settling into lazy repose.

"What are friends for, Frankie? After all, you and me, we've been best buds for how long now?"

Frankie closed her eyes, as if she were too exhausted to engage in any unnecessary conversation. After several seconds, she opened her eyes and turned her head slowly in Regina's direction. "I don't know, Reg. My brain is fried."

"I don't know either," Regina said, looking at her, then at Callie. "But it's been a really long time. We moved here when I was pregnant with Billy. That would mean—"

"Reg," Frankie said, cutting her off. "Didn't you say you were on your way to the grocery store?"

"Well, yeah," Regina said, with a hint of indignation. "Just wanted to say hello first. See what you needed. Just wanted to tell you that my Hal had an *accident* last night."

"An accident? What the hell happened?" Frankie asked, lurching forward. "Why didn't you tell me that right away?"

"I was going to," Regina said. "But then Paulie brought your mom home, and you were tied up with hearin' this bad news."

"It's bad news, all right," Frankie said, trying to keep her personal anguish under control. "But certainly not a surprise. So tell me about Hal."

"Well," Regina said, happy to have the floor despite the inappropriate timing, "last night, my Hal, he goes with Riley Burke to some place he ain't never been before...*Will's Tavern,* I think was the name...over in Riley's neighborhood. Anyway, the bar was all fulled up, so Hal gets a beer, then takes a seat at a table to wait for Riley, who's talkin' to some friends at the bar. Well, soon as Hal sits down, he sees this table of people looking his way...good-lookin' folks...and they're laughin' real hard. Hal figures they must be makin' fun of his beer belly, which, I must say, was kinda protrudin' from that old Heineken T-shirt he was wearin'. Anyway, he tries ignorin' them, but they keep looking at him, laughin' even harder. Finally, Hal, he can't take it no more, so he yells somethin' real nasty at them. Then, one of the men, he gets up, walks over to Hal, and socks him real hard in the jaw. Turns out, no one was looking at Hal after all. There was a TV over his head, and they were all watchin' some blooper show. Hal, he didn't know the TV was there, dumb fuck."

Callie and Frankie shared a look, then burst out laughing.

"It's pretty damn funny, ain't it?" Regina said. "Just don't tell Hal I spilled the beans; it would hurt his manly pride...for whatever that's worth."

"Your secret is safe," Frankie said. "I doubt if either Callie or I will be talking to Hal anytime soon."

"No, I don't think so," Callie said, smiling.

"So what can I get for you at the store?" Regina asked.

"Nothing," Frankie said. "I'm fine. And seeing how you're walking, you don't need to be carrying back any heavy stuff on my account. Not being pregnant, and not in this weather."

"I thought you said you needed some milk," Regina said, sounding as if she were disappointed.

"I've got more than I thought I did," Frankie said, not wanting to give her an excuse to return. "I'm really okay."

Regina turned to Callie. "You need something?"

Callie smiled politely. "No. Thank you, Regina."

"All rightie then," Regina said, rising and walking to the door. "It's off to the grocery for me."

"Where's your umbrella?" Frankie asked.

"Oh, yeah," Regina said, glancing toward the front window. "Guess I better stop home first and get that sucker, huh? See ya, Frankie. Tell your mom I send my love. Take care, Callie."

Frankie waited until Regina had closed the door behind her, then turned to Callie. "She's got a good heart, Reggie, and she means well. But sometimes she can be a little...well, you know. Anyway, the point is, I guess maybe I overreacted yesterday."

"No," Callie said. "You had every right to be angry, and it was me who should have kept her big mouth shut. I don't even remember what I was going to say, but I'm sure it was unnecessary and unwarranted. That's why I'm here, Frankie. I want to apologize."

"Forget it," Frankie said, embarrassed. "It's no big deal. Besides, Reg did make some really lame comment about your ring and all. I can see why you might've taken offense."

"Oh that. I didn't take it personally," Callie said. "She was just being—"

"Reg," Frankie said.

They both laughed.

"You would know better than I would," Callie said. "After all, I've only just had the pleasure."

"You should meet 'her Hal,' " Frankie said, attempting a smile, but little else.

Callie grabbed a sofa pillow and put it on her lap. Sensing that she was not the only one who had wanted to clear up the previous day's dissension, she felt good. But on the heels of Regina's peculiar suspicion, Callie thought better of finishing the apology she had rehearsed on the way over. Callie was not dignifying Regina's suppositions by weighing their validity, but still, she intuited that even the smallest attempt to explain Paulie's visit would only serve to aggravate the underlying tension, and that was the very last thing she wanted.

Besides, Frankie was clearly distracted by the morning's events, and despite Callie's strong desire to resolve the past, she realized that Ruby, not herself, was Frankie's immediate priority. To confront Frankie with anything but concern for Cavalese family problems would be ill timed and selfish, at best.

"What can I do for you?" Callie asked. "I can see how much you're hurting."

Frankie looked at her but said nothing. She needed Callie, and that made her feel vulnerable. More than anything, however, she was frightened, for despite her best efforts to remain estranged, Frankie found herself forming an attachment to Callie—one that unmistakably resembled the bond they'd shared so many years ago. But what were Callie's intentions? Did she want to ease her guilt, then walk away with a clear conscience and the memory of a bittersweet reunion stuffed in her back pocket? Frankie had no idea, but she was too proud to ask and way too proud to expose her concern.

"There's nothing you can do for me," Frankie finally said. "I'll deal with it."

Callie pressed on. "But this news...that the chemotherapy isn't working..."

"Like I just told Reg, I was expecting it. But I kept praying for a miracle anyway. Guess God didn't hear me."

"Oh Frankie..."

Frankie, ruffled by the sound of intimacy, turned away. The sound of thunder rolled in the distance, and Frankie, startled, looked toward the front window as if someone had banged on it to get her attention.

"How's your mother handling this?" Callie asked delicately.

"How does anyone handle the fact that all hope is gone?" Frankie said, still looking away. "How would you handle it if you knew the Grim Reaper was lurking 'round the corner, waitin' for you?"

"I'm sorry. I guess that was a stupid question."

"When Paulie brought Ma home, she was so sick she didn't say nothin'," Frankie continued, looking at Callie. "And by the time I got upstairs to see her, she was already asleep. You know, sometimes I wish I could just trade places with her."

"Frankie, I know how much you're hurting. But please...don't talk that way."

"You got a husband, two kids, and probably a little black book filled with friends you can call. Me, I got a part-time brother and a part-time father, neither of whom can deal with anything emotional, and I got crazy Reg with her big heart and dumb stories. Oh, and this elegant palace."

You've got *me*, Callie wanted to say, but knew that it would be a mistake. A bolt of lightning cracked, momentarily illuminating the gray room. Callie shuddered but didn't let it distract her from continuing the conversation.

"I'm not going to pretend that I know what it feels like to be you,

Frankie. But don't assume that I'm always covered in the support department, just because I've got a husband and kids."

"You got someone to put his arms around you when you're sad, don't you?"

"I suppose," Callie answered uncomfortably.

"And you got someone to tell your problems to, someone to say good night and good morning to, don't you?"

"Yes, I do," Callie said, casting her eyes downward, as if she were ashamed of being loved.

"That's what I thought," Frankie said matter-of-factly.

"Haven't there been men in your life?" Callie asked.

"Only one that really meant anything to me," Frankie said, playing with the cuticles on her right hand. "His name was Johnny DeMarzo, and we dated for three years." Frankie looked up. "Can you guess what our song was?"

"I haven't the foggiest..." Callie said. "Oh wait, I know. 'Frankie and Johnny'. 'Frankie and Johnny were lovers, oh Lordy how they could love, they swore to be true to each other, true as the stars above'...that one, right?"

Frankie laughed. "Yeah. Pretty dumb, ain't it? Well, we liked it, except Johnny didn't particularly care for the part that says 'He was her man, but he was doin' her wrong.' "

"Did he?" Callie asked. "Did he do you wrong?"

"I don't think so," Frankie said, refocusing on her cuticles. "But I'll never know for sure. Stuff just happened, that's all."

"Like what?"

"Like Ma," Frankie replied. "Like Ma not wanting me to move away with Johnny when he got transferred. Like her finding fault with him so I'd stay put." A clap of thunder sounded, only this time, it was closer. "Gee, I hope Reg ain't walkin' in this storm. Hope the girl had sense to stay inside till this blows over."

"I hope so too," Callie said, looking out the front window at the rain. "I don't quite understand, Frankie. How did your mother destroy the relationship?"

"Oh...she started comin' to me with stories about Johnny. You know, this friend of hers saw him here with this broad or that one; another one seen him kissin' his ex in the car. You know, crap like that. She just put a lot of doubt in my head. Every chance she got. Told me Johnny's cheatin' would only get worse, and that only a fool would stay with a man like that."

"Did you believe her?"

"I didn't know what to believe. But her suspicions finally split us up, that's for damn sure. No man's gonna hang around for long if his woman don't trust him. Not someone like Johnny, anyway."

"How can you be sure that your mother didn't have your best interest at heart? Or that what she told you wasn't true?"

Frankie switched her attention to the cuticles on her left hand, glancing up at Callie only occasionally. " 'Cause Ma liked Johnny just fine before he got transferred to Florida and wanted to take me with him. And because she's had a fear of me cuttin' loose ever since I can remember. Always layin' guilt trips on me, tellin' me how she'd be so alone in the world if I went away. You know, shit like that. Trust me, Callie, I know my mother. The worst part is, that she's never stopped hassling me since all that happened, and it'll be twelve years Johnny's been gone. I don't know what I've done…or what I haven't done. But she's been hard on me. Real hard. Can't please her no matter what I do. And God knows I've tried."

"I'm very sorry to hear that," Callie said. "It's tough. Loving someone and resenting them at the same time."

Frankie looked up at her. "That rings familiar, Mason."

"Wasn't there anyone after that?" Callie asked, pretending not to catch the intentional ambiguity of Frankie's remark.

"Just men. "Men that didn't mean anything. Men that are no more."

"I'm so sorry."

"The only ones I meet now," Frankie said, "are in my dreams. You see, sometimes I have these dreams, and they're so real…so vivid, and in them I meet these really terrific guys. Handsome, sensitive types…that really care about me. But then I realize I'm dreaming, and that they're not real people… just fictitious people that my brain's cooked up to tease me with. So in my dream, I'll say to a guy: 'Hey good lookin', listen, much as I truly love you, we can't be together, because you're not real; I'm making you up.' And then, I hope that he'll tell me I'm wrong, that he *is* real, and that he'll give me his name and address so I can find him once I wake up. I pray that he does exist and that miraculously…we're just two people having the same dream…two people that God has put together in the most incredible way. But instead of answering me, and telling me what I want to hear…he goes mute and starts to fade away. Sometimes, he just turns into another person altogether. It depends on the dream. Anyway, about that time's when I wake up…you know how a dream can still feel real once you open your eyes? Well, sometimes I get up, still thinking he might exist, but after a little time passes, and I'm wide awake, I realize how silly and ridiculous the whole thing is, and then I feel like a major idiot. So, after that, I go about my miserable day, feeling like I've lost this really great friend that I never even had. Damn, Mason, I can't believe I'm telling you this. I ain't never told nobody this before."

Callie was struck by the simplicity of Frankie's words, yet haunted by their message. She smiled lovingly at her friend, unfazed by the rumbling of thunder as it rattled the living room walls. "There's nothing idiotic about you," Callie said pointedly. "And what you just told me; I think it's beautiful, I really do."

Frankie, once again uncomfortable by the swell of sentimentality, slunk away from the conversation, absorbed in random thoughts as the thump of her quickly beating heart blended with the force of the pounding rain.

As if on either end of a thick elastic band, Callie and Frankie had been pulling in opposite directions, afraid to get close but not able to go very far. But then, off-guard for a moment, they had both let go, and with great alacrity, had gone charging forward toward one another. It was too much, too soon, and wisely, both knew that for the moment, pleasantries and anecdotes would be a better choice of linguistic fare, for there was only so much gut-wrenching intimacy either one could manage that rainy day.

And so, as the storm raged on with no end in sight, Frankie regaled Callie with her favorite Regina stories, while Callie told stories about Jackson and the twins and for the first time showed Frankie their photographs. After a good hour had passed, Callie opted to graciously slip away, and to give Frankie some time alone. Frankie, sorry to see her go, but grateful for the time to rest, walked Callie to the door and bade her good-bye.

Frankie had been alone for all of ten minutes, her eyes closed for only eight, when Ruby's scream sent her flying upstairs.

"Ma!" Frankie said breathlessly, as she raced into Ruby's room. "Are you all right?"

A clap of thunder responded on Ruby's behalf, and as Frankie rushed to her mother's bedside, Ruby cowered and covered her face with the sheet.

"Ma," Frankie said, sitting down on the bed next to her. "It's okay. I'm here now."

Ruby's frail, thin hands shook as she gripped the top of the sheet. Seconds later, the thunder spoke again, this time more angrily, and Ruby's body bounced an inch or so upward, as if she were convulsing or receiving an electrical shock.

Frankie gently pulled the sheet away from Ruby's face. "Look, Ma, it's me."

Ruby, disoriented and frightened, attempted to cover her face again, but Frankie's calm, steady hands would not allow it.

"It's just a storm," Frankie said quietly. "Remember what you used to tell me when I was little…when I was afraid? You told me that God was bowling, and that he'd just knocked all the pins down…that's what made it so noisy up there."

Ruby looked quizzically at Frankie, then a change came over her, as if she were suddenly cognizant of her surroundings. Seconds later, a bolt of lightning cracked in the sky, sending a frenzied streak of light through Ruby's darkened room.

"How did I explain *that*?" Ruby asked weakly.

"The lightning?"

Ruby nodded.

"You used to tell me that God was shining his flashlight down on me, to make sure I was all right."

"God's hand don't seem so steady now."

Frankie laughed. "No, Ma. I guess not. But that don't stop him from watching over us."

"Did you feel better after I talked to you?" Ruby asked. "You know, when you were a little girl. Did I calm you down?"

"Oh, always," Frankie said, as she gently stroked her mother's forehead.

"That's good," Ruby said, her voice trailing off.

"Ma," Frankie said, trying to keep her alert. "Tell me what's wrong. Why did you scream before? Was it the storm that scared you?"

"Only partly," Ruby said, as if she were struggling to remember. "I think it was the dream."

"You had a bad dream?"

A look of clarity, then fear, appeared on Ruby's face. "I was at the train station, standing in line at the ticket window, and I was surrounded on both sides by suitcases. Everything I owned was packed away. Then, it was my turn to be waited on, and the man at the window...he was wearing a red bow tie and a blue hat...he asked me what I wanted."

"Yeah, Ma?" Frankie said, as she tenderly took Ruby's right hand in hers.

Ruby's voice began to tremble as the significance of her dream became clear. "I...I told him a needed a ticket. He asked me where I was going, but I told him I didn't know. So he stood on his tiptoes and peered down through the glass partition at my luggage. Then he says, laughing: 'Lady, for someone who don't know where she's going, you sure as hell packed a lotta stuff.' "

A thunderclap sounded, punctuating Ruby's words with a forceful bang. "Oh, God, Frankie," Ruby cried, "I'm going away...only I don't know where. I got no destination. All I know is that I ain't never comin' back. Help me, Frankie, I'm so scared."

"Oh, Ma," Frankie said, fighting back the tears. "Oh, Ma."

Putting one hand gently behind each of her mother's shoulders, Frankie bent down and pulled the fragile woman to her. Ruby nestled her face in Frankie's chest, sobbing, finally, without regard for useless pride, while above, the wild skies thrashed and the rain teemed down with unabashed fury.

Frankie pictured herself at Ruby's train station, waving good-bye, having no idea what train her mother was taking, knowing only that she held a one-way ticket. Ironically, it had been little more than an hour ago, when Frankie had spoken so freely with Callie about the power of dreams; now, here she was, wide awake, and in the middle of someone else's nightmare.

"It'll be okay, Ma," Frankie said, gently rubbing Ruby's back as she watched the rain through the front window. "I'm right here with you."

After several minutes, the sobbing stopped, and the sound of thunder softened as it grew distant. It was then that Frankie found the courage to say what had been impossible before: "I love you, Ma. I really do." And as she carefully drew her mother away from her, to gauge her reaction, she saw that Ruby's eyes were closed tight. "Sweet dreams, Ma," Frankie said. "I'm right here with you."

CHAPTER 8

"Hold on, I'm coming!" Callie yelled as she hurried down the stairs.

"Is that a promise?" Paulie asked Callie as she opened the front door.

"What?…Oh…you're disgusting," Callie said, catching her breath.

Paulie stood in the doorway and grinned at her. "Wanna let me in, babe? It's wet out here."

"There's an awning over your head. It'll protect you."

"Oh, c'mon babe," Paulie said, clasping his hands together playfully. "It's blowin' like crazy out here. Look! I'm begging you."

"All right," Callie said, stepping out of the way so he could enter. "Come in."

Paulie hurried inside, shaking the rain off him like a dog who'd just been spritzed by a hose. "Man, I'm soaked."

"Do you need a towel?" Callie asked, stepping away from him.

"Only if you'll dry me off," Paulie said, winking at her.

"Give me a break, will you?" Callie said. She started to take a seat on the couch, then quickly opted for the armchair, hoping that would dissuade Paulie from getting too close to her. He watched with amusement.

"I don't bite, babe. I swear."

"All dogs bite. At one time or another. And will you stop calling me 'babe'?"

"Sure, babe," Paulie said, making himself comfortable on the couch. "Anything you say."

Callie looked at him defiantly, as if that would protect her from any inappropriate feelings she might have toward him. But her first order of concern was Frankie, and the anger she would feel if, once again, she discovered her brother in Callie's presence. Paulie's attentions made her feel guilty, as if she were keeping something that belonged to someone else. He had no business being at Emily's house with her. His place was next door, with his emotionally overwrought sister and his dying mother, but for some reason or another, he preferred exchanging flirtatious banter with

Callie. And the worst part of it all, although she was loath to confess it: being with him made her feel good.

But why? She had a loving husband who clearly adored her. Lately he'd been distracted by pressures at work, but he never ignored her. Was she so selfish that she couldn't accept anything less than Jackson's full attention? Did she not remember how much she loved this man? Why had the sight of this salacious egotist before her caused such a stir inside — just because his eyes twinkled as he showered her with questionable praise? Was she so deprived that she needed conversation, steeped in sexual innuendo, to make her feel alive? Had she sunk so low that she'd forgotten how to say no? Of course not, she told herself. So, why, then, was she not only giving as good as she was getting, but working overtime to convince herself she had done nothing wrong, and that any clever repartee on her part was only a device to discourage this suitor's affections? Callie knew better. If she truly had no use for this man, then getting rid of him would not take the arduous effort that it now seemed to require.

"Why are you here, Paulie? Again?"

Paulie smiled. "Because it's where you are."

Callie crossed her arms and glared at him. "That's not a good reason."

"Only one I've got, babe." Paulie reached into his T-shirt pocket and pulled out a pack of cigarettes.

"Not here," Callie said quickly, letting her arms drop to her side. "My God, your mother is dying of lung cancer. Doesn't that give you any incentive to stop smoking?"

Paulie spied an ashtray, way across the room on a small table, then jumped up to fetch it.

"Paulie…"

Grabbing the ashtray, he rushed back to reclaim his seat, then put the ashtray on the coffee table in front of him. "Just one, okay, babe? My nerves are shot."

"I said no."

"You've made your point. You don't like smoking. Fine. Now, may I have my cigarette? Thanks, babe."

"Go ahead," Callie said, frustrated. "Smoke the damn thing."

Paulie's mouth turned upward, in a quick, victorious smile. Callie noticed and shot him a dirty look as he pulled a silver lighter from his right jeans pocket.

"All right. You've had your fun; you've got your cigarette. *Now,* are you going to tell me why you're here?"

Paulie's laughing eyes grew serious. Slowly, as if for dramatic effect, he lit his cigarette, took a long drag, then watched the smoke as it swirled through the air. After several moments had passed, he turned to face Callie. "I'm here because you do something to me that no babe out there in the streets can do. You make me feel that it's possible to have a quality woman in my life. And secondly, because I could use a friend right now."

Callie didn't know what to say. Responding to Paulie was simpler when he was being a smart ass. "Paulie, I-I…"

"We both know you're married, Callie-fornia," Paulie said, taking another drag. "Let's not talk about that right now."

Callie sighed in exasperation. She leaned forward and looked at him intently. "What exactly *should* we talk about then? My God, Paulie, I told you yesterday. You should be next door with your family, not here with me. Frankie's had it up to here, and your mom, well, no one knows how much longer she has. Don't you want to be with her as much as you can?"

"Damn it," Paulie said, sounding agitated and defensive. "I was with her this morning, when the doctor gave her the final death sentence. How much more fucking togetherness can I deal with? All the way home in the car, all she talked about was my old man, how he was stolen from her, and how she was going to die without ever seeing him again. That's all she ever talks about to me. I can't take it. I don't know what the hell to do for her."

"Does it make you feel inadequate because you can't help her?" Callie asked thoughtfully.

Paulie reeled back in horror. He wasn't used to having that word used to describe him in any context. "Hell no! What are you talking about?"

"Look, you work for your father, don't you?" Callie asked, trying to rephrase her point.

"Sure. What of it?" Paulie asked, taking a nervous drag from his cigarette.

"I don't pretend to know what's in your mother's head," Callie said cautiously. "But it seems to me that she harps on the subject so much because she wants you to intervene. Her pride won't allow her to contact him directly or even to ask you or Frankie to do so on her behalf. You're the person closest to your dad; you see him almost every day. She's hoping you'll ask him to come visit her. Can't you see that?"

"You're wrong, Callie-fornia. Ma's made it clear that she don't want no part of Pop while he's still married to 'that bitch.' And he isn't getting a divorce any time soon, unfortunately."

"Paulie," Callie said adamantly, "trust me on this one. She *wants* you to arrange a visit, despite all that. That much, even *I* can figure out. Can't you do that for her?"

"I don't know," Paulie said, flicking his cigarette into the small round ashtray. "My old man, he can't talk about Ma. Gets all nervous and shit, then clams up."

"Guilt?" Callie asked, crossing her legs and leaning back as if she were a trained therapist.

"Whatever. You're the smart one. You figure it out."

"I just did," Callie said, smiling at him.

Paulie stubbed his cigarette out in the ashtray and leaned back on the couch. "I like you, Callie-fornia. You're one fine broad."

"Woman," Callie said. "Not broad. Woman. One fine woman."

"Listen, what do I know?" Paulie said with a slight grin, as he reached into his left pants pocket for a mint. "When I turned sixteen, my old man told me he was sending me abroad for my birthday." Paulie popped the mint into his mouth. "Dumb kid, I packed my bags thinkin' I was going to London…maybe Paris. Two days later, a hooker shows up at my door. Says, 'Hi, Paulie, happy birthday.' And I've been dealin' with 'broads' like that ever since."

Callie laughed. "Real cute story. Now, why don't I believe it?"

"Suit yourself," Paulie said, sprawling seductively on the couch. "But it's true."

Callie watched admiringly as Paulie's finely chiseled body sank into the plush sofa cushions. Then, realizing that he was following her eyes with his, she sat up straight and quickly changed the subject. "Look, Paulie, I'd hate for Frankie to find you here again."

"Christ, Callie-fornia. She's my sister, not my damn wife. I don't have one of those. Listening to you talk, you'd think that Mary—"

"Never mind," Callie said abruptly. "I just think you should be somewhere else. Not here."

Paulie slowly pulled himself into an upright position, then stood up. "Yeah, okay. I'll go. But I'm warning you. I'll be back."

"Just think about what I said, will you? Do this one last thing for your mother. I really believe you'll be glad you did."

Callie rose to see him to the door. Paulie stepped around the coffee table and stood face to face with her. Without a word, and without warning, he put his lips to hers and kissed her: gently, as if she were a waking princess, then passionately, as if he had only one chance to make her fall in love with him. Callie went numb. She wanted to fight him. She wanted to scream Jackson's name and throw him out of the house. But she could only kiss him back…fleetingly, but not without feeling. Then, as if her good sense had been rudely awakened from an unscheduled nap, she yanked herself backwards, and with soft despair, pleaded with him to go.

Callie couldn't wait to see Jackson that evening. The sooner she did, the sooner she could find a way to assuage her guilt. She had to let Jackson know how much she loved him, or more to the point, to remind herself how much she loved him.

When she arrived home at six forty-five that evening, she found Jackson in the den: music in his ears, gin in his glass, feet on the table, and cat on his lap.

"Hello, darling," Callie greeted him. "How nice to see you and Hungry getting along so well."

Before Jackson could respond, Hungry jumped off his lap, ran over to Callie, and began rubbing against her left leg.

"So much for that friendship," Jackson said, as his head swayed dreamily to Mozart. "Where's my boy, Cobbles?"

Callie bent down, scooped up Hungry in her arms, then unloaded a barrage of kisses on the top of the cat's head. "Good girl. Mommy's so happy to see you." Hungry squirmed as she let out a small whine. Callie, holding the cat a bit tighter, planted five more kisses on her. Hungry protested by turning up the volume, then pressed her back paws into Callie's chest. "All right, then. Be like that, you loveless feline. Go find your brother and tell him Daddy wants to see him."

"Meow!" Hungry mewed, as she sprang free and made a run for it. "Meow!" she repeated, as she took cover under a chair.

Callie laughed and walked over to Jackson. She sat down next to him on the couch, threw her arms around his shoulders, and kissed him right smack in the middle of Mozart's Concerto in D Minor.

"My, that was tasty!" Jackson said, grinning. "What did I do to deserve that?" He paused. "Oh no! You didn't have an accident with the BMW, did you?"

Callie pulled away angrily. "Of course not! Why in the world would you say that?"

Jackson laid his martini on the coffee table and shifted his position to face her. "Lighten up, sweetie. I was only kidding."

"I just don't know why you would even joke about that," Callie shot back nervously.

Jackson shook his head in confusion. "Callie...I was *teasing*. It's just that...well, the way you just kissed me now...that's the way you usually kiss me when you're feeling guilty about something...or we've had a fight."

Callie jumped up and walked over to the bar. "That's ridiculous. Where's the wine?"

Jackson picked up his martini and took a sip. "The Zinfandel is gone. There's a nice Beaujolais there you might want to open. If you prefer white, there's an open bottle of Chardonnay underneath, in the ice box."

Callie looked around until she spied the bottle of Beaujolais. "I prefer the red tonight."

"May I open that for you?" Jackson asked.

"No, thanks," Callie said, picking up the corkscrew. "Stay put. I can do it."

"Okay," Jackson said, quietly reabsorbing himself in the music.

Callie took a small knife, peeled the dark red seal from the top of the wine bottle, then inserted the corkscrew. Her mind was racing and her heart was thumping so loud she was sure Jackson could hear her internal rumblings. Her very own one-note symphony. Callie even had a name for it: Guilt in G Flat. She twisted the spiral further into the cork as she assessed the situation. Operation Seduction was failing miserably, and Callie knew it had no chance of succeeding if she continued to wear her betrayal so boldly.

"Jack, honey...oh damn!"

"What's wrong?" Jackson said, coming out of his musical trance.

Callie loosened a piece of cork from the spiral, then threw it angrily across the room. Hungry, eyeing the wayward cork, sprinted out from under the chair and rushed to pursue her quarry.

"Nothing. The damn cork just broke in half, that's all. I should've just had a glass of the white. I can't do anything right." Jackson downed the last sip of his drink, then carried his empty glass to the bar. Resting it on the counter, he put his right arm around Callie's right shoulder and gave her a squeeze. "Relax, my love. We've weathered worse storms than this. What we have here...is a case of dry cork and harried wife. Sit down, and I, your humble servant, will cater to your every need. And, while I'm at it, I think I'll make myself another drink. Wouldn't want you to tipple alone." Jackson laughed and kissed Callie on the left cheek.

"Thanks, honey," Callie said, handing him the corkscrew. "I really appreciate it."

"Go," Jackson said. "Sit down. I'll be right there, and together, we will revel in the beauty of Wolfgang's music."

Callie took a seat on the couch while Jackson fixed the drinks and watched Hungry as she batted half a cork around the floor. Callie was in no mood for "reveling" while Wolfgang, Fred, or anyone else delighted her with his musical genius. She wanted to talk: she needed Jackson to tell her that she was a good wife and that he loved her. She needed immediate reassurance that their diminished quality time of late was nothing personal, and that his seeming lack of interest in her problems was merely the result of being tired, stressed, and overworked.

Jackson would not have argued that the verbal confirmation of these sentiments was important. However, having stated them multiple times already, the need for ongoing clarification escaped him. In fact, her needs often mystified him altogether, made him feel inadequate, as if he were incapable of being the loving husband he'd always prided himself on being. "If you do it right the first time," Jackson's father had taught him, "then you won't have to keep doing it again." With those words to guide him, Jackson reasoned that Callie's constant need for verification must surely indicate his initial (and subsequent) failings in the role he cherished most.

"Wine, madam," Jackson said, as he handed Callie her glass. "And for me, zee martini." Jackson took a seat next to his wife. "Oh, I forgot to tell you, the kids called a while ago. They're doing great. Molls really wanted to talk to you. Girl stuff, I suppose. Maybe she's fallen in love. Oh damn, I hope not."

Callie put her drink on the table. "I should go call her back."

"Don't bother. They were on their way into Bar Harbor with a group of friends for the evening. Molly wants you to call in the morning. She and Stephen will both be around then."

"Oh, okay," Callie said, disappointed. "I wish I'd been here when they called." Callie leaned back on the couch and sighed. "I really miss those kids."

"Here comes your girl," Jackson said. "And she's got a present for you."

Callie let a small smile pass her lips when she saw Hungry, with the piece of cork clenched between her teeth, making her way for Callie's lap. Dropping her gift upon arrival, Hungry circled the area twice, then snuggled in for a nap. She had only been there for half a minute when Cobbles, who hadn't been seen for hours, came speeding toward Jackson's lap. Hungry looked up at him, as if to say, "Don't mess with me," then closed her eyes. Anxious for his own share of affection, Cobbles made himself cozy on Jackson's lap. As Wolfgang's music filled the air, four creatures, two human, two feline, considered their own agendas, and for what seemed an eternity to Callie, and a brief interlude to Jackson, no one spoke (or mewed) a word.

Wednesday nights at the Blue Lights were usually busier, but for a dismal, rainy evening, business was surprisingly good. Veronica, the regular bartender, a tall black woman with wide hips and long, beautiful braids, moved effortlessly down the bar as she refilled glasses and schmoozed with her regular clientele. When she saw Paulie standing midway down the bar, holding the handful of money she had requested, she walked quickly over to meet him.

"Here you go, babe," Paulie said to her, laying a stack of one-dollar bills, along with several rolls of quarters, on the bar. "Anything else?"

"How 'bout a smile from my handsome boss?" Veronica said, taking the money and putting it into the cash register drawer. "It ain't like you to be so down. What's the matter, baby?"

"My mother's dying," Paulie said, walking toward the empty end of the bar and taking a seat.

Veronica cracked open a roll of quarters, shut the drawer, then followed Paulie to his seat. She stopped in front of him and squinted her eyes in contemplation. "I know she is, honey. But it's something else. And don't try to tell me differently. I know you too long, Paulie Cavalese."

"Suit yourself," Paulie said, pulling a cigarette out of his shirt pocket. "If you wouldn't mind, Ronnie, I'll take that drink now."

"It's not like you to be so quiet," Veronica said with a lilt in her voice, as she pulled a bottle of scotch from the shelf behind her and poured Paulie a drink. "Something's eatin' at you."

"Whatever you say," Paulie said, lighting his cigarette and looking toward the end of the bar. "Annie's waving at you. Better go see what she wants — before she starts running her mouth and you end up bashing her with the vodka bottle."

"Wouldn't I love that!" Veronica said devilishly, as she set Paulie's drink on the bar and headed toward Annie Cavalese.

"The bitch," as Ruby called her, Louie's wife, could usually be found at the service end of the bar, cavorting with the male customers and offering unwelcome advice to the bartender on duty, which was usually Veronica. At sixty-six, Annie was still a good-looking woman, though the nightlife had taken a serious toll on her assets. Annie blamed this demise on her invisible parents, Father Time and Mother Nature, disinclined to admit that a lifetime of excessive drinking and smoking might have had something to do with her current state of degeneration. Often, she would go overboard in her attempts to mask the tricks of time, by choosing tight jeans and wild, streaked hair as an antidote for the creeping effects of age, although doing so only served to promote her insecurities, not obscure them. But despite her surprising, and often controversial, choices, she still had gorgeous blue eyes and a radiant smile. Looking at her, one could only imagine just how beautiful she once used to be.

Paulie had as little contact with Annie as possible. He pretended to like her more than he really did, only because getting along with her facilitated his job as club manager. The fact that she was his father's wife brought her only a modicum of respect. After all, how much respect had she shown for his family when she "stole" Louie away? To Paulie, Annie was shallow and vain, and loved the bar and the life more than she loved Louie.

Frankie, on the other hand, never pretended at all. She let Annie know exactly how she felt and avoided her the best she could. Unfortunately, most of Frankie's interaction with her father took place in the Blue Lights or at his home, so dodging Annie was difficult. For everyone's sake, Frankie was amicable, but her loyalty to Ruby was so intense that she could never have offered friendship or forgiveness, even if she had wanted to. What Frankie most resented was Annie's intrusion in her relationship with Louie. This was especially problematic when she visited her father at home. Annie seemed intent on monitoring her husband's visits with his daughter and often editorialized on conversations that were none of her business. Sometimes, Frankie chalked her intrusiveness up to the fact that Annie had no children of her own and therefore needed to flex her maternal muscles at Frankie's expense. But that theory was usually nixed, as it was Frankie's very strong opinion that

Annie *had* no maternal instinct, and that anything resembling such a creature was merely the woman's obsessive need to control and to be the center of attention. But what really disturbed Frankie, and Paulie too, was their father's refusal to take a stand and to put his intrusive wife in her place.

Paulie took a drag from his cigarette as he watched Annie in animated conversation with Veronica. He couldn't hear what was being said; he only knew that Annie had no business saying it, and that Veronica, who did stellar work, didn't need bartending tips from the owner's wife. Some nights, when he was feeling confrontational, he would intervene on Veronica's behalf, but that was more often out of boredom than anything else, and a need to release his pent-up frustration toward Annie. On this particular evening, with the day's events weighing heavily on his mind (especially the kiss), he had no desire make idle conversation with anyone.

It was not like Paulie to sit at the bar and brood over a woman, especially one as unavailable as Callie Mason Hethers. What was it about her that attracted him so much? Her beauty, he mused. No, it was much more than that. Paulie had no trouble getting beautiful women. Was it her ability to challenge him, to put him in his place, and to see through his protests and flimsy excuses? Maybe. He wasn't sure. But what he had told her earlier was true, and for Paulie, incredibly honest. She made him feel as if he could have someone worthwhile in his life, which didn't say much for the hoards of women he had entertained since puberty. In fact, Paulie had always avoided "worthwhile" women. So what had changed? Paulie thought about his conversations with Callie; he thought again about their kiss. Then, taking another drag from his cigarette, he motioned for Veronica to refill his glass.

"You ready to talk?" Veronica asked, as she poured his drink.

Paulie took a sip of his scotch and pretended not to hear her question. "What did she want?" he asked, nodding his head in Annie's direction.

Veronica rolled her eyes. "Not enough lemons and limes in the bins. Wants me to cut more up, case we get busy all of a sudden. I keep telling her they'll only go bad. We ain't gonna *get* that busy. Not tonight.

Besides, I got more than I need. But damn…she knows better than I do. Always does."

Paulie smiled. "So you cut more fruit?"

"Hell, no!" Veronica said, with mock indignation. "I know you're not talking to me, Paulie Cavalese. You know I don't pay that woman no mind."

"Good for you," Paulie said, crushing out his cigarette.

Veronica picked up the ashtray, cleaned it, and put it back on the bar. "Where the hell are you tonight, anyway? I see you sittin' in front of me, but your head is somewhere else…up in a cloud…far away from here."

Paulie picked up a stack of beer coasters with his right hand and lazily let them drop, watching them as they scattered. "You don't ask my whereabouts, I won't ask about yours."

Veronica shook her head and straightened the coasters. "In addition to bein' smart, now you're gonna go messin' up my bar."

"I love you, Ronnie," Paulie said, taking another sip of his drink. "You're so beautiful."

"Yeah, yeah," Veronica said, as she motioned to a customer that she'd be right there. She looked toward the front door. "Hey, here comes your old man. Maybe he can get through to you. I know I can't."

As she walked away, Paulie swiveled around in the bar stool and signaled to get his father's attention. Louie, who seemed surprised to be summoned, walked over to greet him.

"Hey, son," Louie said, giving Paulie a quick embrace and a manly pat on the back. "How ya doin' tonight?"

"Sit down, Pop," Paulie said. "I wanna talk to you."

Louie ran his right hand through his thick mass of salt-and-pepper hair, then waved hello to his wife at the opposite end of the bar, who was too busy talking to notice him. "Whew! Sure is wet out there. Supposed to be nice tomorrow, though. That's what they say. Well, we'll wait and see."

"Yeah, right," Paulie said, motioning to Veronica to bring Louie a beer.

Louie took a seat on the bar stool next to Paulie. "Spoke to Frankie earlier. She told me about your mother…and the chemotherapy. I'm sorry. I really am. Truthfully, I expected your sister to sound even worse than she did. Said she had a nice visit with an old friend today…and that it really helped her."

Veronica put a frosted glass in front of Louie, poured a beer into it, then went about her business.

"What else did Mary Frances say?" Paulie asked curiously.

"Not much," Louie said, taking a sip from the head of the beer, to stop it from spilling over. "Annie had just come in with the groceries. Needed my help, so I had to hang up. So, who was this old friend, anyway? Whoever she is oughta come around more often. Brightened Frankie's spirits. I like to see that. My little girl's been so—"

"Callie Mason," Paulie said, playing with the coasters that Veronica had just straightened. "You remember her, don't you?"

Louie looked stunned. "You're talking about the kid who lived next door? Emily's niece?"

"Who else would I mean?"

Louie looked toward the opposite end of the bar and watched as his wife flirted with Marv, the piano player, who was just returning from his break. "What in God's name did she come back for?"

Paulie was taken aback by his father's incredulity. "To pack up Emily's house. It's been sold. Why the surprise, Pop?"

"Nothing," Louie said, staring into his beer. "Nothing at all. Just didn't expect to hear her name again…not after so many years. Never thought she'd show in Rainytown again…that's all."

Paulie looked perplexed. "I'm surprised you've even thought about her at all. It's not like you two ever really had a personal connection."

Louie took a big gulp from his beer glass. "I think about lots of things from those days, Paulie. She was my kid's best friend. Meant the world to Frankie. Why shouldn't I contemplate someone who meant so much to my little girl? What's the problem with that? You gonna tell me who and what I'm allowed to think about?"

Paulie reached for another cigarette as the notes from Marv's piano filled the room. "Never mind."

"You don't think Frankie would bring her over here, do you?" Louie asked.

"No way," Paulie responded, lighting up his cigarette. "Why ya askin', Pop?"

"No reason," Louie said, with one eye on Paulie and another on his flirtatious wife. "Just don't think this would be a good place for her, that's all. Don't you bring her over here neither."

"That's crazy. Listen, Pop—"

Louie swiveled in his chair to face the piano and began softly singing to the music that Marv had just started playing. "Where somebody waits for me, sugar's sweet, so is she, bye, bye, blackbird."

"I need to talk to you about something," Paulie said impatiently.

Louie continued to croon. "No one here can love or understand me, oh, what hard luck stories they all hand me—"

"Pop, can you hold up on the blackbird for a minute?"

"Make my bed and light the light, I'll be home, late tonight, blackbird… What's wrong with a little music? Good for your soul. Hell, you should know that. You're a musician, ain't you?" Louie turned around to face Paulie. "All right, son. What's so important you can't wait for the damn song to finish?"

Paulie clutched his glass, as if it would somehow give him courage. "It's Ma. I was wondering if you could go see her."

"Oh, geez…I don't know, Paulie. I don't see no sense in stirrin' up old memories," Louie said, before taking a swig of his beer.

Paulie looked at Annie, then at his father. "Afraid *she* won't like it?"

Louie shook his head. "Oh shit, you're startin' with that nonsense about Annie again."

Paulie slammed his glass down on the bar. "I'm not startin' anything, Pop. I'm just askin' you to go see Ma. Before she dies. Say your goodbyes. Settle some things between you, so she can go in peace. Doesn't she deserve that?"

"Your mother should've moved on years ago. It ain't my responsibility to ease her burden before she dies."

Paulie looked him in the eyes. "I never said it was your responsibility. Just asked if you'd do it, is all. If you won't do it for Ma, would you do it for me…or Frankie? Hell, do it for yourself. You never did apologize to her for running out on us. For leavin' her to raise us all alone."

Louie grabbed his glass and stood up. "You don't know everything what your mother and I discussed; don't think for a minute that you do. 'Sides, I don't need to hear this crap from you, Paulie. I got enough on my mind without worryin' about makin' amends with your mother. I don't know what's gotten into you, but this ain't my son talkin'. Hell, you sound like a woman…all this rot about apologizing…going in peace. Crap. Good ole female crap. Next you're gonna be askin' me to 'explore my feelings.' Crap! You hear me, son? Crap! Now, if you don't mind, I'm gonna go see what the *boys* are up to. Leave this garbage to the ladies, son. Be a man." Louie downed the last sip of his beer, put his glass back on the bar, then hurried off to join a group of his cronies in the back of the room.

Paulie sighed in disgust and crushed out the cigarette he had just lit. He was half off the bar stool, intent on heading to the back office for some solace and bill paying, when Marv began his next number. Paulie hopped back on his seat to listen. Now it was his turn to sing along, although he did so silently. Callie-fornia, here I come. Right back where I started from. Paulie smiled to himself and downed his drink. You're one fine, babe, Callie-fornia. And you ain't heard the last of me yet.

"Callie-fornia" was none too pleased with Wolfgang Amadeus Mozart. Two glasses of wine and a plate of hot hors d'oeuvres later, his music was still cutting into her time with Jackson. And, after two martinis, Jackson's capacity for serious conversation was rapidly diminishing. As for the feline lap-sitters, they had long since left. Annoyed by human movement (but unaffected by Mozart), they had found that chairs make better beds than people, because furniture does not squirm to reposition itself or get up to use the bathroom.

"Fantastic!" Jackson declared, as the final note of the Mozart CD had finished. "Can you imagine how much more that man could've accomplished had he lived past the age of thirty-five?"

"Hard to imagine," Callie said tonelessly. Who cares, she said wordlessly.

Jackson jumped up and walked over to his massive CD collection on the wall. "Hmmm," he mumbled to himself. "I wonder if George will come out to play." He turned to Callie. "How 'bout it, my dear? A little 'Rhapsody in Blue'?"

"Jackson," Callie said with an edge to her voice. "I have nothing against Gershwin, or any other composer, but couldn't we spend a little less time 'reveling' in their musical genius and a little more time together…talking?"

"What do you want to talk about?" Jackson asked, as he slid Wolfgang out of the machine and snapped him back into his case.

"About us. Things in general. About what I've been going through these past few days in Rainytown."

"I thought we talked about all that last night," Jackson said, as he inserted George into the disc tray. "I was under the impression that I gave you some good advice. Figure out what you want from the relationship with Frankie, then go forward."

"Yes, but—"

"Full steam ahead," Jackson bellowed. "Onward and upward."

"Oh, no. Please don't tell me you're drunk," Callie said.

Jackson turned around and grinned at her. "All right, my little chickadee." As the first few notes of "Rhapsody in Blue" filled the air, Jackson opened his arms wide, as if to embrace them. "Melodious orgasm! I love it!"

"For Christ's sake. Will you sit down and behave yourself?"

Jackson danced merrily over to the couch and flung himself down. "As you wish, my dear." He snuggled up next to her. "Ah, you are in the mood for romance!"

"I'm not so sure anymore," Callie said, annoyed by his obvious intoxication.

"I can fix that." Jackson reached over with his left hand and began fumbling with the buttons on Callie's shirt. To his consternation, his fingers would not cooperate with his intentions. "Hmmm…perhaps this is more difficult than I thought. Perhaps this is a job for—"

"Screw Naked Matador!" Callie said angrily.

"Exactly what I had in mind!" Jackson said jovially.

"And the bull he rode in on," added Callie.

"Sorry, my dear," Jackson said farcically. "But that's where I draw the line."

"Can't we have anything that remotely resembles a conversation?" Callie asked, trying to ignore what she had deemed as lunacy.

Jackson looked at her without responding, then seemed to sober for an instant. "How about then…we talk about *my* day? Do you want to hear about every glitch in the Seattle project? Or about Joely's meltdown before the board meeting? Because I'll be more than happy to share every miserable detail with you. I will share, share to your heart's content."

"I'm not interested," Callie said flatly. "Not at this moment, anyway."

"Ah ha!" Jackson exclaimed, jumping up from the couch and walking over to the bar. "Just as I thought! You want to talk about your day, but to hell with mine!"

Frustrated, Callie turned around to see what he was up to. "You're not going to make a *third* martini, are you?"

"Your powers of observation are to be commended." Jackson picked up a bottle of gin and poured a healthy shot into the martini pitcher.

Callie stood up abruptly, as if doing so would somehow serve as a speed bump and slow him down. "Jackson, it wasn't that long ago that you and I could talk to each other. For the past couple of months, I've felt like a stranger in your midst. What's happened to us? My God, we used to be so good together."

"Nothing happened." Jackson poured a drop of vermouth into the pitcher. "And I didn't realize I've been such a lousy husband. Well, excuuuuse me! I'm just an overworked S.O.B. who wants to enjoy himself at the end of a miserable, goddamn day. I deserve that much. What's your problem?"

"You're my problem. Take tonight. I'm trying to get some support from you, and you're too busy conjuring up that old vaudeville team, Tanqueray and Hethers."

Jackson stirred his martini briefly. "And what a fine team they make," he said, dropping two olives into his glass, then filling it with the martini mixture.

Callie plopped back down on the couch, exasperated. "I know you're going to hate this idea, but I've been thinking. Maybe we should see a therapist. You know, someone who specializes in marital relations."

"Martini relations? Wonderful idea!"

"Marital relations!" Callie said angrily.

"Now who is intoxicated!" Jackson said loudly. "For certainly it is not I who has lost his mind, it is you!" Jackson laid his martini on the bar, and began pacing the room dramatically. "Therapists! Sick, malingering sponges...soaking up every toxic nook and cranny of human depravity. And, like their counterpart, the kitchen sponge, they can only clean up so many messes before they themselves are riddled with dirt and bacteria and must be thrown out! Tossed in the trash! Arrivederci, sponges! Good-bye you parasitic beasts! You are too filthy to be of this world! Be gone with you!" Jackson hopped up on the footstool of his recliner and began madly conducting the "orchestra" as if it were a musical footnote to his drunken parlance.

Callie, who was accustomed to his intemperate verbosity, had not seen a performance of this stature in many years. "Would you get down from that damn ottoman before you fall and break your neck?"

"You want me to leave my empire behind? Shame on you, wifely plebe!" Jackson hopped down with a thud and hurried to the bar to retrieve his martini. He picked up the glass and examined it. "Thank you, bartender!" he said to no one at all. "You know just how I require my libation. Very dry. Two olives. Stirred, not shaken." He jerked his head around to look at Callie, who was pouting on the couch. "May I interest you in an olive, ma cherie?"

"For God's sake, cut the drama, will you, Jackson? Let's not make a theatrical production out of olives."

"But olives are dramatic! Just ask the greatest dramatic actor of our time, Sir Lawrence Olive-ier, who was named for one. He will tell you, Larry will."

"I doubt if he'll tell me anything. He's dead," Callie said. "And no, I don't want a damn olive. I hate olives. Besides, they look like eyeballs."

"To eyeballs!" Jackson shouted, raising his glass into the air. "And better yet, to eyeball cocktails. May we all see what we are drinking! Yessiree, I'll drink to that."

Callie made a motion to rise. "I've really had enough of this. I'm not kidding."

Jackson reached into his glass and pulled out an olive. "An eye for an eye, a tooth for a tooth."

"Oh please…" Callie said, standing.

Jackson took the olive and capped it over his front tooth. "Or is it an eye for a tooth? I'm not quite sure."

"I don't know and I don't care," Callie said vehemently, as she drew a mental picture of Paulie, lying sensuously on her aunt's couch. "But I've had enough of you. You're making me sick!"

Jackson, who had appeared immune to injury, stood hurt and confused by his wife's stray arrow and subsequent departure. Unaware that she was taking another man to bed with her, and too tired to follow, he put his glass down on the coffee table, curled up on the couch, and caught the first bus to dreamland.

CHAPTER 9

Except for a few broken tree branches littering the sidewalk, there was no real indication that it had rained so ferociously for the past two days. Grateful for the sun's reemergence, Frankie rehung her plants, swept the porch, then took a few moments to laze in the rocker while the morning sun warmed her face. It was seven forty-five; Ruby was still asleep, and Frankie thought about taking a walk, extricating herself, if only briefly, from the pallid tenor of her life at home. But, she quickly decided, leaving was out of the question: she didn't want Ruby to wake, call for her, and receive no response.

So she sat…and she rocked. Even at rest, she was denied the pleasure of feeling her senses dulling, as she kept her ears open for Ruby and her eyes on the neighborhood. Her emotional strength was nearly spent, and under such circumstances she had even less tolerance for the neighborhood busybodies than usual, who, from all indications, were more interested in Paulie's affairs than in the declining life of Ruby Cavalese.

To them, Frankie was a potential gold mine of information, though talking to her only got them fool's gold, and they resented her ability to see through their "thoughtful" queries. Still, can't fault the gals for trying: they hounded her for years about Paulie's love life (though always under the guise of being "mildly curious"), inquired constantly about the state of affairs between Ruby and Louie (despite the fact that it had been null and void for decades), and now, Frankie had no doubt that Callie's life (past and present) was of supreme interest to them. That, Frankie had intuited from years of experience. In terms of cold, hard proof…well, she had none, but Fat Edna laying on the bell like she had the other day, pretty much said it all. Edna, who rarely budged from her green-and-white folding chair, hadn't personally checked on Ruby for the better part of a year, not since the day Ruby was diagnosed with lung cancer and Edna had responded with a bowl of plastic fruit.

Up and down the street, they readied themselves for the day. House by house, they began to drag their lives outdoors. The rain gone, they crowded their porches with the necessary tools for summer survival: folding chairs, breakfast, televisions, radios, magazines, romance novels, children and grandchildren, cigarettes, beers, sodas, snacks, dogs, cats, newspapers, sunscreen, telephones, an appetite for gossip…and each other.

By eight o'clock, Frankie decided that she'd pushed her luck hard enough and retreated indoors before the well-wishers (a.k.a. dishers) could approach her. She wanted to check on Ruby and was hopeful, though not overly so, that yesterday's poignant moments between the two of them had foretold a kinder end to their troubled history. Watching her mother shrink away was hard enough on Frankie, but not understanding Ruby's anger was even more difficult. For Frankie, the years of sacrifice seemed only to bring resentment, and the more she tried to change things, the more Ruby seemed to disdain her.

"You're awake," Frankie said, peering in the door.

"My eyes are open. I'm talking. Made it to the bathroom and back. Barely. Guess that means I didn't die in my sleep," Ruby said, slowly lifting herself into a sitting position. "Unless maybe *you're* dreamin'."

"Let me help you," Frankie said, scuttling to her mother's side.

"Not much you can do," Ruby lamented.

"I can fluff your pillow," Frankie said, assisting Ruby as she rested her back against the headboard. "And I can wish you a good morning."

"Edna called here last night," Ruby offered, as Frankie positioned the pillow behind her mother's head.

"Really? I didn't hear the phone ring," Frankie said, as she finished with the pillow, then made her way to the window.

"You must've been in the shower. Anyway, she woke me up. Called to tell me that you ignored her the other day. Said you ran inside when you saw her comin' and that you wouldn't answer the door."

Frankie twisted her lips in disgust. "Well, at least she's got something right, the old battle axe."

"So it's true?" Ruby asked, watching Frankie as she pulled open the curtains.

"It's true, Ma," Frankie said, fiddling with the left curtain as it fought to stay closed.

"Good for you," Ruby said, reaching for her remote control on the night table. "She don't care none how I am, anyways. Get this: after tellin' me what you did to her, she says, 'How you doin,' Ruby, okay?' Then, she don't even let me answer. Before I can say anything, tells me she gotta run...*Arlene's* at the door. Don't know why I've always been so worried about Edna's damn feelings. She don't give a good damn 'bout mine. I'm dyin', but she don't have time to talk to me. Can't keep *Arlene* waitin'. *Arlene*...her gripin' buddy. The two of thems always yakking about Stella Trumble and her trucker boyfriend, Dutch. 'They make too much noise when they do it,' 'Stella's bed needs oilin',' 'She yelps like a cat in heat', 'He can't go to sleep without it.' Shit...maybe if Edna'd stop packing down the ice cream and chips, Bud could find his way to the goods and Edna wouldn't have to be so damn jealous of Stella and her fella. Maybe if she took her ear away from the wall...ah...same old, same old, Frankie. Nothin' so nice 'bout neither of them broads."

"Arlene brought you flowers the other day," Frankie reminded her. "That was nice, wasn't it?"

"I guess," Ruby grumbled. "Only they came from Stella's garden."

"But I thought Arlene didn't like Stella," Frankie said, confused. "You just said—"

"I know what I said, Frankie. I said Arlene and Edna like to bitch about Stella. Never said they all weren't friends."

"Sheesh!" Frankie said, rolling her eyes.

"Ah, to hell with all of them," Ruby said, squinting as the sunlight brushed her eyes. "I wonder why the hell Edna came down to visit me anyway."

"Probably to find out what she could about Callie," Frankie said, looking out the window. "That's my opinion, anyway."

"Probably," said Ruby, turning on the television with her remote. "Wow! Will you look at the size of those!"

Frankie turned to see what was on television. "Oh, for God's sake, Ma. What do you care about big-breasted women, anyway? I don't know why they put this garbage on television, anyway."

"My God!" Ruby said, pointing to the screen. "Says she's an M cup! Didn't know the breast alphabet went that high."

"They're probably implants," Frankie said, turning away from the

TV talk show that had absorbed her mother. "What can I bring you to eat?"

"Nope, you're wrong, Frankie. Listen to what she's saying. One-hundred percent natural. Runs in the family. Ain't nobody runnin' nowhere with those overloaded water balloons on their chest. Hard to believe. Who'd want 'em so big, anyway? Not me. I would have had that reduction surgery. Wouldn't you topple over being like that? How could you tell if you had the right shoes on? Imagine havin' 'em so big you couldn't see your own feet!"

Frankie walked over to the television and stood in front of it. "Ma, forget about these women, will you? What will it be for breakfast?"

"Damn it, Frankie. Move!" Ruby said, frantically waving her out of the way. "They're gonna bring on the M-cup's mother. Seventy-five years old and almost as big as her daughter. At that age, they must hang down 'round her ankles like flour sacks, don't you think? C'mon, Frankie. Move! I can't see through you, damn it."

Reluctantly, Frankie stepped out of the way. "Did you hear what Jenny what's-her-name just said, Ma? After the commercial break. Then she'll bring out the old lady. Now, tell me what you want to eat."

"Ah, I don't know. Bring me some vanilla yogurt, I guess. And a little juice."

"Fine," Frankie said, turning to go. "I'll do that right away. And you'll take your meds, right?"

"Frankie, before you leave, I've been wonderin'. Is Callie Mason gonna come see me?"

"Oh...well, I'm sure she'd love to see you," Frankie said, surprised. "I'll mention to her that it'd be okay. I wasn't sure if you were up for visitors, so I didn't suggest it. Your friends from the supermarket have been calling for two weeks. You keep turnin' them down. Even Evelyn...she's practically your closest friend."

"Ah, Frankie," Ruby said, turning her head away. "I can't bear for people to see me like this. Sometimes I can deal with talkin' to them on the phone, but I can't handle visitors. Too tough. I don't want people to remember me like this...or talk about the way I look. Maybe next week I'll feel different. If I even live that long. But today, this is how it is."

"Ma," Frankie said sweetly, straightening Ruby's dresser as she spoke, "your friends don't care about appearances. They just love you and wanna see you."

"*I care*, Frankie," Ruby said, watching a soft drink commercial with interest. "Ain't that actress on one of the soaps? I've seen her before."

Frankie glanced at the TV and then at her mother. "I don't know, Ma. I'm just trying to understand why you want to see Callie but not your own friends."

"It's just different," Ruby said, looking at Frankie. "I ain't seen her since she was a kid…guess I'm just a curious type…no better than Edna, Arlene, and the rest of them."

"You're nothing like them," Frankie said pointedly, as she righted several greeting cards that had fallen down. "I like this card that Sophie sent you. It's beautiful. Look at these roses—"

"When's Paulie comin'?" Ruby interrupted. "And stop fussin' with those cards."

Frankie sighed in exasperation, then walked over to Ruby's bedside. "Later, Ma. Paulie don't get up this early. You know that. He don't get home till three in the mornin' most nights."

"Louie works him too hard. Louie and that bitch. Does she have big boobs, Frankie, like them on the TV? Is that why he cut out on me? What does that bitch have that I don't have…besides my husband? You tell me, Frankie. You've been knowin' that home-wreckin,' man-stealing hussy all these years. What the hell's kept him with her so long? I'm the mother of his children…that son— husband of a bitch. Can't even face me…don't let him come to my funeral, Frankie—"

"Ma," Frankie said, taking a seat on the right side of the bed and putting her hand on Ruby's left shoulder. "You're getting yourself all worked up. Now calm down."

"I mean it," Ruby said, pushing Frankie away from her. "I don't want him takin' the easy way out…tryin' to clear his conscience by puttin' on a black suit and standin' over my coffin like he cares or somethin'. Oh, God, what if he brings *her*?"

"That would never happen, Ma. I swear," Frankie said, taking hold of Ruby's left hand. "Paulie and I wouldn't let it. I promise you."

If he can't see me while I'm still alive, tell him to stay away forever," Ruby said, consumed by her own hysteria. "I'm damn serious, Frankie. I don't want him within miles of the funeral home, or I'll rise outta my coffin and spit in his face!"

"Do you want me to ask him to come visit you now?" Frankie asked, gently squeezing Ruby's hand.

"Not while he's married to that bitch!" Ruby shouted. "How many times I gotta tell you the same damn thing?"

"Please calm down," Frankie said, nodding toward the television. "Look, the show's back on. The old lady's comin' on now. Will you look at her? You're right, Ma. They sure are saggy. Just like flour sacks. Boy, you sure called that one right."

"I mean it," Ruby cried, ignoring the television and Frankie's attempts to refocus her attention. "I don't want neither one of them at my funeral."

"Okay, Ma," Frankie said, reaching over to the night table for the pitcher and pouring a glass of water. "Here, calm down and take your meds…please. I'll be back shortly, okay?" Ruby reluctantly took the glass of water while her eyes, filled with morbid sadness, followed Frankie out of the room.

"Oh, Louie…please come say good-bye," Ruby whimpered, once Frankie was out of earshot. "Please…just say good-bye."

At eight twenty-five, Jackson and his hangover, both of whom had awakened in the den, stumbled groggily upstairs. Unaware that Hungry had left her catnip mouse in the bedroom doorway, he tripped over the cloth rodent, then took an unexpected detour as his right foot rammed the door frame.

"Goddamn son of a bitch!" Jackson screamed, as he leaned against the wall and grabbed his injured foot. "Shit. Goddamn it to hell."

Callie, who'd had a fitful night's sleep, woke easily as Jackson's expletives filled the room. Noticing that his wife's eyes had opened, Jackson turned to her and barked: "Tell your goddamn cat to put her toys away when she's done playing with them. I tripped over that damn mouse of hers and almost crippled myself."

"Next time we have a mother-and-daughter chat," Callie said, rubbing her eyes, "I'll be sure to bring that up."

"Don't be sarcastic," Jackson scolded her. "Not this goddamn early in the morning."

Callie turned to look at the clock radio. "Actually, it's not all that early. You should've been up two hours ago."

"I'm well aware of that," Jackson said harshly, massaging his foot. "Unfortunately, I don't have the luxury of sleeping in until all hours like you do. Someone's got to pay the bills."

Callie did not answer him. She just lay there and looked coldly at him. It was not like Jackson to go for her Achilles' heel, not even with his sore foot. It wasn't often that tempers flared between them, but even when they did, he never attacked her self-esteem. He knew that Callie, being a non-wage earner, had long ago determined her role in the family to be minimal and less important than his. Countless times, he had stated unequivocally, that such was simply her erroneous perception and had no validity. Often, he would laud her successes as both wife and mother, then point out the endless ways in which *her* efforts, on behalf of Hethers & Maynard Construction, had assisted him in the building of a successful, high-profile, community-minded company. But now, for some reason, he had opted to abandon such praise and to use her insecurities as a weapon against her.

As Callie's stare hardened, she flashed back to the early days of their marriage. They had been man and wife for less than two years when Jackson joined the construction business as a junior executive for Hayward & Sons. A month after his hiring, Ernest Hayward had invited his protégé (and very pregnant wife) to a dinner party at their Rosemont estate. Callie, who had been counting on Jackson to help ease her through the evening, was panic-stricken when Ernest Hayward whisked Jackson off to his den of testosterone only seconds after their arrival, leaving Callie and her unborn twins to mix it up with Mrs. Hayward and the assemblage of blue bloods sipping white wine in the living room.

Her self-esteem being tenuous at best, Callie was immediately discomfited by this coterie of women, the preponderance of whom were at least thirty years her senior, and none of whom appeared to have names of their own. In a polite but crisp manner, Mrs. Ernest Hayward introduced Mrs. Jackson Hethers (who was now suddenly stripped of her own first name) to the others: Mrs. Armstrong Badderly, Mrs. Clayton Randolph, Mrs. Delford Collingswood, and Mrs. Henry Allsworth. To complicate an already impossible situation, it turned out that the women *did* have first names and addressed each other using these appellations. Mrs. Badderly was Eunice, Mrs. Randolph was Sarah, Mrs. Collingswood was Mary, Mrs. Allsworth was Helen, and Mrs. Hayward was Nell. But to them, Callie was Mrs. Hethers, and even in her state of pregnant misery, Callie knew that a return formality was expected. Only she had forgotten their names (all except her hostess, Mrs. Hayward) as quickly as she had heard them, the memory of such being further obliterated by the calling of first names among them. There was no choice: she would call no one by name, and if put in an absolute desperate situation, she would simply lapse into early labor.

As if it had been carefully orchestrated, they took turns offering maternal advice and regaling Callie with newborn horror stories as a way of friendly warning. In an attempt to maintain her sanity, she picked out key words to respond to but ignored the whole of what they were saying. Instead, Callie found herself fixated on their various idiosyncrasies, such as the excessive preening of Helen Allsworth, who appeared to be fascinated by her own image in the china cabinet glass. Callie watched as Helen gently pressed her face in strategic places, as if she were a sculptor finishing the bust of an aristocratic icon. That in itself would have been amusing enough to witness, but from Callie's viewpoint, Helen's face in the glass appeared to be a disembodied sphere, rising from the gold-leaf teacup on the third shelf, as if it were trapped inside and trying to find its way out.

"Mrs. Hethers?" her hostess asked. "Didn't you hear Mrs. Collingswood? What was your degree in?"

"Oh," said Callie, turning around. "My degree?"

Mrs. Hayward smiled patronizingly as if she were a first-grade teacher who was giving her student one last chance to get it right before meting out punishment.

"English literature," Callie replied.

"Ah ha ha!" chortled Mary Collingswood. "English literature. Better known as a degree in husband hunting."

As the other women laughed approvingly, Callie shrank inside. Something awful happened to her at that moment: something she couldn't quite put a label on, yet something hurtful enough to diminish her; something to make her take the comment and pack it securely in her baggage for future head trips. She was not good enough to be one of them; she had no talents of her own; she was a joke. They were laughing at her and would always laugh at her. She was no more than a dismal extension of her own deplorable mother.

For years following, she carried that self-admonition with her, despite the fact that she had nothing to confirm it with but the idle laughter of bored society matrons.

"And what was it that you envisioned yourself doing?" Mary Collingswood asked, staring at Callie's belly.

"I thought I might teach someday," Callie said flatly, staring into Mrs. Collingswood's raisin-like eyes.

"Teach!" she replied. "Oh, ho ho no, dear. Not with only a bachelor's degree and twins on the way."

Your eyes look like fat raisins, Callie thought, acknowledging the woman's cruelty with a pleasant nod. *Big, fat raisins, nothing more. I'm surprised you can see out of those wrinkly brown things.*

"And if you want to teach at the college level," Mrs. Collingswood elaborated, "Even a master's degree won't do. No, ho ho, you'll need a doctoral—"

Goobers and Raisinets, Callie thought, thinking of the old candy jingle she had known as a child. The woman's raisin-eyes widened to make a point. *Goobers and Raisinets,* Callie thought, nodding again as if to agree.

"No need to worry, though," Mrs. Collingswood consoled her. "Mr. Hethers is an exceptional young man with a bright future. He'll take good care of you."

Goobers and Raisinets, Callie mused, wondering when Jackson and the men would join them.

Goobers and Raisinets, Callie thought, as she sprang forward in time to find that Jackson *had* joined her, some nineteen years later.

Miraculously, her twins had been born and were all grown up. Only Jackson was no longer in Mr. Hayward's den. He was in their bedroom, leaning against the wall, moaning in agony.

"I'm sorry," he said, letting go of his injured foot. "I didn't mean it, honey. You know I didn't."

"Of course you did," Callie insisted, as visions of Mrs. Collingswood taunted her. "You meant every damn word."

Jackson shrugged, as if to say it was useless to dispute her, then made his way to the shower. Maybe she *had* gotten a degree in husband hunting. Maybe her whole life had been one big joke. Despondent, and minus the wherewithal to weigh her inadequacies further, Callie rolled over, closed her eyes, and waited for Jackson to leave. Fifteen minutes later, with a drowsy thrust of her right arm, she pushed aside the tangled sheets, then spilled out of bed and bedlam with ensuing prejudice toward the innocent day. But as she dragged her slumberous body toward the open window, primed to make the most from her misery, the verdant grounds called to her. Outside, the flowers and plants, so well tended to and so eager to be admired, suggested to Callie a day of trifling fancy in the garden; a day less hopeless and gray than she had feared. All of the colors of her world were vibrant, and the landscape, lit perfectly by the sun, waited in place as if it were posing for a portrait. It was a glorious day, eager to detain Callie with the sweet essence of its flowers and the winsome song of its birds. But once fully awake, despite the temptation, she was bright with anticipation for adventures that lay elsewhere. She looked again at the magical garden that was hers and wondered what she had done, or would ever do, to deserve such elysian fields.

A quick shower and a long phone call to her children later, Callie was on her way.

She had no business resenting Regina's presence; she knew that. To expect Regina to disappear, just because she had suddenly fallen back into Frankie's life for an indeterminate period of time, was selfish and unfair. Caring for Frankie the way she did, she should've been happy that there was someone just across the street who loved her friend so much. But what should be and what is often reside in separate solar systems she told herself.

"Here she is again," Regina declared gleefully, noticing Callie through the dark gray screen. "Come on in and join us."

Callie programmed a smile as she pushed open the Cavalese's squeaky old door. "Hello, Regina. Hi, Frankie. How are you both today?"

Regina, lying back on the couch, had her flip-flopped feet propped up on the coffee table and was wearing a pink maternity shirt with a large red arrow that pointed to the word "Baby" on her stomach. Indicating the general area of the fetus with her right forefinger, Regina answered Callie's question (apparently, the arrow was no substitute for a proper directional): "I'm fine. 'Cept he's kickin' up a storm today. My Hal says he practicin' for a field goal."

"I see," Callie said, with forced enthusiasm. "Well, your Hal's probably right."

"Hi, Mason," Frankie said, slumped on top of her favorite armchair with her feet dangling off to the left side. "Nice day out there, ain't it?" She let a slight grin form on her lips; it was Frankie's way of letting Callie know that she was taking a mildly perverse pleasure in observing the dynamics between her and Regina.

"Park it here!" Regina instructed Callie, cocking her head toward the empty space on the couch. "Join the party."

Callie wanted to leave, and Frankie wanted to laugh, but neither chose a discernible reaction. Instead, Callie took a seat and said nothing.

"I'm dyin' to know," Regina asked, turning to Callie. "Did your feet swell when you were preggers? Look at mine! Hal says I've got elephantitis."

Callie neither cared to answer nor to observe Regina's swollen feet.

"Tell Hal he's got elephantitis of the brain," Frankie offered angrily, an obvious sentiment left over from a previous conversation. "Tell him to take care of that swelled head of his and stop worryin' about your feet. And while you're at it, tell him that if it weren't for his swelled dick, you wouldn't be this way in the first place!"

Regina howled with laughter, while Callie let loose an affectionate grin.

"You know," Callie said, seeing an opportunity to escape, "it's quite obvious that I've interrupted something private here. Honestly, I just came to say hello before I start the day's packing. Why don't I let you ladies—"

"Nonsense," Frankie said emphatically, then smiled at Callie. "Stay and chat."

Callie squinted her eyes in Frankie's direction, as if to say, Thanks a lot; I'll get you for that, and Frankie returned the look with an implicitly understood "You're welcome; give it your best shot." And then they turned away from one another, each aware that their mutual penchant for wordless communication was still fully operational, just as if all the lost yesterdays had never happened.

"So did they?" Regina wanted to know, playfully jabbing Callie in the right arm with her balled fist. "Did your tootsies swell?"

Frankie's smile ran for cover, hiding from retribution behind her own right palm. Again, Callie squinted with mock threat at her friend, as if to up the revenge ante.

"I really don't remember, Regina," Callie said, rubbing her offended arm in response. "It was a long time ago. I just remember being big…really big…and terribly uncomfortable. That's all."

"No stretch marks?" Regina asked.

Callie winced. "It was a long time ago, Regina." She turned to face Frankie. "How's your mom today?"

Regina looked disappointed at the turn in conversation.

"Okay, I guess. I mean…okay for how she is," Frankie faltered. "It could be a lot worse. She was in a decent state of mind this morning, as her state of minds go."

"I'd really like to see her," Regina said, making a circular rubbing motion on her stomach. "I keep askin' you; you keep blowin' me off."

Frankie was annoyed. "Reg, don't take it so personal. I keep telling you that. You know Ma likes you. She cares a lot more about you than them down the street, that's for sure. I've told you a hundred times; it's not that she don't wanna see you—"

"Then why do I feel a but comin' on bigger than the one I'm sittin' on?" Regina said, lifting her feet off the table, as if she no longer felt at home. "So let's have it. But what?"

"Oh, Reg," Frankie said, swinging her feet around to the front of the chair and following Regina's example. "She just don't want people to see *her*! Don't you get it? I don't necessarily agree with her, but I ain't the sick one. She's got the right to see or not to see anyone she wants. For Christ's sake, stop takin' it so personal and layin' your disappointment on me. I'm tired of you makin' me feel bad. You don't think I got enough headache of my own?"

Regina, embarrassed, stood up. "I gotta walk Steffie over to Raucher Street. Bethie just got a backyard pool, and Steffie's invited for lunch and a swim." Regina would not look at her friend. "See yous later." Kicking open the screen door, she left in a blaze of sunlight, letting a burst of blinding yellow escape into the Cavalese living room.

Frankie squinted. "I wasn't trying to be mean, I swear. It's just that I can only take so much."

"I know," Callie said, moving closer as she occupied Regina's vacant seat on the couch. "It's not your fault that your mother doesn't want to see anyone. I can understand your frustration. Really."

"Well," Frankie hedged. "Actually, there is someone she wants to see. You. She asked me this morning if you'd pay her a visit."

"Oh, Frankie. I'd love to see her. I was going to ask you, but...when? When can I see her?" Callie asked eagerly.

"Tomorrow afternoon probably'd be good," Frankie said. "Does that work okay for you?"

"Just perfectly," Callie said. "As it turns out, I've got a dental appointment and some other errands to tend to this afternoon, so I won't be around much today as it is. But I'm really looking forward to seeing her."

"Be prepared," Frankie warned. "She don't look too good. She's real thin and don't got no hair."

"It's okay," Callie reassured her. "I've seen cancer patients before. I used to volunteer at the hospital."

"Oh," Frankie said, her reaction imperceptible to Callie.

Callie felt like kicking herself, convinced that she must've come off like some vapid society matron, like Mary Collingswood, who labored under the mistaken impression that only poor people got sick, and that by volunteering, one was excused from having to deal with tragedy on a more personal basis. Meaning to offer empathy, she'd inadvertently bragged about her privilege as if she were an unfeeling despot who had momentarily purged her airs as a perceived show of respect to the underclasses. When it came to matters of self-deprecation, Callie was a master, and had Frankie not interrupted one of her more admirable efforts, Callie might have continued to berate herself until the ground below rumbled violently and then swallowed her whole.

"You okay, Mason?" Frankie said, gently nudging her friend's right arm.

"What?...Oh..." Callie said, as reality conked her on the head. "What did you say?"

"Must have been those big words I used," Frankie mumbled to herself. "I said, Mason, are you okay?"

"I heard that," Callie said, playfully pointing a finger at Frankie. "And I'm fine. Thank you."

Frankie let her head fall onto the back of the armchair with a soft thump. She looked at Callie disbelievingly. "Nah, I don't think so. You weren't the same when you came in here a while ago, and there was more to it than Reg and her swollen feet."

"Tootsies," Callie corrected her.

Frankie laughed. "So what's wrong?"

"Things at home," Callie said. "Jackson and I didn't have too good an evening last night. And we had an even worse morning."

Frankie's eyes grew wide as she considered what Callie had said.

"Don't look so surprised," Callie chided her. "My life is far from perfect, you know."

"Well, it's a lot closer than mine is," Frankie said with a tinge of resentment. "At least you're within shouting distance from it."

Callie crossed her arms and turned away with a look that said "Forget it; I can't talk to you." Immediately, Frankie regretted having reached into her arsenal of smart comebacks. "I'm sorry. I really am. You know I didn't mean it, Callie."

Callie looked at the black-and-gold watch on her left wrist. "Gee, it's not even noon, and this is the second nasty remark that's been yanked back from me with a rousing chorus of 'You know I didn't mean that.' Well, as I told my dear husband earlier, 'No, I don't know that.' " Callie stirred in her seat and made motions to leave. "I shouldn't have come. I keep forgetting how much you still resent me. I don't even know what I'm doing here. It's just that I've been so happy to see you again. And yes, I feel guilty as hell for what I did to you…what I did to *us*…but I'm not here because of guilt. I'm only here because I like being with you and I care about you." Then, with an angry swipe, Callie wiped a few tears from her right eye with the back of her right hand.

"Mason—" Frankie said pleadingly.

"I should go," Callie said.

"No, please don't," Frankie said, reaching over and touching Callie's hand. "I really like it when you're here."

"Really? I hadn't noticed." She paused, then bit her lip. "I don't blame you, Frankie. Not at all. I'd be some kind of idiot to think that you'd want to hear any of my problems. If I were you, I'd resent me too. Who wants to listen to the poor little rich girl having her tantrum…even if she *was* persuaded to share what ailed her."

"As my brother likes to say…Touché," Frankie said. "I did ask you, didn't I? But you're wrong about one thing, Mason. I don't see you as the poor little rich girl. I know it may seem like that…but you know how I am. I still have this big mouth that doesn't always work in sync with my brain. You see, it's supposed to wait for a signal from above…you know, sort of an all-clear that says it's safe to proceed, but instead—"

"Your parts are all in perfect working order," Callie assured her. "It's me who's off balance."

Frankie put her hands to her hips. "You wanna debate this, Mason? 'Cause I guarantee you I'm more out of whack than you are. I'm not quite sure how we can settle this, but there must be a way."

Callie laughed, then turned to watch the long beams of sunlight as they filtered through the window blinds. She was reminded of her Charleston Light, the red-and-white striped lighthouse by the South Carolina seashore where she and Jackson had spent their first married vacation.

Frankie studied her friend's descent into silence, then spoke:

"Where you drifting off to?"

Surprised, Callie turned around. "Oh…South Carolina. By the seashore. Jackson's parents' friends used to have a summerhouse down there. They let us have it for a week that first summer we were married. The light coming through the window made me think of the lighthouse there…and of that time…and how the hell did you know that I went drifting anywhere?"

"Time hasn't changed what I know about you," Frankie said matter-of-factly, clasping her hands behind her head and leaning back. "You used to get that same faraway look in your eyes when we'd talk about the future. You know, about the guys we'd marry or the trips we'd take before gettin' hitched. You used to get that same look you had just now, one like you were tryin' to picture how things might be, sort of giving yourself a preview of coming events." Frankie paused, then swallowed. "Of course, as we got older, I thought maybe you were driftin' off because you didn't see us being friends no more and you couldn't bear to tell me that."

Callie twirled her wedding ring and looked wistfully at Frankie. "Somehow, I think a part of me always feared that circumstances would separate us…and that scared the hell out of me. So I only listened to the part of me that said you were my very best friend and that *nothing*, not money, time, distance, or men…could pull us apart." Callie straightened in her seat. "Nothing worth having is effortless, Frankie. I was misguided to think that way. Nothing in this life maintains itself without a helping hand or a loving heart. And sometimes, even a loving heart just isn't enough."

Frankie looked deep into Callie's eyes as she spoke. She started to say something but realized in time that Callie had not finished.

Callie laughed nervously. "I guess I thought of Charleston Light just now because it was that week in South Carolina that I realized what I had done to our friendship. There I was, happily married to the love of my life, and I hadn't shared any of it with you. Not the romance, the marriage…nothing. I had completely shut you out. I remember, it was the first full day of our vacation. The weather was perfect. Jack and I were lying on the beach. He was reading some political thriller, and I was watching the gulls overhead. I still recall being struck by how effortlessly they seemed to soar, and I remember thinking how my friendship with you used to be that easy, and how for so many years, there were no outside influences to get in the way. Life was just easy, like the flight of the gulls. Then, later that evening, I was sitting out on the upstairs balcony of the house where we were staying. I was sipping lemonade, and Jack was in the shower, cursing because he'd gotten shampoo in his eyes. I could hear him, but I didn't pay any attention. He was just being a baby, and besides, I was too busy watching the gulls. They were flying so close to me…and at eye level. The more I watched, the more I realized that flying wasn't nearly as easy for them as it had seemed from my previous vantage point on the beach. Maybe it was my imagination, but they all had looks of pained determination on their faces, and the flapping of their wings suddenly didn't seem so easy. I could *see* the effort it took for them to stay airborne. Then it occurred to me that just because you have wings, that doesn't mean you can fly…or do it so with ease. You have to use your wings properly. You have to use all of God's gifts carefully, or you stand to lose them. Anyway, once again, I thought of you. I realized, that without wanting to, I'd clipped our wings and that our friendship, something I had treasured beyond words, was probably gone forever."

Frankie drew a deep breath and sighed. "I don't mean to kick a Hallmark moment in the ass, Callie. And it ain't that I don't appreciate what you've just said. It's just that I got a problem with that last part…about not having wanted to clip our wings. Quite frankly, I think you did wanna clip 'em. I think I represented everything you were ashamed of…growing up in this neighborhood, your lost alcoholic mother, *me* as your best friend, fucking Flern Elementary as your grade school alma mater…c'mon, Mason, life wasn't as damn easy like you seemed to remember it. And as for our friendship, I mean, even if I'd been willing to make the effort for both of us, do you really think it would've been enough to keep us together? Fact is, you didn't want me in your damn life. Ain't that what it boils down to…all said and done?"

Callie considered what Frankie had said, then looked away guiltily. Frankie interpreted the look as an admission of truth, leaving her victorious and crushed all in the same instant, not knowing whether to fight for being right or to fight for a friend. And while Frankie pondered the inequity of pride and forgiveness, Callie moved on to another beach, one at the Jersey shore, years later, when the twins were fourteen and anxious to extricate themselves from all parental ties. Jackson, she remembered, had stayed in Philadelphia to work, and she had come down with the kids, who were at the stage where being seen with their parents was a teenage taboo.

Callie remembered one day in particular. It was around four o'clock in the afternoon. She was sitting on the beach reading Balzac's *Cousin Bette* and trying to ignore the sounds of clinking glasses and high-pitched laughter that were drifting downwind from the oceanfront balcony of Del and Liza Collingswood. The Collingswoods owned a home just two doors down from the Hethers' family house. Perhaps it was just Callie's emotional scars that had been brought on by Mary Collingswood, Del Jr.'s mother, but Callie could never warm up to anyone in the Collingswood family. Especially "Health-Club Liza," as Callie called her, Mary's daughter-in-law, who, when she wasn't training in the club, was tanning her muscled body. Callie also referred to her as the over-baked potato, especially on days when Liza lay on the beach, slathering her browned skin with deep-tanning "sour cream."

From the polish on her nails to the detailing on her car, it was all about money, prestige and power. Who had it, who didn't, who was getting it, who was losing it. Everything in Liza's life revolved around money. Callie used to muse that Liza's attitude was like a Southern accent. You may not have one, but two minutes around those who do and you've picked it up—just because it's too easy to assimilate, and such a simple way to fit in. And so, when she could, Callie politely refused Liza's invitations, despite the fact that, for all her disdain, she liked being a part of the crowd and loved Southern accents.

On that particular afternoon, as she listened to sounds of the party she had declined, a soft breeze gathered momentum, distracting her from the lure of frivolity above. Marking her place, Callie put Balzac in the beach bag and pulled out her date book and pen. Opening quickly to the writing tablet inside the back cover, she set out to write a love poem to Jackson, something she had tried only once before, on their honeymoon. She was missing him terribly and wanted to put it into words. To her surprise, an allegoric memoir emerged instead.

She imagined herself a gull, who one day met up with the breeze, a talky, wifty kind of guy, who had just blown into town. Not having many friends in the area, he tended to eavesdrop on the gulls…especially during cocktail hour. And so he told Callie, he had heard the other gulls talking about her: they were saying that she wasn't good enough, that she fluttered too distantly. Having an air of civility, the breeze wanted to warn her: the other gulls wanted no part of her, though often they pretended they did.

Day after day, the gulls would gather on a barnacled rock by the jetty, laughing and eating fish. From behind a cloud, Callie would watch, afraid to join in the fun. One day, being "gullible" (she couldn't resist), she responded to an invitation to join them. But suddenly, just as she had landed on the jetty, an angry sky and a reckless wave washed away the party. Instinctively, the other gulls linked their wings and flew to safety, but Callie was left for dead. An hour later, among broken shells and bottles, she lay with strands of seaweed wrapped around her body like tangled string. She listened as the other gulls heard tell of her death. There was no remorse, only laughter and the gobbling of fish.

And that was as far as she got, for when she looked up, Del Collingswood Jr., in his plaid shorts and pale yellow polo shirt, was standing by her side, grinning, his outstretched right arm offering Callie a frosty-glassed drink.

"Have something tall and cool," he said gallantly. "By the name of Tom Collins. Here, I'll fold your chair for you. You'll join us for supper. We're grilling steaks."

Reluctantly, Callie took the drink and smiled. But before she could protest or agree to join the party, Del had gathered her belongings and was heading toward the Collingswood home with them. As she followed behind, ruing her passive acceptance to eat steak with the over-baked potato, she called herself a hypocrite and a phony as a stray thought of Frankie ran across her mind. Here she was, joining a party of people she didn't even like, yet still missing the best friend she years ago left behind.

"You're right," Callie said to Frankie, slipping out of her beach clothes and back into the conversation. "I don't suppose there's anything you could have done to keep us together. I was a rotten friend, Frankie. But you never left my heart, for all the good that does us now."

"Yeah, for all the good," Frankie repeated, her voice worn with pain. "Like you said before, 'sometimes a loving heart just ain't enough.' "

Callie let her eyelids droop as her mouth curved into a clown's sad frown.

"Oh, Frankie," she said, choking on the helplessness she felt inside. "I'm so sorry. I wish I could tell you just how much…listen, I've got to take care of some things for my kids. College stuff. You know…oh never mind. Listen, I'll probably see you tomorrow." Callie did not want to leave, but she didn't know how to stay.

Frankie, too upset to even feign emotional stability, blinked her eyes in response and turned her head toward the wall as Callie left. She could not bear to watch her friend leave. "I'll *probably* see you tomorrow." What if she'd pushed Callie too far? What if she never came back?

CHAPTER 10

"Ma!" Frankie cried breathlessly, as she rushed into Ruby's room early the next morning. "What the hell are you doing? I thought the damn house was on fire."

Ruby took a long drag off her cigarette as she stared straight ahead at the television. "What does it look like I'm doing?"

"Oh, geez, Ma!" Frankie said, rushing toward her. "I can't believe you're smoking. Give me that damn thing."

Ruby put her arm up in the air to keep Frankie from snatching her cigarette. "Get away, Frankie. You touch this cigarette, you'll die before I do."

"Okay, okay," Frankie said, keeping her eyes on the cigarette, which was precariously close to the wall. "I won't try to stop you."

Ruby lowered her arm and took another drag. "Not only ain't you gonna stop me, you ain't gonna lecture me neither. Ain't nothing these babies can do to me they ain't already done."

Frankie watched her mother nervously, staring at the cigarette as if it were going to explode into flames.

"And I ain't gonna burn nothin' up, Frankie, so get your knickers outta that knot they're in," Ruby said, her face animated as she watched the action on TV.

"Where'd you get the cigarettes, Ma?" Frankie asked, hands on her hips. "Paulie give 'em to ya? Guess he must've. No one else's been here."

"No questions, no lectures, no attitude," Ruby said, dumping an ash into the old sandbag ashtray that rested on her stomach. "Just leave me be. Let me have my smokes and my talk show. That's all I want. You can go about your business now."

Frankie stormed over to the side of the room and grabbed a chair, then dragged it to the side of Ruby's bed by the front window. "You *are* my business. This house is my business. If you're smokin', I'm stayin'. That's the deal, Ma. Take it or leave it."

"Ah...suit yourself," Ruby groaned, as a puff of smoke trailed behind her words. "Just keep a lid on it. I'm watchin'."

On the television, a rather plump, round-faced woman with oodles of short, blah-brown curls had just been introduced by the host. As she sat in her seat, clutching a wad of tissues and trembling with anticipation, "Gilda, Legal Secretary, 58: About To Be Reunited With Husband Who Abandoned Her 25 Years Ago" appeared on the bottom of the screen. Frankie turned cautiously in her seat to look at the bone-thin woman in the bed next to her. As her mother's drawn face twisted sympathetically with Gilda's plight, "Ruby, Dying, 65: Never Got Over Husband Being Stolen 29 Years Ago" flashed across the pale blue of her withered negligee, just in time for Frankie to read the words.

But what about her own life, Frankie wondered, as the focus shifted abruptly to herself. What about Callie, the best friend who had abandoned her a lifetime ago, then dropped, one summer day, back into her own bleak and dreary life? Did Frankie want to forgive her; there was no doubt. Could she forgive her…ah, there lay the rub. To forgive is divine, the lessons said, but somewhere in the jumble of her mind, forgiveness meant letting go, a releasing of the pain that had defined her life, a freeing of sorrow that had kept her at arm's length from happiness. And how, she brooded, does a person maintain her self-respect if she tells another, "I forgive you for all the destruction, for everything you did to screw up my life?" But, if she doesn't offer that forgiveness, will she ever have a chance to be happy? The confusion was maddening, debilitating.

"I just want to know why!" Gilda expounded, as tears of black dribbled down her cheeks. "What did I do wrong? I was a *good* wife, a *good* mother to our little boy," she cried, as the explanatory chyron flashed again. "Since Bill left me, I've never been able to trust a man. Not ever!"

"And you've been married three times since then, haven't you?" the host said delicately, passing her a box of Kleenex.

Gilda wailed as the history of her failed unions hit the airwaves. "I never got any kind of explanation from him. Only divorce papers. He ruined my life!"

As Gilda grabbed a handful of tissues from the proffered box, Frankie anticipated the obvious. "Can you forgive him?" the host pressed on. "Do you think you can forgive him here today, on national television?

It's important, Gilda, it's important to release this terrible burden inside of you. Don't you think you've carried it long enough?"

Gilda sniffed tearfully in agreement. "I just hope I can," she blathered. "But I'm afraid if I do, he'll hurt me all over again."

I'm afraid if I do, she'll hurt me all over again, Frankie thought in unison.

"It's a chance you'll have to take," the host said soothingly. "Frankly, Gilda, I think you'll be a lot happier saying good-bye to the pain. Come on, say it. Say it aloud for all to hear. 'Goodbye, pain. I don't need you any more.' "

What kind of fucking crap is this, Frankie thought as the hapless Gilda repeated the silly words she had been prompted to say.

At least her son of a bitch is willing to face her, Ruby thought angrily, blotting her tears with a Kleenex as well. At least he's willing to come on the TV and talk about it.

Through the spiraling gray masses of smoke, Ruby watched as a potbellied, cowboy-shirted, balding Bill walked circumspectly on stage, trying to drown out the booing audience as he wondered what to say to the quivering mass of jelly rushing toward him.

Ah, Christ, right into his arms that broad flies, Ruby thought unmercifully. Not even one little "you fucking bastard." Kissy-faced wimp; no wonder he split on her.

He probably doesn't even want a reconciliation, Frankie concluded. Probably just doing this to get on TV.

"I'm sorry, Gildie," Bill sobbed, as his denim arms embraced her. "So sorry, baby." Gilda buried her head in his chest, and they cried together. Then he pulled apart, taking a big white handkerchief from his pants pocket and blowing his nose loudly.

That schnoz sure needs a tune-up, Ruby thought. Bet he snores like a bullhorn, too. Ah, shit, look how happy he pretends to be to see her.

"Why don't we all sit down," the host suggested, as a stagehand rushed over with a chair for Bill. "Bill, let's hear your side of the story. Why *did* you walk out on Gilda all those years ago?"

He was young. He was stupid. Temptation got the better of him. Who cares? They're only excuses, Frankie told herself, as she watched the smoke from her mother's cigarette drift out through the open window.

Come on, Ruby shouted silently to the host. Some fuckin' broad stole him away. Ain't that always the case. Don't ask such stupid goddamn questions. She crushed out her cigarette and watched as the embers faded to black. Oh God, look at me, Louie. I got nothin' but pain, pickin' away at me every day. Nasty little men with rusty razors, running through my head, screamin' at me. I got a body full of cancer; I'm gonna die, and some man in a white coat's gonna steal my body, cut it up, and stick it under some microscope for laboratory analyzation. He's gonna take parts of me, different parts, and stuff 'em into jars of formaldehyde…man, that stuff stinks…and then'll stick 'em on a shelf somewhere for some twerpy little med students to dissect in class. I raised your children, damn it; I kept my word. I loved Frankie…oh God, Louie. You wait…wait'll you read the papers. "Dead woman ain't got no heart. Doctors look everywhere. Husband stole it way back when." Damn it, Louie. I don't wanna die like this…give me back my heart. Let me die whole you son of a bitch.

"Gilda," the host said. "Isn't there someone you want to introduce Bill to?"

As Gilda looked lovingly into the eyes of the man who had ruined her life, Bill Jr., a larger, more awkward version of his penitent father, lumbered anxiously onto the stage.

Ruby grabbed her remote control and zapped the Bills and Gilda into oblivion. "All right, Frankie. I ain't gonna smoke no more now. You can go."

Picking up the words she wanted to say, finding them unnecessary to leave behind, Frankie took them, and Ruby's dirty ashtray, down to the kitchen sink.

Callie sat on her aunt's bed and stared blankly into the old marbled mirror on the wall. She had done it again. She had shown Frankie just what kind of coward she really was. "You never left my heart," Callie said aloud, mocking her conversation from the previous morning. "Gee, what a touching sentiment. I'm surprised Frankie didn't jump up and down for joy. I mean, that's a reason to forgive me if I ever heard it. '*You never left my heart, Frankie. I just didn't know how to include you in my life!*' " Callie winced at her reflection, then spat her disillusionment at the glass. "Ugh! You make me sick! I hate you!"

Don't be so cruel to my niece, Emily's photo said sternly from the dresser.

Who's going to stop me? Callie thought bravely.

Emily's smile morphed into a no-nonsense glare, then resumed its former state as if it were merely a photograph, capable only of one fixed expression.

"Okay, you win this round," Callie acquiesced, getting up from the bed. She walked over to the tarnished silver frame and stood defiantly in front of it. "I'll stop putting myself down. But you tell me how I'm supposed to explain things to Frankie. You tell me how I can *ever* make up for what I've done to her."

I wasn't aware you'd set your mind to do so. If that's the case, you'll find a way. You always do. Besides, you're old enough to think clearly now.

I'll never be *that* old, Callie mused. She bristled affectionately at the way her aunt's lessons had a way of following her like a hungry kitten, then felt grateful and lucky as she considered the lessons Anisa might have taught her, had she had the misfortune to be raised by her natural mother.

The feminine squeals of delight outside the window pierced Callie's thoughts like an arrow slamming into its target. The sound of running feet intrigued her. She had no sooner reached the window than she understood the reason for such a commotion. Paulie Cavalese, sunglassed and tanned, leaning against his shiny black sports car, the sun shining down on him like a spotlight, smoking a cigarette as four middle-aged overweight woman came tromping down the street in breathless anticipation of his company. Like a movie star who had become immune to the frantic calling of his name, Paulie appeared oblivious to the rushing onslaught of cattle. But Callie knew better; he was eating it up. It sickened and thrilled her at the same time.

She stood in the window and waited for the show. As the women called his name, they formed an impenetrable semicircle around him.

Paulie dropped his cigarette to the ground, crushed it out with his right foot, then flashed a naughty, welcoming smile to his admirers.

"Oh, for God's sake!" Callie said. "What's he going to do now, sign autographs? This is ridiculous." And as she said it, she felt an odd stir of excitement, an unwanted tinge of empathy for the women. She hated herself for that. She watched as he pulled a mint from his jeans pocket and popped it into his mouth. That's what he had done the day before. Right before he kissed her.

I wonder what they're saying, she thought. Maybe they're telling him how good he looks in those jeans. Maybe…oh God…what am I doing? What the hell do I care what *any* of them are saying?

And with that resolved, Callie marched away from the window. Then, without even contemplating her next move, she grabbed her pocketbook from the bed and headed straight to the bathroom.

As she stood in front of the mirror, blending her taupe shadow until it perfectly highlighted her left eye, she gloated over the fact that Paulie found her, not those women on the street, so completely irresistible.

"Let there be light!" Paulie exclaimed as he entered the Cavalese home. The old screen door slammed behind him, as if to add emphasis to his words. "It's like a goddamn tunnel in here. Only without the headlights coming at you."

Frankie, making her way into the living room from the kitchen, glared impatiently at him. "Paulie…"

He flipped on a wall switch and then reached for the floor lamp. "It's no wonder you're so depressed, Mary Frances. Everything in this place is the same color. There, that's better. You're multicolored again."

"I'm a friggin' rainbow," Frankie said, sliding into her favorite armchair as she turned from the light. "Minus the pot of gold."

"Damn, you're in a bad—"

"Don't even start on me," Frankie said harshly. "You try living in this hole. You'd be one color, too: drab. Drab as the day is long. So, how long are you going to visit Ma for today? Three, four minutes? How about extending your visit to six or seven minutes? Or would that kill you?"

"Okay, okay," Paulie said, taking a bitter taste of his just dessert. "Sarcasm duly noted. You're right. I'm the coward; you're the one with all the guts. I know that." He walked over to the family gallery of photos by the steps and began inspecting them.

Frankie looked quizzically at him but didn't respond. He saw her peripherally and felt the sting of her anger.

"I mean that!" he said emphatically, turning around to look at her.

"Maybe," Frankie said quietly. "And maybe not. But even if you do mean it, it's what you do about it that really counts."

"How's she doing today?" Paulie asked, looking sadly at the photograph of his parents as a young couple as Frankie's comment seared his brain.

"I just found her smoking a while ago," Frankie told him. "Listen, she's right. There ain't nothing those cigarettes can do to her they ain't already done, but there is something they can do to this house: burn it down. Now, maybe that wouldn't be such a bad idea, but for the time bein', I ain't got nowhere else to live. So if you don't mind, Paulie…"

"Damn, I'm sorry, Mary Frances. I didn't think…I won't give her any more."

"God only knows how many she's still got stashed away, Paulie. She sure as hell ain't gonna come clean to me about it."

"I'll see what I can do."

"Yeah," Frankie said apathetically. "See what you can do."

Time was slipping away for Paulie, and so was his store of rationalizations. Inadequacy clung to him like a wetsuit. His mother could leave the earth any day, and he would have done nothing for her. He had long stopped fooling his sister about his supposed good-deed doing, and while Ruby pretty much denied her blessed son's shortcomings, her anger over them, like her anger over everything else, ended up in Frankie's lap. So what had happened to cause this sudden, brilliant flash of clarity— this sudden realization that he needed to do more, much more, unless he wanted to be swathed in guilt forever? Callie Hethers? Nah, he didn't like that idea, but the stone, cold truth of it had him convinced otherwise. Something about "a broad" getting through to him had a disconcerting ring to it, even one as classy as Callie.

But suddenly, after his talk with Callie, doing something of value for his mother no longer seemed like a nebulous image off in the distance that he was fighting to recognize. Clarity had awakened in him. His mother's desires were finally clear to him: she wanted to see Louie, with a passion that only her pride could obstruct. But Paulie's attempt at implementing a reconciliation had fallen flat. His father had attempted to emasculate him for merely suggesting such a notion.

"I'm trying, Mary Frances," Paulie said, moving away from the pictures and toward the couch. "I tried to do something for Ma the other night. Only it didn't work."

Frankie was too weary to respond.

"I talked to Pop…about coming to see her. You know, to say their goodbyes. Settle things between them."

Frankie perked up. "Really? What did he say?"

"Practically called me a pussy," Paulie said, taking a seat. "Told me not to talk like a goddamned woman, or something like that."

Frankie looked disgusted. "Oh, Christ. The old man's worse than you are."

"In what way?" Paulie asked defensively.

"Denial. Big time. Who do you think taught you to be so good at it? You are going to try again, I hope."

"Of course I am," Paulie said, miffed that his intentions weren't obvious. "I've just gotta figure out what to say. I gotta take a different tact next time. Just damned if I know what it'll be."

"Yeah," Frankie moaned, as she wondered just how much verbal castration her brother could tolerate. "Just don't be too long about it, okay? And don't give up if Pop tries to pussify you again. There's too much at stake for Ma. Okay?"

"Okay," Paulie said wearily. "I hear you, Mary Frances."

As if she knew it was now okay to interrupt, Ruby rang her bell. Frankie bolted upright in her seat, as if she had been programmed for automatic response.

"Stay there," Paulie said, rising. "I'll take care of her. Just relax. Get out the house. I'll stick around."

Three hours had passed since Callie had color-corrected the brown shades on her eyelids and avoided the boxing of personal items and knickknacks from Emily's bedroom that she had planned on tending to that morning. Everything was exactly in the same place as she had found it earlier: Still neat, still orderly, and still covered with the ghostly dust of a bygone era.

Had she really wasted three hours angrily flipping through old yearbooks, trying to identify and remember people she couldn't care less about, all the time pretending not to be waiting for Paulie Cavalese to ring the downstairs bell? Had she really made up her face so spectacularly just to brood in a dusty old bedroom about an obnoxious hunk who wasn't nearly as fine a man as the one she had married, the man she was in love with? Like a jilted, angry lover, she seethed inside: where the hell was he? Had he given up the chase—so quickly?

At first, she told herself that perhaps he had listened to her good advice from the previous day and *was* spending more time with his mother. He'd be over to see her later. But when she got up the nerve to look out the window and saw an old brown, dented Dodge where Paulie's sports car had been parked, she filled with a self-loathing so large it crushed her soul. To her own surprise, she found herself cursing the mammoth rust on the near-dead Dart, following the zig-zaggy pattern of corrosion with her eyes, and cursing the Rainytown standards that for years had shamed her. And once again, of course, she felt ashamed of being ashamed.

A few minutes after one o'clock, she appeared at the Cavaleses' front door.

"I was just coming to look for you," Frankie said pleasantly, opening the screen door for Callie. "Thought you might want to have a bite of lunch with me. Paulie did some shopping for me this morning; I've got plenty of everything."

"Oh," Callie said nonchalantly. "Paulie's been here? I thought he didn't do mornings."

"Depends on how much night he's done previously." Frankie laughed. "You know what I mean. He must've had an early night last night, 'cause he was here by ten, and believe it or not, stayed with Ma for over two hours. Watched talk shows with her and held her hand. Personally, I'd rather see them use the time to work out more important things, but him just bein' there with her, well, it made her happy, and I got some time for me. Alone time. God knows I need it, Mason."

Callie prayed that her interest in Paulie was properly camouflaged. "So, I assume he went out for lunch. He'll be back later?" Callie secretly chastised herself for being too selfish to seize this opportunity to talk about Frankie's needs. It would have been a perfect opportunity to provide an outlet for Frankie's myriad frustrations, but no, finding out about Paulie was much more important.

Oh, what a wretched wench she was! Married and lusting after a rogue like Paulie. Desperate for forgiveness from Frankie, yet, at that moment in time, she was too selfish to interrupt her torrid, ludicrous desires to extend kindness to a deserving friend.

"No, I don't think so," Frankie said, walking toward the kitchen. "Didn't say nothin' about coming back. Hell, staying two hours was a record. Who am I to push? 'Sides, I think he wanted to go in early tonight to talk to the old man."

Callie was dying to probe but managed to repress the urge. She followed Frankie into the kitchen and took a seat. Inside her head, a confused internal dialogue took control, and Callie sat there struggling to understand her own feelings. Why was she angry at Paulie for doing exactly what she had insisted he do, stay away from her and spend more time with his family? Who was he to her but the good-looking younger brother of an old friend — some charmer who knew how to smear on the praise like a three-year-old making his first peanut butter sandwich? Why did she feel so betrayed? Why didn't he come over to see her when he'd finished visiting with Ruby? Had she only managed to hold his interest for a millisecond? Was the game over? Was she so flawed that he'd already lost interest, just like Jackson was doing? Oh, God. Just like Jackson was doing! No, no. Jackson was not losing interest. No. He couldn't be. My God, she thought, my life is ridiculous.

Frankie pulled out a chair and took a seat at the table with Callie. "Listen, before we decide on lunch, there's that little matter that we discussed yesterday morning. You know, seein' my ma. You think you're up for it?"

How could Callie possibly refuse Ruby's request? Besides, this was someone she had grown up with, a second mother of sorts. She truly did want to see her. And, despite the painful circumstances of the reunion, maybe she could spend an unselfish moment helping someone, which might help to balance out the sinful karma she was creating.

"Ma really wants to see you," Frankie reiterated before Callie could answer. "Don't let that stuff with Reg scare you off. Ma's only got a little time left, and I can't worry about Reg's feelings right now. Sorry if that sounds selfish."

"Oh, God. Not at all, Frankie. Not at all. I'd be happy to visit with your mom. I couldn't imagine *not* doing so. It's been such a long time."

"Too long," Frankie said wistfully. "Too long."

Callie smiled uneasily.

"Okay then, we'll have a nice, long lunch, and when Ma wakes up later this afternoon, you two can have your visit."

"Sounds perfect," Callie said.

"By the way, Mason," Frankie said, as if she were truly perplexed. "There's something I've been meaning to ask you."

"And that is…?"

"What's with all this war paint you've got on today? You don't normally look like this. I mean, I know you put on globs of makeup like normal folks put on underwear, but what's with this 'glamour babe' look, especially when you ain't supposed to be doin' nothing but packin' boxes?"

Callie's face fell, and as Frankie watched it do so, an image of Paulie flashed through her mind as Callie's earlier questions about his whereabouts replayed simultaneously.

Oh shit, Frankie thought. Not Mason, too!

Callie scrambled to collect herself and began speaking quickly. "I know. I look ridiculously over made up. I was going to take a break from packing and pay an obligatory visit to some society matron, but then I remembered she was vacationing on the Cape, so I just stayed here and kept working. You're probably wondering why I'd make myself up this way for someone like that, but this woman, Mary Collingswood, well, she's always comparing me to her daughter-in-law, Liza, and me, being an idiot that I am, I always let her intimidate me, and so I keep this ridiculous competition going by doing things like this. I'm so embarrassed. I must look so stupid."

Frankie looked at her blankly, not knowing whether to laugh or think her a liar. Sadly, the competition story was as truthful as ever, but, as they both knew, lust for Paulie was the real answer to Frankie's question.

Frankie laughed and let the subject drop. "You're some piece of work, Mason. I can't believe you let broads like that get to you. You need more time with me. I'll set you straight. I'll teach you what matters in this life."

Realizing that she had made an unintentional plea for continued friendship, Frankie felt a wave of embarrassment, the kind one feels when unexpectedly seen naked, but she ignored the feeling. "I'm starved. C'mon, Mason. Let's figure out what we're gonna pig out on today. I've got some corkscrew and penne pasta salad—that'll be right up your alley!"

CHAPTER 11

"You can go up now, Mason. She's awake. She's waiting for you." Frankie said as her feet touched the landing. "She's anxious to see you."

The levity that had accompanied lunch, when the women had played with tricolored fusilli and made various phallic references to pasta shapes, had not managed to linger post-repast or, in essence, to double as a delay tactic for Callie's reunion with Ruby. So, with nothing to mask or eradicate her fear, Callie fumbled nervously with it, becoming Frankie-like as she sat in the dark, mulling over what the next few minutes might bring and not daring to think beyond that.

Callie looked up at her. "Aren't you going to come upstairs with me?"

"You don't need no introduction. And neither does she. Just go up there."

Frankie watched as Callie swallowed the lump in her throat. "I'm sorry, Mason. I know this shit ain't easy for you. It ain't easy for me, and I should be used to it. But I promise you, it'll be okay. Just go."

"Right," Callie said stoically, as if she were going off to war, then rose from the couch and walked slowly toward the stairs.

Frankie rubbed Callie's back affectionately as they passed one another. "You'll do fine, Mason."

Callie climbed the stairs and stood in front of Ruby's door, which was slightly ajar. She could hear the sounds of a TV talk show blaring inside. "You come near my baby's daddy one more time, bitch, I'll blow your bleeping head off!"

"Please watch your language. We're on television," the host admonished. "Sorry," the woman said sulkily. "But I ain't takin' no more harassment from this ugly-assed bitch no more! She needs to find her own man — not that no man with a face prettier than a bulldog's would want her nasty bleep!"

"*Your* man wanted it, my sistah! He wanted it real bad! But he is *my* man now, and he is *hot* for me now, baby! Oh, yes! You heah me? As

God is my witness!" the new voice chimed in gleefully. "Tellin' it like it is and lovin' ev'ry moment!"

"I'll kill your bleepin' ass, bitch!" the first woman screamed, as sounds of furniture being shuffled took center stage. "Lyin' bitch! That's what God's witnessing. Your lyin' ass! Nuttin' else! Check yourself out! You sho' ain't nothin' to look at! Hmmmph!"

"Oh, please, and you think you all that, Ms. Gorilla face," the second woman said. "Bleep, any bleepin' mirror'll tell the truth 'bout your ass. Seeings how one don't break the second yo' ugly face comes in front of it and give yo ugly ass seven more years o' bad luck!" She laughed uproariously.

"I'll kill you, bitch!" the first woman screamed even louder. "I'll kill your bleepin' mother-bleepin' ass!"

As the host informed the audience that they were cutting away to a commercial break, Callie knew her time had come. This was all too strange. Ruby, like Emily, seemed dead to her. She could no more imagine finding Ruby alive inside the room than she could imagine finding her aunt alive next door. The voices on television — they seemed real. Ruby did not. She couldn't possibly be.

Callie knocked lightly on the door. There was no response. Slowly, she pushed the door open and peered in. Ruby, donning her black wig and a frilly-collared pink nightgown, grabbed the remote control and hit the off button. Callie didn't even realize the special treatment Ruby was bestowing on her.

The shriveled woman in the bed smiled brightly, taking in Callie from head to toe with her eyes, almost the same way her son had done.

"Hello, Mrs. C.," Callie said, suddenly wanting to burst into tears at the sight of her. "I'm so happy to see you."

Ruby's weak arms raised simultaneously to receive a hug. Biting her lip, Callie put her arms around the woman who was once her second mother and tried to shake off the chills of fear and sadness as they raced through her body.

"Take a seat," Ruby told her, straightening her wig.

Callie started to reach for the chair by the wall.

"No, no, honey," Ruby told her. "Sit here on the bed with me."

"Sure, Mrs. C. Whatever you'd like," she said, obliging. Callie noticed that Ruby was staring at her, as if she were awed by her appearance.

"Paulie weren't lyin'," Ruby said. "You sure are one beautiful woman."

"He said 'woman'?" Callie asked, her curiosity piqued.

"Well, no." Ruby laughed. "My son only knows the word 'babe.' But I got a feeling that for you, he might just enhance his vocabulary."

They shared a laugh. Now what the hell do I say, Callie fretted.

Ruby reached over and squeezed Callie's right hand. Callie could feel the dry flakiness of her skin, but still, her touch, both weak and determined, felt warm and motherly. It made her want to cry.

"I know this ain't easy for you, seein' me like this," Ruby said gently. "And I know you don't know what the hell to say to me. Can't tell me I look great, 'cause, face it, I'm dyin' and I look like shit."

"Oh, God!" Callie cried, as the tears started coming.

Ruby, angry with herself, shook her head in disgust. "Oh, honey, I'm sorry. I'm so used to tellin' it like it is with my kids, I forget who I'm talkin' to here. You're a real lady. You don't need to hear me talk like this!"

"Mrs. C., please! Please, don't put me on any pedestal. I don't belong there. You don't have to treat me any differently than you do Frankie or Paulie. I'm not the queen—"

"But you sure look like one," Ruby blurted out. "You are quite the beauty, Callie Mason. Too bad my Frankie couldn't have turned out like you."

"Mrs. C.," Callie said emphatically, trying to ignore the slight to Frankie. "I'm no queen. I'm just me with a new last name, a husband, and two kids. It's just that I haven't seen you in twenty-three years, and I need a little time to adjust. I can handle it. Tell me how you're feeling, please."

"Callie, honey, there ain't that much time left. Now, we can talk about dry mouth and all the pretty sores inside of it, or we can discuss bloody stools, leg cramps, and nausea. Take your pick. But I'd rather talk about stuff that really counts."

Callie was not doing well. "It's just that, well, if you're suffering so, you might need to talk, you know, to get it out of your system."

Ruby laughed. "If talkin' would get this cancer and its nasty cousins outta my system, I'd run off at the mouth till the cows came home. But that ain't gonna happen. So let's use our time to talk about what really matters. Can we do that?"

What really matters, Callie repeated silently. I'll be damned if I know.

"C'mon," Ruby coaxed gently. "Tell me all about yourself. Pick up right where we left off."

For the next half hour, Callie, in her newfound role as raconteur, delighted Ruby with the highlights of the past twenty-three years — from meeting Jackson and marrying him, to giving birth to Stephen and Molly, to playing the oft-reluctant hostess to Jackson's colleagues as his career spiraled upwards, along with an abbreviated version of how Jackson came to be CEO of his own major company.

Ruby's eyes never stopped dancing. It was as if her very own celebrity had stepped right through the television screen, hunkered down on the bed with her, and was giving her a private audience. Callie, while painstakingly trying to give Ruby what she wanted, was delicately pressing her to talk about the Cavalese family, especially Frankie. But for the time being, Ruby wasn't interested in talking about what she already knew; she wanted the vicarious glamour and newness that Callie seemed to effortlessly provide.

"It sure is nice to hear a pretty lady tell a pretty story," Ruby said. "Look at me, spending the last of my days watchin' lowlifes cuss the living daylights outta one another. What the hell for?"

"Then why do you do it?" Callie asked sensitively.

" 'Cause I don't want the girls from the supermarket comin' over here slobberin' over me, anymore than I wanna see Fat Edna Murphy and them broads down the street."

"But they're your friends," Callie protested respectfully.

"Not them neighbors. Gossip-mongering, nosy old dames," Ruby corrected her. "Wanna know this; wanna know that. Wanna know all about Paulie and poor Frankie. Then they take that rubbish home and have it for dinner. Well, they can cook up whatever they like, but I ain't supplyin' no ingredients. You understand, Callie? These lowlifes on the TV; they keep me company. I see them; they can't see me. That's the way I like it. I know their business; they don't know mine. Nuttin' else Frankie can do for me; I've taken too much from that girl already." Ruby thought for a moment. "Nope. This is best for everyone."

Callie made a mental note that she did not include Paulie in this declaration.

Ruby suddenly grew quiet and wistful. After several long seconds, she looked Callie dead in the eye. "Do you really care for my Frankie?" she asked. "I mean, really, really care?"

Callie could see she was tiring. "Of course I care for her," Callie said, determined to be believed. "Very, very much. Much more than I could ever expect you or Frankie to believe after what I've done to her."

"Good," Ruby said. "That's what I needed to know. Listen, Callie Mason, forget the past. Just close the door on it."

"But—"

"No time to argue about it," Ruby told her. "I've got some serious decisions to make here, and I just needed to know."

"Know what, Mrs. C.?" Callie asked curiously.

"Know if you're planning to stick around in my Frankie's life, once you're done with your packing or whatever it is you're doing here. You gonna want my girl as your friend, like you did when you was kids, or is this just like an extended class reunion to you? You know, see your old friends, stay a while, then go your separate ways. I gotta know, honey."

Something big was brewing in Ruby's mind. Callie could sense it. This was more than just wanting to make sure that Frankie had a good friend. Something was up.

"I can't speak for Frankie, Mrs. C. But as for me, I've never wanted or needed a friendship more in my life. And that is from my heart. I mean that."

Ruby studied her face, looking past her eyes and into her soul. "I believe you."

"You know, I think you need to rest now," Callie said gently. "You look very tired."

"I want you to come back and see me again. Very soon. I may have a very important favor to ask of you."

"Anything," Callie said.

"I ain't never asked nobody a favor like this before. I'm not sure if I can do it or if it's even fair of me to ask. But you may be the only one to help me. Now, please, don't mention anything about this to Frankie."

"I won't," Callie told her. "And I don't care what the favor is, I will do it for you."

"You may be sorry you said that," Ruby told her. "I need to think on this. You come back soon. Okay?"

"Tomorrow if you want me, Mrs. C. Anything for you."

Callie reached down and kissed Ruby's forehead, and by the time she was standing upright again, she saw that Ruby had nodded off.

When Callie came downstairs, she found Frankie standing by the family photo gallery, mesmerized by the youthful photo of her parents. As if awakened from a deep sleep, she looked at Callie with inquisitive eyes but said nothing. It was at that very pregnant moment that pride, snatching up all the past hurts it could grab, stepped aside and allowed two best friends, so filled with love and an intense desire to truly reconcile, to have their due embrace.

Frankie began sobbing onto Callie's shoulder. "Did you see? Did you see how bad she looks? She's failing more every day. What am I going to do when she goes? Who am I going to be? A supermarket clerk with a dead mother? That's all I'm going to be, Callie. Oh, God, that's all I'm going to be."

"No, you won't," Callie said with conviction, trying to stop her own tears as she led her to the couch. "Come on, let's sit down."

Frankie looked up at Callie, whose streaked face looked like a child's finger-painting experiment. Frankie grabbed some tissues from the coffee table, handing them to her. "See, there's a real downside to dousing on all of that war paint. Can't cry when you need to."

They laughed through their tears as Callie wiped her face and as Frankie used her one of her arms to wipe her tears. "See, you can dry quicker this way, too. Now if you tried this, your arm would look like that filthy paint box you carried around for years."

"No way," Callie said. "I remember that thing. That was *your* filthy paint box."

"The hell it was, Mason. Your aunt gave that thing to you and you used it so much that all the colors ran together into one giant smushed mess!"

Callie looked at her in mock defiance. "One giant smushed mess, huh? Well, if that was the case, then it definitely had to be yours."

Teary-eyed but beyond crying, the women looked sorrowfully at one another. Frankie managed to smile briefly, but it only served as a preamble to a prolonged frown. Callie squeezed her friend's hand and held it.

Now it was Frankie's turn to flip the pages back in time. It was springtime, and the girls were in the ninth grade. With Ruby's help, Frankie had managed to save enough money to buy a new outfit for the spring dance. Finding the courage to abandon her tomboy façade, Frankie had chosen a beautiful dress — it had a scoop neck and a beautiful print of orange poppies bursting in a lush green meadow with a white background. She remembered telling Callie about it. "It sounds really ugly, but it's not. It's just one of those things you have to see on, you know." Callie knew just what she meant. When Frankie modeled it for her, Callie told Frankie that she was sure to knock Vinnie Salamino's socks off, provided he remembered to wear them.

On the Friday afternoon before the dance, Frankie's feet were so light in anticipation that she practically floated down the hallway, talking excitedly to Callie about the upcoming date. But then, Angela Diamond, the mini-skirted, black-haired, gum-popping diva of the ninth grade, stopped Frankie abruptly, right in front of Vinnie Salamino's locker, where she had just slipped a note in the door for him.

"Yo! Cavalese!" she chortled, then popped a big pink bubble. "A little birdie told me that you actually think my Vinnie is your date for tomorrow night."

"He asked me to the dance," Frankie said assuredly. "And I said yes."

Angela cracked her gum, flung her head back, and laughed. "Cavalese, listen. We had a little lover's quarrel, ya know, and in whacha call a split second of stupidity, he might've said somethin' to indicate he was offerin' up an invite. But trust me, sweetie, you're gonna have one long wait if you think my Vinnie's coming to take you anywhere. Do I make myself clear? So if you, like, bought anything special to wear, not that someone like you would even think to do that, you better get your money back. Gee, I'd hate to see you dribble a milkshake on your new party frock; they'd never take it back then. On second thought, I think Woolworth's is pretty good about takin' stuff back. I wouldn't know from personal experience, though. Well, take care. Have fun tomorrow night. Maybe there's a good movie on television."

The light in Frankie's eyes shut off, and her spirit went dead as Angela and her coterie of carbon copies danced lithely away, giggling at the cruel monologue Angela had just delivered. Vinnie was the first boy Frankie had really taken a liking to, despite the fact that he was completely unworthy of her affections.

Callie said a few words of consolation to Frankie, then rushed off to find Vinnie Salamino and force the coward to confirm the betrayal, which he did. When Callie came to find Frankie, she had not moved from the spot in the hallway where the bad news had been delivered. In fact, she was standing so still, Callie told her (weeks later), that she looked like a cryogenically frozen hall monitor. By that time, Frankie had gotten over Vinnie Salamino and had managed to laugh.

But there was nothing funny about anything the day that it all happened. That night, and the next, the girls sat, just like they were doing now, on the couch, as Callie wordlessly comforted her friend. But the most important part of all, Frankie suddenly remembered, was that Callie had canceled her own date so that Frankie wouldn't be left home alone. At first, Callie had tried to convince Frankie that the two of them should attend the dance together, but Frankie's humiliation was too great to even consider it. And that was just fine with Callie. They would stay home together.

What a supreme sacrifice to make for a friend, Frankie recollected. But that was my friend Callie.

"We can't sit and frown like this forever," Callie said, interrupting Frankie's time traveling.

"No, guess not," Frankie said. "Let's stand on our heads. Then we'll be smiling."

They joined together in a laugh.

"Thanks, Mason. For everything. You know what I was just remembering?"

"What? That smushed mess of a paint box you had?"

"Yours!" Frankie returned in mock sternness. "No, something else."

"You gotta take my Hal's poll," the voice said, breaking the sound barrier, as the body that owned it burst unexpectedly into the Cavalese living room.

Startled, Frankie and Callie looked up at her.

"Oh, hi, Callie," Regina said, trying to conceal the envy she felt at finding Callie with her best friend...*again.* "You might as well take the poll, too."

"What now?" Frankie asked impatiently.

"Excuse me," Regina said, her tolerance for rejection weakening daily. "Am I interrupting something here?"

"What is it, Reg?"

Regina gripped the arm of Frankie's favorite chair and delicately lowered her big belly into comfort. "Get ready to howl!" she warned jovially.

Frankie blew air between her lips in disgust while Callie politely refrained from showing any annoyance at all. It was a skill she had mastered quite well over the years.

"My Hal came up with this poll last night at dinner. I'm his official vote getter. Okay, here goes: whattya think most people do when they're driving, besides actually watch the road: A, they sing with the radio; B, they pick their nose; or C, they check themselves out in the rearview mirror?"

"How about D?" Callie said. "Talk on their cell phones."

Regina looked annoyed. "That ain't one of the choices. Besides, not everyone 'round here carries one of them except for Frankie's hotshot brother."

"Callie does," Frankie goaded her.

"Just answer the poll," Regina demanded, her agitation clear.

"How the hell should I know, Reg? It depends on whether the

person likes the song on the radio, has a booger up their nose, or is prepping for a hot date. It's not something I ever think about, you know?"

"Well, just for the record," Regina said, "my kids voted for nose pickin', and Hal and I voted for singing. Hal said your brother probably does C, check himself out in the mirror."

"Whatever," Frankie said dryly.

"It's a real howl, don't you think?" Regina said, determined to validate her husband's contribution to the world of humor.

"Oh, it's a genuine Hal, all right."

"Well, sorry I bothered you," Regina said defensively. "I won't say no more. I was gonna tell you about the great name my Hal came up with for the bar he's gonna own someday, 'Hal's Bayou,' but you probably don't care nothing about that either."

"Reg, listen," Frankie explained. "Just ten minutes ago, Callie came downstairs from seeing Ma, for the first time in all these years. Ma's not gonna hang on for too long, and neither one of us is in a real cheerful mood. Can you respect that?"

"Oh, sure. Sorry," Regina said. "Just thought you'd appreciate a little tension breaker." She looked at Callie. "So *you* saw Mrs. Cavalese, huh?"

"Yes," Callie said. "I did."

Regina turned to Frankie. "She still don't wanna see me, huh?"

Frankie was angry. "I told you it's nothing personal. Stop heaping your portion of shit on my plate. I got enough!"

"Well, later for you, alligator," Regina said, pushing down on the arm of the chair to lift herself up. "I'm sorry I tried to be friendly, spread a little cheer and all that."

As the old screen door opened and slammed shut, Callie turned to Frankie and took her hand. "I'm here for you. It's going to be okay. I'm really here now."

Callie was solemn on the ride home. Her early morning foolishness over Paulie seemed to have filed itself under "dead and buried," while her visit with Ruby had rightly guided her toward life's more pressing matters.

She shook Paulie off like a chill on a blustery day. Safe and secure now, Callie's focus returned to Ruby and the impending favor that seemed to dominate the dying woman's thoughts. If it wasn't Callie's intervention with Louie she was after, what else could it possibly be? To look after Frankie after she died? No, that wasn't it. She'd already assured Ruby that she wanted this friendship on a permanent basis. Besides, looking after Frankie would not be a favor.

She needed to stop this growing obsession with the Cavalese family. Jackson: that's who she should be thinking about. Suddenly, the relationship with her husband needed more mending than the one with her long-estranged friend.

Why was her happy marriage of almost two decades suddenly disintegrating? Maybe she had been too complacent, hadn't worked hard enough on maintaining a happy home, or of late, maybe she hadn't given Jackson's business problems the recognition they deserved. Or perhaps it was just the strain of missing her children. Why did she suddenly feel more like a member of Frankie's family than her own?

Jackson's car was in the driveway when she pulled in. He was probably in the den, she thought, with Fred, George, or some other dead composer, savoring his martini and delighting in the genius of his idols.

Callie parked her car and rushed inside to find the picture nothing like the one she had just painted. The bar in the den hadn't even been touched.

"Mr. Hethers went straight up to the bedroom," Rosa said, standing right behind Callie.

"My God, Rosa! Don't sneak up on me like that! You scared the hell out of me!" Callie said, angrier and angrier about the live-in housekeeper situation.

Rosa didn't even bother apologizing. "Steve called earlier. Guess Mr. Hethers probably went upstairs to call him back. Molly's working a double shift today. One of the other girls quit last minute, and Molly's been a trooper and pitching in. Of course, her uncle Cole is paying her special wages and all. Mister Steve is going camping this weekend with his buddies. Wanted you and Mr. Hethers to know he'd be incommunicado.

Me and Steve. Had a nice talk, we did."

Callie was incensed. Not only was Rosa invading her space and her privacy, but she did not want to hear her children's news from anyone but Molly or Stephen. At the very least, from Jackson.

Refusing to thank Rosa for her intended kindness, Callie stormed up the stairs, leaving her bewildered housekeeper in the proverbial dust.

Callie ran down the hall, rushing toward the bedroom.

"Tell that brother of mine that time and a half won't do it. Double time. Okay, sweetie? Be sure to get a good night's sleep when this marathon shift ends. Oh, and I hope you told your brother to beware of moose and not to make eye contact with one if they cross paths. The moose will take it as a sign of aggress...yeah, okay, I'm sure you both know much more about moose than your old man. Love you, Molls. Tell Steve to call when he gets back and let us know he's safe. Sorry I missed him. Bye, honey."

"Wait!" Callie shrieked, entering the bedroom.

"Sorry," Jackson said, hanging up the phone. "She's already hung up."

"Okay, fine. I'll just call her back," Callie said, reaching for the phone.

"Wait until later," Jackson advised. "There was a party of seven unloading their car in the lot as we spoke. I'm sure Molls has her hands full right now. She's way too busy to talk to you right now."

Just like you've been, Callie thought, angry at the cold shoulder.

"Okay, I'll call her later," Callie said resignedly. "Rosa said Steve was going camping for the weekend."

"In Acadia with two buddies," Jackson added. "Left hours ago."

"Darn. I want to talk to my children. I miss them."

"Me too," Jackson said, loosening his tie. "Miss 'em like crazy."

"Jack," Callie said, "I know we've discussed this before, but can we please reassess the Rosa situation? Does she have to live here? I feel so exposed, so naked when she's around. The kids are grown, gone this summer, off to school in the fall...our needs are different now."

"She's got her own suite," Jackson reminded her. "She's not in your way."

"But she is!" Callie protested.

"Am I to infer that you want *me* to tell her to find a new home after having devoted years of her life our service?"

"We're not sending her off to prison," Callie said adamantly. "We're not firing her, either."

"We have the extra living suite here. She's got her own kitchen, her own bathroom, her own living area. She's got a separate entrance, for Christ's sake. You act as if she's your roommate or something."

"It doesn't matter if she's got the entire mother-in-law suite or the Taj Mahal to herself. She's in our part of the house all the damn long day."

Jackson looked at her incredulously. "I can't believe we're even having a conversation as stupid as this! She works in 'our part of the house.' Where the hell should she be? Doing jigsaw puzzles in her living room? Cleaning the neighbors' homes and collecting a salary from us?"

"I just wish she lived elsewhere," Callie pouted. "Then maybe she'd leave earlier and I wouldn't feel so infringed upon. She thinks she's doing us a favor by staying late some nights, but it's such an invasion of privacy. I think she's just lonely."

Jackson shrugged. He was in no frame of mind to deal with something so trivial when his company's future was so precarious. His patience had quit for the day. "Are you prepared to pay her rent elsewhere? Do you have the money for that?"

"Okay, Jack. You want to play nasty now. Attacking my Achilles' heel."

"As if that were your only weak spot," Jackson retorted. "It used to be very convenient for you that Rosa lived here. You had a built-in babysitter. Someone was always here to greet the repairman, to accept deliveries, and whatever else was needed."

"It's no longer convenient, " Callie said.

"I don't want to argue about this," Jackson said. "And I really don't want to deal with this now."

"Oh, Jack! How did we even get into this? Can't we just start this evening over again?"

Jackson didn't bother responding.

"Hi, honey. I'm home," Callie said cheerfully, kissing him on the cheek.

"Good evening, Callie," Jackson said brusquely, annoyed by the futility and the silliness of the charade.

Callie felt the rebuff and let her mind drift back to that morning. The events she had tried to disentangle herself from began to replay in her mind. Paulie, roughish and debonair, leaning against his sports car as the neighborhood fan club came to fawn. Paulie's charm was creeping its way back into her head and she was determined to put out a no-trespassing sign and mean it this time. A romantic evening with her husband could easily erase Mr. Cavalese from her mind. She just had to get past Jackson's alternating anger and apathy. Perhaps some pleasant conversation would start the wheels of romance rolling.

"Jack, today was so incredible. I saw Ruby Cavalese, Frankie's mom, for the first time. You know that she's dying of cancer, and so it was heartbreaking, but I felt so happy that she's still in this world and that we had the chance to reunite. It's hard to put into words what I feel, but I want so much to share all this with you. Oh, and I think Frankie and I entered new territory today. I think we're really and truly friends again. Isn't that wonderful?" Callie said, her eyes begging for positive feedback.

Jackson looked at her, stone-faced. "And how was *your* day, Jack? I've been so concerned. I know you've had some major setbacks with the Seattle project and that you've been pushed to the limit. Have you been able to resolve any of the problems? How did today go? Any progress? Any news?"

"Sorry!" Callie snapped angrily, as Jackson continued to shed his work clothes. "What makes you so sure I wasn't going to ask about the situation at work? It's just that I had a really important day, and everything just sort of spilled out of me. I hadn't forgotten about you."

"Callie," Jackson said, draping his shirt neatly over a chair, "you've become so self-absorbed that I don't even know you anymore. It's been only five days since you went back to that place—"

"Rainytown!" Callie interrupted. I wish you wouldn't call it 'that place!' "

"You mean like you used to do?" Jackson challenged her.

Callie looked down at the floor. She didn't want to touch that one.

"As I was saying," Jackson continued, "it's been five days since you went back to your old home, and I barely recognize you."

"Why? Because I'm suddenly not the ever-compliant, how-was-your-day-dear wife? Because now I actually have some overwhelming concerns of my own to occupy my thoughts?"

Jackson pulled a gray T-shirt from his dresser and put it on. "I'll be leaving for Seattle in a day or two."

Oh, Jack. No!"

"I have a company that's going to be nothing but rubble if I don't take swift and severe action to kick the butts that need kicking and fix the problems that need fixing. I'm sorry, but I can't stick around to help you work out your 'overwhelming concerns.' I've got too damn many of my own." Jackson unbuckled his belt, took off his pants and flung them on top of the shirt he had more delicately placed on the chair just seconds earlier. He reached into his dresser drawer for a pair of shorts, put them on, then turned to his wife. "Anything else?"

"Jack, please!" Callie pleaded.

"I'll be out by the pool if Seattle calls on the house phone. Make your own dinner plans."

As he left the room, Callie sank onto the bed and stared morosely into the mirror over Jackson's dresser. It's true, she thought. He *is* losing interest in me. He's *lost* interest in me. I've been nothing but a prop to him all of these years. I've completely outlived my usefulness. Oh, God…

CHAPTER 12

Veronica scooped up the five-dollar bill that Russ Tompkins had left her and stuffed it into her jar. She grabbed a wet cloth and began to wipe down the bar, when she noticed Paulie, looking agitated and out of sorts.

"Hey, baby! You got your days mixed up? This is Friday night, remember? You're off tonight. You've got another twenty-four hours before you need to show that handsome face of yours."

"Where is he?" Paulie asked impatiently.

"Who? Your old man?" Veronica lifted an ashtray and dumped Russ Tompkins' cigar stump into the trashcan. "Man, RT smokes one nasty cigar."

"You've got to acquire a nose for it," Paulie said. "But I like the one you already have. I'd hate to see you trade it in for another one; it's so cute."

Veronica winked at him. "You're a doll baby. But I'll tell you, having to inhale this toxic shit is worth every nickel of the Abe Lincoln RT leaves me. But lately I'm thinking I might require a different president if I have to breathe in just one more of these nasty sticks. I'm thinking Andrew Jackson would look handsome in my jar, even though it *was* ole Abe that freed the slaves. I'll always be indebted to Abe for that. But still…Andrew's the president I'd like to see a lot more of. Come to me, Andy!"

Paulie laughed. Veronica had a way with him. "You didn't answer my question. Where is he?"

"Don't know, sugar. He dropped *her* off and said he'd be back in a bit. You know what I'm thinking?"

"What?" Paulie asked. "That the old man's off doing the widow Sampson?"

"You and that mind of yours!" Veronica laughed. "No, I'm thinking that Lincoln freed the slaves, and here I am, five nights a week, taking orders from Annie Cavalese. What's wrong with this picture?"

"You don't take orders from anyone," Paulie told her. "You're just good at pretending that you do." Paulie looked down the bar at Annie. "Maybe she knows when Pop's coming back."

"Hey, when you go talk to the old witch, ask her if it ain't true. Ask her if Louie ain't off zoomin' Rita Sampson. Just for the hell of it," Veronica said devilishly. "C'mon, just for fun. Let's see what the ole bat'll say about that."

"Make your own fun," Paulie told her, then smiled affectionately.

Veronica watched tenderly as Paulie walked to the end of the bar where Annie sat. Veronica had had a crush on Paulie as long as she could remember, but she often told him that she was awfully glad she lived with her man, Charlie. "I'd have thrown your butt out in a heartbeat," she'd often tell him. "I need a man that's only got eyes for me."

Annie's ice blue eyes gazed suspiciously at Paulie as he sat down next to her. She took a long drag of her cigarette before she spoke.

"Evenin', Paulie," she said coolly. "What brings you here tonight? You leave something or someone behind last night? Or do you just like spending time with your dear step ma-ma?"

"You ain't no ma-ma of mine. What's with the attitude, Annie? You don't even know what I want."

"Hell, yeah, I do!" she said, as a generous portion of drink slid down her throat. "You're lookin' for my husband."

"No, I'm looking for my father," Paulie corrected her. He hated it when she did that, and she usually pulled the "my husband" routine when she felt especially threatened. Paulie reached into his shirt pocket and pulled out a cigarette. Before he could locate a lighter, the cocoa-colored hand with the beautifully manicured nails was reaching over the bar to light his cigarette.

"Thanks, babe," Paulie said.

Veronica winked. "Don't forget to ask," she said.

Annie looked at Veronica and then at Paulie. "What the hell's she talking about?"

"It's got nothing to do with you," Paulie said, as he observed Ronnie laughing over the predicament she'd just put him in.

"Why don't I believe you?" Annie said angrily, noticing Veronica's obvious mirth.

"Your problem," Paulie said. "Where's Louie?"

"Your problem," Annie snapped back in retaliation.

Paulie laughed. "Are you sure of that? Maybe not." He smiled an evil smile, as if to say, "I know something you don't know."

Despite the fact that Annie knew exactly where her husband was, her increasing paranoia about other women always made her come unglued. Louie was her security, and when it was threatened in any way, she lashed out.

Paulie was having too much fun to stop. "It's nine o'clock. Do you know where your husband is?"

"Damn right I do, smart ass!" she said, giving him exactly what he wanted. "He's stopped over at Duke's Taproom. Duke just came back to work. Out for months. Heart attack. Okay? That's what you want to know? Satisfied, Mr. Paul Anthony Cavalese?"

"When will he be back?"

"When he gets back! That's when," Annie growled. "But he doesn't need to come back if you're going to hound him about seeing Ruby again."

Paulie was livid that Annie dared even speak his mother's name, and even angrier that his father had confided Paulie's request to his bitter, compassionless wife. Paulie understood the dynamics of his father's actions better than he would have liked, recognizing some of the same unfortunate traits in himself. He was certain that his father told Annie in an act of cowardice, hoping, but not admitting to himself, that she would actually order him to stay away, thus making it all the easier for him to avoid having to make a decision. Paulie became increasingly anxious and disturbed, feeling as if electricity, not blood, were streaming through his veins.

Damn it, he thought. It's the same old story; Pop's letting this bitch call the shots. No way. Not now. This time, the story ain't gonna end the way Annie writes it. I've got to make that stubborn old coward give Ma the happy ending to her sad life that she deserves. He's fucking got to! Damn it. When's he coming back?

Paulie took a drag of his cigarette, stifled his desire to bestow "Step Ma-Ma" with a hearty expletive or two, and walked to his end of the bar, where Ronnie had a beer waiting.

"Love you, Ronnie," he said, acknowledging her keen ability to know his needs before he did.

She smiled and walked away. She also knew when to leave him alone.

He took a seat, balled his left hand into a fist, and began nervously, but softly, pounding the bar. The sun was setting on his mother's life, and he was fretting over Louie's wife. I can't think about that woman, he told himself. Just Ma. I've got to concentrate on Ma.

As if the angst over his mother's imminent death and his predicament with Louie weren't enough, Paulie resurrected a long-dormant jeremiad and began to brutally chastise himself for the man he had been. He could have done so much more for his mother…and his sister. How could he have let his sister, who'd been denied opportunities for a normal life since the day she graduated from high school, take on the burden of almost singlehandedly tending to their dying mother? Even if his cavorting and his poor attendance record were in truth a disguise for his pain and fear, and not simply the activities of a selfish man, it didn't matter. He'd hurt everyone, and now the weight of his actions fell heaviest on himself.

As the sands of the hourglass rushed downward like tears, and he had one last shot at thanking his mother for loving him, for devoting her life to him, he'd be damned if his father's alcoholic wife was going to deny Ruby, Frankie, Louie or himself that one last stab at peace.

He crushed out his cigarette and looked at it, bent and half-smoked in the ashtray. Maybe he would quit. He didn't even enjoy smoking anymore. Not since he learned it was killing his mother. Not since he found himself clearing his throat more often and popping mints to get rid of the stale taste in his mouth. But he couldn't think about smoking right now; he was too stressed out to even consider quitting. Not now, anyway. So he thought about Callie and indulged himself in a moment of erotic fantasy, but even his lust for her was overshadowed by the mission at hand.

"Hey, Moscatelli!" Louie yelled over the crowd. "Pretty fancy new babe you got outside. Just saw her."

"I call her Portia," Al Moscatelli yelled back. "Ain't she the fieriest red broad you ever did see? You oughta see her engine. Whoa, baby! I just love to turn her on."

"A car's the only goddamn thing an old geezer like you could turn on," a woman's voice replied loudly. Louie laughed, as did Moscatelli's table of cronies, until he saw Paulie at the bar, motioning to him. With some trepidation, he went over to join him. It was Friday night at the Blue Lights, which meant it was filled to capacity, and at least tonight, private conversations were not as likely to be overheard.

"Son," Louie said, patting Paulie on the back. "What are you in for tonight?" It did not escape Paulie's notice that his customary hug was absent from his father's greeting.

"To see you," Paulie said.

"I told Paulie you'd gone over to see Duke," Annie said, suddenly standing by Louie, wrapping a possessive right arm around his waist. "How's the old boy doing, honey?"

"Looks great," Louie said, pleased at the attention his wife was paying him. "Lost fifty pounds, he did. Hardly recognized him without the beer belly, though I must say the weight loss does show his age a bit more. When the fat goes out, in come the wrinkles. But Dukie's just fine."

"Well, I'm very glad to hear that. That's great. May I join you fellas for a drink?" Annie said sweetly, caressing the left side of Louie's face as she brushed a wisp of his salt-and-pepper hair to the side. She glanced at Paulie, defying him to stop her with a victorious glint in her eyes.

But Annie's game was not won. In a fortuitous flash, Louie's attention was suddenly diverted as Al Moscatelli approached Louie, anxious to continue bragging about his new Porsche. Seizing the opportunity when he saw it, Paulie yanked Annie from her husband's side, sinking his fingers into the skin on her left arm.

"You're hurting me, damn you!" she hissed. "Let go of me or I'll scream so everyone in this motherfucking bar can hear me."

Paulie was seething with rage. "You listen to me, you goddamned bitch. You even *think* about fucking in my family affairs, and I'll make sure Louie knows as much about your business as Ronnie and I do. You think we don't see who slips you vials and pills on a nightly basis? You think we haven't seen you 'excuse' yourself to the 'little girls' room' and then run out to the parking lot when you think nobody's looking? What's the going rate for a blow job, 'Step Ma-Ma?' One, two, three lines of coke?"

"Fuck you!" Annie said angrily as she turned on her heels and walked back to her seat. "Damn that fucking kid," she muttered to herself. "Damn him and that nosy black bitch to hell."

Paulie had been holding that trump card for years, and he couldn't have found a better opportunity to play it. He felt a swell of triumph in spite of the miserable circumstances surrounding it.

"Where's Annie?" Louie asked Paulie, as Al walked back to his table.

"Back to her throne; she's holding court. Her admirers couldn't wait," Paulie told him.

"Yeah, yeah," Louie said, accustomed to his wife's behavior as he looked down at the end of the bar and saw that she was already flirting with another man. "So what's up?"

Paulie sat down and faced his father, stiff-lipped and ready for what had to be done. "Pop, let's not play games. You know what I want. And we both know that you probably wanna see Ma as much as she wants to see you. I know that because we're a lot alike. Mary Frances reminds me of that all the time. And I know that if you don't go and see Ma, you'll regret it the minute she dies. That could be tomorrow; that could be next week. I don't know. The doctor said she may need oxygen soon. If that's the case, we'll have to get a hospital bed put into the dining room or wherever we can make room in that downstairs dungeon of a house. Wouldn't it be better to see her now, in her bedroom, while she still has an ounce of dignity left?

"Damn, Pop, Ma worked her ass off in that supermarket for years. After you left she took on a night job, doing surveys for some magazine from the phone at home; sometimes she'd take other jobs, selling newspaper subscriptions or cheap cosmetics to people who'd curse at her and slam the phone in her ear. But once in a while, she'd have a good night, so she kept on keepin' on. For us. Ma didn't tell me till I was over twenty-one that she'd always wanted to be a nurse. Don't think she wanted me to know while I was still a kid. Well, I guess she gave up that dream to be your wife, and what did you do but take off with the first hussy that crooked her little finger at you."

"Paulie..." Louie warned.

"I don't know how much money you gave Ma to raise me and

Mary Frances, but it wasn't damn near enough. Hell no. Shit, I'll bet you think I'm here because Ma begged me to come get you. Well, you'd be wrong. Ma's got more pride than a stubborn old man like yourself."

"I ain't so old," Louie interrupted him.

"It's not your age that makes you old," Paulie said. "Chronologically, I guess you're a fucking spring chicken. It's your attitude, Pop."

"Ahhh…"

Paulie continued. "No, Ma would never ask me to come looking for you. She says as long as you're married to Annie, she doesn't wanna know from you. But Mary Frances and I know better than that. Ma wants to see you again more than anything in this world."

Louie muttered something inaudibly under his breath.

"Damn, you took so much from her, Pop. Can't you give something back? Can't you give something to your children, like the satisfaction of knowing that their mother's dying wish was granted? Don't *you* want the satisfaction of knowing you made amends? Don't you want to send the mother of your children off to meet her maker in peace? Don't you want that for yourself?"

Louie looked blankly at him.

"Damn," Paulie said in frustration. "I just don't know how to get through to you. I don't know what else I could possibly say."

Louie glared at him. "You can say nothing. You've said it all, and I've heard this female load of rubbish for the last time." Louie looked down at the end of the bar to see what his wife was doing and found her coming on to Ben Jones, the retired prizefighter, a good-looking black man with a strong build and finely chiseled features. His blood roiled. He was "pissed off in stereo," as he used to say when two things went wrong simultaneously. He turned to Paulie sternly, determined to release his anger and reclaim his masculinity, which had been suddenly crushed by two of the three people closest to him.

"You know what I'm seeing here?" Louie said to Paulie. "I'm seeing my son, who I think has become a transsexual, give me a pile of crap I ain't got no intention of dealing with. Not now, not in this lifetime."

Paulie was imploding with rage but held his tongue as Louie's fear-induced castigation played out.

"I told you the first time, and I'll tell you again. I got no time for this goddamn women's 'feel good' bullshit. I raised a man, and now look what the fuck I got. Another daughter. Fucking Paula. My Frankie's got more balls than you do."

Paulie had never, in his entire lifetime, actually considered hurting his own father. It was a sick and horrible feeling. He held his arms down at his sides, trying to control himself, but his fists were clenched, and he could feel the sweat in his palms as his fury escalated.

"You didn't raise up anybody," Paulie countered verbally, hoping the urge to physically attack Louie would pass. "You took a hike. It's Ma that raised up a man, one who finally got around to acting like one, but you're too caught up in that hussy of a wife you have to take notice."

"Bullshit!" Louie sniped, watching intently as Ben Jones stroked Annie's hair and she giggled, making a face that looked as if she were having an orgasm on the bar stool. Louie seethed. "Listen to all that bullshit you just laid on me. You sound like some hoity-toity new age guru bitch like you see on TV."

"The hell I do!" Paulie snapped, breaking Louie's gaze and forcing him to look at the person speaking to him. "I'm nothin' like that. But you know what, I'd rather be whatever the fuck you just called me than a pussy-whipped loser like my old man!"

"Fuck you, Paulie! Fuck you! Now, get the fuck out of my bar!" Even over the din of the Friday night chatter, Louie's words were clearly heard. "Get the fuck out! Do you hear me? Fuck you! And don't come back! You're fired. Fuck you!"

Veronica wiped a tear from her eye as she saw the wreckage on Paulie's face as he hastily rushed to the front door, chased by expletives, failure, and prying eyes. She felt his pain as if it were her own; he'd been her closest friend for a very long time.

He let the door slam behind him. He had every intention of returning the following night for his shift. His father's temper had fired him dozens of times, but never before in a center-stage production. Paulie was so despondent over his mother's impending death that he almost didn't care who heard Louie's tortured condemnation. He had grown up enough to realize that it was not his masculinity that had been called to task in public; it was his father's.

As he walked along the boulevard, he stumbled on an empty beer can. Always one to be a good guy and pick up litter that others had left behind, Paulie's good deed doing left him. He stepped on the can and crushed it, then kicked it as hard as he could, watching with pleasure as the can flew across the street, whacking Portia on her rear, right above her back left tire. Paulie kicked another can out of his path and walked on.

He was now sure of one thing. His father cared; Ruby was definitely on his mind. Louie Cavalese, like a lot of people, wouldn't react so violently to something that had no meaning to him, even though some of that anger was actually meant for his strumpet of a wife. But still, Paulie knew that Louie's guilt over leaving his family was enormous. Paulie had seen proof of it a hundred different ways over the years. He knew Louie wasn't happy with Annie. How could any man be happy with a broken-down alcoholic of a wife, especially one of such wanton morality who trifled brazenly with every man who came out to play, while simultaneously doing everything in her power to deny her husband the same pleasure with other women. Part of Louie still loved Annie, but Paulie rarely acknowledged that. It made him sick. He only recognized that his father loved showing off Annie's beauty (what was left of it) and knew that Louie lamented the fact that his marriage was nothing more than an old building, still standing but poorly maintained. A little charm in the architecture, a little character in the porch, but too many broken windows and too much peeling paint to want to live there anymore. But extricating himself from the marriage wasn't an option for his father. Louie was too proud, for one, probably still loved the miserable wench, and he certainly didn't want the courts to give Annie half of the Blue Lights.

Paulie walked on, glancing in the window of a consignment shop and noticing how dirty the mannequin in the window looked. She had a black smudge on her left cheek, a missing left earlobe, and two of the fingers on her right hand had been snapped in half. I'd rather have her for a stepmother, he thought, spitting on the sidewalk. Passing O'Hanagan's Grocery, he wanted to tell the six young teens loitering outside how stupid they looked smoking their cigarettes. But to what end? To hear a retaliatory fusillade of fuck-yous from some punks wearing pants big enough to accommodate the entire neighborhood? Forget it. The echoes of his father's discontent and rage still hollered in his head.

Candy's Crystal Palace. Now, there was a hole, he thought, as he stood outside the gauche beauty salon looking at the lavender lace curtains in the window. Damn, every broad comes out of this hole looks like a goddamn whore. No wonder. Probably a fuckin' brothel; Candy's probably a whore like her momma Crystal was. No fuckin' doubt these broads tease a lot more than hair. Shit. They'll never get near what I got. I'm savin' that for Callie-fornia.

He kept walking. He crossed the street, heading away from the glare of street lamps and toward his apartment four blocks away. He had spoken his piece. He wished he'd intervened earlier; he wished he'd been a better brother to Frankie, but he hadn't. So be it. Some things he could change; others he could not. Everything was in God's hands now…and Louie's.

CHAPTER 13

"Wake up, Callie," Jackson said, standing by the bed and gently nudging her. "Phone call."

"Molly?" Callie asked with groggy enthusiasm. "At this hour?"

"Your friend Frankie Cavalese," Jackson said. "She sounds like a very nice person."

"She is," Callie said. "Did she sound upset?"

"Not particularly. She introduced herself, was quite cordial, and asked if she was disturbing me."

"And you told her…?"

"I told her to go to hell," Jackson said with clear disgust. "Jesus, Cal, I just told you she was nice and cordial. Why would you expect any less from me in return? I'm a damn nice guy, or have you forgotten that?"

"I'm sorry, honey. You're absolutely right," Callie said, climbing out of bed. "I'm just so afraid of anything on my end ever hurting Frankie again."

"Stop being so paranoid," Jackson said, kissing her on the top of the head. "We're all human. Don't try for superwoman; you'll never make it. Now, speaking of going to hell, that's where I'll be if you need me."

Callie's mind went elsewhere as she wondered about Frankie's call. "Oh, I'm so sorry you have to work," she said eventually, realizing what he had meant, but her response had come too late. He was gone.

Callie walked around the bed to the phone, which was on Jackson's nightstand, and released the hold button. "Frankie?"

"Yeah, it's me. Listen, I'm sorry to call you at home…and so damn early."

"We're friends," Callie said, "and I want you to call me any time you need me. Please, no apologies. When Jack told me you were on the phone, I was worried that your mom—"

"She's still hanging in there," Frankie said. "Still her feisty self. That's why I'm calling, actually. She's been hounding me all last night and this morning about having you come back again. She's totally fixated on it.

Do you think you could visit her again this afternoon? I'd have called later, but I'm headed out."

"Of course," Callie said. "In fact, I'd already planned to be over your way in about an hour or so. I want to get the rest of my aunt's personal effects packed so that I can hire the movers to haul it all out and then get the cleaning service in there. Then, believe it or not, I'll be all finished!"

Frankie panicked, wondering what impact this might have on the friendship, but put it out of her mind.

"How about you let me bring lunch for us today?" Callie said.

"Fine," Frankie replied, "but I might not be back until twelve thirty or one o'clock. I have an appointment. I'll be a while. Believe it or not, Paulie's here, so better bring enough food for three."

"My pleasure," Callie said, ashamed of the grin on her face that only she could see. "I'll bring plenty. Something I can bring for your mom?"

"Pudding," Frankie said. "She'll eat pudding. Specially if it comes from you. No butterscotch, though. She hates butterscotch. Anything else'll do just fine."

"Great. I'll see you later, then," Callie said.

"Roger, Mason."

Enervated no more, Callie galloped to the shower, anxiously pondering what adventures the day might bring. As she shed her nightshirt and stepped into the shower stall, it suddenly occurred to her: who the hell is Roger Mason?

After a nice long chat with Molly, and a very special errand that needed running, Callie arrived in Rainytown around ten fifteen. Working solidly for over two hours (the most productive two hours she'd yet to spend there), she glanced at her watch for the hundredth time, happy that it was finally cooperating with her wishes, and read twelve thirty, thus giving her permission to head next door. Frankie had specifically said that she wouldn't be home any earlier, so Callie hadn't wanted to risk showing up too soon. She neither wanted to interrupt Paulie's time with his mother nor have her motives questioned by an early arrival.

"Mary Frances said you'd been showing up 'round this time," Paulie told her, lying on the couch. "I saw you pull up a few hours ago. Poor thing. You've been counting the minutes until it was okay to come over. It must've seemed like an eternity."

"In your dreams," Callie said, feeling naked and defenseless. "How did you stumble upon that absurd deduction?"

Paulie sat up and glanced at his watch. "Well, for one, look at the time. Twelve thirty on the nose. Couldn't stay away another second, could you?"

"Oh, please..." Callie protested, "Is that the best you can do?"

Paulie got up and walked over to her without saying another word. Wrapping his arms around her, he pulled her close and kissed her passionately on the mouth. "How's that?" he said, looking into her eyes. "Better?"

She was shocked and enthralled, and Paulie, being "babe literate," knew exactly what he was reading. "I wanted to give you that yesterday, but there wasn't time. You waited for me to come over, didn't you?"

Callie was in a quandary. Not only had her eyes given her away, her full acceptance of the kiss would not lend credence to any denials she might make.

"You shouldn't have done that just now," she said, avoiding his question, almost breathless.

Paulie walked back to the couch and stretched out again. "But I did," he said in an atypically languid tone. "And you enjoyed it every bit as much as I did. So don't bother pretending otherwise. Then you'll be lying to two people. I'm tired of lies, and I'm tired of bullshit."

"I only said you shouldn't have done that," she said defensively, taking a seat.

"Whatever," Paulie said, gazing aimlessly at the ceiling.

"Looks like a chunk of your machismo is missing," Callie said. "Something happen?"

"Yeah, a wild dog bit me in the groin." Paulie sat up. "I did what you suggested. Not because you told me to do it, but because you were right. Because I finally saw the light, and it was fucking blinding."

Callie looked confused. Paulie paused before explaining. "I spoke to my old man, Callie, *twice,* about seeing Ma. Shot me down, tried to humiliate me right there in the damn club for all his friends to witness. Called me a bunch of bullshit names. Called me fucking *Paula*," Paulie said, getting angrier as he recalled the scene to Callie. "Can you believe that? Fucking fired me too, not that he meant it, but damn, I said and did everything I could do to get through to that stubborn old pussy-whipped bastard. And that's what I got. Fucking *Paula*. I'm a goddamned woman to him because I ask him to come visit Ma."

"Oh, God, I'm so sorry. Are you absolutely sure you didn't make any inroads with him? Maybe he was just too proud to let you see how he really felt," Callie suggested. "Sounds like you hit a big nerve because he's had the same thought all along but was trying to suppress it. Denial is a comfortable place, you know. Think that could be it?"

"I don't know," Paulie said wearily. "I don't know a damn thing. I just spent time with Ma. She's sleeping now, but when I was with her earlier, just like always, she talked about Pa, then persisted in her usual bullshit about not wanting to see him while he's 'still married to the bitch.' Asked about you coming to see her, though. Several times. I told her there's no way you could stay away, not with me in the house. I told her you needed some fucking passion in your life and that I was the man for the job."

"You told her nothing of the sort," Callie said.

"As you like it," Paulie said.

"How Shakespearean," Callie replied.

"What?" Paulie said distractedly.

"Nothing," Callie replied, angry at herself for making a reference Paulie might not identify with. "Oh my God! Look!"

"Ho-lee shit!" Paulie exclaimed, looking through the old screen door. "Mary Frances Cavalese, get your butt in here. Damn, girl, I've been telling you for years that you had babe potential. You look awesome, Sis."

Callie's mouth hung open. "Frankie. You look stunning!"

"Think so?" Frankie said, beaming. "I do look pretty good if I say so myself."

Frankie had been totally transformed. Her untrimmed brown hair had been cut to her shoulders, layered and highlighted with just enough red to make it shine. She was wearing a brand-new pair of navy shorts with a matching striped shirt, and to Callie's utter amazement, had makeup on her face, thin gold hoops in her ears, and beautiful leather sandals on her feet.

"I'm in awe," Callie said. "You look like a million bucks. What made you decide to do this?"

"A gift from my brother," Frankie said. "I also had a facial, full body massage...loved that, manicure, pedicure...the works. Sure felt great."

"I've only been offering this to her for years," Paulie added. "She's just now taking me up on it."

"Oh, really," Callie said, already knowing part of the answer to the question she was about to ask. "And what happened today to make you finally accept?"

Frankie's eyes narrowed as she looked at Paulie, warning him to be quiet.

Callie laughed. "I see, so this was a birthday present."

"Damn it, Paulie," Frankie said. "You promised!"

Callie smiled and walked over to Frankie. She stood in front of her friend and took both her hands in hers. "He didn't tell me anything. He didn't have to. I could never forget your birthday, and I never have." Callie tried to fight her proclivity to overly emote. "You don't know how badly I wanted to call you every year and let you know I remembered, that I was thinking of you, that I missed you, that I was sorry, and that I hoped you were happy. And now, I finally have a chance to do that."

Frankie was speechless. Callie reached into her pants pocket and pulled out a small, beautifully wrapped box. "Happy birthday, my friend."

Even Paulie was amazed, transfixed by the interaction between the two. "Open it, Mary Frances, don't just stare at it."

"I'm pretending I'm you," Frankie quipped. "Lookin' at myself in the mirror."

Callie laughed, and Paulie gave her a playful dirty look. Frankie bit her lip and nervously opened the box. As she took the gold paper off, a black velvet jewelry box was revealed, the kind that snaps shut and is lined with satin bearing the imprint of a fancy jeweler's name. The kind of box she'd never owned in her life. She looked at Callie, then at the box.

"Go on," Callie said gently. "Open it."

"Sure there's not one of those snake things in there?" Frankie teased. "Those things that look like cloth-covered Slinkys that pop up and make you scream?"

Callie smiled. "The box isn't big enough for that. But thanks for the suggestion; it may come in handy some time."

Frankie opened the box and let out a gasp. "Oh, Callie. You remembered my dream. It's just like I pictured it, only much more beautiful." Frankie held the gold heart-shaped locket and chain in the palm of her hand. "It's engraved. MFC. What beautiful letters. So graceful and flowing. Like they were meant for a princess."

"They were," Callie said. "Here, let me hold the box. Open the locket."

Frankie looked at her, as if to say, "There's more?" She snapped the locket open and saw on the right side a photo of the girls together when they were ten, smiling broadly with their arms draped around each other's shoulders.

"I left the right side empty," Callie said. "I thought you might want to put a picture of your mom in there."

"Oh, shit," Frankie said, as the tears began to roll. "I knew I shouldn't have let them put this war paint on my face. Damn, now *I'm* going to look like that smushed paint box of yours!"

Callie laughed. "You look beautiful. And it was *your* paint box! Not mine."

"I'm just overwhelmed," Frankie said, as she reached out to hug Callie. "Thank you, thank you so much. You remembered, all these years, how I'd always dreamed of having a gold locket. And just for the record, Mason, I never forgot your birthday either. Especially since you're four months older than me."

Paulie, sensing the need for the women to have some time alone together, excused himself and went upstairs.

Frankie was enthralled. She managed to stop the tears, but her heart was beating like crazy. This was real. Callie was real. Their friendship had been genuinely renewed, and she finally believed it deep in her heart.

"Let's sit down," Frankie said, taking Callie by the wrist and leading her to the couch. "I'm so blown away; I just don't know what else to say."

"Well, you can tell me what finally made you accept your brother's offer for a makeover. You've told me he's been hounding you about it for years."

"Yeah, that he has," Frankie said. "It was a couple of things, I guess. Or maybe a combination of things. But it was you and Ma. You being back here, back in my life, gave me some kind of hope that maybe my life wasn't over. Maybe it was okay to look good. And damn, you lookin' like Miss America every day and me looking like Fat Edna and those rumpled old hags, well, that was kind of like a stick of dynamite exploding up my ass, you know?"

Callie burst out laughing.

"Well, you asked," Frankie said.

"Oh, I absolutely did," Callie said, still chuckling. "I've really missed your unique and to-the-point responses. You're still as funny as ever, Frankie. So tell me, what were you going to say about your mother?"

"I know how worried Ma is about me. I'm sure that's why she wants to see you so much. She needs to assure herself I won't be alone when she's gone. I know it. What else could it possibly be? And I thought, you know, maybe if she sees me looking like this, it'll put some of her fears to rest. Maybe if I stop looking like an alien from the planet Sloppier Than Shit, Ma will know I can make it in this world."

"She's going to be overjoyed when she sees you," Callie said. "Simply overjoyed. And I think you're right; I really believe your new look will help to allay some of her fears."

"Enough about me," Frankie said abruptly. "How are you doing? Things any better at home?"

"Well, Molly and I finally got a chance to have a long talk this morning. She was a little out of it at first, worked a double shift yesterday, but she managed to wake up for a heart-to heart with her old mom. She's in semi-lust with some guy from New Hampshire named Julian who's got a ponytail and a pierced nose. He wants to be the first woodworker to fly to the moon and wants Molls to go with him." Callie laughed. "I'm glad she's going to art school in Chicago, though God only knows who she'll meet there."

Frankie smiled mechanically. Callie remembered and suddenly felt angry with herself again. "*You* wanted to do something in art, didn't you, Frankie? You wanted to work with children, if I remember correctly."

"That dream's dead in the water," Frankie lamented.

"Oh, don't be so sure," Callie said. "It doesn't have to be."

Frankie quickly changed the subject. "What about your son? Did you speak with him as well?"

"Steve's camping out in Acadia National Park this weekend. I'll catch him on Monday. At least, I hope I will."

"You really miss your kids a lot, don't you?"

"Big time," Callie said, "and even more because things with Jack are so tenuous right now. His business is a mess; we're a mess…oh Frankie, for the first time in all these years of marriage, I'm truly scared that he—"

"Happy birthday to you, happy birthday to you, happy birthday dear Frankie, happy birthday to you!"

It was inevitable. Regina was bound to appear at the most inopportune moment possible. But this time, she had her daughter with her, who was holding a bouquet of balloons and a gift, while her mother carefully held a homemade birthday cake in a yellow Tupperware container with both hands. Regina and Callie looked at each other. Being unhappy to see one another was beginning to become a habit, that and the mutual dislike that was escalating with each visit.

"Oh, hi, Callie," Regina said irritably, as she walked over to the dining room table and put the cake down. "This is my daughter, Steffie."

Callie smiled broadly. "Hi, Steffie, it's a pleasure to meet you. Those sure are a pretty handful of balloons you've got there."

"My daddy blowed them up," Steffie told her.

"I see," Callie said, as she noticed that Frankie was trying to get her attention. Callie refused to turn her head. She knew what Frankie wanted — to make her stomach hurt from suppressing a laugh. "That's pretty impressive, Steffie."

"Daddy said it made his cheeks hurt," Steffie added.

"I'll bet it did," Callie said, finding the torture unbearable. "Listen, Steffie, it was sure nice meeting you. I've got to go next door for a bit. Frankie, I'll be back in a while with lunch. Regina, nice to see you."

Regina's eyes followed her angrily out the door. Then, as if for the first time, she noticed Frankie's new look. "Well, I see you're even startin' to *look* like her now," she said.

"Reg, what the hell are you talking about?"

"What do you think I'm talking about? Callie. Every day you get friendlier and friendlier. Closer and closer. Every time I come over for a visit, *she's* already here. And now look at you. Lookin' so Main-Line-ish and all; just like *her*."

"I look human for a change," Frankie said. "That's all. Human beings come from all over, you know. Even Rainytown."

Regina wasn't buying it. "Steffie, go home and help Daddy make lunch."

"But Mommy," Steffie protested. "I wanna see Frankie open her present."

Regina's mood was fierce. "Open the gift for the kid's sake," she muttered to Frankie.

"Oh, for me?" Frankie said cheerfully, as Steffie handed her the box.

"How exciting." Frankie quickly ripped off the recycled Mickey Mouse wrapping. "What do we have here?"

"It's a candle in a holder," Steffie explained excitedly. "See the house painted on the glass? When you light the candle, it looks like the windows are all lit up like in real life. Mommy got it from the Avon lady. It's really cool. We have one, too."

"Well, I just love it!" Frankie told her. "Thank you both so much. Now, come here and give me a birthday hug."

Steffie, who adored Frankie, couldn't get her hug fast enough. "Wow, that's a cool heart necklace," Steffie said. "Did that really pretty lady just give it to you?"

Regina's eyes were burning with pain. "Steffie, you saw Frankie open her gift. Now, Mommy has to talk to Frankie alone. So you go and help Daddy...now!"

"Okay," Steffie said. "Bye, Frankie. Happy birthday."

"Thanks, little sweetie," Frankie called after her. "I love my candle. And you, too!"

Regina just stood there and stared at her. Frankie was not going to tolerate whatever Regina had in mind. Not today.

"Do you want to sit down, Reg?" Frankie asked impatiently. "I know your back must be killing you."

"Yeah, why not? Let's sit at the table. By the cake I made for you. Chocolate. Your favorite. Or did *she* already bring you one? Oh, I guess you wouldn't know. What did she say...oh yeah, she'll be back later with lunch. Well, la dee dah!"

"Oh, for Christ's sake, Reg," Frankie said, as they took a seat. "What's with you? I'm not allowed to have another friend?"

"She's back in your life less than a week," Regina said accusingly, "and you got no time for me anymore, won't let me see your mom, you're all spiffed up looking just like her, and now she's giving you a damn gold locket for your birthday. It's probably got more carrots than a hutch full of rabbits. Guess you two will have a real good laugh over my stupid Avon candle."

Frankie bit her lip to stop herself from going ballistic. She counted to three, then looked squarely at Regina. "You might say, 'Gee, Frankie, you look so nice. What a lovely necklace you're wearing.' That would be the *nice* thing to do. Especially on my birthday. And as for this bullshit about seeing my mother, you know I have absolutely no control over her wishes, and you also know I've had it up to here trying to explain that to you."

Regina's anger had been festering for days; rationalizing with her was impossible. Her spirited façade had broken and was now about to splinter into a million sharp pieces. "Know what my Hal said?" Regina said with a vengeance, as if she couldn't wait to get the words out. "He said the writing was on the wall, and that I was diluting myself if I thought you and me were gonna be friends much longer."

Frankie wanted to suggest that Hal dilute his own self, but she didn't think this was the best time for a comment about Hal's beer consumption or to correct Regina's word usage.

"Know what me and Hal think?" Regina said, as Paulie made his way downstairs unseen. "We think you're doing to me exactly what *she* did to you. She dumped you because you embarrassed her, and now I embarrass you! You ain't got the time of day for me no more. No, not since your old friend 'Mason' came crawling back on her society hands and knees. And guess what, when she dumps you again, don't look for 'good ole Reg' to comfort you because I'll be too busy with my other friends — the ones that know how to appreciate me. And furthermore, maybe I don't want you bein' Steffie's godmother no more. Maybe my Hal don't want it neither. How do you like them rotten apples, Frankie?"

"That's it," Paulie said sharply, as he reached the landing. "Regina, make tracks. You're history."

"Oh, so now your hotshot brother's throwing me out. The love of your life. The whole neighborhood knows how bad you got it for your own brother!" Regina ripped into Frankie. "It ain't right, Frankie, you know that, don't you?"

Frankie was flabbergasted by the accusation. It took her a moment to take in the fact that Regina was actually serious. "How dare you even suggest such filth to me? That's a goddamn lie," Frankie thundered. "Stupid, fucking gossip from a bunch of mindless biddies who don't have anything better to do than spread filthy dirt. How many people have *you* told that shit to? How do you know *what* the whole neighborhood thinks if you haven't been discussing it with them? And why didn't you set them straight, bein' the good friend you say you were? Well, no 'good friend' would come and do this to me on my birthday or any day, 'specially when my mother's upstairs dying. Get the hell out of here, Regina. Take your fucking cake and feed it to your fat husband."

"I got a lot more to say to you," Regina said vehemently, picking up the cake.

Paulie walked over and grabbed her by the arm, just as he had grabbed Annie the night before, and led her over to the door. "I'm going to ask you nicely, Regina. Get the fuck out of this house."

Paulie opened the screen door and held it open until she was outside. Had she not been pregnant, he might have been even less chivalrous and just let the door hit her on the backside. Regina ran crying down the steps. As she reached the curb, she tripped over a sun-dried mound of dog feces and lost her balance, sending the cake flying into the street. Luckily, Regina safely grabbed onto a street lamp, avoiding a fall and any harm to herself and her unborn baby. Paulie felt a fleeting twinge of guilt imagining what might have happened, but Regina was just fine physically, and when she sat on the curb and began bawling, he couldn't help but think she deserved it. He watched in amusement as a powder blue '79 Lincoln Continental came down the street, smashing the cake with the front left tire and flattening the large domed cake cover with the back right.

Well, all isn't lost, Paulie thought. At least she's got a new Frisbee out of the deal.

Regina let out a scream as she watched, while Paulie shook his head in disgust as Hal Cunningham, with a stomach bigger than his pregnant wife's, came running out of the house. Jell-O, with legs, Paulie thought. He turned to look at his sister. She was standing by the dining table, frozen, in complete devastation. He walked over to her.

"Is she right, Paulie?" Frankie said softly, "Am I—"

"Hush," Paulie said, wrapping his arms around his sister. "She was completely out of line and completely wrong. And she had absolutely no business choosing today to run off about all the worthless shit on her mind. To hell with her. She never meant to you what Callie did, and you know that. She's been a pain in your ass since she moved into this neighborhood. I don't know how you tolerated her as long as you did. That damn woman makes me nuts, running off at the mouth constantly about 'her fucking Hal.' Ma's got days to live, and instead of thinking about you, she's all pissed off because Ma doesn't want to see her. Hell, if I were near death, I wouldn't want her appearing in the final act either. And those things she said about you and me: if she was a man, I'd have punched her for it. And if she wasn't pregnant, I'd at least have enjoyed thinking about it. Hell no. She's no friend of yours, Mary Frances. Trust me on that!"

Frankie cried softly onto his shoulder. "But I was wrong to let her think I felt the same way. Maybe I should have…"

Paulie stroked her hair tenderly. "Don't be so hard on yourself. You didn't have many people to talk to; I certainly wasn't there like I should have been. It'll be all right, Mary Frances. You and me are family; I'm always gonna be here for you. And Callie will be too. That girl's sincere. She loves you. We both do. Just put that Cunningham broad out of your mind. C'mon. Callie's going to be back soon with lunch."

"Oh, God!" Frankie said, breaking the embrace. "Callie! I've got to fix myself up. No way can I let her see me like this!"

"Go then," Paulie said, kissing her on the cheek.

He waited until Frankie had gone upstairs, then walked to the front door, just in time to see Hal Cunningham grab a handful of gooey Pillsbury road kill and gobble it down at the precise moment he was sure no one was watching.

Frankie stared solemnly at her reflection in the bathroom mirror and wondered just exactly who she was. It wasn't the face and the hair she didn't recognize; it was the woman inside. *Was* she truly some kind of hypocrite and not the decent and caring person she'd always prided herself on being? Had she really treated Regina so terribly? Was there any validity to Regina's myriad accusations?

Frankie had had inklings long before Callie's return that Regina could be possessive and jealous, but with so few people in Frankie's life (except for work friends that Regina didn't know), there was no one to really threaten Regina's security. Frankie knew Regina hated Callie from day one, but Regina played friendly because she thought Callie would eventually go away, and though Regina would never admit it, Callie's wealth and status impressed her. But mostly, being one of the rare few on the block to even speak with Callie gave Regina a twisted sort of prestige — something to offer the gossip seekers in return for whatever pretended friendship they felt beholden to offer in return.

Frankie rued the fact that she'd shed even one tear over Regina's tirade. But the accusations had been so hideous, and Frankie was so tired, and Ruby was dying…and the old kick-ass tomboy in her was too weary to keep it all inside.

She opened the medicine cabinet and pulled out a small jar of foundation and dusted it off. The lid was on very tight, and when she finally twisted it open, some of the makeup spilled on the sink. Normally, that would have been worth a "damn it" or two, but Frankie was too shell-shocked by what had just taken place to react verbally. She grabbed a hand towel, moistened it, cleaned up the sink, then retouched her make-up where her tears had left streaks. She washed her hands, dried them on the same towel, put the foundation away, and resumed staring blankly at herself.

Frankie thought she knew herself inside and out; now she was filled with doubts. Had Callie seen her the way she'd always seen Regina? An embarrassing but kind-hearted buffoon with a rotten habit of showing up unannounced for the sole purpose of blathering on incessantly about the latest foolishness in her family? Of course not. There was no parallel there at all. But how *did* Callie see her all those years ago, once they had graduated from high school? When exactly was it that Callie had made the decision to excommunicate Frankie from her life? Frankie hated to end the honeymoon, but if she and Callie were to have a solid future as friends, she needed to know the truth. The Bible was right. The truth would set her free.

Her focus shifted back to Regina. Everything Paulie said about her was true. She had been a pain in the ass since the day she moved in. So why had Frankie put up with her? Why did she enable the friendship to continue year after year? Why did she agree to be Regina's child's godmother? Why did she let Regina tell the world that they were best friends? That answer was an easy one: she didn't really care. It made Regina happy. Why tell her otherwise? Besides, Frankie was lonely; Regina filled a small part of that empty space. But to Frankie's mind, they had never really been close. The relationship was ninety percent superficial, comprised mostly of Frankie's listening to tales of the bumbling, blundering, and boozing Hal Cunningham. It was only after Callie had returned to Rainytown and partaken in hearing the daily recitations of the insipid Hal Chronicles that Regina's babbling had served any kind of purpose.

Frankie grabbed a small brush and began fiddling with her hair in front. She wondered how it would look after she washed it herself. Would it even resemble what the hairdresser had done? Why had she let herself go as she did? My God, she wasn't a bad-looking woman at all. Why had she chosen to emulate every frump on the block? Even the language she spoke was lazy and sloppy. She was certainly no grammarian, but she'd been better educated than one would know by listening to her talk. Why had she chosen to soak in all the negativity around her and speak as if she had no more than an eighth-grade education? Because her mother had fallen into the same stupid trap?

Depression, Frankie concluded, putting the brush down. What did Ma have 'cept me and Paulie? Who cared how we spoke? What the hell did I have in my life that mattered?

Paulie mattered, especially with so few people to really care about. She adored him — even when she was furious with him. But she adored him as a sister loves a brother, not in the vile way in which Regina and the rest of Rainytown had presumably imagined. How sick! How twisted! How could someone who called herself a friend *ever* believe such a thing? How could someone who called herself a friend hassle her daily about visiting with her dying mother, knowing it only added to Frankie's misery. Paulie was right. To hell with her. And to hell with Rainytown. It was time to move on.

Frankie moved a tendril of hair away from her ear. She liked the way gold looked on her. It made her feel feminine. She still had the gold bracelet Johnny had given her, but she'd stopped wearing it years ago. Too painful.

Well, whoever the hell I am, Frankie thought, I'm not going to let Regina Cunningham destroy me. I'm going downstairs and have my lunch with Mason.

She took one last look in the mirror. "Happy birthday to me," she said flatly, and headed for the stairs.

CHAPTER 14

"You're not staying for lunch?" Frankie said disappointedly, as she watched Callie packing a lunch-to-go for Paulie on the kitchen counter.

"I'm sorry, Mary Frances," Paulie said, leaning wearily against the wall. "I'm wiped. After last night's fiasco and getting up so early this morning, I can barely keep my eyes open. And God only knows what'll be waiting for me when I go into work tonight. I really need to rest this afternoon. I'm sorry."

"Oh, God, don't apologize," Frankie implored. "Of course, you need to rest."

Paulie smiled. "You and Callie-fornia here can use some private time anyway. I just feel bad that I've gotta be at the club tonight…on your birthday. I'd really like to spend it with you, or at least stay here with Ma so you could go out and have a good time."

"You've already given me a wonderful birthday present," Frankie told him. "And as for going out and having a good time, I don't think that would even be possible. This is my last birthday with Ma…" Frankie choked up and her eyes began to water, but she stopped the tears just in time. "This is the last birthday I'll ever have with Ma, and I want to spend it with her. Okay? So don't worry about me."

"How can I not worry?" Paulie said. "Especially after what just happened?"

Callie stopped spooning out her basmati rice salad, looked at Paulie, then at Frankie. "What's going on? What did I miss?"

"Hurricane Regina," Paulie said. "Blew in and blew out. Major damage."

"What in the world happened?" Callie asked, as she finished what she was doing. "Did it have something to do with me?"

"I'll tell you about it over lunch," Frankie said.

Callie loaded up several plastic containers of food, a spinach parmesan baguette, and a bag of grapes, then put them in a shopping bag for Paulie. "Here you go," she said, handing the package to him. "Enjoy."

"I'm sure I will," he said wickedly, licking his lips behind his sister's back. "I'm sure it's delicious. The sample you gave me earlier was wonderful. I just can't wait to taste the whole package."

Callie tried to stare him down in a vain attempt to make him stop his sexual taunting, but he looked right back at her in a way that only turned her on more. God, how was it possible this man had such power over her libido?

"Well, you take care, Paulie," Callie said, verbally trying to push him out of the kitchen.

Her efforts only made him laugh. "Thanks for lunch, babe. I'll be seeing you." He threw his arms around Frankie and gave her a big hug. "I love you, Mary Frances, don't ever forget that. Talk to you later."

And with a wink, intended for both women, he was gone.

"I don't think I've eaten at the dining room table in a hundred years," Frankie said ten minutes into lunch. "It feels so weird. But this food you brought is delicious."

"Well, eating at the kitchen table on your birthday just didn't seem right," Callie said. "This just seems more…"

"What?" Frankie said, trying to manage the mouthful of food she'd just taken in. "Palatial?"

They shared a laugh. "Something like that," Callie said. "All jokes aside, what in God's name happened with Regina? I know that she wasn't too happy to see me today, but there was a rage in her eyes I'd never seen before. It was like the woman who comes over and tells all of those goofy stories about her husband was gone, and her evil twin had showed up instead."

"Right you are," Frankie said. "Reginastein. Minus the neck bolts. I have a sneaking suspicion she'd just devoured New York for lunch. Did you see her stomach? You could tell — she had just eaten the Big Apple and hadn't digested it yet. I was tempted to yell 'Taxi!' to see what happened, but I didn't want her hurling yellow cabs all over the living room."

"You're very funny," Callie said, "but I wish you'd be serious. From what Paulie said, it sounds more like she devoured you."

"Tried to," Frankie said, tearing off a piece of the second baguette Callie had brought. "This is fabulous."

"Frankie..."

"Yeah," Frankie replied, relishing her food.

"Would you stop stalling and talk to me?"

"Goofing around is easier," Frankie told her, as soon as she'd swallowed the bread. "What happened here was really ugly."

"Let me hear it," Callie said. "Please."

Frankie let out a long sigh. "Oh, you're gonna hear it, all right. I just needed to prepare myself before reliving it again."

Frankie had always been good at telling it like it is. When they were girls, Callie couldn't wait to meet up with Frankie after school and listen while she told her anything and everything that happened of interest while they were separated during the day. Frankie had always been a good storyteller, never embellishing the facts, but always making the most out of them. Callie would listen enthusiastically as Frankie described a conversation overheard in the hallway, a fight that had taken place in a corner of the lunchroom, or the fate of an unruly student who'd acted up in class. Callie, of course, had her own share of tales to tell, but she didn't have the same caustic humor or the same amazing ability to describe someone's face down to the last pimple on her chin.

Frankie, still in possession of a passion for the raw truth, gave Callie a nail-biting description of the events and conversation that had taken place after Callie had gone next door. Fighting the urge to comment until Frankie had finished, Callie could not contain herself any longer when Frankie related the accusations regarding her supposed feelings for Paulie.

"She said *what*?" Callie screamed in horror.

"You heard me, Mason. She said I had a thing for my brother, and oh, how did she put it, 'That ain't right, Frankie, you know that, don't you?' I wonder how many people she's blabbed that disgusting lie to...my 'friend,' Regina."

"Oh, God," Callie said. "That must have been what she was trying to tell me."

"What?" Frankie exclaimed. "You *knew* about this and didn't tell me?"

"Hold on," Callie said. "Believe me, Frankie, if she'd made any accusations as blatantly as she'd made them to you, I would have told you in a heartbeat. It was back when I first met her, around the beginning of the week. She mumbled something to me about you having 'funny feelings for your brother,' and then you walked in and she shut up. I didn't know what the hell she was trying to tell me, and after mulling it over for a few seconds, I just forgot about it. I believe you had news about your mom, and whatever Regina was blabbing about really wasn't of any importance to me."

"Damn. If I hadn't come in, she would've told you the whole filthy lie."

"Maybe," Callie said, not wanting to be the one to crucify Regina.

"You know," Frankie said, "in a way, I'm really glad to hear that. I mean, I'm feeling bad about some of the things she said, but if that's the kind of shit she's been doing behind my back, it kind of lets me off the hook a little. I felt guilty that I'd let her go on for so many years thinking I cared like she did, but look, when it comes down to it, I had more respect for her in some ways than she did for me. You know?"

"You've got a very valid point. It makes a lot of sense — at least to me, for whatever that's worth."

"It's worth a lot, Mason," Frankie said with a self-conscious smile.

They talked in length for another twenty minutes about the things Regina had said. It was an awkward path for Callie to walk, negating the accusations Regina had made while avoiding self-incrimination by way of any comparisons. What was Callie to say? Oh no, Frankie, you didn't come close to treating her the rotten way I treated you. The touchiness of the subject had not escaped either one of them, but it was also cathartic at some level, too.

Frankie remembered the promise she had made to herself earlier in the bathroom. She had to ask.

"Callie," Frankie began. "I want us to go on forever as friends. Just like we swore we'd do when we were kids. But all this stuff today with Reg, well, it just brought up some questions that I've got to know the answers to, not so I can ream you out, but so we can put the past where it belongs, behind us."

"I'm so glad you feel that way. Believe me, I need to get this out as much as you need to know about it. Go ahead. Tell me what you want to know."

Frankie picked up a chilled green bean and took a bite. "I like these. What did you say they were?"

"Garlic green beans," Callie said, feeling every bit of the tension. "Marinated in extra virgin olive oil."

"How does one get to be an extra virgin?" Frankie joked.

"You not only don't do it," Callie humored her, "you don't even *think* about it. Now, can we get on with this, please?"

"Okay," Frankie said, preparing herself for action. "What I want to know is…when was it, I mean, do you remember the precise moment that you decided our lives just didn't connect anymore, that you didn't want me as your friend anymore, that I just didn't fit into your new life? Do you remember what you were thinking?"

Frankie's question stung Callie more than she had anticipated it would. She picked up a napkin and daintily wiped the tears from her eyes. "Oh, Frankie, that's what I've always wanted to tell you. It was *never* like that. It wasn't you. It was them. It was me."

"Sorry, Mason, I'm not following."

"Of course you're not," Callie said. "Listen, you've got to understand something. My trust fund, which you know I was granted access to after graduation, left me very well off. My father's name alone got me into a school that probably never would have given me the time of day otherwise. I didn't even want to go to that school, but it was his wish for me, and I wanted to honor it. So I went to his alma mater and moved into this expensive apartment community that the fund stipulated I live in. Well, living there, it threw me into the company of girls who had grown up being rich, who had completely different values than I did. I'll admit, there were times when it felt okay, even glamorous and exciting, but most of the time I felt like a big phony. Like a fake. Like I was a spy about to be discovered, and if that happened, I'd be killed. So I had to keep up the pretense, which was so stupid, because I was pretending to be someone I didn't even want to be. It's not like I admired them. Yeah, maybe I wished I'd taken weekend trips on my family's yacht or tasted French Champagne in Paris, but not because those things were important to me, but because having done them would have made me more a part of the crowd."

Now it was Frankie's turn to be riveted by one of Callie's stories. Even as Callie spoke, the layers of resentment she'd harbored for so many years began to slowly peel away. Frankie continued to pick at the green beans, but never once taking her eyes off Callie. Words lie, Frankie believed, but eyes tell the truth.

"The college I went to was in this beautiful setting, up on a hill, in this pretty little place, about an hour or so from here. Sometimes we'd all go into town for a movie, or to hang at this coffee shop where the guys from the neighboring military academy would often be. And, of course, being in town, away from the campus, meant that we weren't isolated anymore. The population was more diverse." Callie began to feel angry as she remembered. "People of all races, religions, and financial brackets actually walked among us. Imagine that!" she said sarcastically.

"Yeah, I'm getting the picture," Frankie said. "Go on."

"Well, these so-called friends of mine, they'd say the most horrible things about people. I remember one evening: it was still early, when the group of us passed this young girl. She was wearing secondhand clothing that was far too big for her, and on top of whatever dress she had on was this kind of seaweed-green sweater with a big patch on both elbows. She couldn't have been more than sixteen, if that, and she was dragging her kid brother, poor thing, who was practically dressed in rags, to the grocery store. He was complaining that he wanted to stay at home and watch television, and she told him he couldn't. He was too young to be left alone. Then he complained that he wanted hamburger and fries for dinner, and she told him they didn't have money for that. He kept hounding her, and suddenly she burst into tears, telling him that it wasn't her fault their father had died, and that she didn't like their mom having to work all night cleaning offices any more than he did. He still kept at her, saying that it wasn't fair. He wanted to do what other children did. I will never forget what she said after that. She looked at him square in the eyes and said, 'I'm a kid, too, Donny.' And the boy looked up at her, as if he suddenly realized that life was no better for her either, and didn't say another word as they rushed past us.

"It was so heartbreaking, Frankie. I wanted to reach into my wallet and give them enough money to eat hamburger for a month, or whatever else they wanted. But the worst of it was, when we got to the coffee shop and sat down at the table, the girls I was with starting laughing at them. Making fun of the poor girl's clothing, calling the boy Oliver Twist, and suggesting that they buy gruel for dinner because it was cheaper than hamburger meat. Wondering if 'Oliver' would want 'some more.' They even made fun of the seaweed-green sweater. They called it puke green. That's why I remember the color after all of these years. They were awful. They nicknamed her 'Patch' and then burst out laughing at the barbarity of their words. When I didn't laugh along with them, this one girl, Elaine Wadsworth, punched me in the arm and told me I had no sense of humor, and everyone agreed with her. I should have spoken up right then and there. But I didn't.

"Criticizing people less fortunate than themselves was their favorite past time. And me, eighteen-years old and having nobody else to turn to, I just put up with it. I didn't join in on that, Frankie; you've got to believe me. But I tolerated it, which I suppose is just as bad. I even went to Nantucket one summer with one of my nicer roommates and her family. I didn't care about sailing, but I didn't know how to refuse when her mother invited me. I just wanted to be back here with you. But I got sucked into the whole scene. Young and stupid. God, I wish I could go back and change everything."

"Keep going, Mason. You're doing just fine. Don't nail yourself to the cross because you went sailing in Nantucket. Sheesh!"

"Yeah, but all that being said," Callie explained, "I missed you like nobody's business. Every day I wished it could be just you and me again. I wished you could be out there on that sailboat with me instead of Gayle Lucretia Winston. I wondered what you were doing, how you were, how Paulie and your mom were doing."

"Then why didn't you at least write to me more often? Did these people check your mail for socially unacceptable zip codes or what?"

"Of course not," Callie said, tearing up again. "Oh, Frankie, I'm so ashamed. I was too afraid that if we kept in touch regularly, it would be inevitable that the subject of a visit would come up. I had all the money in the world to pay for your transportation, but I couldn't subject you to these people. I just couldn't."

"How did you feel about subjecting yourself to the fallout *after* a visit with me?" Frankie asked sharply.

Callie looked down at her plate and played with her silverware. "It was both things, Frankie. I was afraid they'd hurt you and that afterwards, I'd be left alone at school to fend for myself. I didn't like them, but I didn't want to be an outcast. It was not an eclectic group. There weren't different types of people to pick and choose from. It's like I just said: I was young and stupid. But I never would have been embarrassed by you; I would have been embarrassed for you to see how low I had sunk."

"But when you came home for Christmas, we made plans. You were like the old Callie," Frankie stressed. "I never imagined you'd just go away forever."

"Oh, God, Frankie. I didn't either. I *was* the old Callie when you saw me; that's what I'm trying to tell you. It's when I returned to that toxic environment that I lost control of my own life. Or I gave it away. However you care to phrase it. I don't know."

"Okay, Callie," Frankie said with a wisdom shining in her eyes. "Let's say I can accept that. In all honesty, I can't tell you that I might not have felt exactly like you if the situations were reversed, though I'm inclined to say I probably wouldn't have. But what about after you met Jackson, and after you graduated? No time for me then, either?"

"Jackson." Callie smiled, remembering. "I met him when I was a junior. His best friend, Harley Stephens, was going to the military academy, and Jack and I met in town one weekend, in the park, during a volleyball game. He was so handsome with his thick blond hair and to-die-for smile. And my 'friends' were so green with envy that he took a liking to me and not to them. Call it an added perk to meeting the greatest guy in the world. He was wonderful; so different from the other guys. But what I liked best about him was that he was so funny. He just kept cracking everyone up. He was funny — like you. That's really what drew him to me."

Frankie looked as if she wanted to cry, but she grabbed another green bean instead.

"I knew he was wealthy; they all were, but he wasn't preoccupied or even concerned with that kind of stuff. I remember him buying some flowers from this little old man who had a cart in the park, and he walked right up to this elderly lady walking through the park and handed her the bouquet. Frankie, her eyes lit up as if Prince Charming had just proposed to her. She was glowing. I was practically moved to tears and the rest of them, they started teasing Jack, asking him what kind of drugs he was on or if someone had laced his iced tea with LSD. To them, doing something nice for someone of a lower social status, especially a total stranger, was tantamount to insanity. Jack just brushed them off with some smart-ass comment, and I remember thinking, 'They're too stupid to even figure out that he's insulting them.' "

"I'll bet you started to fall for him even more after that," Frankie said, sipping her Chardonnay.

"Right again, my friend," Callie said. "Jack's got an amazing wit; he didn't care what people thought of him, and they all loved him anyway. I envied that. I respected that. And I kept thinking that he had so many of the same wonderful qualities that you did."

Frankie suddenly felt sick to her stomach — and angry. "Then why, Mason, why didn't you come back to me then, or after you got married? I can understand you not wanting me to mix with those dumb bitches from school, but if Jack and me had, what did you say, 'so many of the same wonderful qualities,' why didn't I ever hear from you again? Why didn't you introduce us? Damn it. Damn you."

"Frankie..."

"I'm sorry. Go on with your story. I didn't mean to freak out like that. I just couldn't help myself."

"You're entitled," Callie said, slipping into a comfortable suit of self-loathing. "I'm so sorry."

"Damn, Mason. Screw the apologies. Just tell me the rest. I'll tally up how many apologies are necessary, okay?"

"Okay," Callie said with a thin smile. "Well, it was like I told you. Jack wasn't a snob; he isn't a snob. I'll admit, he has a low tolerance for stupidity and laziness, but that's not based on anyone's color, background, or bank account. Anyway, despite Jack being the great guy he is, he comes from a world of people very much like those I went to school with. Some of them were okay, even nice, like his brother Cole; he's a great guy. But he had a contingent of relatives and cousins that were even more vicious than the girls from school. Frankie, I had every intention of inviting you to my wedding. In fact, I wanted you to be my maid of honor, though I wasn't sure by that point you'd even think of accepting, let alone want to talk to me again."

"So what happened?" Frankie asked. "Jackson nixed the deal?"

"God, no!" Callie said emphatically. "He was all for it. In fact, I remember what he said, 'That's a swell idea, Cal,' and I laughed because I'd never heard anyone use the word 'swell' like that except on reruns of *Leave it to Beaver, Father Knows Best*, and old shows like that. I teased him about it for a week."

"So when exactly did I get cut from the wedding, and from your life?"

"Jack's mom, God rest her soul, was a very nice but proper woman, a pillar of Main Line society. She knew my aunt couldn't plan the wedding I was 'predestined' to have and so she took complete control. She told me that I needed to choose my bridesmaids, and asked me to make a list of all of my friends, those witches, from school. Quite frankly, there were only two that I liked at all, and I couldn't very well invite them and not the rest of the ghouls."

Frankie laughed.

"I told Mrs. Hethers that I only had one friend I really cared about, Frankie Cavalese."

"Okay, I got it. You told her all about me, and she threatened to cancel the wedding if I stepped one Rainytown foot into the church."

"How silly," Callie said. "Of course not. She would never have done something like that. But she did tell me that I needed to have at least six bridesmaids, and that if I didn't have friends or relatives to fill the bill, Jack's female cousins and two family friends would do the job. Well, I wasn't thrilled about that, but there was no alternative. And at that point, I was still hoping you'd forgive me and be my maid of honor."

"Yeah, so…"

"So a meeting was arranged for me to get together with Jack's cousins and the other two girls. I'd never met women with so little substance in my life. They were worse than the coven of witches from school. All they talked about was money, wedding gifts, the caliber of people who would be invited, and on and on. 'Gee, I wonder if Aunt Lucille', that was Jack's mother, 'is going to invite the help.' 'I hope not, it would be so sacrilegious to see Mamie and LeRoy being treated as equals. Ugh, can you imagine! Aunt Lucille says they're part of the family, but I hope she doesn't mean that literally.' That's just a brief but disgusting example of their mentality, but I knew right then and there I could never expose you to such shallow, horrible people. Ever. They would have destroyed you, and that would have destroyed me. And no, I would not have been embarrassed by you. Believe me, not in a million years."

"So because they were shallow and racist, you just said, 'Adios, amiga,' and forgot all about me?"

"Frankie, Jack didn't know the kind of people his cousins were back then, and I couldn't upset the apple cart by going to Jack, or his mother, and telling them that I hated these women. They were close friends and members of the Hethers' family, for God's sake. How could I say I didn't want them in my wedding? What reason could I have given? I just wanted Jack. I just wanted to be his wife. I was so in love with him, I *am* so in love with him. But the hurdles back then were overwhelming to me. And even if by some miracle I'd managed to dump those dunderheads, Mrs. Hethers would've found another group just like them to fit the bill, and then I'd be no better off, only more miserable because I'd have made enemies of the first group."

'How 'bout Emily? Didn't you go to her for advice?"

"Of course I did. You knew my aunt, Frankie. She didn't like to tell me what to do; she had a real thing for raising me to make my own decisions. But I do remember her saying one thing, 'Do you think it'll hurt Frankie more to be invited, and to be subjected to those kinds of people, or do you think it'll hurt her more to be left out?'

"I guess that was probably the toughest question I've ever been asked. And you know what? I'm still not sure I did the right thing. I only know that the more time I was forced to spend with those cruel and condescending snobs, the more I was certain that their contemptible behavior would crush you and I couldn't let that happen."

"How about after you got hitched?" Frankie said. "What then? Still no time for your old friend Frankie?"

"After we were married, Jack took a job with this company called Hayward & Sons. He was some kind of junior executive. All the partners were in their late fifties and sixties, and they wanted to groom Jackson to take over some day. Didn't realize he'd start his own business instead. Ha! But the point is, Frankie, our life was comprised of socializing with these men and their wives, awful women most of them, and I just didn't know what to do about you. If I'd suggested having you over for dinner, Jack would've wanted to make a party out of it, and then I'd have to tell him that I didn't want his associates or their wives anywhere near you. I was a newlywed. I was extremely insecure. I'd already abandoned you during my college years. I hadn't invited you to my wedding. What was I supposed to do? Invite you to lunch on the sly? Call you and tell you I was pregnant with twins? Frankie, I was so sick and ashamed that I just tried to put it out of my mind. I didn't know what to do. And it just continued like that, only the shame grew like a malignant tumor over time, and I just didn't know how I'd ever face you again."

"Is that why in all of these years, before Emily moved out, she always went to visit *you*. You never came here once. Not ever. Not that Ma or I ever saw."

Callie looked ashamed. "Emily always insisted on coming to our house. She said that escaping from Rainytown helped her to stay sane. Looking back, I'm guessing she was just trying to keep the peace. I think she knew in her heart that I would find you when I was ready. I don't know for sure and I never will."

"How come you showed up last Monday like you did? Were you finally ready to see me? Biggest surprise of my life. Never thought I'd ever see you again."

"I needed to come. I didn't even think you still lived here. I didn't know what to expect. Part of me expected another family to be living in your house. That's it, Frankie. I'll answer any questions you have. I'll sit on the witness stand forever if I have to. I'm sorry. That's all I can say." Callie bent her head and covered her eyes in the palms of her hands. She felt like a defendant, waiting for the jury's verdict. She couldn't bear to look up. She knew she was facing the death penalty.

"Callie," Frankie said. "Will you look at me, please?"

"I'm so ashamed," Callie cried into her hands. "I can't look at you."

"I have something to say," Frankie said, "and I wish you'd give me the respect of making eye contact with me."

Well, when she put it *that* way, Callie had no choice. She took her hands away, looked up, and burst into hysterics.

Frankie, devoid of expression, was staring at her, with one garlic green bean protruding out of each nostril. "Mason," she said, still stone-faced.

"Yes?" Callie said, her laughter and her tears all wound up together.

Frankie crossed her eyes and managed to make her nose move in such a way that the beans touched each other. "It's time to forgive yourself. Because that's exactly what *I've* just done."

CHAPTER 15

At twelve minutes to three, Ruby rang her bell to let Frankie know she had awakened. Frankie went upstairs to see her mother and to bring her some tapioca pudding, while Callie cleared the lunch dishes from the dining room table. At exactly three o'clock, Frankie returned with an empty bowl and relayed the message to Callie that Ruby was ready to see her. Callie smiled nervously and headed upstairs, anxious to discover the reason for Ruby's apparent desperation to see her again.

Frankie finished cleaning up in the kitchen. Opening the refrigerator to put away the leftovers, she laughed a silent belly laugh noticing the decorated chocolate cake that Callie had left as a surprise. "With love to my friend Frankie on her birthday. Callie." Feeling catty, comical, and angry all at once, she wished Regina could see the cake and choke on it. That would be the icing on the cake, she thought, frustrated that there was no one to share her pun with.

Damn Regina anyway. There was no relationship to be saved, Frankie was fine with that, but she was still reeling from the pain of losing a friendship, even one as flawed as she'd had with Regina. Especially on her birthday. But the vicious lies and the betrayal of trust enraged her. She hated the feeling of venom coursing through her veins. It weakened what little fortitude she had left. But what affected her most deeply was the sadness of losing a godchild whom she truly adored, and so close to the day when she would inevitably lose her own mother.

At three forty-five, Callie descended the stairs, trying to feign a clear state of mind. She found Frankie on the couch, mindlessly flipping through a recent issue of *Redbook*.

"Well," Frankie said, throwing down the magazine. "What did she want? Was it like I thought? Did she want to make sure you were stickin' around in my life? Did she ask you to promise her or what?"

Callie felt her entire body atrophying as she stood in front of Frankie. Her knees felt rubbery, and she was dizzy with disbelief.

"Mason, sit down. You don't look so good."

Callie followed instructions robotically and took a seat.

"There's something weird about you," Frankie said. "Well, you know, weirder than your normal weirdness. What the hell did Ma say to you?"

Callie swallowed the lump in her throat as her brain raced to come up with something. "She was very adamant that you wouldn't be alone. Pretty much like you thought." Callie was amazed she'd even got two sentences out.

"Mason...again, what's up? You weren't like this yesterday when you saw Ma."

"Emotional," Callie choked out. "Old memories. Very emotional." Oh God, she thought, now she was unable to talk in complete sentences.

"I think we need to talk," Frankie said. "Like right now."

"Can't," Callie choked out in a staccato voice, standing up. "Have to meet Jack at home."

"Mason, I hate to push you, but I've heard computerized voices sound more human than you. 'Please listen carefully as our menu options have recently changed.' "

Callie couldn't even laugh as badly as she wanted to. "Frankie, I have to go."

"Callie...please!"

"No, I have to go." Callie pressed in clipped tones. "Now."

"Okay then," Frankie said, perplexed and concerned. "You sure you're all right?"

"Painful memories," Callie said again, trying to offer a credible reason for her behavior. "Emily, you and me, my mother. Painful things. Hard to see your mom like this."

"There's more," Frankie said. "I can feel it. But we can't have much of a discussion if you're breakin' down every third word. Just drive carefully, please."

"Happy birthday," Callie said, hugging her hard. "Love you, Frankie."

"Love you, too, Mason. We'll talk tomorrow."

"Absolutely," Callie assured her, then ran outside and into her BMW just as quickly as her wobbly legs could manage.

The ride home was frightful. There was an accident up ahead on the main road she took home, and traffic had slowed to a crawl. There was no way out of it; she was stuck. She just had to get home. She had to see Jack. He would know how to handle this. She had never imagined Ruby would ask her something like this. Had she known...oh, she didn't know what she would have done had she known. What did it matter? What would it have changed? She'd just been handed the shock of her life and was being asked to do the impossible. And right after she and Frankie had really reconciled and she had been forgiven. What would this news do to Frankie? Especially coming from Callie?

"Oh, God!" Callie screamed in the car. "Oh, God! Tell me what to do!"

After fifteen minutes lost to emergency vehicles and rubbernecking drivers, Callie picked up speed and breathed a sigh of relief. But when she almost hit an eight-year-old boy who'd hopped the curb with his skateboard, it gave her an adrenaline rush unlike anything she'd ever experienced. She realized she had not been concentrating on the road, on her surroundings, and her heart was pounding at the thought of the disaster that had just been averted.

Slow down, Callie, she silently admonished herself. Watch what you're doing. You're far too distracted. Thank God you didn't hit that child. You could have killed him...I hope that scare will teach him to be more careful...what am I thinking...*I* should be more careful...what am I going to do? How can I do what Mrs. C. wants me to do? Just get home to Jack. He'll know how to handle this. He's smart. He'll be able to see this more clearly because he's on the outside. Stay calm...just watch the road.

"Thank God!" she said loudly as she pulled into home twenty minutes later and saw Jack's car parked in its usual spot. "Thank God he's home!"

As she rushed in the front door, she practically tripped on a set of old plaid suitcases by the door. They obviously didn't belong to Jack.

"Mrs. Hethers," Rosa cried, rushing toward her in tears. "I'm so sorry. I have to leave you."

Oh no, Callie thought. It's because of me. Jack must've asked her to move out because I was so insistent. She felt terrible, but at the same time, whatever was wrong with Rosa had happened at an extremely inconvenient time.

"You're not leaving us for good, Rosa?" Callie asked impatiently. "Are you?"

"I'm sorry, I cannot live here anymore," Rosa said, weeping.

I'm horrible, Callie thought. What have I done to this poor woman?

"Why not?" Callie asked, fearful of the well-deserved and terrible answer she was sure to receive.

"My brother-in-law, my sister Gladys' husband, Ernesto, he's dead. He was such a lovely man…my poor sister…"

"Oh, Rosa," Callie said. "I'm so sorry."

"He's been sick for many years," Rosa explained tearfully. "And I always promised my sister I would live with her when the time came. It's very difficult for me to leave you and Mr. Hethers, and of course the children, especially after so many years, but I made this promise to my sister. I gave her my solemn word I would come to live with her when Ernesto passed. She needs me very much."

"I understand," Callie said, feeling grateful she wasn't the cause.

"But in a few weeks, I will come back to work for you, part time, if that is suitable. I just can no longer live here, Mrs. Hethers. In the meantime, if you need help, my cousin Anita, who has filled in for me many a time, can come in two days a week until I can return. If this is not good for you, I will understand if you prefer another situation."

"Oh, no, Rosa. This will be just fine. The kids are in Maine now, and then they'll be going off to college in September. So part-time will be perfect. And we can wait until you're ready to return. I'm just so sorry for your loss. And for your sister's loss, of course."

A horn honked twice outside. "Oh, my cab," Rosa said, flustered. "I must go. I left my sister's phone number and address on the hallway table if you need me for anything."

"We'll be just fine. Let me help you with the luggage," Callie said, reaching for the heaviest bag.

"No, no," Rosa said adamantly. "The driver will do that."

"Please, take this for your cab fare," Callie said, quickly handing her three crushed twenty dollar bills from her wallet.

"Oh, Mrs. Hethers, this is too…"

"You be well," Callie said, hugging her. "Please give your sister our deepest sympathy."

"Thank you, thank you," Rosa said. As she opened the door, a big burly man in a Phillies T-shirt walked in and grabbed the entire set of luggage at once, as if it weighed nothing. Callie gave Rosa one last sympathetic glance, and then raced upstairs to find Jackson.

It was like some twisted sense of déjà vu. As Callie rushed into the bedroom, she nearly tripped again, only this time, she was almost felled by designer luggage with the monogrammed letters JMH.

Callie's logic and reason had broken down. "You're not moving out, too, are you?"

"For God's sake, no!" Jackson said. "I'm going to Seattle. Cal, I told you'd I'd probably be leaving in a day or so. Why do you seem so surprised? And what in the world would make you infer I'm moving out on you?"

"Four suitcases?" Callie asked, wide-eyed.

"Callie…" Jackson groaned intolerantly. He walked over to the luggage and pointed at the first item. "This is a dress bag. It has my suits in it. Next to it is a suitcase; it holds my casual clothing. You know, those rugged manly outfits I wear to the construction sites. Jeans, work shirts. Big leather belts with buckles that advertise my favorite beer. And then, there's my underwear and socks. Can't leave home without them. Oh, and to make sure I stay dry: a rain jacket and an umbrella. Seattle weather, you know."

"All right, Jack…" Callie said, more than getting his point. "You can stop this silliness."

Jackson continued. "In addition, there's my Sony CD Walkman. Fred, George, Johann. You know, those dead guys in square plastic cases. Jogging clothes. Papers. Files. A few books to read. And this little bag, this is where I keep my toiletries. My razor, toothpaste, shampoo, shaving cream, dental floss, aftershave."

"Jackson, this is ludicrous…please stop."

"And this last item is not a suitcase; it's my laptop, and you know that as well as I do. Now, will that suffice? Because I really don't have time for a more detailed inventory. My flight leaves just a little after seven."

"Oh, Jack," Callie cried, "you can't leave now. I need you like I've never needed you before. I had a long visit with Mrs. Cavalese today, and she asked me to do something for her that blew my mind. I feel as if I'm in a black maze and there's no way out. Even the exit is sealed. I'm just alone in a void. Please, you're the only one I can talk to."

"Talk to your friend Frankie," Jackson said, as he gathered some files he'd laid out on the bed. "She'll know what to do. After all, it's her mother."

"No, no. I can't. That's the whole point. I have to make a decision *regarding* Frankie, and it's just not my place to do it. Jack, please stay. Can't you take a later flight? God, please. I need you so much."

Jackson looked at her sternly and took a firm grasp of both her shoulders. "Honey, calm down. I don't know what's upset you so much, but I'm sorry, I've got to go, now. I told you this trip was inevitable, and I told you it would be soon. I truly wish I could help you, but I can't; not now."

"But Jack," Callie protested, "I didn't know *this* would happen. You *have* to help me!"

"Damn it, Callie!" Jackson said, slamming three file folders onto the bureau. "Haven't you heard one word I've said? Aren't you the least bit concerned about the fate of my company? Where's my goddamn ticket?" He reached in his inside coat pocket, felt around, then breathed a sigh of relief. "Aren't you concerned about me? Can't you stop obsessing about your secret life in Rainytown? Maybe you should stay away from there if it's causing you so much grief. See other friends. Hire someone to finish packing up Emily's house."

"I'm done packing," Callie cried. "I've already hired a cleaning service. I'm there now because of Frankie. She's the best friend I've ever had in the world. Jack, today she forgave me for the past."

"Callie, I'm truly glad to hear that," Jackson said. "I know what that means to you, honey, but whatever else it is you want to talk about will simply have to wait. I've got a plane to catch. Oh, and judging from your opening statement, I assume you've talked to Rosa and that you know she's moving out permanently."

"Yes," Callie said despairingly. "I saw her. She told me."

"Well, then you've got your wish," Jackson said. "You'll have all the privacy you need."

"I didn't want it to happen this way," Callie said. "I didn't want some poor man to die!"

"Well, you didn't kill him," Jackson said. "Did you?"

"Oh Jackson, really…"

Jackson reached down and pulled the luggage straps over his shoulders. "Come here, kiss me good-bye," he said, weighed down with baggage.

Callie kissed him and threw her arms around him. "How long will you be gone?"

"I don't know," he said, heading into the hallway. "At least a week. I'll call you as often as I can. Take care, Callie. I mean that. And get some rest."

Callie burst into tears and flung herself on the bed. She felt completely alone. There was nobody to help her. Why had Ruby chosen her to handle this? Why couldn't Ruby do it herself? It wasn't right. But Ruby must've had her reasons. This was what she wanted. This is what she thought was best for Frankie. How could Callie deny her that?

Her life had changed so monumentally in only six days. She was charged with emotions she hadn't felt in years. She could handle all of it; everything except this.

At eight o'clock that Saturday night, Frankie was sitting on the edge of Ruby's bed, holding her hand, trying not to cry, and managing a smile. In just two days, Ruby had lost most of what little verve she had left, but her mind was clear, and she was determined to be Ruby until the very end.

"That Cunningham broad wants to see me so bad…" Ruby said weakly, "go bring her ass here. I'll give her a good-bye she'll never forget."

"I don't think so, Ma." Frankie said. "I shouldn't have even told you about it."

"You didn't have much of a choice, Frankie. I could hear you cussing her out almost like you were on the TV. And I sure could hear your brother 'askin' her nicely' to get the fuck out. Loved that. You didn't have to tell me nothin'. I'm just glad you came clean with the details when I asked. Got my juices flowing again."

"Oh, did it now?" Frankie said. "Well, I'm glad Reg was good for something."

Ruby squeezed Frankie's hand and her expression became serious. "You don't need people like that in your life, Frankie. You've been nothing but a sounding board to her...someone to yak to about that big-bellied walrus she's married to...and as we found out today, someone with a back to talk behind. Promise me, Frankie. Promise me from now on. Only quality people in your life. Like Callie. Move out of this damn town. Find another one and paint it red. Look at you, so beautiful like I knew you could be. I'll take this image of you to heaven. My beautiful Frankie, lookin' like a million bucks. Only wish I had a million to leave you."

"Who the hell is that?" Frankie said, as the sound of the doorbell was clearly heard.

"If it's that Cunningham broad, don't send her away. Send her right upstairs to me. Tell her I'd just *love* to see her," Ruby said, licking her lips in anticipation.

Frankie laughed. "Sorry, Ma. It won't be Regina. She knows I'll kill her if she comes back here. I just hope it ain't Fat Edna, Stella, or Arlene. I have no time for any of those gossip-mongering bitches."

"If it *is* one of them," Ruby instructed, "send 'em to the Cunningham house to have a few brews with Mr. and Mrs. Blubber Gut."

"Yeah, okay, Ma," Frankie said, wondering who in the world it could possibly be. "I'll be right back, most likely *without* whoever's come to call!"

It must be Callie, Frankie thought, as she rushed down the stairs. She was acting so weird when she left, she must've come back to explain.

"My, my, is this *my* Frankie I'm lookin' at? This glamour queen couldn't be my little girl, could it?"

Frankie was speechless. Her jaw dropped as she stood there, gaping, staring at her father who was holding a big plush teddy bear that donned a Happy Birthday T-shirt. Louie tried to smile, but it was one of deep shame and sadness.

"Here, honey, this is for you. I thought this furry guy might be able to provide some TLC, and I kinda figured that's what you'd be needin' most on this birthday."

Frankie was still reeling from the shock of seeing Louie standing in the doorway. He had never come back to the house...for any reason.

"Thanks, Pop," Frankie said, taking the bear and hugging her father. "You're right. This is just what I need. He's adorable. It's just that I didn't expect...please, come in."

Louie slowly walked into the living room, overwhelmed by pangs of nostalgia as if he were someone who'd just stumbled upon an old family photo album and was eagerly revisiting their past. "Whattya know, still got my old Motorola. It don't work, does it? And my recliner...boy, I loved that old chair. 'Course it wasn't so old when I bought it, but I thought it was the greatest thing since sliced bread. Like a throne to a king, you know? Uh huh, sure did love that chair."

Frankie didn't say anything. She just watched him as he looked around the room and recalled his former life.

"Well, I'll be," Louie said. "Still got that crazy mermaid lamp. Your aunt Belle gave us that for a wedding gift. Your mom loved it; can't say as I did. Guess I'm not surprised it's still here."

Frankie's stomach was churning. Louie was so nervous he couldn't compose his next thought. What was he going to say when he ran out of dusty old memories?

Frankie knew she had to take action. Her father's dread would escalate if she didn't make the first move, and he'd end up making a cowardly dash for the door. She'd never forgive herself if she let that happen.

"Well, I sure don't remember this couch," Louie said as if either one of them cared.

"We bought that new, 'bout ten years ago," Frankie said. "The Snooge chewed up both legs on the old one. Pop, listen, you didn't just come to bring Mr. Bear to me, did you?"

"No..." he said, barely above a whisper. "I came...well, you know..."

"Wait here," Frankie said sternly, putting the bear down on the couch. "If you leave this house, I'll never speak to you again. Just let me tell her you're here. I'll only be a minute."

Louie nodded obligingly, then took a seat in his old recliner.

"Who is it?" Ruby said. "You were sure down there long enough. How long does it take to get rid of—"

Frankie eyes began to water. "Ma, you've got a visitor."

"I told you, Frankie, I don't—"

"It's Pop," Frankie said. "Pop's come to see you."

Ruby's eyes filled with joy and disbelief simultaneously. "Louie," she said, as if she could not have possibly heard Frankie correctly. "My Louie's come to see me? You sure about this, Frankie? You wouldn't kid 'bout something like this? I ain't havin' one of them 'near-death experiences,' am I? Am I awake? I'm not dreaming, am I?"

"No, you're not, Ma. Not unless I'm having the same dream. It's true, Pop's here to see you. Shall I send him up?"

"Quick, hand me that damn wig," Ruby said nervously, as Frankie obliged and helped her on with it. "Is it on straight?"

"Fine," Frankie assured her.

"Hand me my lipstick, not that dark red one, the rose-colored one and bring me over that perfume Paulie gave me last year."

Frankie handed her the lipstick. "I'll spray a little on you, Ma, you don't want Pop to choke on the fumes." Or maybe you do, she thought to herself.

"My lipstick look okay?" Ruby asked.

Frankie smiled, wiping a tiny smudge from the left side of Ruby's bottom lip. "You did a good job, Ma. You're a pro." There was a light in Ruby's eyes that Frankie hadn't seen since her childhood. But the image of her mother, not even weighing a hundred pounds, days, maybe hours away from death, yet filled with the excitement of a school girl on prom night, was so emotionally packed she wanted to run out into the night screaming. Collecting herself, she left the room and prayed to God that her father hadn't turned chicken and run.

"Pop?" Frankie called down the stairs.

There was silence.

"Pop?"

I'll kill the son of a…

"I'm here, Frankie," Louie said, appearing on the landing. "Does she want to see me?"

"Every bit as much as you want to see her," Frankie said, vastly relieved.

Frankie waited until her father had made it upstairs. She needed the memory of seeing her mother's smile when he walked in the room. It would comfort her in the days and years ahead. That's all she needed to see. Then she would leave them alone to tend to their private business.

She opened the door for her father and noticed his hands were shaking as he walked in the room. Ruby was resplendent with joy. She was so filled with happiness that for a brief moment, Frankie believed her mother's euphoria might miraculously cure her.

Louie felt lightheaded as he saw the once-beautiful woman he had married. Her arms were no bigger than twigs that litter the lawn after a rain, her face was drawn and dying, and yet her eyes were filled with elation at the sight of the man who had broken every promise he'd ever made to her and who had destroyed her life. Louie felt riddled with guilt and grief, ashamed and disgusted with himself, and totally undeserving of the smile that greeted him and the arms that labored to reach for his touch.

"Hello there, Sunshine," Louie said, smiling as big as he could.

Frankie took one last look at the light in her mother's eyes and closed the bedroom door.

"Oh, Louie," Ruby sobbed. "Look at you, still as handsome as the day I met you."

Louie sat on the bed and took her in his arms. The feel of her bones against his body devastated him. "I don't feel so handsome," he said as they held one another tightly. He released the embrace so he could look into her eyes. "If you wanna know, baby, I feel like the ugliest man in the world."

"Don't say that," Ruby comforted him, as if the years of anger had vanished without a trace. "Ugly is one thing you'll never be."

"Don't be so damn nice to me," Louie told her. "I don't deserve it. I walked out on you and our children. That was ugly. And the words I spoke to our son this week, on the two occasions when he pleaded with me to follow my heart and come here, well, those were some of the ugliest words I've ever spoken to anyone. I can't even believe they came out of this mouth of mine."

"Paulie…he spoke to you about me?" Ruby asked with an obvious pleasure in her voice.

"Loves you, that boy does. And what did I do, I—"

"He'll forgive you," Ruby told him. "Paulie's smart. He knows you were just frightened."

"Ah, damn it, Ruby, stop being so good to me. Tell me what a rotten bastard I am. You're too damn good. That's what made me…" Louie stopped dead in mid sentence.

"Whenever someone stops talking like you just did," Ruby said, "it's because whatever they were gonna say packs a mighty wallop. So you tell me, Louie Cavalese. 'Cause you can see, I got no time or strength to pull it out of you."

Louie contemplated the raw truth she had just hit him with. She was right. There was no time to hem and haw or twist the truth until it was more comfortable to tell. "You wanna know? I'll tell you then. You were too good for me, baby. I didn't feel like I deserved you; I didn't feel worthy."

"What?" Ruby asked him, agitated. "I don't understand, Louie. That don't make sense to me."

"Ah, baby, you know my old lady was a drunk. And my daddy's liver killed him by the time I was thirteen. Found him dead in the fucking gutter near 30th Street Station. It's pretty amazing I never became a drunk myself, but I did something just as bad; I've been keepin' company with drunks my whole life. I hated my mamma and her booze. I hated wakin' up for school and finding some stranger, reeking of stale alcohol, lying naked in my mamma's bed, or passed out on the couch with his pants up on the lampshade or down around his ankles. Between my daddy's liver and my mamma's lovers, I didn't have much of a childhood and didn't learn the things a boy needs to know to grow up with a healthy mind. But you know all about my miserable childhood, and you know it's the reason why I moved out on my eighteenth birthday. I thought I'd go make a new life for myself there in upstate New York, in some one-horse town where my uncle

Harry owned a business. But that was no life, so what did I do? I met the town drunk, Francine Ellen Parker, and then I married her. Got hitched to a bitch who split on me the second week I brought her home to Philly. But my luck sure did change when I met you. Ah, Ruby, you were a beauty: my voluptuous baby with the dark brown hair and liquid-brown eyes. And you sure knew how to work those hips. Oh, I loved to see you walk. Curvy delight, I used to tell my buddies. What a beauty my Ruby was. Still is."

Ruby pouted, and the tears began to fall. "Then why, Louie, why the hell'd you walk out on me and the kids for that other bitch?"

"Because I was a stupid fuck," Louie said. "You were just so much classier and more decent than any woman I'd ever known. Couldn't handle that. All those miserable fights we had. They were my fault, baby. I couldn't handle the dreams you had for us. You weren't askin' for much, either, just a home in the suburbs, a chance to go to nursing school, a trust fund so the kids could go to college some day. My daddy never taught me how to take care of a family, and I didn't get nothin' from my mamma either. I felt like a scared little boy inside a grown man's skin. I was making a halfway decent living, but I didn't know how long my job would last. My daddy's jobs never did. I knew I wasn't a drunk like he was, but I still couldn't visualize myself bein' any better. Never thought I'd have a successful club like the Blue Lights. Not back then. No way. I felt like any day I was gonna fall from that pedestal you had me on. My good looks and wise-ass ways weren't gonna pay our kids' tuition, buy that house, or put you in nursing school. I was too busy feeling sorry for myself to think like a man, to take a second job, or maybe look into some kind of financial aid so you could go to school like we'd agreed. I was a fuck-up, just waitin' to fall from that pedestal and thinkin' about the look in your eyes when you realized who you'd really married. I couldn't take the waiting, babe. So I jumped."

"Right into the arms of that bitch!" Ruby exclaimed, finding her anger again. "Annie Colton."

Louie looked confused.

"What," Ruby said, still observant enough to notice every nuance of his reaction. "You act like you don't remember the name she had before she took yours and stole mine?"

"I'd forgotten," Louie said.

Ruby looked baffled, but it wasn't worth talking about. "Damn you, Louie. Where the hell did you get the idea I had you on a pedestal? I just loved you. Loved you like nobody's business. Why the hell didn't you tell me what you were feeling? We could have worked it out. I had no idea you were hurtin' so bad. Oh, shit, Louie, why did you have to leave me and our children?"

"Told ya, baby, our life, my responsibilities. It just scared the crap out of me," Louie said.

"So you ran off with drunk number two, a bitch who didn't need nothin' but a good fuck and a refill," Ruby said. "A stiff drink and a stiff —"

"Can't argue with you," Louie said. "A yellow-bellied coward I've been. Like I was sayin' before, I don't deserve any kind words from you. Don't say 'em, baby. Don't even think 'em. You know, I worried for years that Paulie was too much like his old man. Some of those women he used to bring around: trash. But I think my son's smarter than I was…yeah, I think he is. Thank the Lord. I'm seeing some changes in him. I think when he finds a good woman, he'll know what to do with her. Just hope he hurries up; can't play the town Romeo forever. Least he never had a family and deserted them like his old man did."

Ruby was quickly losing steam, and she knew it. "I love you, Louie. Still do, you old bastard. You ain't gonna change that fact no matter how much you cuss yourself out."

"If only I could do it differently," Louie said despairingly. "I swear, Ruby, I'd never leave you. I know where I fucked up now. And I know why. But it's too late."

"Some day," Ruby said, "when you leave this world and go to heaven, you're gonna find me waitin' for you."

"I'm not so sure that's the destination the good Lord has in mind for me," Louie told her.

"I'll have had plenty of time to put in a good word for you. You'll be there. And if by some act of madness the Lord sees fit to let that wife of yours enter the pearly gates, too, I need to know, Louie, who you gonna choose then?"

"You, baby," Louie said, weeping, as he embraced her for the second time. "I'd come back right now, if the Lord didn't have other plans for us. I'm so sorry, baby. I'm so sorry."

He felt Ruby weakening and helped her to lie back on the pillow.

"So we got a date, then," Ruby said. "Eternity? You and me?"

"Absolutely," Louie said, his eyes bright with love. "And until that time, I'll know I've got the prettiest angel in heaven looking after me."

Ruby smiled, her eyes closing and then opening again.

"I know you're tired, baby, but there's something else we've got to settle right quick," Louie said. "It can't wait for heaven. Wish it could, but it can't. Frankie. Did you ever tell her?"

"No," Ruby said in a whisper. "I promised you I wouldn't."

"I didn't think so; she never said nothin' to me, but I haven't exactly been available to my little girl. Annie's always lurking around wantin' to know what we're saying to each other. Frankie hates that. So I thought maybe she knew but just wanted to keep her feelings inside, you know, so as to keep Annie out. Frankie does that when she's hurtin'. But I'm thinking she should know, baby. I think it's time." Louie drew a deep breath. "I just can't believe you kept your promises to me when I broke all of mine to you."

"It's what I wanted to do," Ruby said, fighting to keep her eyes open. "Paulie don't know either."

"So I figured," Louie said. "I wasn't sure. You gotta tell her, baby. Before it's time for you to go. You hear me? It needs to come from you."

"Callie Mason was here today," Ruby said softly, her brief exuberance gone. "I told her the story. I asked her to tell Frankie. She's Frankie's best friend, despite the years lost. Frankie still loves her like I still love you. Callie will tell her when the time is right. I couldn't do it, Louie; I couldn't bear to see the look in my Frankie's eyes."

Louie's angst was growing. "Listen, baby, I know I got no right to ask you to do anything or to offer up my opinion. But I feel strongly about this…real strong. You gotta tell Frankie yourself. It's not fair to ask the Mason girl to do it, and it's sure as hell not fair to Frankie to hear it that way. She's gonna have questions that only you can answer. And if you're gone, those questions will haunt that girl all the days of her life. I know you don't want that for her. You see what I'm sayin', baby, it's gotta come from you."

"You're right, Louie. But I can't tell her tonight," Ruby said, slipping into sleep. "Not on her birthday."

"Certainly not," Louie said as he watched her struggling to finish their conversation. Ruby could barely speak another word, much less have an important conversation with her daughter or anyone else. "You'll tell her tomorrow. And then, when Frankie tells Callie, she can just pretend she's hearin' it for the first time. That's what's best, baby."

"Anything for you," Ruby said as her eyes closed for the final time.

For several minutes, Louie held her hand and watched her sleep, hypnotized by the rhythm of the shallow breaths that barely sustained her. "God, I love you, Ruby. I'm so sorry. I love you, baby." He bent down and kissed her goodbye, watching as his tears landed on her face like big fat raindrops. He stood up, and after one final stab of excruciating sorrow pierced his heart, he left the room hurriedly.

When he got downstairs, he looked over at the couch. Frankie had curled up with her birthday bear and was fast asleep. He walked over and kissed her lightly, then slipped out the front door into the night — back into the only world he knew.

CHAPTER 16

"You've gone over that liquor order so many times I've lost count," Ronnie said. "Something wrong with it?"

"I can't concentrate," Paulie said, dropping his pen on the bar. "Can you check this for me?"

"Sure, baby, I don't know why you didn't ask me that an hour ago, 'stead of torturing yourself."

"Manly pride," Paulie said flatly, handing her the papers. "Look at her. She's nervous as a cat tonight. Wherever Pop is, he's not at Duke's Taproom, and the old bat knows it."

"Where do you think he is?" Ronnie asked.

"Anywhere that I'm not. Didn't want to face me after what went down last night. He'll be here on my next night off. You'll see."

"Sooner than that," Veronica said, raising an eyebrow. "Here he is now."

Paulie swiveled in his bar stool just in time to see his father walk through the door, his expression grave, his eyes avoiding everyone but Paulie as he walked straight toward the bar. Paulie remained motionless as he watched his father advance. The sounds of jazz piano and raucous chatter that filled the air had gone mute. Nothing and no one existed but Paulie and his father. Louie's pace seemed slow and measured as he walked, as if he were not real, just a shadowy figure in a cloud of gray mist who would continue walking but never reach his destination.

But Louie did reach his destination, and it was then that Paulie could see he had been crying. Without a word, Louie threw his arms around his son, crushing him with his love and his pain. Veronica, noticing Annie spring from her bar stool like bread popping out of a toaster, tried to warn Paulie with her eyes that she was approaching, but he was oblivious to everything but his father's embrace.

"Where have you been?" Annie asked Louie accusingly, as if his absence had somehow inconvenienced her. "I've been waiting for bloody hours."

As Louie let go of his son, the darkness in his eyes impaled Annie's presence like a dagger through her heart. She felt her blood curdle as he glared at her contemptuously. "What the hell did I do?" she said sharply.

Louie pointed a finger at her, started to say something, then stopped. He took a deep breath. "Leave me alone with my son."

"Oh, shit," Annie barked. "You had to go, didn't you? Stupid old man."

Louie lunged forward, as if he wanted to strangle her, but Paulie held him back. Annie's beleaguered face contorted in disgust. She looked at Louie for a prolonged moment, as if she were going to spit at him, then stormed the length of the long bar back to her seat.

Paulie sat down again, and his father followed suit. Ronnie walked away to give them privacy, and also to make sure that Annie didn't disrupt them again.

Paulie looked sympathetically at his father's hangdog expression. "You saw Ma."

"Yes, son, I saw your mother."

Paulie closed his eyes, as if to thank God, then opened them again and looked at his father. "You're not sorry that you—"

"Son, I'm sorry about almost everything in my life, especially the way I spoke to you the last couple of nights, but one thing I'll never be sorry about is seeing my beautiful Ruby again."

Hearing his father utter those words seemed fantastic to him...if only...no, why torture himself with muddled thoughts of what could have been. His mother had gotten her wish. There was nothing else to contemplate.

"I'm glad, Pop, I'm just so damn glad you went."

"I'll be grateful to you for helping me get there till the day I die," Louie said. "Any lesser son would've given up on me and kicked my ass for the things I said, but you were man enough and smart enough to know what was really going on."

"I wanted to do more than kick your ass, Pop," Paulie told him. "I wanted to bash your fucking face in and break both of your legs."

"I know you did, son. I saw the clenched fists and the veins popping in your neck, and I'm not sure I would have done as well had I been in your shoes."

"Getting through to you was more important than breaking your bones," Paulie said. "But damn, that fucking Paula shit...that was callous, Pop. And that transvestite garbage...that was some sick fucking shit to say to me."

"Oh Lord, don't I know it..." Louie began. "I'm so ashamed. Paulie, you gotta know how..."

Paulie motioned to Ronnie to bring his father a drink. "I know you're sorry," Paulie said. "Save the rambling apology. Just tell me about Ma and don't ever lay that kind of trip on me again or I will break your legs. And your arms too. So, tell me, she was glad to see you?"

"Ah, sure," Louie said. "Gave me a beautiful welcome, one I sure as hell didn't deserve. Thought she might've wanted to bust my lights out, too, just like you did. But she made me feel so loved...oh, Paulie...broke my heart to see my baby all withered and dying...she's going soon, Paulie, real soon...I swear to you, son, if I could've done it all over again...oh shit, I'm so sorry."

"You told Ma what you needed to tell her?" Paulie asked.

"Didn't leave nothin' out," Louie said confidently. "Your ma, she's still sharp upstairs. Wasn't able to stay up with me for too long, but she didn't waste time with any small talk...she made sure we said all that needed sayin'. We both saw to that. Listen, son, I wish I could stay and talk with you some more. I hope you'll understand. I've just gotta get out of here. I'm too broke up inside, and Annie ain't gonna make life any easier for me. But listen, when you close tonight, don't come back for a while. You stay with Frankie and your Ma until...well, just don't come back until it's right. Mike, Ernie, and I will cover everything. And you know you can count on Ronnie. You just take care, son. I'm sorry. I've gotta go. I love you, Paulie."

And as slowly as he had seemed to enter, he was gone in a flash, and Annie, in hot pursuit, rushed toward the door after him. Paulie's outstretched arm stopped her like a gate arm slicing the windshield of a speeding car.

"He wants to be alone. He doesn't want to see you now. That was made abundantly clear to you. So where the fuck do you think you're going?"

"You happy now?" Annie growled. "Got your *Pa* to see your *Ma,* just like you and Frankie wanted. Now look what you've done to him. Just look what the hell you've done to him, you miserable kid!"

"What *I've* done to him?" Paulie seethed, his face distorted by his loathing for her. "It's what he's done to himself. He's falling apart because he's feeling the shame and remorse of having fucked up his life. For having left his kids and the only woman he's ever really loved — only to end up with an old bleary-eyed bitch who's had more traffic in and out of her tunnel than the Lincoln and Holland combined. Then, he almost, and I repeat *almost,* lets stupid pride keep him from saying goodbye to the love of his life. But he finally follows his heart, comes to his senses, and says his piece. And none of your machinations, threats, or childish tantrums will ever change that. Even that worn-out pussy of yours and all the tongue gymnastics in the world won't help you now."

"Damn you to hell!" Annie hissed. "How dare you speak to me with those foul and disgusting words? How dare you interfere in our lives? Your father will never stand for this. You disrespect me; you disrespect him."

"Tell him anything you'd like, Step Ma-Ma, and as I told you the other night, I've got some tales of my own. You don't care about Pop, and sooner or later, if it ain't happened already, he's gonna realize he doesn't give a damn about you either. Go have another drink. Take a look around. It's crowded in here tonight. Go find some down-and-out loser with a hard on. He'll cure what ails both of you…at least for ten minutes. Go on…this place is filled with 'em. Just get out of my face."

Annie gnarled her face contemptuously and walked away.

Paulie resumed his seat at the bar. Veronica was waiting for him. She smiled and held his hand. "Paulie Cavalese, I've never been so proud of you as I am right now. You're one fine man."

Paulie bit his lip and felt a tear sting his cheek. Veronica smiled, then politely excused herself as she meandered down the bar to see what Russ Tompkins was moaning about.

The storm clouds had come swiftly and unexpectedly. As she roamed her lonely manse, Callie could hear rumblings of thunder outside. The cats were huddled together asleep on the sofa in the den, and as tempted as Callie was to wake them for a much-needed cuddle, she knew that any solicitation of affection, especially if it disturbed feline slumber, was not likely to produce the desired results. Both Cobbles and Hungry had clear autonomy in these matters and did not appreciate humans having the audacity to initiate tender moments or lap-sitting sessions. A human's job was only to respond appropriately when called upon. Callie, having learned from experience, tried to find some other way to fill the terrible void inside — one that would not involve hissing, scratching, or dirty looks.

Jackson's abrupt departure had unsettled her, and her longing for Emily depleted her. After a week of sorting through her aunt's possessions, she had seen her childhood flash before her again, and she desperately missed the wise and wonderful woman who had raised her.

She stopped into Stephen's room and sat on his bed, eyeing with pride the trophies he'd won for his myriad endeavors over the years. His favorite was the one Molly had made for him when he had finished his term as president of his senior class. She was so clever and artistic, so thoughtful and devoted to her family. And Stephen, at such a tender age, was so focused and confident. He managed his priorities like a man three times his age. What amazing kids she had. They must've gotten all of their positive traits from Jack…or maybe from Callie's father, Samuel Mason. Certainly not from her.

So where did she go from here? Emotionally exhausted, she lay back on Stephen's pillow, only to hear the distant strains of Mary Collingswood's laughter taunt her. "And if you want to teach at the college level, even a master's degree won't do. No, ho ho, you'll need a doctoral…"

The old woman's condescending predictions, voiced almost twenty years ago, had all come true. What *would* she do with her life now? Did she even want to teach? Could she stand the rigid schedule and the drudgery of going back to school? Could she stand idly by as her children, her husband,

and even Frankie would struggle daily to reach their respective goals? Frankie didn't know it, but Callie would see to it that she never had to return to that supermarket she so hated. She'd been thinking about Frankie's future for days and had come up with several plausible ideas. She was wonderful at helping others. But what about herself? What would *she* do? What *did* she want to do? What *could* she do?

Frankie and Mr. Bear, roused by the thunder from their nap on the couch, headed upstairs to check on Ruby, then downstairs to the kitchen for a slice of birthday cake. Frankie took a couple of phone books and put them on the chair next to her, determined that she and her new friend sit at eye level. "If it wasn't for you, good buddy," she told him, "I'd never believe he was really here. And I'll love you twice as much because you'll always remind me of the night Ma and Pop got together again." Mr. Bear grinned. "The only thing is, you see, I'm thinking that now that Ma's seen Pop, there ain't much more reason for her to stick around, you know?" Frankie reached over, snatched Mr. Bear, then clutched him to her chest. "I'm so scared," she wept. A boom of thunder sounded, and Frankie rose two inches in her chair. "Oh, God, somebody help me! Please!" And as she prayed for comfort, the phone rang as another boom sounded, and it startled her so that Mr. Bear flew up into the air and landed on the bowl of plastic fruit. Frankie grabbed him quickly, wanting to rescue him from anything that may have been contaminated by Edna Murphy, then grabbed the phone with her free hand. "Hello…oh, Callie…I am *so* glad to hear your voice…"

By midnight, Veronica had finally convinced Paulie that he was too distracted and upset to be of any use to anyone. He'd been reticent to agree, but the futility of his presence could no longer be denied when it took him five tries to accurately count out two hundred dollars in tens.

Paulie had left his car at home, as was his usual practice. He preferred the safety of his garage to the uncertainty of the boulevard and the bored teenagers who cruised the streets. Being only four blocks away from his apartment, walking home always helped him to wind down.

As he opened the door to leave the Blue Lights, he was stunned by the intensity of the storm that raged outside. The loud music inside had obliterated any sounds of thunder, leaving the heavy rain as a complete surprise. He grabbed hold of a plastic shopping bag that blew by him in a fortuitous gust of wind, covered his head, and with no thought of running, or going back inside to find an umbrella, he walked the distance home.

Louie had driven downtown, with a mind to get lost in the sounds of New Orleans blues, but when he reached his intended destination, he could not bear the thought of an old crony tapping him on the shoulder with a rousing hello and an offer for a beer. Nor could he bear the thought of facing strangers, even in a haze of smoke and discontent with no words to connect them. And so, he sat in his parked car on a Philadelphia side street, watching as the rain drizzled down his windshield, slowly at first, and then with a pounding motion as the storm's intensity increased, like a million punching fists out for revenge. But neither the tears from his eyes nor the tears from the skies could ease the gut-wrenching self-revulsion that permeated his being. He was plunged so deeply in a sea of self-loathing that he had momentarily contemplated taking his life. But he'd already done enough damage to his children; leaving them now would be the cruelest thing of all. Especially now. And he'd been told once by his mother, when he threatened to take his life at the age of ten because she'd come into his room drunk and naked in front of his friends, that people who commit suicide never make it to heaven. He believed that...even coming from her. So now, having just made a date to meet Ruby in heaven, there was no way he was going to break his final promise to her. The Lord would call him when the time was right.

Ruby, immune to the thunder and thrashing of branches outside her window, slept soundly and deeply. Although she would never remember it in the morning, she dreamed of making love to Louie. It wasn't like the dreams she'd had all her life, the ones where he would walk toward her, and then turn to chalk or ash when she tried to touch him.

This was the real thing, blissful, erotic, and worth all the years of waiting. The way it was in the early years of their marriage when their lovemaking was replete with rapture, mutual idolatry, and an intense hunger to meld together as one erotic entity. As she lay with her head upon his chest, basking in the glow of what they had just shared, she told him softly and sweetly. "I may be dying, baby, but my passion for you is livin' all over again. It's in every cell of my body and soul. Oh, Louie, we could've had so many more beautiful years together. If only…" He stroked her thick, dark hair, then kissed her tenderly and fully on her beautiful lips. "I know, baby," he said. "I know."

CHAPTER 17

By ten o'clock Sunday morning, Callie was dressed, in jeans and a T-shirt, and preparing to leave for the Cavalese home, despite the fact that heavy rain continued to fall. The forecast for the next couple of days was grim, and so there was no sense in waiting for the rain to let up. Besides, Callie was anxious to get to Rainytown.

She and Frankie had spent over three hours on the phone the night before, and despite their blatant disregard for childhood warnings against the dangers of telephone use during thunderstorms, both had survived admirably.

After hearing about Louie's visit and Frankie's subsequent premonition of an imminent death for her mother, Callie had decided she would make every effort to put her dilemma on the back burner, praying that a way out the impossible and sudden predicament would become clear with time. All she wanted to do now was stand vigil with Frankie and Paulie. It was all she could do.

It felt so wonderful to have her best friend back. Callie finally had a confidante. Her recent and ongoing detachment from Jackson had frightened her. For the first time in her life, she was deathly afraid of losing him. She was angry with him, and she was angry with herself. Frankie, using common sense and her innate radar to predict impending doom, had tried to assuage Callie's fears by playing seer and telling her that a separation was *not* in her future, but little progress was made. Callie cleaved to her doubts and fears like a child with a security blanket that could not be wrested from her grip…even at bath time. Repeatedly, she told Frankie that she felt guilty talking about her marital problems when Frankie's mother was dying, but Frankie assured her, ad nauseam, that a change of subject was healthy, not hurtful or selfish. She then reminded Callie that it had been less than two weeks since the death of her aunt Emily, and that Callie, still grieving for her own "mother," was now plunged into the Cavalese tragedy. "Guilt is a two-way street," Frankie told her, "So chill, Mason, 'cause you're making me crazy with this shit."

Dear God, Callie prayed, as she brushed her hair in the bathroom mirror, thank you for giving me back my friend. Thank you for answering my prayers and giving Frankie the courage and the desire to forgive me. Thank you for allowing me to forgive myself…well, almost… And as she was praising God for his gift to her, she dropped her brush on the marble sink as loud chimes sounded throughout the house to let her know that someone was at the door.

"Now, who in the hell could that be?" Callie said, forgetting with whom she had just been conversing. "Maybe it's Rosa. Maybe she forgot her Bible or something."

Callie raced down the grand staircase, contemplating the mystery, only to be sickened by its revelation.

"Liza!" Callie exclaimed, as the socialite with the sopping wet Gucci umbrella invaded her home. "What in the world are you doing here?"

"How socially correct of you, Callie," Liza scoffed, holding her umbrella as if it were a dirty dishrag that should never have touched her hands. "Pul-leeze! Is there somewhere I can put this thing? It's so…wet!"

There sure is, Callie thought. And it's on your person.

"Here," Callie said, taking the unwanted wet item and laying it on the umbrella stand. "Will this do?"

Liza peeled off her Burberry raincoat, oblivious to the puddles she was creating on the floor. "Can you take my coat, please! I'll catch my death if I keep it on. Oh, Callie, don't tell me that you have the central air running. This rain has really cooled things off; you don't need it right now. Where are the controls? I'll turn if off myself."

Callie had no tolerance for Liza Collingswood. She hated her, and she was not about to change the climate in her home for a temporary and unwanted visitor. She didn't know what to do with Liza's wet coat. Normally, she'd have hung it in the pantry off the kitchen, but that would've indicated that Liza was welcome to stay for at least five minutes, and to Callie, that would be five minutes too long.

As Callie stood there, debating how to handle the situation, Liza pouted and rolled her eyes in disgust. "Oh, really, never mind. I'll hold the damn thing. My God, it's cold in here. I feel like I'm at the North Pole."

"It's not cold in here, Liza. You're just all wet!" Callie said, taking satisfaction in the double entendre. "What can I do for you?"

Liza gritted her teeth. She wasn't enjoying this any more than Callie was. "Marge Vandercleef begged off for tennis doubles today. We need a fourth, and you're it."

"I can't do it," Callie said firmly. "Besides, it's pouring outside."

Liza looked condescendingly at her. "Indoor courts, Callie. Really."

"Indoor, outdoor, outer space, wherever. I still can't make it."

"Sure you can. You need a break from…oh wait, where is it you've been going all week…oh yes, *Rainy*town. How appropriate!"

"How do you know where I've been going?" Callie asked, feeling violated.

"Del told me. Ran into Jackson last night at the airport. Del was coming in from Chicago, Jackson was going to…oh, right…Seattle."

Callie was fuming. "And Jackson told Del my whereabouts this week?"

"Well, Del asked how you've been, so naturally Jackson told him that your aunt had died, my condolences, of course, and that you'd been running back to her place all week to clean a house she hadn't even lived in for ten years…or something ludicrous like that. And, oh, I don't know, that it had been very taxing on you and that he was worried, blah blah blah. Well, I'm sure Delford would be absolutely panicked to death…freaked I should say… if I'd suddenly decided to spend an entire week cleaning out a dead person's home, even if she was a relative, but especially in *that* kind of neighborhood. Well, it's obviously something that you felt behooved to do, and for whatever reason I don't think I really want to know."

As if I'd tell you anything, Callie thought irritably.

"Anyway, Jackson said he hoped you'd get a change of scenery today because you needed one. And I agree. So here I am, Callie. And you can't say no because I've called everyone else, and they're all previously engaged."

"Oh, I'm your very last choice," Callie goaded her. "Well, Liza, you should have just used the phone and saved yourself a trip in the rain."

"I had the feeling it might be tough prying you away from your secret life, so I came in person so that you couldn't turn me down. You're it, cookie. No slumming today. Now, grab your tennis duds, and let's head for the club. I'm buying lunch."

Callie picked up Liza's umbrella, which lay horizontally on the stand, and handed it to her in the same position. "Here. Your umbrella. You take care."

Liza cocked her head to one side and opened her mouth until it formed the perfect O. She looked completely dumbfounded, as if being rejected for tennis doubles was akin to being asked for a divorce. But she collected herself quickly and grabbed the umbrella in disgust. "I knew this was a bad idea," she said huffily. "You're such a grand hostess, Callie; so full of grace, wit, and charm. No wonder Jackson told Del he's not sure when he's coming home again." Liza scratched her head. "Or did he say 'if.' My, my, I just can't seem to remember. Bye, Callie. Have a nice day."

Seething, Callie stood in the foyer for over a minute after Liza had gone. "God, I hate her!" she screamed. "How dare she imply…damn her!" Callie turned and ran up the stairs to finish getting ready, when suddenly an equally potent rage toward Jackson developed. "God, he knows I hate the Collingswoods. How could he tell them my business? How could he humiliate me like that? Why would he tell Del such private things, knowing that his over-baked potato of a wife would twist them out of proportion, cut them into little pieces, then serve them like hors d'oeuvres to that crowd of conceited cloneheads? How could he do this to me? Damn him, too!"

Callie reached the bedroom, sat on the bed, and took several deep breaths. Frankie, she told herself. Frankie needs me now. That is my concern right now. My only concern. I will drive safely to Rainytown. I will pay attention to the road. Damn him! Damn her! I *will* calm down. Frankie needs me…

Paulie was just descending the stairs as the doorbell rang. As if on automatic pilot, with no thought to whom it might be, he walked to the door and opened it.

Callie was alarmed to see the tears flowing, without inhibition, down Paulie's cheeks. She came quickly inside as he held the door open for her, took off her raincoat, and hung it on the coat rack by the door. Paulie stood there and stared at her, his pain swelling like deadly poison, and Callie, not knowing if Ruby was dead or alive, reached for him, as he reached for her, and they held each other, deeply and lovingly, for a very long time.

"Let's sit down," Callie said softly, taking his hand and leading him to the couch. "Your mom, is she…"

"She's still here; Mary Frances is with her…" he said, his voice cracking. "I just left them together…I don't think I'll ever see Ma alive again."

"Oh, Paulie…"

Paulie buried his head in her chest and sobbed. She rubbed his back and cried softly, for her pain, for his, for Frankie's and Ruby's. Finally, Paulie lifted his head and spoke to her. "She thanked me for getting Pop here and told me that because of me, she could die a happy woman. Said that she and Pop are spending eternity together in heaven. They made a date…last night. Ma said she felt like a new bride when she woke up this morning. Said she was proud of me…" Paulie choked on his words as he reached for the box of tissues on the coffee table. "Oh, God, Callie. I thought I'd be able to hold it inside…just like I did the night Pop left us…I've done it all my life…why the hell do I have to lose it now?"

"Maybe your brain ran out of storage space," Callie said sweetly.
Paulie tried to smile.

"You may have spent a lifetime holding things in, Paulie, but we both know that doesn't make them go away. It only makes them grow larger."

"Yeah, I know," Paulie said, hating himself for crying. "The pain, it grows like Ma's cancer did. Damn I'm going to miss her."

"You already do," Callie said.

As she sat on Ruby's bed and held her hand, Frankie felt numb, as if her entire body had been shot with Novocain, with only a tiny prickling sensation to remind her that she still existed. The fate that she had spent over two years readying herself for was now upon her, and all her emotional preparedness, her acceptance of the inevitable, and the internal strength that had galvanized her through the long days and nights had disappeared. Frankie was stricken with a dread more powerful than anything she'd ever known.

She looked into her mother's eyes. A light brown film covered her eyes, as if a translucent, taupe-colored curtain had fallen, a precursor or warning that the final, darker curtain would descend before long. There was a strange gel-like substance around Ruby's eyes, sticky and frightening: a messenger of death. Her eyes would open and close, and every so often Frankie could feel the lifeless hand trying to squeeze hers. Ruby was slipping away, there was no mistaking it, but suddenly, Frankie felt a strength emerging from her mother, one that was inconsistent with approaching death.

"Frankie," Ruby said softly, finding a voice after several minutes of silence between them. "Try not to interrupt me. I'm racing against God's clock, and I gotta get this out. You know those deathbed confessions you see in the movies and on TV? Well, I'm gonna make one now."

Frankie eyes widened. She couldn't begin to imagine what secrets her mother could possibly have that couldn't have been told before. She could see her mother bracing to make an important revelation and believed that God had temporarily given her enough fortitude to sustain herself until the job was done.

"You know your pop didn't have a good growing up," Ruby told her. Her voice was low and faint.

"I know," Frankie said, confused, as to why Ruby found this of import. "They found his daddy dead by the train station and his mamma just drank all the time. But Ma, why does this matter…"

"That's right," Ruby said weakly, relieved that Frankie knew that much. "And sometimes when people live in bad situations, instead of doing better for themselves, they go out and find more of the same, 'cause it's all that they know."

"That's why Pop left you for Annie," Frankie said.

"You mean 'the bitch,' " Ruby said, turning up the volume as best she could. "Yeah, but that don't matter now. Listen to me, Frankie. Before that bitch there was another one. Your father married her when he was very young, before he met me."

Frankie's jaw dropped. "Pop was married before you? No, Ma…"

"Let me talk," Ruby insisted, straining with every word. "Your pop moved to upstate New York to get away from his mamma. He married a woman there named Francine Ellen Parker."

As Ruby spoke the name Francine, a chill shot up Frankie's spine.

"And they had a baby together," Ruby said, looking straight into Frankie's eyes.

Frankie swallowed a lump in her throat, and her eyes welled with tears. The hand that was holding Ruby's began to shake uncontrollably. "Ma, I don't think you should tell me anymore. I don't think—"

"Your pop brought her and the baby girl—"

"Oh, God!" Frankie blurted out.

"He brought her and the baby girl to Philadelphia right after the birth. But after two weeks, bitch number one left him for some boozer boyfriend from back home. Didn't want nothin' to do with your pop or their daughter."

Frankie began crying. "Ma, I don't like this story. Please don't tell me anymore."

Ruby looked at her sternly. "Frankie, listen to me. You need to know this, and you need to hear it from me." Ruby stopped talking momentarily. Her breath was labored, and it took her a while to begin speaking again. Frankie waited patiently. The words were becoming increasingly difficult to get out, but Ruby plodded on. "Now, shortly after your daddy divorced that good-for-nothing, he met me. I was workin' in a hospital, as a receptionist in the clinic, and I was planning to go to nursing school the following fall. That was my dream, and I had it all planned out. But I fell so madly in love with your pop, my handsome Louie, that all I wanted to do right then was marry him. I told him I would raise his little girl as my own, and he promised that if I held off on my schooling for a bit, till the baby was older, he'd work hard to pay my tuition."

Frankie's entire body had gone numb. She couldn't even feel the prickling sensation anymore.

"Well," Ruby said softly, her eyes fluttering, "some things work out, and some things don't. What worked out for me was that I couldn't have loved this little girl anymore if I'd given birth to her myself. I loved her every bit as much as the little boy that came along a few years later."

"No, Ma," Frankie cried. "You're mixing something up; you know this isn't right."

"I'm dyin', Frankie; I ain't delusional," Ruby maintained, determined to be believed. "Oh, honey, I wish I could hold you while you cried this out. I'd hold you forever, baby. But I can't. Your brother, your pop, and your friend Callie will have do that. You've just got to listen to me."

"I just can't believe you're not my—"

"I'm your ma, Frankie," Ruby said with conviction. "You ain't my blood but you're my heart. Don't you ever question that."

Frankie sat there, sobbing. She could see that Ruby had more to say, but by this point, she had become almost too frightened to hear it.

"Frankie," Ruby said feebly, "tellin' you what I just did; that was the easy part. What I gotta say next is harder, 'cause I could have controlled this part, I could have done better by you."

"What do you mean, Ma?" Frankie asked, her thoughts spinning like a wayward top.

"I didn't figure it out till just a few weeks ago. It came to me, very slowly, and only a few days ago was I really able to admit to myself the terrible damage I did."

"What damage, Ma?" Frankie asked.

"I didn't treat you right, Frankie. You know I didn't. I cozied up to denial for all the years that you were sufferin'. Ain't no secret there. Hell, I didn't mean to, but I made you pay just like I'd paid. I deprived you of a life. I kept you here in this damn house out of some kind of guilt. You might've been married to Johnny by now with kids of your own, or maybe be an art teacher somewhere…I don't know. I only know that I kept you here to wallow in my misery with me; I was cruel to you when you gave me everything a daughter had to give. You devoted your life to nurse me when

I took sick. Ain't that funny, you ended up being the nurse in the family. Oh, Frankie, I talked so bad to you."

"It's okay, Ma," Frankie said, "Please hush now. You don't have to go on."

Ruby was weakening, but her unyielding desire not to quit kept her going. "Remember the other day, Frankie, when I told you that your pop loved you so much he used to say you hung the moon? Then, like some mean old woman, I told you the moon was crooked, making it sound like I didn't think you could do nothin' right, and like I didn't love you like your pop does or that I don't see you for the wonderful woman you are. Oh, Frankie, the moon ain't crooked. It looks as the eyes see it, and now mine see clearly. You did a beautiful job hangin' that moon, baby girl, and next time you look up into that sky, you be proud. Proud of everything you've done and proud of who you are. I'm not sorry that other woman gave birth to you. Only damn thing she ever did right in her life. I couldn't imagine anyone but you for my little girl. I love you, Frankie...and I'm sorry I failed you. And I'm sorry I threw the oatmeal...I'm so ashamed..." Ruby's reprieve was over. She began to fade again. "Frankie," she said feebly. "Hand me that mirror; I wanna say goodbye to myself."

Frankie laughed and cried at the same time. It was just like her mother to say something silly like that, like an artist, signing her signature on the painting of her life at the precise moment it was finished. "Sure, Ma," Frankie said, giving Ruby the hand mirror that lay on the table by her bedside pharmacy. She put the mirror in Ruby's hands and kept hers there. "Here, Ma, I'll hold it for you so you can see."

Ruby looked into the mirror. The lines of age and sickness were gone. Her skin was now aglow with a warm beige color, and there was a soft pink hue on her cheeks. The clouds had left her eyes, and they were again bright with hope and love. There was no wig, no bald head, only a thick, beautiful head of dark chestnut brown hair, flowing copiously onto her shoulders. In the mirror's reflection, she saw the angel behind her, extending an arm, her smile warm and inviting, and brimming with unconditional love.

Frankie held the mirror for several moments after her mother's hands had dropped. She turned it face down on the night table, taking care not to catch a glimpse of her own reflection. Everything made sense. Nothing made sense. She pulled the blankets up to her mother's shoulders to keep her warm. She didn't know how to stop caring for her. She bent down and kissed her mother, as her hand slid down the side of Ruby's face.

She had isolated Ruby's revelation to another part of her mind, to deal with at another time. The tears fell, but she did not weep. She imagined Ruby walking into the light, greeted by loved ones in gleaming capes of gold and white, their eyes sparkling with joy as they met hers. She imagined the gardens of heaven, so vibrant with every color in God's creation, wishing she could see the awe and the wonder on her mother's face as it all came into view. She looked down at Ruby. The death mask was gone. Agony had turned to ecstasy as she left one world and entered another. She must be in the gardens now, Frankie thought…she must be so amazed by all the beautiful colors…she must feel so good. So alive.

Downstairs, Callie and Paulie sat silently on the couch, lost in their own thoughts. Callie's left hand rested over Paulie's right hand as they listened to the rain as it made a tapping sound against the awning outside.

CHAPTER 18

"She's gone," Paulie suddenly said with a start.

"How do you know that?" Callie asked.

"I just do. I can feel the emptiness. Ma's left us, Callie."

As Callie was about to respond, she and Paulie turned toward the stairs. Gripping the railing with both of her hands, pushing them downward in a sliding motion, was Frankie, staring straight ahead, intoxicated with pain and navigating the climb downstairs with slow precision. Paulie looked at Callie, his glum expression confirming everything, then resumed watching his sister's agonized descent. He thought of going to her but sensed her need to make the trip alone.

Callie was immediately consumed with the debilitating grief she'd felt only two weeks ago. She was certain that Frankie had to be suffering the same feelings of loss and disbelief as she had felt when Emily died. It was a simultaneous feeling of torture and panic, of an emptiness as vast as the ocean. Callie remembered feeling as though she were trapped in some parallel universe, able to see only a distorted, blurred world around her. It was a world where walls were made from dying embers and would crumble if touched, where floors and ceilings undulated in a dizzy rhythm, and where people were gaseous shadows that moved like ghosts passing in the night as swirls of light encircled them in a mad-brained fury.

As Frankie reached the landing, Paulie ran over to her, catching her in his arms, just as she was about to collapse. "Paulie," she cried, "Ma's gone. She's gone."

Paulie, holding on to his sister, sat on the first step and cradled her in his arms as they both wept. Callie watched in torment as Frankie and Paulie mourned their mother. It was such a horrible, helpless feeling. She didn't know whether to just leave them be or to say something. After several minutes, she walked over to them and stood silently. Paulie nudged Frankie, to let her know Callie was there.

"I'm so sorry, Frankie. I'm so sorry for both of you," Callie said. "I just don't have the words…"

"There are none…" Frankie choked.

"I need to go see Ma," Paulie said to Frankie. "Will you be okay with Callie?"

Frankie nodded her head affirmatively as Paulie helped her stand up. Callie and Frankie embraced, and Paulie, after taking a monumental breath, headed upstairs for a grim goodbye.

"Can I get you something to drink?" Callie asked Frankie as they took a seat on the couch. "Water?"

Frankie didn't even hear her. "Oh, God, Mason…I can't imagine life without Ma. I feel like I died with her. What am I supposed to do now? I don't even know who I am. I can't stay in this house. I can't go back to that job. I can't handle Edna, Arlene, Stella, and all them coming down here to pay their respects. What if Reg tries to come by? She will, you know. She's banking on this stuff between us blowing over. That's how she thinks. I don't want her stepping foot in this house…ever…oh, God…what am I supposed to do now? I don't know what I'm supposed to do now. I don't want to see people. I just want my Ma back, Callie. I just want Ma!"

Callie held her tightly and stroked her hair. "Listen to me, Frankie. You don't have to do anything you don't want. Don't worry about work now; just be assured you never have to see that supermarket again if you don't want to. And as for people coming down here, you don't have to deal with that either. I don't want to overstep or intrude, but if you tell me who to call and what your wishes are for your mom's funeral services, I'll handle everything and take care of the financial arrangements, too — if you'll permit me to do so. We can hold a reception right at the church after the service or at a local restaurant if you prefer. That might be nicer. I'll call as many people as you want me to. I'll fill the church with your mom's favorite flowers. Whatever I can do. I promise you nothing will be spared to give her a beautiful farewell. Please, let me do this for your family."

"Mason, I can't let you do all that…"

"Frankie, I want to do it. Because I love you. And I loved your mother. Not because I was a stupid idiot and disappeared for twenty-three years. I can guarantee you this is not about assuaging guilt. It's an offer from the heart. I want you to be free to grieve without the burden of having to make funeral arrangements, unless, of course, that's something you want to do. I would really like to handle this for you, but only if you and Paulie are okay with it."

Frankie looked at her, as the tears ran like winding mountain streams down her face. "You know, Mason, I never thought I could let go of the reins for anyone. But I'm kind of on overload right now, and so I'm not gonna fight you. I just don't understand how you can do this for me when you just went through this for your aunt almost yesterday. It's too much."

"Frankie, don't worry. I really want to do this. It's okay. And remember, when my aunt died, I had Jackson to help me. I couldn't have done it alone, either."

Frankie reached for a tissue and blew her nose. "Then I'm just gonna say thanks. I know it'll be just fine with Paulie. And even more so, Ma would think this was just great. Oh, God, I was just thinking I should go tell her. Isn't that stupid? Am I losing my mind?"

"No, honey, you're not losing your mind. It's so natural and normal what you're feeling; it's just horrible to feel it. That's all."

Frankie lay her head on Callie's shoulder and sobbed. Every so often, Ruby's confession would poke its head in the door and remind her that it was real. The death of her mother had crushed her; the thought that another woman had given birth to her had annihilated her. She didn't want to talk about it; she didn't want to ask her father about it; she didn't want to think about it. She didn't want to do anything that would confirm it, but the cold truth nagged at her, pounded at her, not even having the decency to give her a reprieve while her heart was breaking.

And Callie, whose mind was on the same subject, looked at her grieving friend and wondered how she could ever deliver the shattering news. How could she tell Frankie that Ruby was not her biological mother; how could she tell her that some drunk named Francine Ellen Parker had given birth to her and then abandoned her? Maybe she could talk to Louie and he could tell Frankie. Or maybe Paulie would be a better choice. But then she realized that it wasn't so much the messenger, it was the news itself. How much more could Frankie take? And as if that weren't enough, there was Callie's solemn promise to Ruby, the one she swore she'd keep.

They came for Ruby after nightfall. Watching the men from the funeral home take Ruby out the front door was excruciating. Frankie, by this time, appeared catatonic as Callie and Paulie stood on either side of her, holding her steady. She was fading quickly. She had slipped into her own silent world hours ago. Her only wishes, expressed within an hour of her mother's death, were to be left alone in the house after Ruby was gone, and for the phones to be disconnected from the jacks upstairs so nobody could disturb her sleep. She did not want Paulie and Callie to stay. She asked that they understand and leave her in complete solitude. Neither one of them liked the idea, but neither wanted to exacerbate her suffering by disrespecting her wishes.

As soon as the door closed behind the second man from the funeral home, Frankie let out a barely perceptible moan. Paulie held her and kissed her on the forehead. He whispered "I love you, Mary Frances" into her ear, then nodded to Callie, who quietly escorted her grieving friend upstairs.

Paulie peeped out the curtains of the front window as they put his mother into the hearse. Only a light mist was falling now. The news that Ruby had died, unsurprisingly, had spread quickly throughout the neighborhood. Paulie could see Regina, across the street, wailing on the front porch while her three children stood in confused silence and her corpulent spouse tried to console her. Paulie watched as Regina took steps to cross the street toward the Cavalese home, then sighed in relief as "her Hal" displayed some previously untapped good sense and pulled his wife back.

To his right, Paulie saw the dreaded triumvirate, Edna, Stella, and Arlene, making their way down the street, with a brigade of assorted neighbors lagging behind them. The idea of facing any of them sickened him, but he knew if he didn't go outside and say a few words to the hungry throng, they'd ring the bell and bang on the door in pursuit of details. He couldn't allow his sister to be disturbed, so he opted to go outside, make a brief statement, and then ask them to leave Frankie in peace.

Paulie conducted his business in record time. He told the neighbors that Ruby had died peacefully, and that someone would inform them when funeral services would be held. He expertly brushed off the multiple attempts to coddle and comfort him, which he correctly identified as poorly masked excuses to touch his person. He thanked everyone for the expressions of sympathy, then turned back toward the house. It was at that very moment that Regina appeared by his side, still wailing, gushing apologetically, and begging to see Frankie, whom she still referred to as her best friend. Paulie, knowing he had an audience, took Regina gently aside and spoke to her in low but clear, firm tones. He made it abundantly clear that if she cared anything for his sister, she would stay far away. She had hurt Frankie beyond repair, and Frankie did not need her life complicated by Regina's attempts at reconciliation. The desire was not mutual nor would it be in time. He punctuated his statement by making a vehement request that Regina not attend the services for his mother, at which point Regina let out a distressed scream that seized the neighbors with a burning curiosity, then hurried back home and into the waiting arms of her precious Hal.

"Well, here it is," Paulie said gloomily. "If I had a hat, this is where I'd hang the damn thing."

Callie stepped inside the door and looked around. "This is a beautiful apartment. You seem to have an amazing collection of music. And in my humble opinion, incredibly good taste in art. I love this watercolor of the trumpet player. This is such a comfortable place, Paulie, very nicely furnished."

"Here, let me take your raincoat," Paulie said. "And that's a tenor sax. Have a seat."

"Oh, sorry," Callie said, embarrassed. She handed him her coat and took a seat on the leather sofa. It was smooth and worn but had aged well. The leather had been well taken care of, she noticed, probably treated with some kind of special oil on a regular basis. There was something about the lines, something about the way they proudly showed their age. She was reminded of her aunt's beautiful, proud face. Her skin had been so soft, like a baby's, and her wrinkles showed, but did not condemn, the passage of time. A more wise, wonderful woman she had never known. Because of Emily, Callie never carried the burden into her adult years of not having known her biological mother. Emily *was* her mother. But now she was gone, and so was Ruby.

Oh, God, I miss her, Callie silently mourned. Oh, how Frankie and Paulie must miss Mrs. C. I'll miss Mrs. C. I hope Frankie's asleep. I hope she can take a respite from this pain.

Callie never imagined she'd find herself alone with Paulie at his apartment, but there were arrangements that needed to be discussed and two people that did not want to be alone, or out in public, in their present state of bereavement.

"I need a drink," Paulie said, standing in front of her. "I'm having a scotch. Would you like one, or maybe a glass of wine? I'm not sure what I have. I'm not even sure who the hell I am right now. Sorry, Callie-fornia, my brain isn't working."

"Whatever you're having is fine with me," Callie said.

"I'll bring out some cheese or something," Paulie said absentmindedly. "I guess we need to eat something."

"Let me help you," Callie offered.

"No, really. Just stay there. I'll put on a CD for you. Since you like trumpeters, how about Wynton Marsalis?"

"Great," Callie said, not missing his sarcasm but finding the moment inappropriate for their customary exchange of snappy witticisms. "Paulie, please, don't worry about me."

Paulie walked over to his enormous CD collection on the wall. Callie was impressed at his apparent knowledge of each CD's precise location. Without hesitation, he quickly grabbed the selected disc, inserted it into the proper orifice of his elaborate sound system, and then excused himself to the kitchen.

Callie liked the music and couldn't help notice that he'd chosen to play New Orleans blues, music slow and mournful like a funeral dirge. The sounds of the horn, so filled with a passion and spirituality, brought to mind a picture of the old South. She could envision a line of mourners, trudging sullenly and silently down a dirt road. She could see the horse-drawn carriage that led the way, while the coffin in back jostled lightly over the bumpy road, leaving a swell of dust in its wake.

Two glasses of scotch suddenly appeared on the coffee table before her, along with a platter of cheese, crackers, and grapes. "Best I could do under the circumstances," Paulie said apologetically. "I thought I might have some cold cuts, but I'm all out. So, how do you like Wynton?"

Callie gasped. Oh, God, he sounds just like Jackson, she thought. My precious Jack, I wish I knew where we stood. I wish I knew how to fix us. You feel so far away…

"Wynton, Wynton Marsalis," Paulie repeated, as if she hadn't understood.

"Yes, I like him very much," she said. "I'm sorry. My mind was somewhere else."

"Yeah, I know. Probably lingering in the same empty space that mine is in. Pop is a fan of New Orleans jazz … loves this place in Philly where … never mind."

Paulie raised his glass to hers. "To Ma, and to your aunt Emily."

Too choked up to respond, Callie managed a half smile and raised her glass to his.

Paulie took a sip of his drink and sighed heavily. "Do you think Mary Frances is okay? Maybe we should have insisted on staying."

"I think your sister is probably in a deep, deep sleep," Callie told him. "I just hope she stays there until morning."

"Still, I didn't like leaving her alone. But she was so insistent. You don't think she'd—"

"Oh God, Paulie. Don't even think that way. You know Frankie, when she's dealing with pain, sometimes she just can't share her feelings with others, so she goes off into her own little world. She's always been that way. You know that as well as I do. Probably better."

Paulie shook his head and made a face. "Why wouldn't she be able to share Ma's death with me, or with you? That doesn't make sense."

"We can't predict how we're going to grieve when the time comes. I guess she just wanted to be alone tonight. She needed to be. For whatever reason."

Paulie wasn't convinced. "There's something else," he said. "I know my sister, and there's something she's not saying. You know what? I think I need to go back over there and check on her. I don't care what I promised. I'm too worried. Oh shit, who the hell is that? I already spoke to Pop hours ago. Who the hell else would be calling me now?" Wearily, Paulie picked up the black phone on the right end table.

"Yeah, hello," he said, as if defying the invasive caller to speak.

"It's me, Paulie. You can chill. I just wanted you and Mason to know I'm okay. I had some soup and crackers, and I'm going to bed now."

"You were so out of it when we left," Paulie said. "I thought you would have fallen asleep the second Callie took you up to your room."

"Me too," Frankie said. "But I couldn't. Now I'm ready. I'm just calling to make sure you're not going to come over here to spy on me or some nonsense like that. Because if you do, it'll really piss me off."

"Mary Frances, I was just saying to Callie that it seems like something's bothering—"

"You think something's *bothering* me," Frankie exclaimed. "Ma's dead. Isn't that enough, for Christ's sake?"

"I'm sorry. Just calm down, okay? I'm really sorry."

"I'm sorry, too," Frankie said, a bit frightened by her brother's intuitiveness. "Just stay put, Paulie. I mean it. I just need to be alone. It's been so long since I was totally by myself. I just need to feel that space around me. I can't explain it."

Satisfied that his sister was not a candidate for suicide, he relented. "Okay, I'll leave you alone. But I'll be over there in the morning. You can count on that."

"And I'll be waiting for you. I just need this time now. It doesn't mean I don't need you, or Mason either. Tell her that, okay? I love you, Paulie. Mason, too."

"Love *you*, Mary Frances. Sleep well."

"Is she okay?" Callie asked as Paulie hung up the phone. "Well, I know she's not *okay*, but you know what I mean."

"She's going to sleep now, but she wants us to know that her need to be alone tonight doesn't mean she doesn't need us. Oh, and she loves us."

"That's so sweet," Callie said tearfully. "I love her, too."

Feeling more relaxed about Frankie, Paulie and Callie put their heads back on the couch and let the majesty of the music fill them up. When the CD had finished playing, Paulie put five more in the changer, beginning with his favorite Stan Getz recording that played first. For the next couple of hours, the two of them poured through Ruby's phone book and assorted papers, deciding whom to call in the morning, and making a list of everything that needed to be done for the funeral and burial.

Without realizing it, Callie, in a state of sheer exhaustion, lay her head on Paulie's shoulder and fell asleep. His eyes fell closed only moments after hers did, and they stayed in that position until Callie awakened at one a.m. Not wanting to wake Paulie, she attempted a slow rise from the couch, but he felt her moving, and pulled her back down. Face to face in the near darkness, with only a soft light burning next to them, Paulie kissed her lightly on the lips. When she responded, his kiss became more intense, and suddenly she found herself lying on her back, her arms around Paulie as he moved in slow rhythm on top of her while Shirley Horn sang "Here's to Life" as she played her piano, softly and sensually, just for them.

Callie could feel him, so hard against her thigh. Her head was filled with grief and the effects of too much scotch. And there was Shirley, urging them on. But Callie didn't need whiskey or soft music to draw her to Paulie. She'd wanted him since the moment she saw him again, and even though it was not love, or anything close to what she felt for Jackson, it was raw, real, and dangerous, and it left her breathless and vulnerable.

With his left arm, Paulie pushed himself up while his right hand reached underneath his body to unzip his fly. As he expertly forced his pants down, her appetite for him grew ravenous. She could feel all of him now and longed to have him inside of her. Once he was totally exposed, he began to undress Callie in the same manner. Her heart was pounding even harder. But it was so wrong. Within moments, her pants were down and his hand was inside her underwear, touching her in all the right places. It was an ecstasy of the indescribable kind, something unlike any sensation she'd ever felt. He was seconds away from entering her body. Oh, God, what to do. She wanted this man so badly, and if she gave in, it would haunt her forever. She would disintegrate into ash like a paper doll who had foolishly chosen to dance in the fire because the colors of the flame entranced her so.

"Oh, Paulie, please have mercy on me," she begged. "I'm too weak to resist you. My body wants you, but my heart and soul are begging me to say no. This isn't right. Please, Paulie."

He looked at her, crestfallen, then, as if suddenly recognizing her desperation, he sighed and collapsed on top of her. For both of them, it was consolation just to feel each other's naked bodies, pressed together, as they never had before and never would again. She could not ask him to get up. She did not want him to.

"I'm sorry," Paulie whispered, as he pulsated against her thigh. "Just let me lie here until I can move. I'll behave myself, but I'm telling you, babe, this is fucking torture for me. I've never wanted someone more in my life."

Callie ran her right hand through his thick locks of hair. "Me, too," she whispered. "But thank you. Thank you *so* much."

CHAPTER 19

The next day, Monday, by one o'clock, Callie had completed all of the arrangements for Ruby's funeral service. It would be held on Wednesday at Ruby's church. Immediately following the burial, there would be a reception in the private banquet room of a nearby restaurant. Callie ordered flowers for the service, coordinated arrangements with the banquet manager, and called the local newspaper to place an obituary notice. When she was confident that all the details had been finalized, she called Paulie, who was at his sister's house, so that, as arranged, he could make one call to each of Ruby's friends and family members. He wanted to have *all* of the necessary information at hand, including Ruby's handwritten request that donations to the Cancer Society be made in lieu of flowers. The majority of Ruby's female co-workers at the supermarket, many of them unmarried (and many not), had a voracious appetite for Paulie, and each in their own way, labored dreamily under the preposterous misconception that their hunger for him might one day be satisfied. Paulie knew it and wasn't giving anyone *any* reason to warrant a second phone conversation. He was having enough trouble dealing with his grief; he could not tolerate these women using his mother's death as an excuse to invite him over for a home-cooked meal and "sympathy," which he knew was bound to happen no matter how brief he kept the conversation.

Then there was the Rainytown contingent, which neither Paulie nor Callie wanted to deal with, so they had devised a plan to make notification as painless as possible. Callie would make up flyers (on Stephen's computer) containing all the necessary information; then Paulie would insert them into selected mailboxes late at night.

Despite all of the plans going smoothly, Callie and Paulie were having their respective personal difficulties getting through the conversation. Their emotions, which were tangled up with grief over Ruby, concern for Frankie, and lust for one another, enervated them. Callie finally broke the tension by asking Paulie to put his sister on the phone.

Callie was infuriated by what she heard next. As expected, Frankie was broken, barely functioning, but she had gotten a decent night's rest and felt calm and secure when she found Paulie waiting downstairs for her in the morning. Unfortunately, that calm was short-lived. Regina had slipped a long, babbling, misspelled letter under the door, demanding her right to attend Ruby's funeral and insisting that Frankie had been "to tutchy" about Regina's "tempir tantrem" the day before. She ending the letter by expressing the heartfelt sentiment that "true friends and deesent humen beans forgive each uther," then reminded Frankie that she would need Regina's comfort in the days to come because "Callee Masen" wasn't "goin to do no slumming forever," implying that she would be Frankie's sole source of comfort. Regina's inappropriate epistle also contained a postscript that further blathered on with a twisted depiction of Frankie's lonely days ahead if she didn't "shape up" and "come to the good cents her mamma gave her." As Frankie read her the letter, Callie was reminded of Ebenezer Scrooge, being whisked around by the Ghost of Christmas Future, with a sneak peak into the pathos that was to define his mortality should he not drastically alter his life upon waking. That Cunningham woman is scarier than the Dickens, Callie thought to herself when Frankie finished reading, then wondered if it was sacrilegious to pun, even silently, during such tragic times.

As Frankie explained to Callie, she had seen the letter as Regina slid it under the front door, so Paulie had no opportunity to intercept it. But Frankie also made it clear that she would not have wanted the letter intercepted; it helped to drive home the reality that Regina was no one she ever would call "friend" again under any circumstances. So, Frankie, as it turned out, still reeling from Regina's initial attack, had to suffer all over again the childish and boorish ramblings of a defeated, lonely woman.

"Paulie," Frankie told Callie, "wants to kill that bitch."

Callie was horrified by Regina's gall. She told Frankie to hang in as best she could, and promised that she'd be over as soon as she'd finished lunch and typed the flyer for the neighbors.

As Callie sat at her kitchen table, eating the Greek salad she'd picked up on her way back from the church, it occurred to her that it had been only one week since she had returned to Rainytown and had been reunited with the Cavalese family. It was fact but seemed unfathomable to her. It felt more like a month had passed. Like two months. Everything was different. She was different.

Somehow, with Frankie's help, she'd been able to work through her past and gotten to understand herself better. That not-so-easy feat had lifted an onerous burden, one she had expected to carry forever. But there was just such a jumble of feelings to deal with at the moment, and Callie couldn't begin to sort them all out. Not now. There was only one thing that reigned triumphant and clear through all the upheaval: that was the unbridled elation Callie felt at having her best friend back.

But there were so many other things, she bemoaned — things that weren't so easy to embrace. Most important, her marriage had taken a sudden nosedive. Callie couldn't even consider the thought of losing the husband she so adored. So why was she thinking about Paulie? Why was she still clinging to the physical memory of his genitalia pressed against hers — his lips kissing hers, his tongue sliding deliciously around in her mouth, his hands touching her body with such fervent zeal? Why hadn't she lamented her actions the moment she woke up that morning? Had she cheated on Jack? No, she was sure she hadn't. Would Callie mind if Jack found himself in the same position, literally, with another woman? Of course, she'd be outraged and cry for weeks. It would mean the end of life as she knew it.

Nothing was the same. Nothing but her friendship with Frankie seemed right. Emily was no longer in the world, and now Ruby had died, making Callie the executor of her secret. She'd looked at the problem from every angle and still had not a clue what to do. Not telling Frankie would be wrong, and telling her would compound her best friend's already unbearable anguish. She repeatedly thought of turning over the task to Paulie or Louie, but each time she reminded herself that she had promised Ruby that *she* would be the one to tell Frankie, as unfair as it now seemed in retrospect for Ruby to have asked. So when was this revelation supposed to occur? Should she wait for Frankie to get her strength back and then crush her all over again? Would there ever be a *good* time to deliver such news?

Callie sighed and reached for the salt to season the egg in her salad.

After two quick shakes, the phone rang.

"Hello?"

"Hi, honey, can you hear me?"

"Oh, Jack! I'm so glad you called. I can hear you just fine," she said, the guilt beginning to kick in.

"I'm on the twenty-fourth floor of the new bank building. But actually, I'm outside. This building doesn't even have any walls or floors yet. Thank God the rain stopped."

"Jack, please be careful up there…"

"I'm fine. I'm enjoying a beautiful view of Seattle and I'm quite safe. Wait, oh no, I've lost my balance…oh no, who the hell had that banana for lunch? Help me, oh no…goodbye Callie…I lovvvvvve you."

"Jack!" Callie screamed.

"Just kidding, honey. How are you?"

"God, Jackson. You can be such an asshole. Don't ever scare me like that again. It's not the least bit funny. And you were ridiculously melodramatic. I should have known better than to fall for that. No pun intended. Especially with that stupid bit about the banana peel…"

"I'll try for more realism next time," Jackson said. "It was an impromptu thing."

"Don't you dare," Callie warned him.

"You don't sound so good," Jackson asked, his tone growing serious. "Are you okay?"

"Not really. Frankie's mom died yesterday. It's been really rough. And I miss Aunt Emily so darn much. There's so much I want to talk to her about. I feel like an orphan. I *am* an orphan."

"Jesus, I'm sorry, Cal. You're right. I am an asshole. Pretending to be falling off a building when you're grieving for Emily. And now you've lost someone else. I'm sorry. How are Frankie and her brother doing?"

"They're hurting really bad, Jack. I'm taking care of the funeral arrangements. It's something I really want to do for the family."

"That's fine. I'm glad you're doing that. Do whatever needs to be done."

The phone connection began to crackle. "Can you hear me, Jack?"

"Yeah, but it would help if you spoke up," he said loudly.

"Tell me, how is everything out there?" Callie yelled into the receiver. "I'm hoping that your pathetic attempt at humor is a good sign that things have improved."

"Drastically," Jackson said loudly. "I think everything's going to work out, but trust me, it took some doing. This was one of the biggest scares I've ever had. But I'll tell you all about that later, if you're interested. Listen, Cal, I know we've been sailing over some rough seas lately, but I don't think now is the time to work that out. I appreciate your asking about the business. I haven't exactly hidden my feelings about what I perceived, falsely, I hope, as your lack of concern. Right now, my thoughts are about you and your friend Frankie. Tell me what I can do for you."

"Oh, Jackson. There is something you can do for me. It's been on my mind since you left. It's really important; it would make me so deliriously happy. I just don't know if I have the right to ask now, seeing the way our relationship has been and—"

"Callie, we'll work out our marital woes later. You know how much your happiness means to me. Yours and the kids. Now, tell me what I can do for you before we lose our connection or I fall off this damn shell of a building for real."

Callie, who had called in advance to let Frankie know that she was right around the corner, arrived at the Cavalese home midafternoon. Frankie had asked Callie to phone ahead, as she didn't want to make the mistake of opening the door for the wrong person. Peeking discreetly through the blinds, Paulie had been able to verify that Regina, Stella, Arlene, Edna, and at least three other women whom he couldn't identify by name, had come to call. Every last one of them had pounded on the door or rang the bell incessantly, despite the large note he had posted outside: "Family in mourning. Please do not disturb. Notification of services for Ruby Cavalese will be distributed within 24 hours."

Frankie was near hysteria by the time Callie arrived. She was curled up on the couch, holding the birthday bear Louie had given her. "Did you see the note Paulie put on the door? What? Those illiterate bitches can't read? How dare they disrespect us like this! We've asked to be left alone. We told them we'd let them know about the funeral. What the hell do they want from us? God, I fucking hate it here! I want out! I want out of this house! I want out of this Rainyfuckingtown!"

Callie and Paulie exchanged looks of despair. Callie sat down next to Frankie and put her arms around her.

Tears flowed from the tomboy's eyes. "What do they want from us? Tell me, Mason. I really don't know. I don't know anything anymore."

"Grist for the mill, I suppose," Callie said. "They're like tabloid press reporters. They have no respect for *anyone's* privacy. They just want to be the first one to get the 'story.' "

"Well, there ain't no fucking story for them here," Frankie choked. "And if Reg dares show her face one more time, Paulie won't have to deal with her, 'cause I'll be happy to do it myself."

Paulie looked at Callie in complete despair. He had no idea how to calm his sister down. He looked drained as he collapsed into the armchair.

"What am I going to do, Callie?" Frankie went on. "Am I supposed to live in this mausoleum with vultures and rattlesnakes for neighbors? Am I supposed to go back to the courtesy desk of that supermarket for another twenty five-years, refunding money to customers for rotten food and sour milk, giving out rain checks to coupon-crazy shoppers, and selling cartons of cigarettes like the ones that killed my ma: I can't do it. 'Grocery Manager. To the courtesy desk, please.' I hate hearin' my voice go all over the place. Like some faceless robot. You know what, Mason? I don't have an identity anymore. I don't know who the hell I am."

"You're Mary Frances Cavalese," Paulie interjected. "And you're also my sister."

You're half right, Frankie thought, and then she said: "Don't be so sure, Paulie. Maybe I'm not who you thought I was."

Paulie and Callie exchanged confused glances. Callie could see the wheels turning in Paulie's head. Maybe he had been right after all. Could there be something else bothering his sister besides her mother's death? Whatever it was, how could Callie *ever* compound her friend's grief by delivering the shocking news Callie held about Frankie's biological beginnings? She said a silent prayer, asking God to let her know what to do, then continued to comfort her friend.

"Either of you ladies hungry? Thirsty?" Paulie asked.

"I'm fine," Callie said.

"I don't want food. I just want Ma."

"I know you do, Mary Frances," Paulie said gloomily. "So do I, sweetie. More than you know."

"But you have a life, Paulie. I mean, you have a beautiful place to live, you have your music…you might even be famous some day when you get back to playin' again. You've got dreams, and talent. Me, I'm gonna shrivel up and die here. Hell, fuck it. I got no future. I'm already dead."

"Oh God, Sis," Paulie said helplessly.

Callie took both of Frankie's hands in hers. Look at me, Frankie. And listen carefully to what I have to say. I had no intention of bringing this up today, but I think maybe now I should."

Frankie looked confused but curious.

"You don't have to live this life anymore if you don't want to. You don't have to live here, and you don't have to work at the supermarket."

"Oh, really," Frankie said. "And exactly where *am* I going live, and exactly where *am* I going to work?"

"Let's start with the new digs. And I've already discussed this with Jack, and he's fine with it. Happy about it, in fact."

Paulie shrugged off the sound of Jackson's name. It made him want to pound the arm of the chair.

"You remember me telling you about our maid, Rosa? Well, the other night she moved out for good. For years, she'd occupied the mother-in-law suite in our home. It's a self-contained apartment, complete with kitchen and full bath, and a private entrance. She's gone to live with her recently widowed sister, and she'll only be working for us part-time now. So you see, I just hate things to go to waste, and this really is a beautiful apartment. There are these wonderful curved window benches in the living room by the bay window. The bedroom is large and has a huge walk-in closet. The bathroom is done in marble, the kitchen is state-of-the-art. And there's a small dining room perfect for an intimate evening when you meet Mr. Right. In addition, it has central air and thick, plush carpeting. And it's yours to live in for as long as you want. Forever, if you so desire."

"Got one for me, too?" Paulie asked, trying to encourage his sister to go for it. "Damn, nobody's ever offered me a deal like that."

"Oh, Callie, it sounds so wonderful, but I just couldn't live there rent free. I mean, I pay my way. That's who I am. And I could never afford—"

"Frankie, you are family to me. You don't have to pay anything. Besides, if you don't take it, it'll just stay empty. Jack and I certainly don't want to rent it out. And now that the children are grown and soon to be on their own, I have no use, ever, for another live-in maid."

"But still, rent free. That don't, doesn't, sound right."

"Then pay us rent when you settle in with your new job. Do whatever makes you feel comfortable."

"My new job? You must have some kind of fancy supermarket near your house."

"Don't be sarcastic, Mary Frances," Paulie admonished her. "Listen to Callie."

"Yes, there *is* a supermarket not far from our home," Callie said, "but there's also a university. And the university's got a daycare center where my sister-in-law, Cynthia, happens to be the director. Just by chance, we were talking the other day, and she told me that she's looking for a new teacher's aide. You know, someone to help with the children, develop arts and crafts projects, supervise activities, enforce discipline…things like that. When she asked me if I 'knew anyone,' I screamed, 'Yes! I have the perfect person,' but it wasn't the right time to tell you about it."

"Oh my God, Callie!" Frankie said, her joy and her grief scrambling for center stage. "This is too good to happen to someone like me."

"Don't ever say that again, Mary Frances," Paulie said vehemently. "You deserve the best, and that's what Callie-fornia is offering you. Get the hell out of this fucking house. It's yours now. Sell it and get out."

"I don't know what to say," Frankie said.

"Yes would be nice," Callie said. "But let me tell you what else comes with this package."

"A man?" Frankie asked. "That good-looking-dark-haired stallion like I see in my dreams?"

Paulie and Callie laughed.

"Sorry," Callie said. "Mr. Right you'll have to find on your own. But working at the university not only pays you a salary and offers you a chance to meet eligible bachelors, it offers you free tuition if you want to pursue a degree. Maybe in art education, whatever you'd like. You know all of those dreams you thought were down the drain?"

"Looks like some big monster plunger just sucked 'em back up for me," Frankie said tearfully. "This is too much to take. Oh, I wish I could tell Ma. She'd be dancin' in heaven if she could hear this. Right before she died, she told me to go find a good life for myself, to associate with good people, and to be proud."

"You're right, Mary Frances. Ma would be thrilled for you. I can hear her right now, 'Take it, Frankie, you get away from these no-good broads and this no-good place. I mean it, Frankie. You take that Callie Mason up on her offer!' Can't you hear her talking to you?" Paulie asked.

"Yeah, I think I can."

"Does this mean that you accept my offer? Shall I arrange for you to meet Cynthia in a couple of weeks, when you're feeling up to it? I've told her all about you. You're just the kind of person she's looking to hire. 'Someone down to earth with lots of love to give to the children and lots of common sense and smarts to teach them well.' And that's a quote. And by the way, she doesn't need you to start until September. Her current assistant is moving to Chicago. Husband got a transfer. Cynthia said she was a little too uppity and not well suited to work with children. So she's glad she is leaving. She said you sound like a dream come true."

"Oh, yeah, that's me: a dream come true." Frankie looked at her brother for support.

"Your girlfriend's offering you a life, Mary Frances. The best thing you could ever do in Ma's memory, and for yourself, is to take her up on it. Later with the sarcasm."

"Thank you," Frankie said. "Thank you so much. Just wait till Reg sees the "For Sale" sign stuck outside on the railing. Wait'll they all see it. Thank you, Mason. And please tell Jackson I thank him from the bottom of my heart."

Callie looked sweetly at her friend. "You'll get a chance to tell him yourself very soon. I'm *so* glad you said yes. It means the world to me. Having you so close is actually a dream come true for *me*."

Paulie was thrilled for his sister, but hearing the name Jackson again made him want to do inappropriate things.

As happy as Frankie was about the prospect of a new life, it was hard to see beyond her grief. Ruby's deathbed confession had decimated her. She desperately wanted to share the revelation, at least with her brother, but she felt that telling the story would somehow make her waking nightmare all the more real. And, of course, Paulie would immediately go to their father, and Louie's corroboration of Ruby's story would be like a giant rubber stamp branding her brain with big red letters, "Nightmare Confirmed." And her head would become translucent and then everyone would know. They'd read the words and then hound her for details. She'd tell them all to go to hell, but that wouldn't stop them from twisting the truth. She could see them now, sitting in Edna's living room, munching on potato chips and bloating their bellies on beers as they speculated on and embellished the sad beginnings of her pathetic life. Then, their lies would gain momentum, and people everywhere would hear them. Maybe even that awful Francine Ellen Parker, if she was still alive. Maybe she would come and hunt Frankie down. She'd be even worse than Ruby had described her. She'd probably make Annie Cavalese look like a saint. Francine was bound to be one miserable drunk, just like Frankie's stepmother, but at least Annie didn't give birth to a child and then throw her away. And that's the only good thing she could say about the woman whom her mother had called "the bitch" for so many years. Oh, no, Frankie speculated. I hope she doesn't try to come to Ma's funeral.

Her fears continued to escalate. I'm becoming a crazy person, Frankie concluded. If I don't stop these thoughts from spinning in my head, I'll end up like that poor Jane Marie Johnson, that street lady who was let go from the state institution and walks the boulevard. Just like her, I'll be talking to no one while I hunt for scraps of food and whatever other stuff I can find in the trash. Oh, please, I don't want to be crazy. I can't go crazy now. Not ever. I'll have to talk to Paulie. I'll have to tell him before this eats my guts out. I'll do it tonight, after he puts the funeral notices in the mailboxes. I'll talk to him then.

Callie could see that Frankie was not only tiring, she was orbiting in a world of her own. Politely excusing herself, she told Frankie she would call her later, adding that she would be happy to come back if Frankie needed her for any reason at all.

Paulie looked disappointed as Callie hugged Frankie goodbye. Despite the awkward tension between them, he needed her comfort, too. As she passed Paulie on her way out the door, she touched his shoulder, then smiled at him, genuinely and longingly. It was only a matter of seconds, however, before she caught herself openly displaying her hunger for him.

With his back to Frankie, he pursed his lips and blew her a kiss, showing Callie the depth of *his* desire. But he was no longer the quick-witted, overtly flirtatious "You-want-me-babe" Paulie she'd known a week ago. This was a man who had abandoned his clever come-ons for something much more real: true passion and feelings that went beyond carnal desire, but naturally, did not exclude it. Callie felt a rush of eroticism sweep through her body as he returned her unwitting show of emotion. Rattled, she offered him a clumsy, nervous smile, then hurried to her car.

Frankie, totally oblivious to the sparks that had just lit up the gray and gloomy room, told Paulie that she needed to sleep, then asked him to come back later to have dinner with her. She needed to talk to him about something really important. He knew immediately she was going to tell him whatever painful secret he had intuited and felt a sense of relief that his sister had chosen him as a confidant.

"I need to sleep, too," Paulie said to Frankie. "I'd crash here on the couch, but the nosy bitch brigade might come trespassing again. I think I'll go upstairs and grab some Zs in my old room."

"It'll be like old times," Frankie said. "And when you close your eyes, you'll feel Ma watching over you. And then she'll kiss you goodnight. Or in this case, good afternoon."

Paulie bit his lip to keep from crying. He took his sister's hand as they climbed the stairs to their respective bedrooms, each hoping that Frankie's words would go straight to Ruby's ears.

CHAPTER 20

Frankie slept several hours longer than she had thought was possible. When she woke up at nine fifteen to the dark skies outside her window, she was completely disoriented, having no idea what time or day it was. Since Ruby's death, each awakening tendered the formidable task to Frankie of having to once again reacquaint herself with the changes in her life that sleep had temporarily obscured for her. Disremembered in the sanctum of slumber, the recent past, a jumble of vagaries, would gradually congeal, then greet her like a steamroller that was advancing head on. So much had happened in just a week's time: good, bad, horrific, and wonderful. Callie had come back into her life; Regina's mounting insecurities had led to an ugly, bitter attack on Frankie; Ruby and Louie had made their peace with each other; Ruby had died and left Frankie with an unwelcome going-away present and a shattered heart; and Callie had just offered her a new life, far away, in every respect, from Rainytown.

She could barely field the questions her mind was tossing at her like errant baseballs. Would she fit into Callie's world? Would she be an embarrassment? Would she pass muster at her new job if indeed it truly were hers for the asking? Would she and Paulie stay close? Why hadn't Ruby told her the truth before? Was her mother's confession the truth or the delusion of a dying woman? Or was it, perhaps, the delusion of a dying woman's daughter? She reminded herself that the mind's ability to play cruel tricks was not to be underestimated. (If only that were the case.) Was she going crazy, or was she just scratching around in her grief, trying to understand the crushing changes that had taken place in her life while simultaneously fearing the changes to come? Was it bereavement, lunacy, or anger? It *felt* like lunacy; that's all she knew.

But she knew what Ruby would say to all that. She'd have reprimanded Frankie for even considering the possibility that she had come unhinged. Frankie recalled how her mother had prodded her, as only Ruby could do, not letting anything or anyone get in her way. Now fully emerged from her post-sleep haze, Frankie resolved she was indeed lucid and went into the bathroom to douse cold water on her face.

Oh, no! Paulie! Dinner. Our talk, she suddenly remembered, hoping he had not given up on her and left.

Paulie had successfully delivered the funeral notices to the selected addresses. Serendipitously, some rain had fallen just minutes before he had headed out, forcing the porch dwellers inside for the evening and giving him an opportunity to deliver the notices unscathed.

Back at the house, he was sitting on the couch, anxious to talk to his sister. He could hear Frankie stirring upstairs, then the expected sounds, running of water and the flushing of a toilet. What he did not expect to hear was the slamming of the screen door, but when he saw an envelope slide under the front door, there was no doubt who had just delivered the unwelcome communiqué.

Jumping up from the couch, he ran to retrieve the damp paper intruder.

"Don't even *think* about keeping that from me!" Frankie said, midway in her descent downstairs. "Let me see what that bitch has to say now!"

"Mary Frances, do you really think—"

"Paulie, you know how I am, and you know I'm not going to back down, so please, save me the grief of arguing with you. Now, does that damn thing have my name on it?"

"Yeah," Paulie conceded. "Unfortunately, it does."

"Then let me have it, and if any more of this shit slithers its way into this house, don't you dare try to keep it from me."

"I hear you, Mary Frances," he said, handing her the envelope.

"Look at this filthy thing," Frankie said. "A freakin' phone company envelope with potato chip grease all over it. Don't they keep any plain white envelopes in the house? Is this thing vile or what? Hal has beer and chips every night for dessert while he and his gut watch TV. Can you imagine? Hell, forget the gut; his ass spreads quicker than the fucking gossip on this street!"

Paulie chuckled. Frankie was such a live wire. He loved that about her.

Frankie took a seat on the couch, her face poised to do battle, while Paulie sat across from her on the armchair.

"Wait," Frankie said, "you've got to sit next to me while I read this so you can see it. Just hearing it, you don't get the full impact."

Paulie dutifully took a seat next to her. She read aloud: "Frankie: My oh my. Did you realy think that I woodent find out about your mother's funerull service? I have frends on this street you know. Hal says he knows damn well that your hot shot brother avoydid us on purpose."

"No shit, Sherlock," Paulie muttered. "What a pair of idiots! I already told her she wasn't welcome at the funeral. What the hell was there to figure out?"

"We're talking about Hal and Regina," Frankie reminded him. "They just figured out yesterday that you can actually slice bread."

Paulie chuckled. Frankie read on. "Mr. Hot Shot acts so damn soupeereeyore. Well, we all know that he's got checkers in his passed, don't we?"

"Holy shit," Paulie exclaimed. "What a fucking airhead!"

"Checkers in your past, huh? She's got Scrabble for a brain."

"Yeah," Paulie concurred, "but she doesn't have a Monopoly on stupidity."

Frankie and Paulie laughed heartily together. "Good one, Paulie," she said, feeling close to her brother.

"Let's see what else this pea brain has to say," Paulie said. "Keep reading."

"Hey, thanks for ansering my last letter—NOT! I reached out to you, hoping we could fix our fences, and you don't so much as give me no thought. So guess what, Miss Callee Masen the Second all dolled up and too good for your Old Frends, my Hal and me say Fuck You to you, but dispite what I don't feel no more for you, I still loved Mrs. C. and I know she would want me to come and say Good bye to her."

"Like hell she would!" Frankie said angrily. "You should only know what Ma thought of you, you damn bitch!" She continued reading. "So I'll be there, whether you and Mr. Hot Shot Tight Pants Showin Off His Big Dick likes it or not."

Paulie shook his head and rolled his eyes. "Holy Christ." Regina's comment bothered him, only because it made him think of Callie, and the *part* of himself he had not been able to fully share with her.

It's amazing Hal can even find *his* with all that blubber," Frankie continued. "But he obviously manages…somefuckinghow," Frankie said. "He couldn't show his off if he walked the streets butt naked!"

She read on. "Oh, and one more thing thanks for breaking my Steffie's heart. You try to explane to a little girl why her Godmommy don't love her no more. What would you know anyway, you ain't got no kids."

Frankie paused to feel the barb, then pushed it away.

"So, the only thing I got left to say is see you at the church on Wensday, both of yous. If you try to turn me away, you'll both burn in HELL! Then your brother can be a Hot Shot for eturnity. Ha ha. My Hal thought of that. Your very EX-best bud, Regina Cunningham."

"Damn her," Paulie said. "I'll take my chances on Hell. That woman will not enter the church. I'll have Mike and Ernie from the club stand guard. Ernie's the best bouncer we've ever had. Don't worry, Mary Frances, she won't get in. I promise. Being as pregnant as she is, believe me, she won't be hard to spot. As much as I despise that woman, I do respect her pregnancy, and I promise, nothing but her pride will be hurt."

"Thanks, Paulie. I knew I could count on you. And you wouldn't kick her ass even if she weren't pregnant. I know you better than that."

Paulie defied her with a look. "Now, down to the business of dinner. I stopped and picked up some things for us to eat. Why don't we make Ma happy by nourishing ourselves, and then we'll talk. Okay?"

"You really think Ma's gonna know the difference?"

"Sure," Paulie said. "You know Ma wouldn't let a little thing like death keep her from making sure we eat right."

"My stomach feels like it's filled with jumping beans," Frankie said. "I don't know if I *can* eat." She paused. "What I got to tell you, Paulie, it's something really big. I don't know if—"

"I've sensed that all along. I know you've got something important to tell me." He took her hand and led her to the kitchen. "Come on, let's see what your 'hot shot brother' brought for dinner. One thing at a time."

By ten fifteen, dinner had been consumed, and brother and sister were in the living room, sitting side by side on the sofa. Paulie looked into Frankie's soulful eyes wishing he could say or do something, anything, to make the fear and sadness go away. He waited patiently for Frankie to speak, until it became apparent that she was numb and that whatever she wanted to say was not likely forthcoming without some prompting from him.

"Is there something I can do to make this easier for you?" Paulie said. "I feel so damn helpless."

"Me, too."

"Just tell me what it is, honey," Paulie said gently. "I think you need to unburden yourself, and from the look on your face, I don't think there will ever be a perfect time."

"Got that right! There will never be a good time for me to detonate *this* bomb," Frankie said, piquing his curiosity. "Never, Paulie."

He looked at her sympathetically.

"Let me ask you this…" Frankie said. "Do you agree with that old saying, 'Half a loaf is better than none'?"

"Sure, I guess so," Paulie said, mentally scratching his head. "Especially if I were hungry and that's all there was to eat."

"Well then, you won't be too disappointed to hear that you've only got half a sister. Only half of one, Paulie! Got that?"

He wasn't following her. "You mean, you feel like part of you is missing, with Ma gone and all that?"

"No!" Frankie said adamantly. "I mean you got half a damn sister! Or a half sister. Damn, I'm not used to thinking it, much less saying it."

Paulie looked baffled. "Mary—"

"Ma told me before she died that I wasn't her blood, only her heart. She said Pop was married to some drunk named Francine Ellen Parker before he married Ma, and when that boozin' bitch gave birth to me, she left Pa and me too. Then he met Ma, and she took to raising me as her own. She'd really wanted to go to nursing school, and because of me, it didn't happen. She said she didn't like admitting it, but that she'd held me back from finding my own life because raising me up had taken away some of hers."

Now Paulie had gone numb. Frankie had blurted everything out so quickly, and he wasn't one-hundred percent sure he had heard her correctly.

"So, you don't have anything to say?" Frankie said. "You gonna sit there with your mouth open and catch insects for me after what I just told you? Guess I don't need that old fly swatter anymore. I've got something even better."

At that repulsive thought, Paulie closed his mouth. He ran the fingers of his right hand through his slightly wet hair and sighed. "But Ma chose to have *me*. She could have gone to nursing school when you were older, but obviously she wanted children."

"I guess I'd already fucked up her life; damn it, I have no idea. She was so in love with Pop she probably wanted a kid that belonged to both of them, you know? And I guess she still couldn't go after you were older, 'cause Pop had flown the coop and taken his wallet with him."

"Mary Frances, are you sure you heard her right? I mean, I talked to Ma a couple of times before she died, and she was kind of confused about things. Maybe—"

"She was as clear as that goddamned bell she used to ring. Oh, Paulie. Can you believe I actually miss the sound of that thing?"

"I know, Mary Frances. Listen, just start from the beginning and tell me as close as you can remember exactly what Ma said. And try to slow it down a bit."

Frankie's eyes narrowed as she looked at him. "You swear you didn't know none of this before? Don't lie to me, Paulie Cavalese."

"Hell no!" Paulie said adamantly. "I'm fucking flabbergasted; look at my face."

"Okay, then," Frankie said. "I'll tell it best as I can remember it."

It was well after midnight when they finished discussing the situation for the time being. Paulie, finally convinced it was true, couldn't believe he was learning about it for the first time. He wished desperately for his sister that Ruby had not waited so long to tell her, but was thankful that she had in the end. It was important for Frankie to have heard the words from their mother, not just because they were more convincing, but because Frankie would always have the memory of Ruby's loving words that came with her heart-wrenching confession.

"Paulie?"

"Yeah?"

"I just had a thought."

"What is it?"

"Do you think Ma adopted me?" Frankie asked with hope in her eyes. "I mean, do you think she made it legal back then? Or just sort of took me in like a stray cat?"

"I have no idea," Paulie said, "but what I *do* know is that you were never a stray cat to her. Anyway, I'm sure Pop will know about the adoption question."

"Oh, God!" Frankie panicked. "I'd knew you'd want to go to him."

"Why shouldn't I?" Paulie asked.

"Because that will make it all the more real," she wept, burying her head on his shoulder.

"We both need to know what Pop has to say," Paulie said, lifting her head and looking her in the eyes. "And one other thing. If it took not being Ma's biological daughter to get you for my sister, then I'm glad. I hope you'll take that the right way, Mary Frances. I'm glad you're who you are; that's all. You're more of a sister than I could ever hope to have. Hell, I'm the one who's been a half a brother to you. I'm so ashamed. I let you take so much of the burden for Ma. I'll never forgive myself, Mary Frances. Never."

"Let it go," Frankie said.

"How can I?" Paulie asked. "I have no excuse for the way I behaved. I tried to deny my responsibility. Tell myself it was easier for you to take care of things because you lived here, because you could help Ma with, you know, personal things. Because I worked late nights at the Blue Lights and you had taken a leave of absence. There is *so* much more I could have done. And now it's over. I can't make it better. And here you are telling me to let it go. How can you say that, Mary Frances?"

"Because you've changed. Seen the light. And I know how sorry you really are. Not much is clear to me now, but that is. Ever since Mason came back, things changed. We've changed. Callie brought something good into our lives, just by being here. I forgave her for the past, and now I forgive you. Oh, and speaking of Mason, how about a word concerning this thing you've got for her?"

"I was wondering when and if you'd bring that up," Paulie said.

"Well, I'm not blind," Frankie said. "What worries me the most is that the feeling appears to have some mutuality to it."

"Mutuality?"

"Whatever," Frankie said. "Is there a law saying I've got to use the same words all the time?"

Paulie laughed, bypassing the catch in his throat.

"You're avoiding the question," Frankie averred.

"Well, yeah, there is some, uh, *mutuality* involved," Paulie admitted.

Frankie twisted her mouth, then spoke: "I meant it a minute ago when I said I'd forgiven you for everything. But if you fuck up Mason's life, or your own for that matter, I won't forgive you. Mason's a bit shaky now. Don't take advantage of her. You hear me? She's got a good husband and two beautiful children. She's just going through some rough spots right now, you know, losing Emily, her husband and kids being away, trying to figure out what to do with her life…she's extremely vulnerable."

"You think I don't know that, Mary Frances?"

"I'm just letting you know that I've got eyes. And I'm *real* good at math. I can add two and two and come up with four in a heartbeat. So watch your step, Paulie."

"I really care about her, Mary Frances. This isn't just another case of your brother wagging his tongue at some babe."

"I know," Frankie said emphatically. "That's what worries me the most."

"What I'm trying to tell you is that it's *because* I care that I won't take advantage."

"Yeah, well, maybe 'cause you *do* care so much, you won't be able to resist your pretty little 'Callie-fornia.'"

Paulie looked down at the floor.

"Oh, no!" Frankie exclaimed. "Don't tell me that you two have already—"

"We didn't," Paulie said. "Just leave it at that."

Frankie sighed. "Damn, *that* sounds ominous. Well, I've said all I had to say. I'm not going to hound you. And quite frankly, I don't even want to know." She paused, as if reconsidering what she had said. "No, I really do *not* want to know."

"Why don't I stay here tonight with you?" Paulie said. "In case you need someone."

"No thanks, what I need now is to be alone. But I'm glad you were here, Paulie, and I'm really glad I told you."

"You gonna tell Callie?"

"Not yet," Frankie said. "Not until after Ma's funeral. I got enough to deal with now. It was hard enough rehashing it all to you, you know."

"Okay," Paulie said, rising from the couch and kissing her on the top of the head. "You know best. Take care, whole sister of mine. I'll see you tomorrow."

"I love you, Paulie," she replied, "sometimes ass-whole brother of mine."

Paulie winked and smiled. And then he was gone.

CHAPTER 21

"Meow," came the whimpering cry.

"Oh, Hungry," Callie protested sleepily. It's only eight thirty. You can let me sleep a bit longer, can't you?"

"Meooowwww!"

"Please, Hungry," Callie begged. Your mommy didn't get much sleep last night. Just this once, can't you wait?"

"Meeoooowwwwww!" came the impatient reply.

"Oh, Hungry, please stop. You wouldn't be this cruel and deny your mother a few extra winks."

"MEEEEOOOOWWWWW!"

Cobbles watched Hungry as she mewed in vain for breakfast. Not having the patience that his sister did for the futile sport of battling back and forth with a human, Cobbles knew exactly how to remedy the situation and get the desired results. While Hungry continued her pathetic whine from her post at Callie's right side, Cobbles, who sat silently at Callie's left, jumped onto the headboard. Then, with deft precision, he took a flying leap, landing on all fours right on Callie's bladder with a victorious thud.

"Oh, God!" Callie screamed, as she sat straight up in bed and looked at Cobbles. "You think you're real slick, don't you?"

Cobbles' innocent eyes stared back at her. Hungry had stopped mewing and was looking proudly at her brother.

"Okay, you fur balls, you win. But you *will* wait until I use the bathroom!"

"Meow…" Hungry squeaked.

"Don't press your luck," Callie said with a loving scowl as she climbed out of bed. "First things first."

By nine fifteen, the cats had been fed and Callie had showered and dressed, prepared to run some final errands in preparation for Ruby's funeral the next day.

I can't believe tomorrow will be Wednesday, Callie thought. Please, God, let this service go well for Frankie and Paulie. As she stood in the bedroom, looking at her unmade bed, she realized that the changing of linen was two days behind schedule. She really didn't give a damn, but for lack of a good reason not to, she pulled the sheets off the bed and sauntered into the hallway to get a new set. Returning to the bedroom, mindlessly putting the new bottom sheet on the bed, she began to schedule the day in her head. She would finish her chores at home, run her errands, and then spend the day with Frankie. As she tucked the fourth corner of the bottom sheet under the mattress, she noticed two very large lumps moving underneath the sheet.

"Is this 'Torture Mommy Day?' " Callie asked helplessly as the phone rang.

"Hello?"

"Hi, Mason, hope I didn't wake you."

"Oh, no," Callie said. "My furry children took care of that. Listen, I was just figuring out my time schedule for the day, and I should be by your place by early afternoon. I was planning to be there earlier, but I remembered I have to synchronize the arrangements between the movers and cleaning service. You know, make sure the movers come *before* the cleaners. I'm hoping Emily's home will be cleared out by the end of next week at the latest. Anyway, shall I bring lunch? Say about one o'clock, if that's not too late for you?"

There was a pause on the other end.

"Oh, Callie, you're the greatest. And I really want to see you, I *need* to see you, but I can't today. I'm sorry I couldn't let you know earlier. I didn't find out until really late last night."

Callie felt her heart sink. She didn't know what she would do with herself if she didn't go to Rainytown. "What's up?"

"You remember my aunt Belle, Ma's older sister? She lives in Phoenix. Well, she didn't think she was going to be able to make the funeral, mostly due to finances and things, but her kids really pulled together for her at the last minute. They bought her a plane ticket and booked her at the Holiday Inn downtown. She's there now, catching up on a little sleep. She got in early this morning. Paulie's gonna pick her up around noon and bring her by. He'll spend the afternoon with us; then Aunt Belle and I are planning some private time tonight. You'll see her tomorrow."

Callie felt ridiculous as the tears streamed down her face. She was happy for Frankie and Paulie but felt so disappointed, so lost and worthless. Intellectually she knew there was no good reason to feel exiled into obsolescence, but her heart was sundering into pitiful little pieces despite all good reasons to stay whole. What a confused, miserable person she was. Ruby was dead, and she, who had been so blessed in her life, was broken because she didn't know how to fill her day; because her plans had changed and her person was not requested at the Cavalese home.

"I'm *so* happy for you," Callie said, simultaneously trying to chase away the self-loathing. "I know how special Belle's always been to you. It'll do you good to have her there with you. And good for her to be with you."

"Mason," Frankie said, feeling Callie's distress. "It's not that I don't need you, it's just that—"

"Oh, don't be silly," Callie interrupted, trying to fool Frankie into thinking she had erroneously assessed her pain. "I totally understand. Just tell your aunt that I look forward to seeing her again, but, of course, I wish it could be under different circumstances."

"Mason—"

"Frankie, you just take care. I'll be fine. I've got tons to keep me busy around the house. As you'll recall, I'm shy one housekeeper for a while."

"Yeah, well you're also shy three people to mess things up, and I know that's hurting you," Frankie said, realizing that Callie was upset. "I'll try to call you later. I don't know if I'll be able to make it through the night, knowin' Ma's gonna be buried tomorrow." Frankie started to cry.

"You've got my cell phone number if you can't find me here," Callie said, her heart breaking for Frankie. "Use it if you need to. I love you. Take care."

"Bye, Mason," Frankie said. "You're the best. I know you're grieving too, just like me. I haven't forgotten that. You call if you need *me*. Friendship goes both ways."

"Okay," Callie told her, knowing that she would never call Frankie at such a time only to ease her own anguish. "You just take care. We'll talk later."

Callie hung up the phone and looked at the giant lump under the sheet that had been two lumps before the phone rang. She grabbed the corner of the sheet and lifted it up. "Okay, outta here you two! There's plenty of room to play without destroying my sheets."

The cats each gave her a brief, defiant glance, then scurried out of the room to see what mischief they could make elsewhere. She finished making the bed, then took off her shoes, got on top of the freshly made bed, and pulled the summer quilt over her shoulders with every intention of sleeping until noon. But Callie was in such a restless and agitated state that she was only able to sleep for another hour, idling away far less time than she had desired. An hour later, without any feline assistance, she was up and ready to face the day for the second time.

Having tended to her outside errands more quickly than anticipated, Callie was back home by noon, where she was now besieged by overwhelming loneliness. Nobody had called. Nobody needed her. She felt dislocated from civilization. For three hours she tried to occupy her time by doing various chores. The only one that halfway interested her was making an inspection of Rosa's old quarters, to see what needed brightening, fixing, or painting for Frankie's arrival. But she couldn't really throw herself into that project because she feared doing so would jinx the arrival of the new resident. Frankie would change her mind and stay in Rainytown. She couldn't say why, but the idea nagged at her. Maybe it was simply because Frankie's moving in seemed too good to be true.

It was another miserable hot and humid day, so Callie nixed the idea of lounging outside by the pool. Besides, she was too restless to do that anyway. She wondered if it was hot in Seattle and if Jackson was sweltering on top of some building. If he was, she hoped that the building had at least acquired a couple of walls and floors by now. It probably wasn't as hot in Seattle as it was in Philadelphia. Maybe she'd call and find out.

She was thrilled to hear Jackson answer his cell phone, but she could barely hear him in his lively surroundings. He explained he was at lunch with his Seattle colleagues, and that as delighted as he was by her call, he couldn't really talk to her, much less hear her very well. That said, the shrill laughter of a nearby female pierced her heart, suggesting to Callie that they were all laughing at her for being so naïve. The clinking of glasses in the background and general sound of joviality isolated her even more. The last words Jackson said to her had something to do with a fading connection. That was all that she heard before the deadly silence. Knowing Jack, she thought, he'd at least call back on another phone and say goodbye properly. But he was too busy with that woman who Callie had already decided was blond, cunning, and out to steal her husband. Indeed, she told herself, their connection *was* fading.

She considered trying to reach her children, but by this point, was in such a state of melancholy that she didn't want Molly or Stephen to pick up on it.

Ten minutes later, the phone rang. Perking up, she knew that Jackson had excused himself from his raucous surroundings and gone somewhere to speak to her privately. She scolded herself for having doubted him.

"No," she told the caller firmly. She didn't need a new roof on her house.

The rest of the day dragged. The mail brought nothing but bills and circulars. She could hear every tick and tock of the proverbial clock. The day stretched before her as if she were walking for miles and miles on a deserted coastal beach: destination unknown. Cobbles and Hungry, who had joined forces to wreak havoc on her morning, were fast asleep somewhere in the great expanse, probably enjoying marvelous mischief in their dreams, while she, wide awake, was being pulverized and beaten by the worst loneliness she had ever known.

By seven thirty, she was needed again. The cats were awake and wanted to be fed. She obliged without hesitation. They never even said thank you. Why the hell did she love them so much?

By nine fifteen, she was in her car, headed off for salvation in the sticky black night. Destination: supposedly unknown.

"I've made the worst mistake coming here," Callie said breathlessly. "I just didn't know what to do. Just pretend you don't see me, and heaven help me, I'll try to pretend I don't see you."

Paulie, who had opened the door to his apartment wearing nothing but a blue towel, reached for Callie's arm, pulled her inside, then shut the door.

"I shouldn't be here," Callie insisted. "It's just that today has been the loneliest day of my life. I thought the alienation would kill me. I had to get out of the house. I couldn't stand it, Paulie. But to intrude on your privacy, the night before you're burying your mother—"

"Would it help if I told you that I'm glad you're here? What if I told you that I was *very* glad you're here?"

Callie looked into his irreverent brown eyes, then down at the towel.

"I can end the mystery right now," Paulie said. "I'd be happy to show you my wares."

"Oh, God," Callie choked. "Paulie, please, don't."

"Certainly you'd like a little peek," Paulie said wickedly.

Callie bit her tongue. She was not going to answer him.

"Don't you at least want to see what was pulsating against your body the other night?"

Callie sighed breathlessly. "I-I don't think that would be…"

Paulie took hold of the towel and threw it across the room, where it landed on the couch. His verbal braggadocio gone, he watched Callie looking longingly at him.

Callie threw her arms around his naked body and began to unravel. "My God, Paulie, you should have thrown me out of here. I'm playing Russian roulette with my marriage, and you're sure as hell not helping matters. I know you won't believe me, but as much as I want you, and God help me I do, I didn't come here for this."

Paulie walked her over to the couch and sat down with her. He hadn't forgotten his sister's warnings, but Frankie's admonishment paled next to what he was feeling.

"Mother Nature was kind to you," Callie said, trying to smile.

"You could be even kinder," Paulie told her.

"If you put your clothes on," Callie said, "I'll kiss you."

"And if you kiss me, I'll just want to take them off again."

"Then I won't kiss you," Callie said. She handed Paulie his slightly damp towel. "Please, I know I'm all screwed up and I know that I'm sending you mixed signals, but please forgive me. I just need a friend."

Paulie took the towel, stood up, and put it around his waist. "You're not sending me mixed signals, babe. You want me as much as I want you. But you have a husband you don't want to cheat on, and as much as I hate that, I have to respect it. I guess it makes you the classy babe I fell for in the first place."

"Thank you," Callie said. "Why are you so nice about this? You must think I'm a terrible...oh, I hate that word."

Paulie thought for a second. "Oh, *that* word. Don't worry. It doesn't apply to you. I understand." He thought for a moment. "I fucking hate it, but I understand. Wait there. I'll be back shortly."

"Really," Callie called after him as he left for the bedroom. "I swear, I just came here because I need a friend!"

He returned only moments later in tight shorts and a black T-shirt. "I need a friend, too, Callie-fornia."

Callie smiled at him. Unfortunately, his "clothing" did nothing to quell her desire for him.

"I've had second thoughts on that kiss I turned down," Paulie said.

Without hesitation, Callie put her mouth to his and they kissed deeply and passionately for several minutes until her cell phone rang. They pulled apart reluctantly.

"It's probably Frankie," Callie said gasping for breath. "I told her to use my cell phone if I wasn't home."

"Just don't let her know you're here," Paulie said with mild alarm.

"Don't worry, I won't," Callie said, as she prepared to answer the call.

"Callie, honey, is everything okay? I'm sorry I didn't get back to you earlier. I was stuck with this swarm of gnats the entire day. The only break I got was to go to the men's room, and even then, Denny Sterling followed me to the urinals to continue our conversation. Didn't even have a moment to myself to think about you and the kids. Oh, and Sterling has this wife with the most ghastly laugh you've ever heard. Elmira Nancy. Ever hear such a name? I don't know why the hell he brought her along. She's got a head of long stringy dyed black hair and a small wart on her nose and a bigger one on her chin. The best thing I can say about her is that she'd make a splendid Halloween decoration. My head is still ringing from the sound of her ear-splitting cackle. So, how are you?"

Callie gulped, then looked reluctantly into Paulie's sad eyes as she spoke to Jackson. "I'm just okay. I'm over at the Cavalese house. Mrs. C.'s funeral is tomorrow."

"Tell your friend Frankie that if I were in town, I would be there with you."

"I know you would, Jack," Callie said sweetly. "Thank you."

"Cal, listen, I know we've got some work to do when I get home, but I need you to remember that I very much want things to work out between us. I should be home in about three or four days. We can talk then. Okay, sweetie? I love you."

"Me too," Callie said. "Bye, Jack."

Callie clicked off and put the phone back in her bag.

Paulie looked at her with deep hurt in his eyes. "I guess that's your signal to leave, isn't it?"

"Only if you want it to be, Paulie. I really want to stay here with you."

"Even after a phone call from your husband to remind you how sinful it is for you to be here with me?"

"Paulie, you're one of the most awe-inspiring men I've ever known, and you do something to me that as a married woman, I should be immune to. But with all that lust aside..." Callie took a deep breath, "which sometimes is easier said than done, I care about you. I want to be your friend. We need to deal with our attraction to each other so we can *be* friends. Of course, maybe you're not interested in that, I don't know. But to answer your question, no, I do not want to leave because my husband called. We've both admitted we needed a friend tonight. How 'bout it?"

"Why'd you offer me that kiss?"

Callie looked at him wistfully. "I wanted to feel those luscious lips just one more time. I wanted one more memory for my old age. I could make something up, but that's the truth. I'm sorry. I know I'm a mess."

Paulie straightened in his seat and resumed his manly posturing. "Babe, don't apologize. I had the wherewithal to refuse it. And if you run out of memories, we can always make more."

Callie smiled tenderly at him. "Tell me about your aunt Belle," she said. "How is she doing?"

"Devastated," Paulie said. "Ma was everything to her. Belle did nothing but cry from the moment I picked her up at the airport until the moment I dropped her off a while ago. Mary Frances and I both spent the afternoon with her at the house, then had an early dinner, which Belle barely touched. The two of them were planning to spend the evening alone together, but Belle was so worn out from crying that I suggested taking her back to the hotel when I left. Thank God she agreed to go, Callie-fornia. I didn't know what to do. My sister is so shaken from Ma's death, in ways you can't imagine, and Belle, sweet as she is, was making Mary Frances crazy. Hell, she was making *me* crazy. Going around the house, touching everything, remembering every story behind every object, especially that weird lamp she gave Ma and Pop for a wedding gift. That thing made her crazy with emotion. And it was so hot in there. So dark. So humid. And so damn empty without Ma. And then she wanted to see all the photograph albums and she fucking blubbered over them, turning each page, then turning back again. 'Oh, no, I have to see that picture one more time. Wasn't your mother the most gorgeous woman? Oh, Ruby…my baby sister…' It was tough, Callie-fornia. We're grieving for our own loss, and Belle just needed more consoling than we could handle. I feel guilty saying all this, but she wore us down big time."

"But you got through it," Callie confirmed. "You gave her what she needed."

"Somehow we managed," Paulie said. "A team effort. I guess I've come a long way. Thanks to you. And Mary Frances, of course."

Callie smiled. "And your mother. Don't forget her."

Paulie managed to almost smile. "Belle's leaving tomorrow. After the service and reception, I'll take her straight to the airport. I need to do right by her while she's here. So, enough on all that. How 'bout some blues?" Paulie asked, walking over to his CD collection. "Will you stay a bit longer and keep me company?"

"I kind of like being your friend. Sure, I'd love to stay."

CHAPTER 22

Late Wednesday morning, the limousine arrived at the Cavalese home, taking Frankie, Paulie, Callie, and Belle to Ruby's church. Louie was waiting for them when they arrived, dressed in grief from head to toe. All the years he had spent lying to himself, pretending not to care about the woman he'd left behind, had come back to riddle him with guilt and sorrow so intense it nearly incapacitated him. It was a noticeable strain for him to even rise from the bench outside the church when his family arrived.

Paulie held his father up by the left elbow as Louie looked at Callie for the first time in almost thirty years. "My son told me you were something to see," he said. "And he was right." Louie's eyes began to water as he struggled for self-control. "Paulie was right about more than that," he added.

Paulie looked at Callie, sending her a look that said "thank you," as he knew that without her intervention, he probably would not have approached his father at all regarding Ruby, much less persevered the way he did.

"It's good to see you again, Mr. C.," Callie said sweetly. "I just wish it was for a happier reason. I see you haven't lost your good looks."

"Ah, forget about me," he said morosely. "I'm a haggard old man. Look at this fine stallion of a son I produced. Now, here are some good looks."

Callie took a deep breath as she caught Paulie making a feeble attempt at a wink. Frankie, who caught the entire interchange, shook her head hopelessly as her weeping aunt clung uncomfortably to her right arm. Frankie was convinced she would collapse beneath the weight of her grief and her aunt's neediness, but she was determined not to cry in public. To Frankie, that was akin to being naked. Tears were private. At least for her. She caught hold of a floating curiosity about Regina and wondered if she had gone through with her threat to crash the funeral, but Frankie shrugged off her concern as they all walked into the church together and took their seats in the front pew.

The service was beautiful, though at first, Frankie only heard every three words that were said. She couldn't help but stare at the casket before her, upon which rested a beautiful photo of Ruby that Belle had brought from Arizona—and a red rose. Callie had filled the church with more flowers than Frankie had ever dreamed of; she hoped that Ruby could see them. It was all so beautiful.

Don't be scared, Ma, Frankie told her, trying to take her own advice. She felt her strength waning as she listened to the wails emanating from some of Ruby's co-workers in the back pews. Their plaintive cries made her want to jump out of her skin, especially the copious sobs of Ruby's close friend Evelyn. Why can't they control themselves better, she thought angrily. I can't take it. She wasn't their mother. If I'm not crying, they shouldn't be either.

As Louie tried to pacify Belle, who was forthwith approaching delirium, Paulie reached for the hands of his two favorite women on either side of him. His touch comforted them both. Frankie took a deep breath and sat back. She was now able to concentrate better on the eulogy.

Callie, reliving her aunt's death all over again, found the service even harder to bear than she had anticipated. Paulie's hand in hers gave her strength, just as Jackson's hand had given her strength at Emily's funeral, only she felt an odd, disturbing sensation, as if Paulie had just slipped into Jackson's shoes, like one actor replacing another in a play, and that was all there was to it.

Like his father, Paulie alternated between grief and guilt, involuntarily imagining how much worse it all could have been had Callie not come back into their lives when she did. He had been given a quick lesson in growing up, and as inchoate as his newfound maturity might be, he was grateful for it. He imagined what his mother would want to say to him at that moment. She would tell him to forgive himself, then insist that he pay attention to all of the lovely things being said about her.

Louie, on the other hand, heard nothing but his own voice cursing in his head, calling himself every amoral name he could conjure into his consciousness. For him, there was no reprieve. He had sullied his own good name and hurt the people he loved most in the world. He was a first-class reprobate and Annie was his punishment. He deserved a hundred of her to reprove himself for what he had done to his family, despite the fact that one of her did the job just fine.

When the time came for the pallbearers to carry out the casket, Louie rose from the front pew only to nearly collapse back into it. Paulie caught him just in time, then asked his father if he'd prefer that someone else take his place. Horrified by the mere suggestion, Louie galvanized himself and walked staunchly to take his rightful place. Mike and Ernie, Ruby's boss, Ed, and another male co-worker, Trevor, joined them up front.

Seeing the long, oppressive faces of Paulie and Louie made both Callie and Frankie want to wail like the others. Frankie felt as if there was a knife stuck in her heart that nobody could ever remove.

Callie, as she watched the same agonizing scene, remembered the blues she'd heard at Paulie's apartment the night Ruby died. In her mind, she could hear the music so clearly again; she could see the pained march of the funeral procession as she'd imagined it that first night. But it was nothing like what was taking place before her. These were not strangers in some sad scenario of her own creation. These were people she cared about: dead and alive.

She wanted desperately to somehow extricate Paulie from the picture, to go home with him, and to make love to him until she could make the pain go away, unaware that she hadn't clarified whose pain it was that she wanted to assuage. She did realize, however, that even a "babe" like her did not have the capability to allay such powerful grief from a man who had just lost his beloved mother. And somewhere in her mind amid all of her confusion, she could see Jackson. He was off in the distance, but nonetheless, she could see him brimming with love for her, smiling and waving as he began walking toward the woman whom he had so loved and trusted throughout his entire adult life. She could picture his electric blue eyes, excited to see her again, as he brushed his trademark wisp of blond hair from his eyes. Oh, Jack, Callie moaned silently, this too shall pass. And then she prayed that it would, as she stood, preparing to follow Frankie down the aisle of God's house and into the bright sunshine.

Once out at the burial grounds, about a half hour later, Frankie could feel the eyes watching her every reaction as Ruby was lowered into the ground. She knew they were waiting for her to crack. They wanted to see her snap in half as she fell to the ground screaming for her mother. She could see the malignant anticipation in their eyes. It was so much stronger than their bogus grief. No matter what, she would never allow them the satisfaction of seeing her crumble. Paulie, though not as focused on the sea of fervent, waiting eyes, was as determined as his sister was not to allow any lapse of strength to become public. Louie, who couldn't have cared less what anyone saw or thought, wept as the weeping Belle cleaved to him.

Once the brief service was complete, the family and Callie were first to throw flowers on Ruby's casket as they said their strained and impossible goodbyes to her, then hurried back to the limousine for a brief respite from the invasive stares and the heart-wrenching pain.

Frankie dreaded what came next. The limousine would now take them to the reception. She did not want to see or talk to people. She did not want to answer their questions or accept their condolences. She could not bear to think of the gossip that her father's presence and obvious melancholy would set into motion and she despised herself for letting it rankle her at all.

She could not get it out of her mind that Ruby had not given birth to her but she was not ready to discuss it with her father. That was a separate issue for another time. But it wasn't Louie she dreaded; it was the prying neighbors she hated. And although she genuinely liked most of Ruby's co-workers, she did not want to talk with them or to be asked when she was returning to the courtesy desk. She wasn't. And she sure as hell wasn't going to explain why.

She wanted to scream things to make everyone shriek in horror. She wanted them to shrivel and die, blaspheming their fates as they shrank down to become one with the earth, just as the Wicked Witch of the West had been melted by water into vacuity. All except the cherished few that she loved. They could live.

When the limousine arrived at the restaurant where Callie had

booked a private room for the reception, Frankie steeled herself with the
knowledge that this was the last stop on the day's gruesome journey.
Inside, the reception line was a nightmare for everyone. For Callie, it was
the first time she had to deal with the neighbors. No one, except Millie
Tyson, the block's oldest and kindest resident, had anything at all to say
about Ruby or Emily. The lack of appropriate comportment from the rest
of them appalled and sickened her. They were vastly more interested in
mining for details about her privileged life. What did her husband do?
How did they meet? What kind of home did she live in? How *many* homes
did she have? How many children did she have? Did she own a boat? Were
her towels monogrammed? Had she ever met the president?

Oh, but the apparent dearth of remorse came gushing out of the
same unfeeling parties as they approached Paulie, carrying their lame
collective hope that he would accept their disingenuous condolences while
they lapped up the golden opportunity for the hands-on consolation they
presupposed Ruby's death had provided for them. He fended them off like
a pro, standing rigidly as if he were unable to hug or touch anyone.
Crushed and disappointed, they headed off to the banquet tables to see
what kind of food was being offered, plotting their postsustenance second
tries.

Standing in the crowded room, the first thing Frankie heard was
hearty female laughter, which she recognized as Arlene Humphries. She
couldn't begin to imagine what would justify such an outburst of hilarity.
Frankie felt compelled to approach her, but her attention was diverted
when she happened to glance over at the banquet table. There, she saw
Edna and Stella lowering their pocketbooks under the table, attempting to
nonchalantly brush some of the more expensive hors d'oeuvres into plastic
bags they'd obviously had the foresight to bring for the occasion. She was
so bitter and resentful that she wanted to embarrass them publicly.
Normally, she wouldn't have had any qualms about doing such a thing, but
being on the precipice of complete malfunction, she reluctantly opted to
keep quiet. It would all be over soon. She would be moving out of
Rainytown, and she would never have to see these women again. Let them
stuff their face with death food, Frankie thought. Ma's watching this, I
know she is. I'd love to hear what she's saying. Oh, wouldn't Ma and I get

some mileage out of this. Oh…Ma…

A few yards away, she saw Paulie talking to Ernie and shaking his head in disgust. In theory, she didn't want to care, but she had to know. She walked over to the duo and insisted on hearing what Ernie had to say. Regina and Hal had apparently arrived at the church very early, hoping to slip in unnoticed, but Mike and Ernie had immediately asked them to leave. Regina answered their request with a shocking barrage of expletives, which ceased only at the sight of rapidly approaching clergy. Ashamed and embarrassed, Ernie reported that she quickly left with her husband, whom Mike had commented, appeared more pregnant than his wife did. The satisfaction that Frankie felt from hearing the story helped to abate her anger over the food-pilfering neighbors and the inappropriate laughter of another.

After a half hour, Frankie insisted on leaving. She was fading into nothingness. The world was gray and empty without any Ruby red in it.

Once they arrived back home, Frankie bid farewell to her aunt, then asked the others that she be left alone until tomorrow. Louie begged her to let him stay, but Frankie kindly dismissed him, fearful of what confessions her father might feel compelled to make in his volcanic-like state. Frankie hugged and kissed everyone good-bye, watching and wondering as Callie got into Paulie's car to accompany him and Belle to the airport.

Belle's flight had been delayed for three hours, a terrible postscript to a terrible day. Near virtual collapse, Paulie and Callie promised to stay with her until the flight was confirmed and ready to take off. In the meantime, Paulie bought dinner for the three of them at the airport restaurant, then waited until it was an absolute surety that the aircraft was primed and ready to take his frazzled and distraught aunt back to Arizona. At nine o'clock, the boarding call was finally announced. After another round of hugs and sobs, in the midst of a cluster of angry, exhausted passengers, Paulie and Callie said their final goodbyes to Belle. Emotionally and physically drained, Belle's send-off finally liberated them. Together, they practically flew through the airport to get to the parking garage.

"Whew," Paulie said as he started the engine, "this has been the longest day of my life, and those were the longest three hours of my life. How can anyone cry so continuously like that? Doesn't the human body run out of tears or something?"

"Apparently not," Callie said, fastening her seat belt.

"I just hope for Aunt Belle's sake, and the sake of the person sitting next to her, that she sleeps all the way home."

"I think she will," Callie assured him. "After the day she's had, she was so nervous that her flight home might end up being canceled that she just wound herself up into a ball of hysteria. You were very sweet with her, Paulie. And patient."

Paulie looked embarrassed. "Whatever," he mumbled, then suddenly put the car back into park and turned off the engine. "Listen Callie-fornia, before I pull out of this garage, where exactly are we going?"

"I don't know," Callie told him. "I hadn't thought that far ahead."

"Sure you have," Paulie told her.

Callie looked down at her lap and didn't answer him.

"We both want to go back to my place and make mad, passionate love," Paulie said, lifting her chin and forcing her to look into his eyes. "Don't we?"

Callie remained silent.

"Of course we do. Only we both know that would be a mistake…not that I mind making an occasional mistake."

"But I would mind," Callie said softly. "It would haunt me forever. I'm already feeling—"

"Fine," Paulie said, making an idle clicking sound with his tongue. "Just tell me that it's what you wanted to do; I'll live with that."

"I wanted to," Callie said softly. "I *want* to. But I can't."

"Yeah, and I've grown this damn conscience that won't let me seduce you into it. I'm not so sure I like this new me."

"You'll get used to yourself," Callie said, then laughed. "Besides, Paulie, you haven't exactly embraced monastic life. You're still your wicked self."

"Thank God," Paulie said, feigning great relief. "I was worried. So, where do you want to go? Should I take you back to your car, or do you want to go somewhere and have a drink?"

Callie thought for a minute. "You know where I'd love to go?" she said brightly. "The Blue Lights. Please, Paulie, I'd love to see the club."

"Might as well," Paulie said, turning the key in the ignition again. "I need to check on Pop anyway. He didn't look so good. Hell, I'm not so good myself. God, I miss Ma…"

The club was packed, but Paulie bribed "Cheap Butch" Hanley with a couple of free beers to vacate his bar stool so that Callie could sit in Paulie's usual seat at the front end of the bar.

Marv Jackson's jazz quartet had invigorated the crowd, and Paulie was pleased by the crowd's finger-snapping, toe-tapping, thigh-slapping, drink-lapping response to the music. It had been a while since the group played together. Marv usually played alone, but once or twice a month the quartet got together, and when they did, it was always an event. Sometimes Paulie even played tenor sax with them. But it had been a while since he'd performed, and he felt uneasy about that. He was frightened that his talent would be gone when he tried to play again and despised that insecurity in himself.

But he liked the fact that Callie was seeing the Blue Lights so alive. He liked seeing the light in her eyes and wished she were really his woman. He liked the fact that for one night, most of the regulars would think that she was, but in a way, that just made him feel even sadder.

Paulie introduced Callie to Veronica.

"Hi there," Veronica said. "I saw you at the service today, but we didn't get a chance to meet. I wasn't able to make it to the reception. This funky place was calling; you know how it is. Work, work, and more work!"

Callie smiled. She didn't know how it was. She had no life. "Very nice to meet you, Veronica."

"I'm just glad you were there, Ronnie," Paulie said. "It meant a lot to me, and to Pop and Mary Frances."

"Anything for you, baby. I haven't really had the chance to tell you how very sorry I am. I only met your Ma those few times at the house, but she was so vibrant and so real. And so darn funny. We really hit it off. I'm sorry, baby. I know how much you loved her."

"Thank you," Paulie said. "It's just real hard to believe she's gone. But Ma's at peace now. That's what's important."

"Don't look like your old man's at peace," Veronica said worriedly.

"Where is he, anyway?" Paulie asked, looking around.

"Over there," Veronica said, nodding in Louie's direction. "Sitting at that table in the corner by himself. People keep comin' over to him but he ain't in a talkin' mood. Especially for you-know-who. And the bitch is seething about it. Lots of folks been asking for you, handsome. You up for it?"

Callie could feel the closeness between Veronica and Paulie. She felt envious of their friendship. Whatever they had, it was strong, solid, and lasting.

It didn't take long for the news of Paulie's return to get around. He could see the regulars making moves to come extend their sympathies to him.

"Listen, babe," he said to Callie. "Let me go make the rounds. Tired as I am, the last thing I need is to listen to all these people telling me how sorry they are, but they need to do it, and I need to get it over with. And I've got to check on Pop. Will you be okay here with Veronica?"

"I'm a big girl," Callie said. "I'll be just fine."

Paulie gave Veronica a look. "Don't worry," she responded. "I'll take care of Callie for you. I won't let Russ Tompkins or any of these fools anywhere near her."

Satisfied, Paulie winked at both women and took off.

"So, you look like a wine girl to me," Veronica told Callie. "Am I right? Care for some vino?"

"Another night," Callie said, "you'd be right on target. But tonight, I'm a scotch woman. Johnnie Black, Grouse…whatever twelve year-old you have."

"Got 'em both," Veronica said. "Pinch and a bunch of others, too. Want me to read 'em off?"

"No, thanks, Veronica. That won't be necessary. Johnnie Walker will be just fine," Callie said, thinking of Frankie's lost love, Johnny. "On the rocks, please."

"Coming up," Veronica said with a smile. "Hold on, Clem," she yelled to someone at the end of the bar. I'm good, baby, but I ain't no octopus. Keep your britches on." A few chuckles flowed through the bar crowd. Everyone loved it when Veronica put a smart ass in his place. "I'll be right back with your scotch on the rocks, Callie."

On the rocks, Callie thought. Just like my marriage. My life. God, I'm a mess. An unemployed, useless mess.

Callie looked around the club and tried to guess the different jobs that the patrons might have as she simultaneously castigated herself for having no life. True to her nature, she blotted out her impressive résumé of charitable work and ignored all that she'd done to raise two wonderful children. Now, she theorized, her happiness had always been dependent on other people: Jack, her kids, Emily, her friends. When the people she loved went away, either permanently or temporarily, she felt discarded and empty. If there was no one to need her, she might as well not exist. She didn't know how to like herself unless she was helping someone, and she didn't always know how to help herself.

She continued to look around the room, until she noticed a preponderant number of men returning her glance. She swiveled back into place, facing the bar, and waited for the drink that Veronica put in front of her only seconds later.

"Thank you, Veronica," Callie said graciously.

"Need anything else?"

"Actually, a glass of water on the side would be good. I'm rather thirsty."

"Coming up," Veronica said, grabbing a glass and scooping ice into it.

"Hey, Ronnie," Clem Hawkins yelled from the other end. "I need a clean ashtray."

"Stop smoking!" Veronica suggested loudly. "It won't get dirty so fast."

The bar crowd within earshot laughed.

"Need a Heinie over here," a man's voice demanded.

"Well, you ain't getting' no Heinie over there until this heinie's finished over here," Veronica shot back. The crowd roared. Even Callie had to laugh. She admired Veronica. She could really hold her own; no wonder she and Paulie were such good friends. No wonder he had such immense respect for her.

Veronica placed Callie's water on a cocktail napkin, then headed off to the far end of the bar to do battle with the regulars. Following Veronica with her eyes, it was then that Callie noticed Annie Cavalese. The man who had been fawning over her had left, and the once-obstructed view was now clear. Callie felt a wintry chill crawl up her spine. She knew immediately that the woman eyeing Veronica so contemptuously was the same woman who'd played such an integral part in the break-up of the Cavalese family. But there was more: something odd, something malevolent, something corrupt and cunning; something frighteningly familiar. She had no idea what it could be. Suddenly, Callie gasped as if she had been spooked: Annie Cavalese had noticed *her*. Callie could feel the penetrating chill of her icy light blue eyes. Evil, she thought. She's pure evil. Callie turned to face forward, but her peripheral view could not deny the fact that Annie was still fixated on her.

"Are you okay, Callie-fornia?"

Startled, Callie almost fell off the barstool.

"Hey, babe, calm down. What's got you so rattled? You look like you've seen a ghost."

"That woman, your father's wife. She's evil, and she's staring at me."

Paulie glanced in Annie's direction. He shot her a dirty look, but Annie didn't notice him. She was still staring at Callie.

"Damn, babe, she sure is staring. That bitch is always in my business and she's trying to figure out who you are."

"She's got creepy eyes," Callie said, almost childlike. "She scares me."

"You ain't lyin', honey," Veronica said soothingly, appearing in front of her. "Beautiful but creepy. That's Annie. Don't let her get to you. You're a real knockout. She's never seen you in here before and wants to know who you are. She doesn't like beautiful women; they threaten the crap out of her. Hell, she doesn't like women period. She'll get over it. Ignore her ass."

"Ronnie's right," Paulie said, taking a seat next to Callie that had just been vacated. "Just ignore her."

"How's your father?" Callie asked, trying to shake the steely eyes that were still condemning her from afar.

"He's been better," Paulie told her, disturbed by Annie's almost-catatonic fixation with Callie.

"You can ask him yourself," Veronica said. "Here he comes."

Paulie and Callie turned to see Louie rushing toward them as if the place was on fire. The sense of urgency on his face had momentarily replaced the grief. As he approached the bar, he nodded hello to Callie and pulled Paulie away.

"What's up, Pop?" Paulie said. "What the hell are you doing?"

"I gotta talk to you, Paulie. Right now! Come over here with me."

Paulie started to say something to Callie.

"NOW!" Louie demanded. "Now, Paulie!"

Something was eerily wrong; Paulie could feel it as well.

Louie led Paulie over to a corner table, far from the music, the only table in the place that wasn't vacated. "Sit down," he said forcefully.

"What the...?" Paulie said, obeying his orders.

Louie furiously grabbed a chair and sat down. "Son, didn't I tell you recently never to bring Callie Mason in here?"

"Yeah, but...so what?" Paulie said confusedly.

"I guess I should've been more clear. You obviously didn't think it was a warning worth heeding."

"I remember, Pop, but I thought it was just because you were worried that some of the old geezers, you know, like Clem, Russ, and Moscatelli, might try and hit on her."

"I don't give a goddamn about them, Paulie. Fuck them!"

"What then?" Paulie said. "What the hell—"

"Get Callie Mason out of here this minute! Or you'll be sorry!"

"Why, Pop? What the hell is going on here?" Paulie said irately.

"Listen, son. You get her out of here before Annie figures out who the hell she is. Because if that happens, then you'll all be sorry. Deadly sorry. Especially that lovely Callie."

"I'm sorry, Pop. But I'm not getting this," Paulie said emphatically. "What the fuck is going on here?"

"I'll make it real goddamn clear for you," Louie said passionately. "Annie, that miserable wife of mine, is also Anisa Phillips Mason. Callie's mother. Think you got it now?"

Paulie blanched as his mouth fell open.

"When I spoke to your Ma before she died," Louie said, "she referred to Annie as Annie Colton. I thought, 'Colton, where'd Ruby come up with that name?' I figured she was just confused, bein' that she was dyin' and all. But later I remembered. Your Ma was right about the name. She remembered exactly what she'd been told. I didn't, 'cause it was just a made-up name. I couldn't tell none of you that her name was Phillips or Mason, and because Anisa was such an unusual name, I just started calling her Annie, so no one would be the wiser."

"Pop, I don't understand any of this," Paulie said. "You're not making any sense. This just isn't coming together for me."

"Listen, son. I'll tell you quickly. Annie, *Anisa,* left the drunk hospital against doctor's orders, back when you were just a boy. After wandering for God knows how long, she finally came to Rainytown, lookin' to get Callie back. Hell, she didn't even really care about the kid; she just wanted to take something from Emily; she needed a fight, something to get her blood flowing. My guess is that she was too scared to confront Emily or Callie. Wouldn't have known what the hell to do with Callie had she gotten her anyway. So she lurked around the neighborhood, tryin' to figure out what to do. She was often there in the early morning when Callie and Frankie were just heading off to school. I used to see her around on my way to work, and for a while, I just assumed she lived on the next block. She was one beautiful woman back then, Paulie, but she didn't have your Ma's class. And good-for-nothing idiot that I was, I let her lure me into her web."

"How the hell could you do that, Pop? Let someone like her take you from Ma, and from Mary Frances and me? Damn you!"

"Because with Annie, your stupid, insecure Pop didn't feel like he had to be someone special. He didn't have to worry about doing right by a deserving and wonderful woman like your Ma. Bloody coward I was. Bloody unforgivable jackass. So I took up with Annie, tangled myself up in her walk and her talk, in the wild sex we were having, and just became downright obsessed with her. I swear, Paulie, I thought the affair would eventually end, part of me even prayed that it would, but when Annie gave me an ultimatum…her way or the highway…God, I'm an unworthy bastard, I agreed to leave my family. At least *I* had regrets, not that *you'd* know it or it means a rat's ass to you that I did, but Annie, she forgot all about her kid. In fact, it wasn't until right before I left your mother that Annie told me that Emily Phillips' niece was her daughter, Callie. Real casual like, as if she were talking about the weather or something."

"And that didn't bother you?" Paulie asked angrily. "The fact that she was the type of woman who could just throw her child away like that? Deny Callie's existence just to satisfy her pussy?"

Louie laughed disgustedly. "Hell, son, I was throwin' my family away to satisfy *my* johnson…breaking *my* vows and promises to your mother. Who was I to judge her?"

"Oh shit, Pop. I can't believe this. Goddamn you."

Louie stood up and Paulie followed his lead. "Goddamn me all you'd like…later. Right now, just get Callie the hell out of here, NOW! If Annie recognizes Callie, that lovely lady won't ever have peace again."

"I hear you, Pop," Paulie said, still reeling from the shock as he and his father advanced quickly toward the bar. "We're out of here."

"Come on, babe," Paulie said grabbing Callie by the arm. "We've got to go!"

Callie didn't protest or ask any questions. She just knew it had something to do with the sinister woman at the end of the bar. She held onto Paulie and didn't look back.

CHAPTER 23

There was silence on the drive back to Rainytown. Paulie was still adjusting to the shock, and Callie was too afraid to question what had just happened. But when Paulie pulled into the parking space behind her car, she managed to call up her courage and ask him.

"Paulie…"

"Yeah, babe," Paulie said as if he were far away. "What is it?"

"That woman, your father's wife…there was something so awful about her…something that made my flesh crawl. I didn't like being in the same place as she was, but your father liked it even less. He wanted us to leave because of her. I know it. But why?"

Paulie knew she deserved the truth, but he decided it would be better coming from his sister than him. "Because she's a miserable, nasty drunk. And you are way too beautiful to sit at *her* bar. Just like Ronnie said. And Pop, well, he was really afraid she was going to make a scene, you know, because of the way she was staring at you and all."

"He could see that from where he was sitting?" Callie inquired.

"Trust me, Callie-fornia, he watches that bitch like a hawk. He knew she was gearing up to attack."

"Not to take what you've said lightly, but there must be more to this. I can feel it, Paulie."

"I'll wait until you get your car started, babe." Paulie kissed her gently on the cheek. "Thank you for everything you've done for us. I'm sure Mary Frances will want to see you in the morning. It's been a long day. Take care, okay?"

"Paulie…"

"I've got to go inside and take care of something. I'm sure I'll see you tomorrow, too."

Something had obviously and profoundly unsettled Paulie, and Callie knew it was useless to pursue the matter, at least for the time being. "Okay, Paulie, you take care, too. I'm so sorry about your mother. I hope you know I loved her, too."

"I know you did. I'm sure your aunt is taking good care of her now. Showing her the ropes up there. You know."

Callie's eyes began to get misty. "I'm sure. That would be Aunt Emily. Goodnight, Paulie."

Paulie sat in his car until Callie had started her car and pulled away. He remembered his sister's admonishment to give her space for the evening, but he hoped she wouldn't mind his emergency intrusion.

He found Frankie sitting on the couch. Her eyes were red from crying, and she was clutching her mother's afghan. "Oh, Paulie, I'm so glad to see you. I wanted to call you and tell you I'd changed my mind, that I wanted you to come by, but I didn't know what you were doing and—"

"You were afraid I was up to no good with Callie."

"I guess I was," Frankie said. "Can you blame me?"

"We were together, Mary Frances, but not in the way you were worried we'd be." Paulie explained the airport ordeal to her and how they'd ended up at the club when it was all over.

"You're a really good guy," Frankie said. "I don't know what I would've done if it had been me taking Aunt Belle to meet her plane. I never would've held up. Never."

"It was nothing, Mary Frances. What you did for Ma all this time: that was something special—something worth talking about."

"I keep waiting to hear Ma's bell ringing," Frankie said as tears rolled down her cheeks. "But it's so quiet in here...no screams from the television. Nothing. Every night at nine o'clock, Aunt Belle used to call Ma, and they'd talk for five or ten minutes, if Ma had the strength. Aunt Belle would call right at six o'clock her time. And when they hung up, Ma'd drift off to sleep, feeling more content. They were really close."

"I know," Paulie said wearily as he took a seat in the armchair. "Belle told me. I've lost count how many times she told me."

"Tell me she isn't really gone, Paulie."

"I wish I could, Mary Frances. You know I do."

"I miss her so much."

"Me, too," Paulie said. "Me, too."

Frankie suddenly remembered Paulie had mentioned being at the Blue Lights with Callie. "You didn't stay at the club very long, did you? Too exhausted?"

"I've never been more exhausted in my life," Paulie said. "But that wasn't the reason. It had to do with Annie."

"What the hell did that bitch do now?" Frankie said, getting her ire up.

"Mary Frances, I want you to listen to me. I found out something tonight. It doesn't concern us directly, not at the moment anyway; right now it concerns Callie, and it's as big as the secret Ma told you. I don't know what to do with it. I don't even know if I should tell you, today of all days, but one of us has to tell Callie. It wouldn't be right to keep it from her."

"One of us has to tell *Callie*? Well, damn, Paulie, you can't dangle *that* bone in front of me and expect me to wait until I feel better to deal with it. What the hell is going on?"

"I think maybe tomorrow would be a better time to talk about it. I'm really wiped."

"Well, you should have thought of that before you brought it up to me. So spill, Paulie."

"Okay, but first I pour," Paulie said as he got up and walked over to the liquor cabinet. He grabbed a rock glass, helped himself to a generous shot of Irish whiskey, then sat down again. Frankie stared at him with intense anticipation. She noticed that she hadn't seen him smoke since Ruby's death, but she didn't want to mention it. If Paulie had found the strength to quit, congratulating him on doing so, or on trying to do so, might only serve to whet his appetite for a cigarette. She could see him fidgeting with the arm of the chair; she knew she was right. It was difficult, but he was doing it.

After several minutes of silence, Paulie began to retell the evening's events. He described the way Annie had transfixed her glance on Callie, how spooked Callie had been, and how even he, who thought he'd seen every incarnation of the witch's contemptible face, had been startled by the intensity of Annie's venomous, unbroken gaze.

Frankie could feel the goose bumps on her arm and the hair tingle on the back of her neck as Paulie spoke. She knew something wicked was coming.

Paulie took a large swig of whiskey, then paused for strength. He then continued, telling Frankie how their father had come storming toward the bar demanding that Paulie follow him to the quietest corner of the room.

Frankie reached out her arm for Paulie's glass. He handed it to her and waited until she took a swig for herself, then began speaking again. He told her how insistent Louie had been that he take Callie out of the club immediately, then warned him that they'd all be sorry if Annie recognized her, and on and on.

Frankie took another swig of her brother's drink, then passed it back to him. She had no idea where Paulie was going with this, just as the same story had baffled Paulie only a half hour ago.

When Paulie finally repeated his father's words, "Annie, that miserable wife of mine, is also Anisa Phillips Mason. Callie's mother," Frankie gasped and covered her mouth with her hand, as if someone was coming toward her brandishing a deadly scythe. She was too horrified and frightened to speak.

Paulie plodded along. He explained how their father's insecurities had led at first to a sexual dalliance with Anisa and then flowered into a full-fledged obsession that resulted in the break-up of their family.

"I can't believe that bitch is Callie's mother," Frankie said. "But now that I think about it, they do resemble one another quite a lot. I might have noticed it, but I only see pure evil when I look at Annie, and I see only beauty when I look at Callie."

"I feel the same way," Paulie said.

"You," Frankie said adamantly, "see *too much* beauty when you look at Callie."

Paulie wanted to laugh, but he couldn't.

"I don't understand," Frankie said. "How did they meet one another?"

"Oh, this is rich," Paulie said. "Step Ma-Ma split from the alcohol recovery program she was in and eventually slithered into Rainytown to put dibs on Callie-fornia. She didn't have the courage to knock on Emily's door, so she lurked in the shadows until she found something a lot more interesting than her daughter: our pop."

"After all these years, I still don't understand how he could have gone for someone like her."

"It's like Ma explained the last time we spoke. It's all making sense now. The night Pop came to say good-bye, he told Ma that way back when, he couldn't deal with the pedestal he thought she'd put him on. He told Ma he'd been so afraid of falling that he jumped. The pressure of not wanting to disappoint her and of meeting his promises was too much for him. That's probably why they argued so much in the later years. Ma's love and expectations for the future made him feel worthless. It was easier to leave her, to fight with her, than to disappoint her the other way. You know, reject someone before they can reject you. People do it all the time."

"God, what a waste! What a damn, stupid waste!" Frankie said angrily. "The only good thing that came out of this was that Callie never had to deal with that monster for her mother, and that I had her for a best friend all my growing up years."

"That is a good thing," Paulie said. "Mary Frances…do you think I'm like Pop was?"

"Of course not," Frankie consoled him.

Paulie thought for a moment. "Oh, come on, think about it. You know I am. Look at my track record! Until Callie-fornia showed up, I couldn't even *think* of being with a classy woman like her. I was a master at dealing with tramps and worthless bitches that had little to offer me. I didn't have to worry about being a stand-up guy or doing anything to make myself or anyone else proud of me. Not until Callie-fornia—"

"Trying to seduce another man's wife isn't exactly being a 'stand-up guy,' " Frankie pointed out. "But I get your drift."

"Touché," Paulie said. "You see, I'm rotten all the way through."

"Oh be quiet," Frankie insisted. "You are not. At least I don't think…"

"We didn't sleep together, Mary Frances, okay?"

"All right, then I guess I can continue defending you." She paused. "But I know you did some shit with her," she mumbled under her breath.

Paulie shot her a look, polished off his drink, then got up to refill his glass.

"Well, Paulie, whatever regrets you have now are just that. Regrets.

Time to move on. You haven't always done your best…far from it," Frankie said, turning to face him as he walked back from the liquor cabinet, "but at least your mistakes never involved deserting a wife and kids or destroying lives. And miracle of miracles, you never even got one of those broads pregnant."

"Oh, I made sure of that," Paulie said. "Real sure."

"I guess you're right," Frankie said. "Maybe the apple didn't fall all that far from the tree, but you're a better man now than Pop was back then. Maybe because you had a loving Ma to raise you and Pop didn't. That can make a lot of difference."

"You're right, Mary Frances. I think it did. I hope Ma heard what you just said. It would make her really happy."

Frankie managed a smile.

"Look, I've got to get some sleep," he said, then drank the small shot he'd just poured. "A hot shower and a soft bed. That's what I need."

"I guess we're making progress," Frankie said. At least you said *hot* shower."

Paulie started to respond to the comment but proffered a dirty look instead. "So, what do we do about Callie?"

"She has to be told," Frankie said. "It's not pleasant news, it downright sucks, but we have no right to keep it from her."

"I thought you should tell her, not me," Paulie said.

"Yeah, it should definitely be me. I'll call her over here in the late morning."

"Are you sure you're up to it, Mary Frances? It *can* wait a few days."

"No," Frankie said adamantly. "The longer secrets stay secret, the harder they hurt. I'll tell her tomorrow."

"Hi, Mom, it's Molly. No, I'm not lost in the mountains; there's just been a lot of excitement around here. One of our guests, Mrs. Cady, had a heart attack right here in the lobby, and Steve gave her CPR and it saved her life. Is that unreal or what? Two television stations came to interview him, and he was written up in two papers. One's called *The Daily Moose.* Is that a riot or what? Don't worry, I've saved copies for you. Don't be angry that I didn't call sooner. This only happened two days ago, and it's been a madhouse here. I wanted to wait until I had a sec to really talk, you know. Sorry you're not there. I wanted to personally give you the good news that your son is a hero. He must take after you, Mom. You're always helping someone. I'll bet you've saved a life or two just by doing what you do for people in the hospitals. I don't think I ever told you how proud I am of you. You've told me a million times how proud you are of me; I'm sorry I haven't returned the compliment sooner. Well, I'm getting like really super gushy here, so I'd better stop. Oh, and I'll just die if you save this message or play it for anyone. Don't even tell Dad about it. Promise you won't, okay? Steve sends his love and says he will call you soon — when his fifteen minutes of fame are up. He's kidding, of course, but I'm sure he'll have more than fifteen minutes the way he's going. I'm really missing you, Mom. Steve is too. You're the greatest. Hope you're not too lonely with Dad gone and all. I sure miss him, too. We'll talk soon. Bye."

"Oh, Molly," Callie sighed. "You can't know how perfect your timing was, or how much I love you and your brother."

"Beep."

"Hi, honey, it's me. I was hoping to hear your voice, but I just remembered that today was your friend Frankie's mom's funeral. Hope everyone pulled through it okay. I know it must have been draining for you, coming so close to Emily's death. I'm sorry, honey. I should be there for you. I can't *wait* to come home. Had another business dinner with Denny Sterling last night, and he brought Elmira Nancy along. I've never been so embarrassed to be in anyone's company in my life. The people at the next table actually asked to be moved because she was so loud. And Sterling, he's actually proud of this insufferable bag of wind that he's legally bound himself to. I'll tell you, Cal, I never felt so lucky to be married to a woman like you than I did after that evening. And not that it took *Elmira Nancy,* God, still can't stomach that name, to make me see that. I've known it all the years we've been together; she just put it in a new light for me. I miss you. Can't wait to ravish you! I'll get home as soon as I can. Love you, honey."

"*Beep.* End of messages."

"Oh, Jack," Callie cried, lying down on the bed. "I love you, too. So much. I don't know how I could have let myself get so out of control. But it's something I'll have to live with. Something I'll have to forgive myself for. I came so close to doing something that would have been *so* wrong. I *did* do things that were wrong. I don't know why, Jack. I was so confused. But maybe in some way what I did made me realize what I had and what I stood to lose. I love you so much."

Callie was exhausted. She snuggled into her bed, pulling the pink-and-green summer quilt over her shoulders. She put her troubles behind her, and allowed herself just to bask in the calm and comfort of Molly and Jack's messages. Her life wasn't so grim and worthless after all. Finally, feeling some true inner peace, the long day took its toll on her, and she instantly fell into a state of repose.

The next thing she knew, Jack, Molly, Stephen, Emily…and even Cobbles and Hungry were sitting on the bed, their eyes were filled with love for Callie. She felt so safe, so secure. Nothing could ever hurt her again. They were all dressed in their best clothing. Callie didn't know where they were going, only that she wasn't ready yet. But nobody complained or attempted to hurry her. They all just smiled and waited patiently for her to get ready.

She sat down at the makeup mirror to fix her face. She heard Jack tell her how beautiful she was, only when she turned around to throw him a kiss, he had become Louie Cavalese. And Emily had somehow become Ruby and seemed angry and scornful of her. Callie tried to shrug it off. She picked up her eye pencil, but as she went to apply it, she saw two icy blue eyes surrounded by dark gray circles staring back at her in the glass. It was not her face. *She* was still young and beautiful; the face in the mirror, with threatening eyes, flaring nostrils, and bitterness oozing from every pore, was evil and ugly.

The room got very quiet. Callie looked over at the bed for support. Only Cobbles and Hungry remained. They were whining. They wanted food. She looked in the mirror again. The left upper lip of the face was snarling at her, like a dog on the verge of attack. Suddenly, Paulie appeared at her side holding out his hand to her.

"Come on, babe, we're out of here."

"Who is that in the mirror?" Callie screamed at him. "Is that me? Is that who I've become? What happened to my family? Where's Jackson? Where are my children?"

"We've got to go, babe," Paulie said. "Now!"

Callie's face was dripping with sweat as she opened her eyes. Oh my God, that evil Annie Cavalese. Why can't I get her out of my mind? Is this my punishment for having wanted Paulie? Am I no better than she is? Why did I see her face where mine should be? Why? Oh, Lord, help me!

Go back to sleep, dear, she heard Emily say. Lie down, close your eyes, and just go to sleep.

Before Emily had finished her sentence, Callie had drifted off again, and this time, to sleep soundly through the night.

CHAPTER 24

Paulie opened the door of the Cavalese home to let Callie in. "Hi, babe, how are you? Did you get a decent night's sleep?"

"I suppose so, after that nightmare was finished."

"Come in," Paulie said. "I can't leave this door wide open. They're still lurking. I'll leave it open a crack, just to get some air in this place. What nightmare are you talking about? Are you referring to what happened at the club?"

Callie sighed and leaned against the railing. "No, it was a *real* nightmare, and it was about your horrible stepmother. I dreamed that I looked in the mirror and saw her face where mine should be."

The color washed out from Paulie's face in an instant. "Oh, shit, Callie-fornia. I can't believe you just said that."

"Why? Paulie, what the hell is going on? Frankie sounded rather urgent when she called, and now you look completely freaked."

"Mary Frances is waiting for you upstairs, in her bedroom. She'll explain things to you."

"I hope she hasn't changed her mind about moving into my house," Callie said.

"No, babe, she's really looking forward to her new life. It's helping to get her through all of this. Go on. I'll talk to you later." He gave her a kiss on the cheek, then nodded upwards.

"I'm going," Callie told him. "But I have the most terrible sense of dread."

"It'll be okay," Paulie called after her. "Oh damn, poor thing! Who needs news like this?" he mumbled to himself.

"Hi, Mason," Frankie said sitting on her bed, leaning up against the wall. "Sit down, here on the bed like we used to do."

"It's been a long time since I've been in this room," Callie said, taking a seat as she looked around, her eyes taking in the memories.

"Look here," Frankie said pointing. "See all of these dents in the wallpaper? That's from rapping out that horse code to you every night."

"Horse code!" Callie said, delighted to remember. "I'd forgotten. That was Paulie's dream child...but we stole it from him." She paused. "But you didn't call me over here for this right now, did you?"

"No," Frankie said. "I didn't."

"And you didn't call me over here because you needed comforting, did you?"

"I do need comforting," Frankie said. "But no, that's not why I called."

"Frankie, please. No twenty questions. You and Paulie are acting really weird, and I'm feeling more uneasy by the second."

"I know, Mason. There's just no easy way to tell you this..."

"Like you always tell me, Frankie. Just cut to the chase."

"Okay. I will. First, you need to know that Paulie told me what happened last night at the club."

"You mean how that repugnant step-monster of yours was staring me down? How your father pulled Paulie aside and urged him to get me out of there?"

"Yeah, that," Frankie said quietly.

"There's a lot more to it, isn't there?" Callie wanted to know. "I tried to get it out of Paulie last night, but he just ignored my questions and told me to go home and get some sleep. God, Frankie, I was just telling Paulie, I had the most chilling nightmare about that woman. I looked in my makeup mirror and saw her face looking back at me."

"Oh, my God!" Frankie screamed. "If that isn't too creepy, I don't know what is!"

"Why do you say 'creepy'?" Callie said, her heart racing. "Why?"

"Annie Cavalese," Frankie said slowly. "She had another name once. It was..."

Tears flowed down Callie's cheeks. She put her left hand up in a halting motion. "Don't say another word, Frankie. You don't have to. It all just clicked in. Everything makes sense now. No wonder she seemed so familiar; no wonder I seemed so familiar to her. And my dream, my *nightmare,* oh God...no wonder she looked so familiar...I hate her, Frankie! I hate her with everything inside of me!"

"Callie..."

"Oh, God, no!" Callie screamed, pounding the mattress. "No! Not that evil woman! No! You know, I've never allowed myself to say it aloud, but secretly I'd hoped she changed. Wherever she was, I hoped she was a decent human being. But she's not even human, much less decent. It makes me sick knowing that that sideshow horror gave birth to me. What does that make me? A freak, just like she is! Oh, no!"

"Mason, please! That's ridiculous," Frankie shouted, thinking of the drunk who'd given birth to her. "We are all are own people. And it took more than one person to make us. But mostly, we are what we make of ourselves."

Paulie, still downstairs, could hear the screaming. He felt sick to his stomach and started to cry. Upstairs, Frankie was crying too, as she witnessed Callie's agony.

"I can't bear to think about her," Callie cried. "It makes me too ill. But I remember her now. I do. It's the same face of the woman who never loved me, who shoved me into the arms of babysitters and nannies and made my father leave the country just to get away from her. The same woman who brought stranger after stranger into my home and told me to 'find something to do' and to 'get lost.' She's evil, and I hate her!"

"I understand," Frankie said gently.

"Paulie!" Callie screamed. "Please, come up here!"

Paulie wiped the tears from his eyes and raced upstairs to Frankie's room. Callie could see he'd been crying. The look on his face verified everything Frankie had just told her.

"It's true," Callie addressed Paulie. "Annie. She's Anisa, isn't she? That's why you wouldn't talk to me last night. That's why you were so quiet on the ride back."

Paulie just looked at her, his eyes answering her question.

"How did she come to be your father's wife? I don't understand."

Paulie sat down on the bed and held her hand. "When she left the hospital she was in, against doctor's orders, she came here to look for you."

"But I don't understand," Callie said. "There was a time when I wanted to know her. I asked Aunt Emily to find her. My God, she hated to do it, but she made the call because she loved me that much. They told her Anisa had been long gone, but that she always used to tell people that someday she'd come and find her daughter. She made it sound like she really wanted me…even loved me. How could she make it to Rainytown and *not* find me?"

"She found you," Frankie said. "But she found Pop, too, and she liked him a whole lot more."

Callie looked sick. She leaned her head against Paulie's chest.

"You were lucky, babe," Paulie said as he stroked her hair. "Imagine if she had taken you away from Emily. She'd have destroyed you. Even if she'd tried and failed, she would have made your life miserable."

Callie looked up at Paulie, then at Frankie. "You're right, I was lucky. But at your family's expense."

"Don't think that way," Paulie said. "From what we know now about Pop back then, if it hadn't been Annie, it would have been someone else. Trust me."

"He's right," Frankie said gently. "It would have been."

Callie looked urgently at Paulie. "Please tell me she didn't recognize me. Please, Paulie."

"Don't worry. I called Pop this morning. He casually mentioned to her that you were a friend of mine visiting from out of town. He even made up some other name for you, just to be safe."

"Did she buy it?" Callie asked.

"Oh, yeah. She mumbled something about how you looked familiar, like some 'bitch' who'd come in once before to invade her territory."

"Maybe her subconscious recognized you, too," Frankie added, "but her brain is so clouded by booze that she'd never figure it out. You're gone. That's all that matters to her."

"Mary Frances is right, Callie-fornia. Listen, I'm going to leave you two alone," Paulie said. "I've got to make a quick run to the bank. I'll see you both in a bit." He kissed both women goodbye and left.

"I hope you're not angry that I told you," Frankie said. "But it would be wrong to keep something so important from you, even if it's the last thing you wanted to hear."

"I'm glad you told me," Callie said. "I probably would have figured it out after a few more rounds of nightmares. Believe me, it was much more palatable coming from my best friend."

"Good," Frankie said. "I'm relieved. I couldn't live with myself it I'd kept it from you for even a day."

Callie covered her face with both hands and began to sob. Frankie's words kicked her in the conscience as she remembered the promise she'd made to Ruby. Considering what Frankie had just said, how could she not tell her now? She had asked God to let her know when the time was right; He had listened, and the time was now.

But the secret Callie held was even more painful than the one Frankie had just revealed. Callie had always known who her mother was; she had always assumed she was still a drunk, if she were even alive; she just didn't know that her mother and Annie Cavalese were one and the same person. It was horrifying to get such news, to even *think* of Anisa again, but how could she tell Frankie, who just lost her beloved mother, that some other woman, also an uncaring alcoholic, had given birth to her? How could she tell Frankie that Ruby was not her biological mother? How could she tell her such a shocking thing the day after Ruby's funeral? Ever!

Callie struggled with what to do. She battled back and forth with whether or not to tell her, but kept coming back to God and the plea she had made to Him. He had given her a sign, just as she'd asked Him to do. She had to believe that. She had to do this. Now. There would never be a "good" time. This was it.

Frankie watched her friend's tortured eyes, having no idea what to do for her. She had no way of knowing that Callie was thinking about her.

"Hey, Mason," Frankie said, "you know what just occurred to me?"

"No," Callie said, grabbing a tissue from the nightstand. "What?"

"This makes you and me stepsisters. And it makes you and Paulie *brother* and sister!"

The emphasis of Frankie's last sentence did not escape Callie's attention. She was not the least bit surprised that Frankie had noticed the attraction between them.

"You've always been my sister," Callie said tearfully. "And I don't need Annie Anisa whatever her name is to make that a reality."

Frankie smiled briefly.

"Look, Frankie. I have something to tell you, too. Only it's going to hit you a lot harder than this news has hit me."

Frankie looked at her confusedly. What else could there possibly be? Hadn't she had enough unpleasant surprises lately? "Jesus, what now? Well, go on, tell me."

"Do you remember the second time I came here to visit with your mother?" Callie asked. "The day she was so adamant about seeing me?"

"Sure, I remember," Frankie said. "She bugged me for hours about bringing you back. I think she was real nervous about whether you'd be there for me when she was gone."

"That was only a small part of it," Callie said, still sick over her own discovery.

"That's the day you were really weirded out," Frankie said. "You could barely talk, and you went running out of here. You said you were all choked up with emotion or something."

"I was, Frankie, but it was a lot more than I let on."

"Well, what the hell was it, Mason?"

"Your ma, she'd been keeping a secret from you throughout your entire lifetime. She was dying, and she wanted you to know what it was, but she was too afraid to tell you. Too afraid to see the pain in your eyes. She'd asked me on the first visit if I'd be willing to do her a really big favor. I promised her I'd do anything she asked. When I came back the next day, I was literally flabbergasted by what she told me and by what she wanted me to do for her."

Frankie's mouth dropped open as she pieced together what had happened. *It was Pop,* Frankie thought to herself. *I'll bet Pop convinced Ma to tell me herself before she died. Mason's known all this time, and she didn't tell me. How can she call herself my friend and have kept something so important from me?* Frankie became inflamed with rage. *If this thing with Annie hadn't come up, would Mason have told me at all? Probably not!*

"Oh, Frankie," Callie said. "This is so hard—"

"Save it, Mason!" Frankie barked.

Callie was stunned. Frankie's animosity had hit her right between the eyes. "Frankie...I—"

"When were you gonna tell me that Ma wasn't my biological

mother and that some Annie-Cavalese-type broad named Francine Ellen Parker was! When, Mason? When the cows came home? When little winged piggies dotted the Rainytown sky?"

"Oh my God," Callie gasped. "You already know!"

"Yeah, I know," Frankie said bitterly. "Ma told me right before she died. I'm sure Pop talked her into it that night he came to say goodbye to her and set things right again. It broke my heart, Mason, but it doesn't change the fact that Ma was my mother. My only mother!"

"I understand," Callie said desperately. "Just as Emily was *my* only mother."

"Don't you *dare* try to sympathize with me now. You should have told me immediately, Mason. The minute you found out. You had no way of knowing I'd find out. You should have told me so that I could've talked to Ma about it while she was still alive. But you were willing to let me wait until she was dead to hear this shit. When I couldn't hear Ma's side of the story. How could you do this?"

"Frankie, please!" Callie cried. "Can't you see the position I was in? Your mother made me swear up and down to uphold her wishes. I know she was frightened and dying, but she put me in a terrible position. What in the world would you have done if you were me?"

"I would have told you! I would never keep something like this from you. I think I've just proved that to you. Don't you think so, Mason? Don't you think I've just proved it to you?"

"Oh, Frankie, you're not being fair to me! I know you told me the truth about Anisa as soon as possible, but you didn't have to break someone's dying wish to do it!"

"Damn you, Mason. If I hadn't just told you about Annie being who she is, when the fuck *would* you have told me about Ma? Huh? Can you answer that?"

"I don't know," Callie said weakly. "I was going to talk to Jack about it when he got home."

"You were going to wait until *Jackson* came home? What, you can't fucking think without him? What kind of wimp are you, anyway? Is this what rich women do? Let their husbands think for them when their troubles extend beyond what shade of lipstick to wear?"

Callie shuddered at Frankie's sarcastic remarks. "No, of course not! I just wanted his input. Is that so wrong? And what the hell does it have to do with how much money I have? I thought you were over that kind of crass and stupid talk. The fact is, Frankie, I just didn't know when or how to tell you. I would have told you soon, though. I'm sure of that. Probably when you moved into our house and felt secure."

"Secure? In your world?" Frankie said. "Never! I'm not going anywhere, as I'm sure must be apparent by now. I don't need you, your fancy apartment, or your sister-in-law's job. I'd rather live out my life in this miserable place than accept *anything* from you. I should have never let you back into my life. So beat it! You're dismissed."

Callie stood up, weeping. "Frankie, are you trying to hurt me for all those years ago? Are you finally exacting your true revenge?"

"I told you I forgave you for that," Frankie said. "I meant it. Are you calling me a liar now?"

"No!" Callie said vehemently. "I just can't help but wonder, though. If our friendship was so important to you, the way you swore that it was, how can you just 'dismiss' me like this? Where did our friendship go? Our bond? Everything we've just worked so hard to rebuild?"

"Who the fuck knows?" Frankie said. "Where do lost socks go? It's a mystery. No one knows. They just disappear. Just like you're going to do. Now! Get out!"

"Frankie, please! You're not thinking straight. You've just lost your mother, and you're grieving. You're not being rational. Please calm down."

Frankie shot up from the bed and began chasing Callie down the stairs. Once downstairs, Callie opened the front door, then turned to Frankie to make one final plea, but she was given no opportunity to do so.

"Get out of my house, Mason! Do you hear me, get the fuck out!"

Callie ran down the steps to her car, sobbing wildly. She didn't even notice that Paulie had just pulled up in front of her. She just had to get out of there. He tried to get her attention, but she'd already jumped in her BMW, turned on the motor, and gone screeching out of the parking spot.

"Mary Frances!" Paulie screamed, rushing into the house. "What the hell was wrong with Callie?"

"I told her to get the fuck out!" Frankie screamed back at him.

"You told her what? Why?" Paulie asked, appalled. "How could you do that? What the hell is wrong with you?"

"Never mind, Paulie. Go find your precious little Callie-fornia and screw her brains out until she feels better. Just leave me alone!"

"Are you crazy?"

"Yeah, I'm fucking crazy! Isn't that obvious? Now, go, Paulie! Now!"

Hurt and stunned, Paulie looked down at the floor and shook his head despairingly. He took one last look at his sister, who was glaring at him defiantly from the third step, waiting for him to leave. "Close the door behind you!" Frankie screamed.

Paulie looked at her as tears rolled freely down his face. And as he slammed the door shut behind him, Frankie collapsed on the stairs. "Oh, God," she cried, "What the hell did I just do? I've lost everyone. Help me, Ma. I don't know what to do."

As she turned onto her street, Callie thanked God for driving her home safely. He must have put me on autopilot, she thought, as the tears streamed down her face. I don't know how I made it here. It had to be God.

It was only one o'clock in the afternoon, but the skies had darkened. A storm was on the way, and there was a heaviness lurking in the air. Callie's eyes were so filled with tears that the familiar sights on her street became a blur to her. Intensely distraught, she almost turned up her neighbor's driveway before reaching her own. The images and sounds of Frankie chasing her out of the house tormented her, like the call in the middle of the night telling her that Emily had died unexpectedly. It all hurt way too much to be real.

When she pulled into her own driveway, her first reaction was that she must have been hallucinating. "Oh, please tell me I'm not dreaming!" she called upward to the rumbling sky. "Oh, thank you, God, thank you!"

Callie jumped out of the car, fumbled with her house keys, then ran charging into the house. "Jackson! Where are you? Are you here? Jack!"

Jackson, quickly recognizing the hysteria in her voice, came bounding down the stairs. He got a chill as he saw his wife's tear-stained face, laden with smudges of black, brown, and taupe, her right arm covered in makeup where he assumed she must've tried to wipe her face. Even her shirt was wet and stained.

"Callie, my God!" he said in horror, fearing the worst. "Baby, what happened to you! Did someone *hurt* you?"

"Oh, Jack!" she cried, falling into his arms. "When I saw your car outside, well, I've just never been so glad to know you were home in all my life."

Jackson clutched her tightly to his chest. "I came home early. I missed you too much to stay away another day. Now, tell me what happened, but just tell me you weren't attacked." He could not bring himself to say the word "raped."

"No, honey. Nobody touched me. It's not that. But it's all so awful. Every bit of it. It was worse than any nightmare could ever be," she sobbed, her voice partially muffled as she pressed even closer to him.

"Come on, honey," he said, deeply concerned. "Let's go upstairs, okay? We'll talk there."

Callie looked up at him and shook her head affirmatively. "Oh, God, Jack, everything I'd worked for is all gone, but I'm *so* glad you're home. I love you so much."

Jackson sat her down on the bed, took a seat next to her, and put his arm securely around her. With his free hand, he grabbed a handful of tissues and began to wipe her face.

Callie continued to cry hysterically. She couldn't help but compare herself to poor Belle. Aren't we a pair, she thought.

"Sweetie, you've got to tell me what happened," Jackson pleaded.

"How did your trip go?" Callie sobbed. "Was it a success?"

"Oh, Cal, I appreciate the interest, but neither one of us gives a flying fig about that right now. Baby, please. What happened?"

Tearfully, Callie began to tell him the story, beginning from her initial reunion with Frankie and the subsequent reconciliation. When she reached the part about Anisa, Jackson reacted in horror, until he realized that there was a lot more to his wife's traumatized state of mind than seeing her lost mother again.

"Oh, hell!" Jackson said, when Callie had finished the story. "It's all my fault."

"Your fault?" Callie said, still sobbing. "How in the world do you figure that?"

"When I was leaving for Seattle, you told me that Mrs. Cavalese had asked something tremendous of you, something you didn't know how to handle. If only I hadn't been so brusque with you, we could have at least opened the conversation and maybe finished it later over the phone. But I just pushed you away, and now, this incident with Frankie. Oh, Callie, I finally understand just how much this all means to you. I didn't give you the respect you deserved."

"Don't say that, Jackson," Callie said, thinking of Paulie.

"But it's true," Jackson insisted. "I didn't."

"And I didn't give you the peace of mind or the respect you asked of me. I was so selfish, only wanting to talk about my problems."

"Cal, you've been such a joy to me our entire marriage that I unknowingly took you for granted. I wasn't used to you having serious problems or concerns. Hell, I was the big man, the CEO. I was the one with *real* problems."

"But they were real. The company was in trouble and you were so incredibly stressed out. And when you came home at night, just wanting to relax, I made it impossible for you to enjoy your music. The music that you love so much—the music that soothes your soul. It was awful of me." Callie protested, feeling an intense need to beat herself up.

Jackson smiled and put his hand under her chin, looking her straight in the eyes. "I can't imagine a worse thing to do to one's spouse," he said teasingly. "Maybe it's not too late. Maybe I can still file a police report."

"Oh, Jack, no jokes. Not now," Callie pleaded.

"Not ever?" he said, smiling.

"You know, my precious weeping willow," he said, caressing her sad face. "This isn't the end. Frankie just buried her mother yesterday, and a few days before that, discovered an incredibly disconcerting truth about her parentage. And from what you've told me, she's taken care of her mother since the day she took ill. And add what happened with that crazy neighbor friend of hers, I can't imagine that she wasn't overwrought with emotion, and unfortunately, took it out on you. I don't think it's over, honey. I really don't. I think she just lost it for a moment. The dam just broke, and, unfortunately, you're the one that got wet. She'll come around."

"No, Jack! You're wrong! She despises me," Callie told him. "I've betrayed her trust for the final time. You don't know her; she's tough. She means what she says."

"Oh, Cal," Jackson said, rocking her slowly in his arms. "You'll see, baby. It'll be okay."

Jackson held Callie in his arms for a long time. When the tears and the trembling had subsided, he stood up in front of her, then flashed his winning smile, only in a softer, more tender way than he usually did. Slowly, he removed the teal blue Polo shirt he was wearing and put it on the bed. Without taking his eyes off Callie, he removed his belt and then the rest of his clothing. He grabbed hold of her hands and stood her up, then, looking lovingly into her eyes and seeing the love returned twofold, he undressed her, slowly and gently. Then, without a word, he kissed her on the lips and led her to the shower.

As the water beat down on them, wrapped in each other's arms, they both felt immersed in sheer ecstasy. Jackson delicately scrubbed Callie's face until it was pink, then with a soft cloth and her favorite almond body wash, gently went over every inch of her body. When he had finished, she did the same for him, only she had merely covered sixty percent of his body when Naked Wet Matador suddenly turned off the shower, grabbed his terrycloth cape, and carried his señora to bed.

Jackson exhilarated her. The joy of rediscovering her immense love for him, the feel of his rhapsodic touch, could not even begin to compare with the purely carnal desire she'd had for Paulie. This was her heart, the father of her children, her lifetime love.

Thunder crashed outside, coinciding with Jackson's plunge deep into her body. And he, feeling every bit the deep and abiding love that she did, reached a paradise that even Naked Matador had never known before.

❖ ❖ ❖

Frankie had come undone. It was as if an evil doppelgänger had broken into her home, bound and gagged her, then devastated her best friend and her grieving brother while she watched in horror, leaving nothing behind but the shattered remains of her life. The glass that once mirrored her reflection, an image of someone Frankie could respect, now lay on the floor like a million shiny shards. Never, she thought, not by the most skilled of craftsmen, not by all the king's horses and all the king's men, could anyone ever put her together again. And then, as the Humpty Dumpty nursery rhyme repeated itself in her head, she cried for the big egg who'd fallen off the wall and lost his life.

What a horrible story, she thought. Why do people read it to their children? It's too sad. God, poor Humpty! I hope you're in heaven with Ma. She could use a good egg like you.

Frankie still hadn't moved from the step she'd been on when she erased Paulie from the scene over an hour ago. He'd been so loving and wonderful lately. What had he done to deserve such treatment? Showed concern for the woman Frankie had just thrown out of her house, out of her life? He'd lost his mother, too. He was in a state of terrible anguish, and look how horrendously she'd treated him. He would never forgive her. Her attack on him was completely unjustified.

But Callie was another story. Frankie still felt justified in her anger toward her. She felt a deep sense of betrayal. It hurt. But did it warrant the way she treated Callie, after all they'd done to put their friendship back on track, after all that Callie had done for Frankie and her family? She didn't know. Probably not. But she still could not accept the fact that Callie had kept such vital information from her, and might've done so forever had the Anisa situation not come to light.

Regina's vile accusations, uninvited, nosedived back into her head. What kind of behavior could Frankie possibly have exhibited to elicit such false and vicious ruminations?

Nothing she told herself, angry that she was paying any credence whatsoever to such ugliness. They're projecting their own desires for Paulie on me, she thought. They're angry that I can get close to my own brother and they can't.

Frankie felt a strong wave of nausea in the pit of her stomach.

Could *she* have been envious of Callie simply because of the special attention Paulie had shown toward her? Could Frankie have denied her own hurt feelings to such an extent that they manifested as blinding fury, then masqueraded as rage toward another matter entirely? How could the mind trip up like that? Wouldn't she know how she felt or where her anger was really coming from? Could her mother's languishing in the throes of death have overshadowed her true feelings temporarily? Was she unknowingly disturbed because Paulie and Callie shared something separate and apart from her, something they had no business sharing? Had it hurt her to see Paulie divvy up his attention to include both her and Callie? No, Frankie would not get jealous over something like that. It shouldn't matter that Paulie felt something special for her friend…Paulie never pushed Frankie away…had he? Well, there was that day when she found him at Emily's house…

She felt herself puffing up with anger, trading contemplation for rage, then rage for confusion. There was no one left to comfort her or to help her make sense of things. She'd chased everyone away. She was all alone, sealed inside her wretched tomb of a home, buried alive. She'd even sent Louie away, fearful that he might confirm something she already knew to be true.

The walls encroached on her space. The distance between the banister and the wall grew shorter. The house hated her too, for all the years of neglect, and now was going to choke her to death with its gray, gnarled fingers that had disguised themselves for years as stairway spindles. She would be punished for having kept the light out. She had killed all of the color. She had forced others into the darkness that had been her life. Now she was going to pay.

CHAPTER 25

As comforting and as thrilling as Jackson's homecoming had been for her, Callie was still deeply depressed when she woke up Friday morning. She picked up the note Jackson had left her on the bed. "I love you. Don't ever forget that. I'll be home early. Call me on my cell if you need me. XOXOXO! Jackson."

She was inordinately lucky to have a man like him, but still, her life could never go back to the way it had been just short of two weeks ago. After twenty-three years, she had found her best friend again, and doing so filled her with an abundance of life's simplest, yet most precious gifts. But now there was a big, gaping hole, leaving her dispossessed of all she had just received. Nature is so illogical, Callie thought. How is it possible for a heart to feel so empty, yet be so filled with pain?

She had no idea how to fix things; she just knew she could not allow them to stay broken. But it would be impossible to approach Frankie. Her stubborn pride would insist on an encore performance, even *if* she'd had a change of heart, which Callie highly doubted as she replayed Frankie's violent reaction to her "revelation."

Nothing made sense. Frankie and Callie had been through so much together; they had come so far together. Their bond was far too special to just ignore. Callie couldn't live with that.

But for the moment, it was Frankie, not her, whom Callie was most worried about. If Frankie stayed in that dreary house and went back to her old job, it would destroy her, like a slow cancer shutting her down a little more each day. She must feel *so* alone, Callie thought. God, please watch over her. You too, Paulie. Don't let her do anything stupid. And be there. She really needs you.

Frankie walked down the stairs in a daze. From start to finish, none of it seemed real. She had waited up until late at night, hoping Paulie would recognize her foolish attack on him as uncontrollable grief and come back.

But she'd pushed him too far. He hadn't returned. He hadn't called. She was sure he didn't care.

As she reached the landing, Frankie heard a familiar sound coming from the porch. Someone was rocking in the chair. For a milli-second, she thought it was Ruby, who'd often rocked peacefully after tending to her plants.

Ma's dead, Frankie thought. I can't forget that again 'cause it hurts too much to remember. Paulie, she thought elatedly, it's got to be Paulie. I can't believe he's just sitting out there. He'll have the whole neighborhood on the porch if he doesn't come in soon.

Without stopping to consider any more alternatives, Frankie opened the front door and stepped out onto the porch.

"Oh, shit!" Frankie exclaimed. "Reg!"

Regina slowly rocked in the chair. "Frankie, I gotta talk to you. It's important."

"Reg, can't you just leave me in peace?" Frankie begged wearily.

"You ain't in peace," Regina told her. "Your Ma ain't buried a whole day when everything I predicted has come true."

"What the hell are you talking about?" Frankie said disgustedly.

"Callie Mason," Regina said. "I heard you throwing her diamond-studded butt out on the street yesterday. Yep, saw her crying her eyes out as she got into her fancy car and peeled outta here. Surprised she didn't kiss a tree the way she was driving."

Frankie winced. It made her sick that Regina had witnessed the scene, and even sicker to worry that Callie might not have made it home all right. With Jackson and the kids out of town, and the maid temporarily away, who would know to worry if Callie hadn't made it home? Oh, God, Frankie thought. What have I done?

"You sure were screaming at her," Regina added happily. "Get the fuck—"

"How is any of this your business?" Frankie interrupted.

"You talk to me," Regina baited her. "I'll tell you."

Frankie just glowered at her.

"You keep turnin' me down, Frankie; I'll keep comin' back. Like a bad penny. You might as well let me have my say."

Frankie grabbed a folding chair that had been resting on the side of the porch. Unfolding it, she dusted it off, then sat down angrily. "Okay, Reg, say what you have to say."

"I told you Callie Mason would dump you again," Regina boasted. "What did she do? Tell you she couldn't see you much anymore, now that she'd done her good-deed doing? I hear she gave your Ma one fancy funeral. Guess her charity work was done after that, huh?"

"You couldn't be more wrong, Reg," Frankie said. "And for the last time, it's none of your business. If that's what you came here to say, then get lost."

"I'm sorry," Regina softened. "It's just that you and me, we were best buds before she came back. She ruined everything for us, Frankie. I tried to like her at first because she was your friend, but every day, you became less and less interested in me. She pushed me out of your life. You both did."

Frankie didn't respond to her comment. She just looked away, watching Regina's children as they played in the small yard. "I hope you put lots of sunscreen on Steffie today," Frankie said. "The sun's really bright."

"Hal Junior!" Regina yelled across the street. "Take Steffie inside and put some more of the number 30 lotion on her. Be careful not to get it in her eyes, and make sure you don't forget no parts of her body that ain't covered with clothes. Same thing for you and Billy. Any of yous get burned, your ass is grass!"

"Ah, Mom," Hal Jr. whined. "That's your job!"

"You know I ain't in no shape to be movin' around, Hal. Don't sass me. Do what I say. 'Sides, you see I'm talking to Frankie here, don't you?"

Hal Jr. shrugged and herded his siblings inside the house.

"Thanks for the reminder," Regina said to Frankie, feeling confident that things were returning to normal. "Listen, Frankie, I came here to apologize. I didn't mean what I said about you not bein' Steffie's godmother no more. I was just really hurt. I swear to God I didn't mean it."

"It's better that I'm not her godmother," Frankie said. "As much as it saddens me. It's for the best."

"Oh, Frankie, you're just sayin' that because you're hurt. I'd get down on my knees and apologize if I could physically do it."

"Apologize for what, Reg?" Frankie asked her mechanically.

"For saying those things I said on your birthday, for sayin' Steffie wasn't your godchild no more, for writin' you those mean letters. I was just hurt, Frankie. Didn't you ever say really mean things to someone you loved because you were hurt?"

Oh yeah, Frankie thought to herself. I'm the champ. Nobody can beat me in that department. Not even you, Regina.

"Well, Frankie, you gonna forgive me?"

"Reg," Frankie said, watching as the Cunningham kids came out of the house again, "let's for a moment forget about everything that happened since Callie came back to town."

"Boy, oh boy," Regina exclaimed. "Wouldn't I love to do that!"

"Not so fast," Frankie admonished her. "From what you said to me on my birthday, it's quite clear that you'd been trashing me with those filthy lies about me having a thing for my own brother way before Callie came 'round again. What was it that you said? Something about 'everyone knowin' about it and that it wasn't right'?"

Regina yelled across the street. "Hope you did a good job, Hal! Did you put the lid back on the tube?" Hal Jr. looked disgusted as he threw his ball on the ground and ran inside again.

"I don't have all day," Frankie said. "You wanted this conversation so bad. So talk. Answer the damn question."

"Oh, shit, Frankie, it ain't that easy. I wasn't goin' 'round saying things, it's just that other people were sayin' 'em and I sorta started believin' it all."

"Real sweet, Reg. What a friend. It never occurred to you to look beyond the gossip, to think with your own brain, to defend me, seeing how you bragged 'bout knowin' me better than anyone else did? Seeing how you considered me your '*best bud*'?"

"C'mon, Frankie, you know how it is. I know it ain't no good excuse, 'specially when you say it out loud. It all sounds worse 'n all. It's just that I wanted people to like me. I didn't have that many friends bein' kinda new to the neighborhood and all. I couldn't be disagreeing with people and makin' enemies. 'Specially with Edna. She can be a bitch on wheels if she thinks you've crossed her."

"Edna Murphy has no power," Frankie said. "But cowards like you give it to her."

"Oh, Frankie, I'm really sorry. I see now how wrong I was! But I wanted friends so bad! I wanted to be a part of the neighborhood."

"So you just believed all of their lies? How could you, Reg?"

"I-I don't know, Frankie. Maybe because you were always so upset every time Paulie left. Like your lover leavin' you or something."

"No," Frankie said adamantly. "Not like my lover leavin' me. Like my brother leaving me to do everything for Ma when I was tired, frustrated, and on my last nerve."

"But you were always so happy to see him when he'd come back. You couldn't have been that mad."

"Regina, he's my brother. He's very special to me. So he didn't give all he could have, but still, I love him and I was happy to see him. That's all the explanation you need. I can't believe the foul and disgusting conclusions you and all the others drew from that. You even tried to tell Callie about it, didn't you? What did you say? Oh, I remember. Something about me having funny feelings for my brother? Is that right, Reg?"

Regina looked ashamed and rubbed her stomach as she watched Billy's ball go into the street. "Look both ways before you go after that, Billy!" She turned to Frankie. "I'm sorry. I guess that wasn't right. I don't know why I said that to Callie. She sure has a big mouth, damn her."

"Callie only brought it up to me after I told her what happened on my birthday. She wasn't the one with the big mouth."

"Guess not," Regina said dejectedly. "I'm sorry. It really wasn't about you, Frankie. I swear, I just wanted to be liked."

"Again, I ask you the same question: did your need to be liked require you to trash the person you considered to be your best friend?"

Regina started to cry. "Ain't you never gonna forgive me, Frankie? I'm sorry about everything. I'm sorry about givin' you so much grief all the time about seeing your ma. I know you didn't have no control over it. It's just that...oh, never mind. Can't we just forget this whole thing and be best buds again?"

Frankie shook her head wearily. She had so little left in her. "Reg, I have an apology to make to you."

Regina wiped the tears from her eyes with her arm and looked hopefully at Frankie.

"I haven't had a real happy life," Frankie said. "And when you moved in all those years ago, you were nice, someone to spend time with in the neighborhood and have a few laughs. But, Reg, I didn't feel about you like you did about me. You just started telling everyone right off the bat that we were 'best buds,' and I didn't want to embarrass you or tell you that I didn't feel the same. I guess I didn't think it mattered if I set you straight or not. I didn't see the point in hurting you unnecessarily. In hindsight, I guess I was wrong."

Regina started to cry again. "What are you sayin' now, Frankie? That you never really liked me?"

"No, of course not, Reg. I liked you a lot. But you weren't a *best friend* to me. You were more like a friend to just have fun with, you know, shoot the breeze with. Doesn't mean I didn't care about you. I cared a lot. You just weren't my best friend. That's all."

"You mean like a best friend like Callie Mason was? Someone who dumped you for twenty-three years? You mean I wasn't *that* kind of friend!"

"Reg, I can't explain it, and if I somehow found the words, they wouldn't be what you wanted to hear anyway. I wish you and your family all the best. No hard feelings. But that's all I can do for you."

"Why'd you agree to be Steffie's godmother if I was no more than just some friendly neighbor to you?"

"Because you asked me to, and at the time, I didn't consider all of the possible ramifications. And I love kids, and she was such a beautiful baby." Frankie blinked back the tears. She didn't want Regina to see her feeling sentimental. "Once again, I was wrong. I just didn't wanna hurt you, Reg. But now, I can't lie anymore. I can't pretend. I'm sorry. Whatever we had, it's gone now. You have to accept that." Frankie got up, folded her chair, and put it back where she'd found it.

"But Frankie! You and me. We live right across the street from one another. And we probably will forever. We *gotta* be friends!"

Frankie cringed at the thought. "Sorry, Reg. That's all I've got to say. If you wanna stay out here to rock and roll, feel free. I need to be alone now. Just understand one thing: I meant every word I said. I'm not going to change my mind, so please, respect that and move on. I'm hurting more now than you could possibly imagine. I would consider it a great favor if you just let me be."

Regina, her face distorted by pain, turned away as Frankie said her final words. Too upset to go home, she continued to rock and sob once Frankie was back inside, secretly hoping her pitiable cries would somehow convince Frankie to change her mind.

For Frankie, she felt a great sense of relief that she had properly and quietly ended the relationship. She realized that her feelings for Regina weren't as completely dead as she'd thought, but she had no second thoughts about her decision to move on. She felt sorry for Regina and mused that maybe one day she'd miss her silly Hal stories. But the warm feelings ended there. Except maybe for Steffie. That was another loss she would learn to live with.

All she was certain of now was that she had to make things right with Paulie. Then she'd think about Callie…maybe. And then again…maybe not.

The sound of the key in the lock woke Frankie about three o'clock in the afternoon. After she'd come inside from her talk with Regina, she had lain on the couch, looking drearily at the chipped paint on the ceiling, until the Sandman had alleviated her misery by taking her out for a long snooze. When she woke up to find Paulie standing over her, she had no idea what time of day it was, and it took a few seconds to even remember what had transpired between them the day before.

Frankie's eyes darted to the big wooden clock on the front wall between the windows. She now had assessed that it was afternoon. Paulie gave her an odd once-over, then took a seat in the armchair, where he sat motionless, staring blankly at her.

Frankie broke the silence. "Would it mean anything to you if I said that I was really and truly sorry for every miserable word I spoke to you, and that I love you, and that I'm so glad you came back here…even if it is to rip me into a million pieces?"

"Don't be stupid," Paulie said flatly.

"You're really angry at me, aren't you?"

"Oh no, I'm as happy as a lark." He took a long pause as if he wanted to choose his words carefully. "I didn't deserve that heap of shit you threw at me yesterday, Mary Frances. Not by a long shot."

"No, of course you didn't. Please, Paulie. Please forgive me. I just couldn't take anymore," Frankie pleaded. "I'm so sorry. Do you forgive me?"

"Jury's still out. Why don't you start by telling me what happened? I can't wait to hear why you told your best friend, who had just given our mother a beautiful funeral, and who'd just learned some terribly disturbing personal news, who'd only recently buried her beloved aunt, to get the fuck out of your house. You know, I kicked that one around all night. Couldn't come up with a thing."

"So you didn't talk to Callie then?"

"No!" Paulie said angrily. "Goddamn it, Mary Frances. I told you to leave that shit alone."

"Sorry," Frankie said. "That was a stupid thing to say."

"We agree there," Paulie said, taking a hard tack with her. "Is there any beer in the fridge?"

"Should be. If you put it there, I haven't touched it."

"I'll be right back."

Frankie fidgeted in her seat while Paulie went to the kitchen. She wondered how her story would sound to him. She wondered how it would sound to herself. Would Paulie understand? Maybe…if he wasn't so inclined to defend Callie. There it was again: the nagging thought of that bond between them. Then she remembered what Regina had said about the way Callie drove off. Was her best friend lying dead somewhere? No, she couldn't be. Someone would have called. But the thought still disquieted her.

"Okay, Mary Frances," Paulie said, taking his seat. He quickly licked some foam from the beer that was spilling over the side of the bottle. "Let's hear it."

Frankie looked around the room as if she hoped the walls would speak for her. Anything to get out of telling Paulie the story. But she could see he was growing impatient, and not wanting to push him any further, she related the horror story from the previous afternoon. When she finished, she was unnerved by the lack of any perceptible change of expression on her brother's face. She felt as though nothing she'd said had made any difference to him at all. He wasn't talking and his silence only heightened her angst and anticipation of his reaction.

"You're going to defend her, aren't you?" Frankie finally blurted out.

Paulie just continued to look at her. He took a swig of his beer and looked thoughtfully at her. "Oh, Mary Frances," he said helplessly. "This is your closest friend we're talking about. It's not about taking sides. You've both, hell, we've *all* been under tremendous emotional strain. And shit happens. You've got to make it right."

"What does that mean? That you don't think Callie did anything wrong by withholding that information from me?"

Paulie leaned back in the chair and sighed. "Mary Frances, first of all, I forgive you for what you said to me yesterday. God only knows you've forgiven me for enough shit. But like I told Pop about calling me fucking Paula and spouting all that other garbage to me: you're off the hook *this* time; just don't ever go there again. Okay?"

"Paulie," Frankie said desperately. "When have I ever done something like that before? You know that's not me."

"No," Paulie said firmly. "I don't know anything right now. Ma's gone and you've kicked Callie-fornia out of your life. I'm sure she's as fucking miserable about it as you are. What are you going to do about it?"

"Why should *I* do anything about it?" Frankie said. "If that's the kind of friend she is, maybe I don't want anything to do with her."

"We're talking about Callie, Mary Frances. Not Regina Cunningham. Callie loves you. She respects you. She'd never purposely hurt you."

"Oh, but I purposely hurt her, did I?" Frankie countered angrily. "Well, didn't you?"

"She deserved it, Paulie. How could she keep such a thing from me? I wouldn't have done that to her."

"Can we turn on a fucking light in here?"

"Whatever," Frankie said, standing up and turning on the floor lamp. "Okay, satisfied?"

"Barely. Now you listen to me, Mary F., 'cause I'm not going to repeat the same things over and over again. You know how that bores me."

Wouldn't want to bore you, Frankie wanted to say, but judiciously decided to lose the wisecracks.

Paulie continued. "You can't say for sure *what* you would have done in Callie's position. I don't care what you think you might have done, you don't know. When I spoke to Pop yesterday, you know, to find out if Evil Step Ma-Ma had recognized Callie-fornia, we talked about this whole mess. I asked him why the hell he and Ma chose to keep this from you. I told him I was pissed that you had to hear such fucked-up news only moments before your mother's death. I told him how damn wrong that was. They *both* should have told you years ago!"

"You got that right," Frankie said, fighting back tears. "So what the hell happened? Why didn't they?"

"To hear Pop tell it, supposedly, they had originally talked about telling you when you were eighteen or so. But when Pop left us, he was feeling so guilty about what he'd done that he didn't want to spring more bad news on you — ever — especially news like you weren't Ma's biological daughter. So he begged her to keep silent. Well, you know Ma, she let her whole damn life go to hell waiting for him to come back to her. Despite his betrayal to her, she didn't want to break her promise to *him*. Damned if I understand, but like Pop said, he didn't deserve that kind of respect. But Ma gave it to him anyway. To me, that still doesn't explain why they never chose to tell you down the road, but I guess there's never really a good time to lay that kind of trip on someone. But still: they should have; they owed you that. So you think about this, Mary Frances, and tell me if you really think that Callie deserves the blame for all of this. Don't you think you're being really unfair to her? Making her a scapegoat for something our parents did...or *didn't* do?"

Frankie was confused. She had no idea how to respond, but she couldn't shake her anger at Callie. She had trusted Callie with her life, she had made herself vulnerable to her once again, and as much as she told herself that they were starting over with a clean slate, perhaps she'd been mistaken.

Frankie searched her soul for an answer to Paulie's question. Maybe there was more residual anger inside her than she'd realized. Maybe she *was* jealous of Paulie's affection for Callie, or maybe she just needed to scream and yell, releasing the demons that had taken shelter in her mind long ago, demons that circumstance had forced to remain mute until now. Had Callie been right? *Was* Frankie finally exacting her revenge? No! Absolutely not. She'd forgiven Callie, and she'd meant it. She was not some head case reacting viscerally to a situation with no comprehension of her own feelings. It was simple: Callie had played God with her life. Callie had deliberately chosen to keep a life-altering secret from her. Callie was dead wrong, and Frankie had every right to be furious. There was nothing more to it.

"I'm not saying Ma and Pop didn't fuck up royally," Frankie answered him, having thought it out. "But the two aren't mutually exclusive, you know? Mason still did wrong by me. Big time."

Paulie slammed his beer bottle on the end table. "Mary Frances, listen to me. How was Callie to know that if she told you right away, you wouldn't curse the hell out of her for having laid such a trip on you right after Ma's death? She was in an impossible situation. Can't you see that? God rest her soul, but Ma was way wrong to ask Callie-fornia to be the one to tell you."

"She should have refused Ma the favor then," Frankie said. "Why the hell did she agree to do this in the first place?"

"Oh, you know how persuasive Ma can be, I mean, was," Paulie corrected himself sadly. "And Callie didn't exactly have time to think it all through. There was no time left. What was she supposed to do? Say 'Listen, Mrs. C., let me get back to you next week on that'? She did it because Ma begged her to do it. Can't you just accept that? You don't want to blame Ma because she's dead, so you're heaping all of your anger on Callie."

Frankie stared at the wall clock and watched the minute hand as it made short, staccato leaps from one second to the next. She followed the motion with her eyes until the repetition of the movement became almost hypnotic to her, and she could feel her breathing slowing down.

Paulie, who could sense that she was copping out on the conversation, grew frustrated. "So, can't you see that Callie was in an impossible situation and Ma put her there?"

Frankie looked at him as if he were a stranger. There was a chilling, lost look in her eyes that didn't seem to comprehend the entirety of what had been said. Not only was it atypical of Frankie to be so out of tune, it was as if she were another person entirely.

"Mary Frances! Are you fucking possessed? Look at me! Answer me!" Paulie said with fierce agitation.

Frankie stared ahead with a dreamlike glaze in her eyes. "I thought Mason and I were traveling down the same road together, you know, going in the same direction, to the same place," she said softly. "But I was wrong, wasn't I, Paulie?"

Paulie picked up his bottle and polished off the beer. "You're freaking me out, Mary Frances," he said, as he got up and walked into the kitchen to get another one. Paulie reentered the living room with a fresh bottle. "Let me tell you something. Just because you hit a bump in the road, or maybe even a pothole or two, doesn't mean you're going in the wrong direction. It's called life."

"Yeah, well, Callie don't want me in hers anyway," Frankie said scornfully. "She just got all caught up in the moment. Felt sorry for me with Ma dying and all. That's why she offered her home to me, talked about that job and all. She didn't really care. Hell, Regina was right. She just wanted to do her good deeds and keep on walking."

Paulie's eyes almost bulged out of his head. "No, she didn't walk, she fucking ran! Because you literally chased her out of your house. She wasn't going anywhere, and you goddamn well know it. Now you're gonna go from blaming Callie for something that's not her fault to doubting her sincerity and her love for you. That sucks, Mary Frances. What kind of friend are *you*? And if you think that Cunningham broad was right, go square things with her. She'll take you back in a heartbeat."

"I don't want Regina in my life. We had a talk today, a rather civil one, and I told her so. I wished her well and apologized for letting her believe I felt the same way about our friendship as she did all these years."

"Fine. Good for you. But I don't want to talk about her. I want to help my sister, but fuckin' A, you are making this so hard for me, Mary Frances. You're the most stubborn goddamn woman I've ever known."

Frankie sat up with a start. "How come you've always called me Mary Frances? How come you never called me Frankie like everyone else did?"

Paulie looked surprised by the question. "I can't believe you don't know that. Don't you remember that bully on the Raucher Street named Frankie Corronado, Jr.? I hated that asshole from the day I first met him in kindergarten. No way I was going to call my sister by the same name. And to this day, I'm glad I didn't. You were a pretty little girl who didn't know it, and now you're a pretty woman who doesn't know it either. Gee, you sure waited a long time to ask me that question. I thought you knew all about that years ago."

"Maybe I forgot," Frankie said, as if it suddenly didn't matter again.

"Mary Frances, have I gotten through to you at all?" Paulie asked desperately.

Frankie looked dumbfounded. "I'm so confused, Paulie. And I'm really dizzy and I have a headache."

"What have you eaten today?" Paulie asked.

Frankie thought for a moment. "I guess nothing," she said. "It slipped my mind."

"No wonder you're like this. Is there any food out there?" he said getting up.

"Lots," Frankie said. "But I'll just have a raspberry yogurt and a bran muffin. My stomach's in knots. I can't eat anything heavier than that."

"Okay, stay there," Paulie said, walking toward the kitchen. "I'll get it for you."

"Thanks, Paulie."

"Here," Paulie said a minute later, laying a tray with juice, yogurt, and a muffin on the coffee table in front of her. "Maybe this will put the common sense back into your head."

Frankie picked up the yogurt and removed the lid. She picked up the spoon to take the first bite. "Who the hell could that be?" she said, putting the yogurt down.

Paulie and Frankie looked cautiously at one another. Paulie walked to a section of the living room where he could catch a glimpse of the person ringing the doorbell through the blinds. "I have no idea who it is," he said. "It's not someone from *this* neighborhood. Not dressed like that. It's some blond guy I've never seen before in my life."

Frankie gasped. "Oh, God, Paulie. I don't know which one of us he's come to shoot, but you'd better let him in."

Paulie looked confusedly at her. "What the hell are you talking about?"

"You'll see," Frankie said. "Just open the door."

CHAPTER 26

Paulie was staring vacantly at the handsome blond stranger with the thick locks of hair and the tailored clothing, when the caller's identity swiftly dawned on him. He swallowed a lump in his throat that felt as if it were an orange, and the sick feeling in the pit of his stomach seemed to mark the spot were the "orange" had landed.

"Is something wrong?" the visitor said. "Please don't tell me I look like an FBI agent. God, I'd hate that. Ever meet one of them? They're so deadpan and robotic."

He's making a joke. Thank God, Frankie thought as she listened to the one-sided conversation. That means Callie got home safely.

"No," Paulie said, staring skeptically at him. "Why do you ask?"

"You have that odd look of fear on your face. I figured you might have been expecting one of our government's finest," the visitor said, grinning.

"No, not really," Paulie said suspiciously, anxious to ascertain his motive.

"Paulie, for God's sake, invite him in," Frankie yelled from the couch.

"Why don't you come in?" Paulie said, trying to hide his nervousness and doing a lousy job of it.

"Don't you want to see some ID?" the visitor asked.

"I don't think I need it," Paulie said. "You must be Callie-fo, I mean, Callie's husband."

"Jackson Hethers," he said, extending his hand. "And you must be Frankie's brother. I'm sorry, I don't—"

"Paulie Cavalese," came forth the choked reply. "Come inside."

Frankie wanted to cry for joy when Jackson walked in the house. He was more gorgeous than the photos Callie had showed her; he was exactly like the man Callie always swore she'd marry some day. Handsome and debonair with "very twinkly eyes." They must look wonderful together, Frankie thought, feeling happiness for the friend she was so convinced she could never forgive.

Jackson smiled broadly at Frankie. "You must be Frankie. I'm so delighted to meet you. You have no idea how much I've heard your name over the years."

"Really?" Frankie said, extending her hand to him.

"Yes, really. And I'd rather have a hug," Jackson said. "If you don't mind. I feel like we're old friends."

Frankie had no qualms about hugging him. Doing so was comfortable for her; she felt as if she already knew him, too.

Paulie continued to stare at Jackson.

Jackson could sense Paulie's discomfort, and that rattled *him*, but he masked his feelings with humor. "I'd hug you, too, Paulie, but I'd rather get to know you first."

Paulie attempted a weak laugh. He wondered if Jackson could see the sweat on his brow, then he got angry at himself for letting himself be intimidated at all.

"Oh, please, sit down!" Frankie said graciously. "Where are my manners? Can I get you a drink or something?"

Jackson took a seat on the couch next to Frankie. "Thank you. And, no, I don't need anything. I'm fine."

You sure are, Frankie thought to herself. Mason did all right for herself. Good for her.

"I'd like to tell you both how very sorry I am to hear about your mother. Callie told me she was a wonderful woman. She spoke of her many times over the years." He looked at Frankie. "Said she had lots of spunk; just like you. I wish I could have known her. Please, accept my deepest sympathy."

"Thank you, Jackson," Frankie said. "That's very kind of you."

"Yes, thank you," Paulie said, fidgeting awkwardly with something in his pocket.

Paulie was now making Frankie nervous, just standing there stupidly, as if he were waiting for Jackson to punch him out or vice versa. "Sit down, Paulie," Frankie urged strongly, indicating the armchair with a nod.

Jackson picked up on the interchange between them, and Frankie noticed that he had. Quickly, she tried to allay any possible suspicion. "My brother's on the shy side. You've got to forgive him."

Jackson took a good look at Paulie. "Now that, I never would have guessed. Not in a million years. I've always prided myself on being an intuitive guy. Guess I scored a big fat zero here," he said with a sardonic twist to his words.

Oh, shit, Paulie thought. Callie-fornia must have spilled everything and he's just here to fuck with me. Wants to see how much of this I can take.

This isn't my imagination, Jackson told himself. Something isn't right here. He was uncomfortably distracted from the purpose of his visit: to express his condolences and to appeal to Frankie on Callie's behalf. But Paulie, sitting silently in the chair in his dark, tight clothes, reminded Jackson of Mr. July on Joely's Hunkiest Guys of the Year calendar.

Frankie sensed what was going on, but she had no idea how to blot out the suspicions she was convinced Jackson had. "It was really nice of you to come all the way to Rainytown to express your condolences," Frankie said to Jackson.

Jackson turned to her. "I needed to do that, Frankie. And to be completely honest, I came here for both you and Callie. I wasn't home from Seattle a half hour yesterday when my wife came charging hysterically into the house. Quite frankly, she looked so brutal I was afraid someone had attacked her."

"Oh, no," Frankie said. "I did."

"I meant physically," Jackson said. "I'm sure you never laid a hand on her." He turned quickly to Paulie to catch his reaction. Can I say the same for you, he thought.

It was as if Paulie could hear his thoughts. This guy is really out to fuck with me. Damn it, Callie-fornia, how much did you tell him? *Did* you tell him? Paulie suddenly remembered the story of *The Tell-Tale Heart* that he'd read in high school. Maybe he doesn't know anything. Maybe I'm just hearing the dead man's heart beat under the floorboards. Damn it! I've got to mellow before *I'm* the one that tells him. Maybe Pop was right. Maybe I am fucking Paula, cracking under this rich guy's gaze like a chicken-shit broad. Damn.

"Of course I never laid a hand on Callie," Frankie said, feeling the tension mount between the two men. "But if I had, it wouldn't have hurt as much as what I said."

"Callie's separation from you has been an albatross around her neck since the day I met her," Jackson said. "It's haunted her for years. Maybe she should have tried to contact you before; I don't know. I do know that my wife has her insecurities, and if anything kept her from reestablishing contact, it was insecurity, not a lack of caring. But what I know for sure is that I've never seen her hurt like this, Frankie. She can't bear the thought of having regained your friendship only to lose it again. I hope you'll pardon me for being presumptuous, but I have to believe...I suppose I *want* to believe...that you feel the same way."

Frankie picked up her spoon and dug it into the yogurt. She didn't know how to respond.

"She does feel the same way," Paulie said. "She's just got a little pride problem."

"And my brother has a big mouth," Frankie said, evil-eyeing him.

Jackson laughed. "See? I knew he wasn't shy after all."

Paulie swallowed another lump in his throat. This guy doesn't let go. Damn. What the fuck does he know?

Jackson looked at Frankie and smiled understandingly. He was well aware that this was a difficult thing to talk about, especially to a stranger. He watched as she put a spoonful of yogurt in her mouth. "That stuff is good for you. I have one every morning. Raspberry's my favorite, too."

"Yeah, I like yogurt," Frankie said. "But I wouldn't eat it for years. After high school, I worked at this diner, and my boss told me one day that part of yogurt is actually alive."

"I believe it's the bacteria," Jackson said.

"Yeah, well, it totally freaked me out!"

"Culture shock," Jackson said with a grin.

"Mason said you were funny," Frankie said.

"Does that mean I pass muster?" Jackson asked.

"Only if it's Grey Poupon," Frankie shot back at him.

They both laughed out loud while Paulie remained stone-faced.

"So," Jackson said, ambling back into uncomfortable territory. "Do you think you might consider working things out with Callie?"

"I don't know," Frankie said. "I just can't get over the fact that she kept such important news from me. I think I would have told her immediately."

"I understand. Maybe you both have different ways of handling difficult situations. And maybe you don't. But just because you *think* you would've handled things differently in the same situation, is that a reason to end this relationship forever?"

Frankie looked at him brokenly. "I don't know, Jackson. I just don't know. I'm sorry for some of the things I said to her, I really am, but I can't apologize for how I feel. And for the record, you're starting to sound like my brother, throwing your logic in my face and expecting me to just up and change my mind."

Jackson glanced over at Paulie. "Well, I'm glad to hear we're on the same page where this situation is concerned."

Paulie nodded uncomfortably. What the hell did he mean by *that*, he wondered.

"I'm not going to push you, Frankie. I just want to let you know that Callie would welcome you back with open arms. And that both of us, not just Callie, would really love for you to come occupy Rosa's old apartment. That's another reason I came here today. I wanted to extend that invitation personally so that you'd understand just how much you're truly wanted in our home. I sincerely hope, no, I pray, that you'll reconsider."

"I can't promise anything," Frankie said. "I really don't think I can reconsider. I just feel dead inside."

"And if you stay here, Mary Frances, you will be dead inside. You're half dead already."

"Paulie, please."

Paulie turned to Jackson. "She'll think about it. Don't worry, I'll help her think about it."

"I appreciate that. Thank you. Well, I'll leave you alone now. You're grieving for your mother, and you don't need me putting unnecessary pressure on you. But I'll say it one last time: you and Callie really need each other. I wish I could fulfill all of her needs, but I can't. No one person can fulfill all of another person's needs. Life doesn't work that way. Anyway, Callie needs her best girlfriend in her life, just like I believe you do."

Jackson stood up, and Frankie started to rise as well. "Stay there, Frankie, don't get up. I'm not going to say goodbye, just 'see you soon.' Oh, and by the way, I'm having the apartment painted today, just in case." Jackson winked at her. "You take care. Here's my card. Call me anywhere, anytime. Got that?"

"Thanks, Jackson," Frankie said, taking the card. "You're really a great guy. I'm glad Mason has you."

"Hethers," he said with a grin. "But you can call her anything you want, just as long as you call." Jackson turned to Paulie. "Hey, Paulie, you know anything about cars?"

"Sure," Paulie said. "Lots. Why?"

"Walk me outside then, if you will. I have a question about my Jag."

Oh shit, Frankie said to herself. He's gonna nail Paulie to the cross.

Car question my ass, Paulie thought to himself. "Sure, no problem."

The two men walked outside and Frankie went nervously back to her yogurt.

"So, what's the question you wanted to ask me," Paulie said, as they stood together on the sidewalk. "Something about your car?"

Jackson pointed to his car. "Do you like that color?" he said. "I'm trading it in for a newer model soon, and I was wondering if I should go with something lighter."

Paulie stared at him skeptically. "Newer model, huh?"

"Yeah, I'm thinking about it. In fact, I'm wondering if Callie had recently considered trading hers in for a newer model. But she may prefer something darker."

Paulie was growing agitated with Jackson's word dance and double entendres. "Excuse me," Paulie said bluntly. "Just what the hell are you trying to say to me? I'll be glad to hear you out, but I'm not going to stand here and play fucking mind games with you. Got that?"

"Sorry," Jackson said, unprepared for the frank response. "I'm not trying to be an idiot. I just don't know exactly how to handle this."

"Handle what?" Paulie asked impatiently.

"This situation. Look, my wife and I had a wonderful reunion last night," Jackson began uncomfortably.

Paulie felt sick to his stomach just picturing them together. "That's really none of my business. I can't imagine why you feel the need to tell me this."

Jackson ignored his comment and proceeded to talk. "And I think our relationship is stronger than ever, because for the first time in our lives, we both realized that we'd taken our very solid marriage for granted. We've both learned how easily a marriage can crumble if you don't take the necessary steps to fix those little things when they start to go wrong. You know, it's sort of like losing a shingle from the roof and not bothering to replace it. Before you know it, you've lost more shingles, and then you've got three inches of rain in your bedroom and you've ruined the ceiling below. I'm sure you see my point. Cal and I have still got issues to deal with; I'm not kidding myself, but I believe we're back on solid ground now."

"Again," Paulie said strongly, "you're telling me this because…"

Jackson took a good look at Paulie. He saw a strong, potent, exceptionally handsome man whom he preferred not to have as a complication in his life.

"You're staring," Paulie said, finding his courage again. Now it was Jackson who was feeling a bit shaky.

"Let me put it this way," Jackson said. "If I went home now and told my wife that you and I had a private talk, what kind of reaction do you think I'd get?"

Paulie kicked a rock by his right foot. Jackson was making him angry. "She's your wife. What the fuck are you asking me for?"

Jackson held his own. "So, do you have any problem with me doing that?"

Paulie needed a moment to consider this one. Going on the assumption that Callie had not confessed anything, and considering the incredible strain she was under, Paulie feared that Jackson's question might just lead her to believe that Jackson had heard the entire story from him. And then what would she do? Paulie wondered. She'd fucking lose it, he told himself, expose everything unnecessarily, and then watch her marriage go south. Then she'd blame him. Not that Paulie wouldn't like her marital status to change for his own selfish reasons, but he knew that wasn't what Callie wanted. She wanted her husband and her family. He couldn't make her happy forever the way Jackson could. He knew that. He needed to be the friend he'd claimed to be and do everything in his power to help preserve her marriage.

"I said, would you have any problem with me doing that?" Jackson repeated.

"What if I said that I did?" Paulie asked him straightforwardly. "Would it make any difference?"

"Yes," Jackson said, dropping the pretense. "It might make *all* the difference."

"Why don't we take a seat inside your car? We can talk without interruption. You can't be too careful on this street. It holds a Guinness world record for nosy."

Jackson laughed. "Sure thing," he said, as he opened the passenger side of his car and let Paulie in. "So I've heard tell." Paulie drew a long breath as Jackson walked around and got into the driver's seat and closed the door. "Okay, Paulie. I'm listening."

"I grew up with Callie," Paulie began. "I've known her since I was three and she was six."

"I'm well aware of that," Jackson said. "She's talked to me about your entire family, many times. You are all a very special part of her life."

"Did she tell you I had a terrible crush on her when I was about eleven or so? In fact, it grew in intensity as I got older and lasted throughout my teen years. Quite frankly, Callie put the H in hormones for me."

Jackson made a face. "So glad to know that my wife originally jump-started your libido," Jackson said. "What of it?"

"Didn't she ever mention my crush on her back then?"

"Sounds vaguely familiar, though I'm sure she described it more delicately than you just have. Unfortunately, I suppose I didn't feel the same need to pay the rapt attention to her childhood chronicles that I do now. Is this something you feel I need to know…the history of your adolescent hormones?"

"You asked me to be upfront with you," Paulie said. "That's what I'm doing, starting from the beginning."

Jackson shrugged. "Yeah, okay. Go on, then."

"Well, from the moment I saw her again, that first day she came back, close to two weeks ago, that babe, I mean, Callie, melted my heart all over again."

"And you did exactly *what* about it?"

"Oh, I don't know. Flirted, tossed a few sexual innuendoes in her lap. Told her to check out my many assets."

"And how did she respond?" Jackson asked flatly, unappreciative of Paulie's vaunted disposition.

"Oh, she pushed me away; tossed some clever insults at me; tried to deny any and all attraction."

"So I am to infer from that comment that she *was* attracted to you?"

"Couldn't help herself," Paulie said, enjoying himself. "Look at me."

"Jesus Christ. Are you always this much of an asshole?"

"No," Paulie said wryly. "Only on select occasions. I'm actually quite a humble Adonis."

"I said 'asshole,' " Jackson corrected him. "Not Adonis."

"I must have misheard you," Paulie taunted him. "But to answer your question, I really am a very humble guy."

"And I'm the goddamn queen of England," Jackson muttered. "So, this attraction, I'm sure you didn't let it stop there, did you?" he asked irritably.

"Nope. Can't say that I did," Paulie responded cavalierly.

Just fucking wonderful, Jackson thought. "So what the hell happened?"

"Look, I'm going to lay it on the line for you, Jack. Your wife was attracted to me, and I was most definitely attracted to her. I took advantage of her weaknesses, of the friction between the two of you and your absence, and I maybe got a kiss or two out of the deal. But then we became friends. Callie was instrumental in helping me to grow up. She begged me to open my eyes and realize that my mother, despite her many denials, wanted nothing more in this life than to see our pop one more time. I listened to her, and God knows it took some doing, but with her good advice behind me, I made it happen. On a more personal front, no, we never made love. You have my word on that. Callie made it very clear that her husband and her children were the most important people in the world to her. I respected her immensely for that, and despite the asshole I appear to be, I didn't push for more. I was just someone filling a temporary void in her life during an extremely painful time in mine, and as I just said, from that grew friendship, nothing else. And that's it."

Paulie stopped talking to gauge Jackson's reaction to his semi-true, out-of-sequence rendition of what had happened. Despite the altering of facts and the reinvented time chronology, Paulie was truthful about what mattered most: they did not make love (almost didn't count,) and Callie had indeed chosen Jackson. There was never any question about that.

"And that's all there is to it," Jackson said. "You're not leaving anything out."

"Well, yeah, I left shit out. You don't need to know every word spoken between us. You just need to know that you've got one fine babe for a wife who loves the hell out of you and who has remained faithful to you." Paulie hoped Jackson wouldn't ask for his definition of "faithful."

"All right," Jackson conceded. "I'm going to take your word for it. Quite selfishly, it won't do me or my marriage much good to foment a stir over this and complicate our lives any further."

"Does that mean you won't mention this conversation to Callie?"

"No, I won't. I can live with this, especially since I feel partially responsible for pushing her away when she needed me. I didn't mean to; my company was falling apart. I felt Callie was unsympathetic and totally absorbed in her own problems, and…oh, it doesn't matter. We just lost each other for a while. I see no reason at all to tell Callie what I know. It would devastate her to find out that I even suspected anything, especially since I have your word that nothing happened."

"My word is worth something," Paulie said, taking a more serious tone.

"I believe you. And Callie's been through enough heartache of late. Confronting her with this would serve no purpose at all. I plan to do everything I can on my part to make our marriage strong again. Telling Callie what I know would only make that all the more difficult. She'd never be able to let her guilt go, and that alone could destroy us. Besides, Paulie, I really *do* want to like you. After all, in some weird sense, I guess you are my new brother-in-law."

Paulie rolled his eyes. "Well, if you put it like that…"

"And you do have a twisted sense of humor, which I'm sure I'll appreciate more fully when I'm not the brunt of it," Jackson continued. "I pray that your sister and my wife will find their way to become friends again. And when that happens, I don't want there to be any awkwardness between us. I mean that."

"Thanks, Jackson. I honestly *do* feel the same way. And let me reassure you that your wife and I are truly *just* friends. That's the best I can do for you. Now, if you'd do something for me?"

"Sure, what's that?" Jackson asked.

"Tell me what made you suspicious in the first place. What exactly led you to believe that something had gone down between Callie and me?"

"Nothing," Jackson said. "Not until you opened the door with that Oh-shit-deer-caught-in-the-headlights look on your face when you saw me. You didn't really hold your cool as well as I'd expect a guy like you to do."

"You caught me off guard," Paulie said, lighting up. "And what do you mean by 'a guy like you'?"

"Hell, I don't know," Jackson said. "You look like one of those studs on my secretary's calendar, minus the fig leaf. I put that image together with the unfortunate image I had of the sad and vulnerable wife I left behind, adding in, of course, your rather nervous behavior, your sister's reaction to your behavior, and voilà, that's all it took."

"We're square now?" Paulie said, reaching for the door handle.

"Yes, we are," Jackson said, extending his hand.

Paulie and Jackson exchanged a solid handshake. "Just take care of her," Paulie asked. "I just want to know she's happy."

"Thanks," Jackson said, as Paulie opened the door to get out. "You're okay...for someone who knows how to royally piss off a guy!"

Paulie acknowledged the comment with a smile, but it soon faded as he watched Jackson drive off, knowing he was on his way home to Callie. He told himself that all was not so grim. Callie's husband was a good guy; he clearly loved her. Paulie could walk away with his pride and honor intact. He'd done all he could to ensure Callie's happiness.

"So, did he kick your behind?" Frankie asked Paulie before he'd even made it completely inside the house.

"Nah," Paulie said. "He was just trying to find out if it needed kickin'."

"Translation?" Frankie asked.

"I told him what I told you, Mary Frances. There was an attraction—"

"With *mutuality* to it," Frankie said.

"Whatever," Paulie said. "You and that stupid word. I told him that we had not made love, we had become friends, and that he and the kids were the most important thing in Callie-fornia's life. Okay?"

"You referred to her as 'Callie-fornia'?"

"Hell, no, Mary Frances. Get real. Are you satisfied now?"

"Yeah, sure," Frankie said. "It doesn't really matter anyway."

"What does that mean?" Paulie said, turning on the floor lamp that Frankie had turned off again in his absence. "That you're not going to reconcile with Callie? What's with this goddamn darkness you insist on living in? You remind me of one of those light bulb jokes Ma liked so much."

"What in the world are you talking about?" Frankie asked.

"Oh, you remember those jokes. Ma loved the one her friend Sophie Levin told her. How many Jewish mothers does it take to screw in a light bulb?"

"Yeah, yeah...I know," Frankie groaned. "None. 'I'll just sit here alone in the dark.'"

"That's you, all right," Paulie said. "Alone in the dark."

"At least a Jewish mother has kids," Frankie said flatly. "I got nothing."

"Because you're choosing to have nothing. It's all your doing. So you have fun sitting here, Mary Frances. Play the fucking martyr. Feel sorry for yourself. I'd do almost anything for you, you know that, but I'm not going to sit here in the dark with you and pretend I'm the phantom of the opera. You've just got to be right, don't you? You'd rather sit here and sulk because Callie made a decision that you *think* you disagree with. Truth be told, Mary F., you haven't been in her position, so you can't really say, can you? But you'd rather rot away in the cold, black hell of this house than look toward the light and see the wonderful life you could have waiting for you. A job, a beautiful new home, a best friend, maybe a family of your own someday."

"You and Jackson," Frankie said angrily. "Two peas in a holier-than-thou pod. This entire situation is just *so* simple to both of you, isn't it? Nobody understands what it took for me to trust Callie again, and neither one of you understands what it felt like to be hurt again. I can't get over the feeling that she played God by deciding when and if I should ever hear this news. I can't get over feeling like she thinks I'm beneath her somehow. I feel like one of her charity cases at the hospital."

"That's not fair. Whenever she told you about Ma, even if it had been right away, it still would have required making a decision to do so, wouldn't it have? I'm sorry, Mary Frances, you've put Callie between a rock and a hard place. And the hard place is your head. You're so goddamn stubborn. I'm going home for a while before I go back to work. You call me if you want to talk. But I've got about two brain cells left after trying to knock sense into your head. So call me only if you feel like being reasonable. See ya." Paulie opened the front door and walked outside.

"They just don't understand," Frankie said, as she heard the sound of Paulie's sports car engine outside. "Nobody gets it but me."

CHAPTER 27

Callie lay in the chaise lounge, luxuriating in the feel of the sun's rays on her body. It was just the kind of day she loved: a cloudless cerulean sky with a bright, warm sun to bask in. A pitcher of lemonade and a good, absorbing novel, she thought, would be the perfect complement to such a glorious day. But her heart hurt too much to think about anything but what grieved her, and there was no writer in the world who was good enough to refocus her attention elsewhere. And although it appealed to her, she hadn't the energy to go inside and prepare some citrus libation.

The sunlight danced on the pool water, enticing little beams of delightful illumination that would tempt even the staunchest of poolside sitters to take a dip. Callie loved the pool; she was a superb swimmer, but nothing about the sparkling light show remotely interested her.

She glanced over at the plants along the side of the house that Eduardo nurtured so well. How lucky she was to live on such luscious grounds and to enjoy a taste of tropical paradise in her own surroundings. In the distance, at her neighbor's farm, she could see the palomino looking in her direction. Mr. Ed, her kids had always called him; they had loved to visit him when they were younger. It's not that they'd lost their equestrian spirit as they grew older, but their lives were filled with so many friends and functions, not to mention adult responsibilities, that the simple joys of spending time with a neighbor's horse no longer fit into their schedules. But this was an exciting time for them. They were having a wonderful summer in Maine and would be going off to college soon, where a world of opportunity and new friends awaited them. New friends, Callie thought as she steamrolled into self-deprecation. Sure, they'll make new friends. But they won't ignore the old ones. Not like I did.

She often daydreamed about her children and their respective futures. It gave her a brief hiatus from thinking about her own, but nothing could eclipse what was foremost in her mind. She'd waited twenty-three years to make things right with Frankie, and when she was finally able to do so, she had discovered to her delight that the connection between them was still as strong as ever. To lose that connection all over again was simply unendurable. But she alone could not correct it. She could disseminate the proper pleas and invitations, but she did not have the power to elicit a response, much less one involving any reciprocity of feelings.

She looked at the lounge chair next to her and imagined Frankie sharing in this beautiful day with her, finally getting a break from the gloom that had dominated her life. Oh, Frankie, please come back into my life.

Callie wasn't looking for a shadow; she was an independent woman. When existing in her usual state of mind, she enjoyed her time alone and didn't really understand people who couldn't enjoy the pleasures of solitude. But that didn't negate the need for a best friend to share her life with, to go shopping with, to understand her when no one else could, to push her when she needed pushing, and to love her when she couldn't love herself. Even more so, she needed and wanted to give all of those gifts to someone else. If anything was clear to Callie, it was the fact that nobody but Frankie had ever come close to being that person, and nobody ever would.

"Hello, my sweet, depressed baby," Jackson said, appearing at her side.

"Hi, honey," Callie said, managing a smile. "Where have you been? I thought you were going to work out."

"I did, too," Jack said as he stood by her chair, "but I remembered something that needed doing in the office. I figured it was worth an hour out of my Saturday because it would take four hours on Monday with the usual interruptions."

"I'm just sorry you had to go in on the weekend at all," Callie said, making a visor with her hand to block the sun as she looked up at him.

"Don't burn your eyeballs, honey. I'll sit down next to you." Jackson pulled up the nearby empty chair and sat down.

"Thanks," Callie said. "It's really bright today. Even with my sunglasses on. But the sun feels good."

"So do you," Jackson said, slipping his right hand under her bikini top. "Real good."

Callie blew him a naughty kiss. "I love you so much, Jackson," she said as he caressed her. "I'm sorry I've been such a mess since you've come back home."

"I take it the mail came. Still no word from Frankie?"

"No," Callie said, her eyes watering. "And it's been two weeks now. I really thought I'd hear something by now."

"So did I," Jackson said with conviction.

"You don't even know her," Callie said. "How could you..."

"That's true," Jackson said. "I don't know her. But I have met her."

Callie looked absolutely stunned.

"The day after I returned from Seattle. I stopped at the Cavalese house on my way home from the office. I wanted to offer my condolences and to try to convince Frankie to work things out with you."

"God, Jackson, why didn't you tell me?"

"I was afraid it would get your hopes up, honey."

"What did Frankie say?" Callie asked eagerly.

"She said she was sorry for the way she spoke to you but just didn't know if she could ever forgive you for not telling her about her mother right away. I really tried to reason with her and explain how minor that seemed in the scheme of things, and that you handled the situation to the best of your ability, but she seemed so fragile and broken, as if she were incapable of fixing anything. She was just so lost. There was simply nothing else I could say to her. I wanted to, Cal, but it would have been invasive and inappropriate."

Callie looked crestfallen. "Oh, dear God, I hope she's okay. I'm so worried about her, Jackson. But what can I do? I have to respect her wishes. It's just that...well, if a handsome devil like you couldn't convince her to forgive me, and if my letter didn't convince her, then I suppose nothing will. The more time that passes, the less likely I am to hear from her. It feels like twenty-three more years have passed this time."

"It's no wonder," Jackson said. "Your two weeks together were extremely intense. Once you find something or someone precious that you've lost, it becomes even more difficult to let it go again because you've learned to cherish it that much more. I understand, sweetie, I really do." Fearful of getting too maudlin, Jackson tried to lighten the conversation. "Well, look at that water! Does it not beg the body to immerse itself in such liquid delight on this hot August day?"

"Go get into your swimsuit," Callie said. "Enjoy yourself. I just don't feel up to it...Jack, what in the world are you doing?"

Callie watched in amazement as Jackson began disrobing by the pool. "You're going to swim naked...in the daytime?"

"Nobody's around, oh prudish one. Unless you count Mr. Ed way over yonder. I've seen his many times; I don't care if he sees mine. As long as he doesn't compare, I can deal with it."

Callie laughed. "You're so incredibly strange at times."

Jackson winked at her, then dived naked into the pool.

"What the hell!" said Callie, removing her bikini top and then the bottom. "Maybe a little fun is just what the doctor ordered."

"Ah, you have made Naked Matador a happy man!" Jackson exclaimed as she jumped into the pool. Have you ever been ravished nautically?"

"Like I just said," Callie said, wrapping her arms around his shoulders and her legs around his. "You are so weird."

"I think you said 'strange,' " Jackson jokingly corrected her. "In fact, 'Incredibly strange,' if I am to quote your sobriquet with precision."

"Weird, strange, peculiar, bizarre. Take your pick, honey. They all work for you." Callie laughed and gave him a kiss.

" I like 'weird.' I'm weird and in love with my beautiful wife," Jackson said. "Oh, Cal, honey, I just want you to be happy."

"Me too," Callie said, clinging buoyantly to him. "I want us all to be."

Misery crushed her like a vise. Despondency, melancholy, and self-loathing had made her a stranger to herself. Paulie stayed away, but he called her every day to see if she was still breathing or if she'd miraculously had a change of mind, but he refused to come to the house anymore. His sister's dark, brooding mood was intolerably morose for him to witness, and the funereal oppression in which she lurked, like a ghost haunting herself, created far too bleak a scene for him to endure, even briefly. But it affected him nonetheless; he carried her disconsolation with him at all times, and dutifully dragged her chains as they entangled with his own.

Frankie was semi-conscious of the effect she was having on Paulie, and naturally more so on her own self-destruction, but she could not see a way out. So deep in her despair, she had stopped hunting for the light, because for Frankie, there was none.

Out on the front porch, she preserved the only color left in her life: the green of her mother's plants. They helped to secure a connection with Ruby, but Frankie felt deader than her mother was.

She put the watering can down and took a seat on the rocking chair. She had long come to realize that Paulie was right; Ruby had put Callie in an untenable situation. Frankie could not accept the fact that it was only her grief that spoke so horribly to Callie and sent her crying into the streets. It was more than grief; it was the monster inside her — a monster so heinous and depraved that it didn't deserve to walk among the living. She was the unwanted child of a drunken failure, and despite Ruby's protestations to the contrary, Frankie's arrival in this world had nixed all chances for Ruby to ever realize her dreams. Ruby hadn't wanted the infant child of her husband's first wife, but she was kind enough to pretend otherwise on her deathbed. Sure, maybe she had come to care for Frankie over the years, but she couldn't have wanted her from the start, and despite her love for Frankie, she had never stopped harboring resentment.

As for Callie, she'd long gone back to her own world and was now likely to remember her reunion with Frankie as something she'd wished had never happened at all. Even if Frankie were now to beg forgiveness, Callie wouldn't be interested. How could Callie ever trust her again? She certainly wouldn't want to live with the fear that if she did something disagreeable to Frankie, the evil monster would emerge and assail her all over again.

Frankie had seen firsthand how much Jackson loved his wife. Certainly, his love and the love of her children were enough to fill Callie's world. She was back where she belonged, far from Rainytown, and the walls that separated her from Frankie grew thicker and taller by the day.

For years, Frankie had enjoyed watching the playful romp of the neighborhood children, but on this day, she could neither see nor hear them. She was oblivious to almost all life as she'd known it, but her pain could not obfuscate the sight of Regina crossing the street with a large white envelope in her hand. As Regina huffed and puffed up the three steps to the porch, Frankie felt every cell of her body shrink.

She was emotionally enervated. She could barely brace herself for any kind of interchange with Regina at all. "Don't tell me you've written me another letter, Reg. I thought we had settled everything between us."

"I didn't write you nothing, Frankie. And I already told you I was sorry for them letters. This one is from your other ex-best bud, Callie Mason. It came almost two weeks ago, by mistake."

Frankie suddenly found her strength again. "And you waited this long to bring it to me?" she said angrily.

Regina unfolded the extra chair and sat down. "Now, Frankie, don't go gettin' your bowels twisted up like a pretzel. It came like two days after you told Callie Mason to 'get the fuck out of your house.' "

Regina's delight in once again quoting Frankie's harsh condemnation of Callie did not escape her notice, but she chose to ignore it. "Why didn't you bring this to me right away?" Frankie demanded harshly.

"Well," Regina said matter-of-factly, "After you tellin' her to get the fuck out and all, I didn't think you were in no hurry to hear from her. And I wasn't feeling so well that day to bring it over."

"You have three able-bodied children," Frankie said vehemently.

"Whatever. I was gonna do it myself, but then it got lost in a stack of Hal's *Field and Stream* magazines, and I just forgot about it. Sheesh, Frankie, what's the big deal? You hate the woman's guts. You told her to get the fuck—"

"Will you stop saying that, Reg? Don't you ever quote me on that again, or I'll fucking kill you!"

Regina looked startled. "Sheesh, Frankie. You're acting like a wild animal or something. You got a real scary look in your eyes…like one of them rapid dogs. Here, take the darn thing."

Rabid, Frankie silently corrected her as she snatched the envelope out of Regina's hands. "You had no right holding my mail, Reg. It's not your place to decide what I want or don't want to see. Do you hear me?"

"Oh, shit," Regina exclaimed. "Don't tell me you still care for her?"

"Whatever I feel or don't feel for Callie," Frankie said, "has absolutely nothing to do with you. As for *our* relationship, I told you, it's over. It won't heal with time, if that's what you're hoping. Stick it with a fork, Reg; it's done! Now, leave me alone."

Regina pretended not to hear her. She was determined to gain Frankie's empathy. "I'm goin' in the hospital on Tuesday morning. They gotta take him by C-section. He's upside down. Breach of contract or something like that."

Frankie rolled her eyes. "Well, I hope everything goes well for you and the baby, Reg," Frankie said. "I mean that sincerely. But don't *ever* hold on to my mail again. And for the record, I don't believe that story about this being lost in Hal's magazines. You waited to bring this over until you had news about your baby, didn't you? It gave you an excuse to come over and make another plea for a friendship that you can't seem to accept no longer exists."

Regina was embarrassed and disappointed that Frankie had seen through her subterfuge so easily. "So, is this my cue to leave?" Regina asked dolefully.

Frankie smiled sarcastically. She was not a willing subject for Regina's attempt at emotional manipulation. "Three stars for you, Reg. That's right. It's time."

Regina put an arm on the railing and pushed herself up. "I was countin' on you bein' there with me, Frankie. Like you were when Steffie was born. It won't be right without you."

"You've got a husband to support you," Frankie said. "And apparently, lots of good friends on the block. Ask Edna to go with you. Goodbye Reg. Have a healthy baby boy."

Frankie held onto the envelope until Regina had gone and was back inside her home. She didn't want Regina to see how anxious she was to open it.

"Oh, God," Frankie said aloud, as her eyes fell upon the contents of the envelope.

She didn't even notice the letter from Callie at first. Only the signed adoption papers and a sealed envelope with her name on it, written in Ruby's handwriting, attached to the documents with a paper clip. Frankie opened the envelope slowly. Ruby's determined yet shaky scrawl made her want to sob.

> My dearest Frankie. By now you know what a big coward I am by letting Callie Mason break this traumatic news to you. I should have done it myself, but I couldn't bear to leave this earth seeing the shock and hurt on my baby's face. I hope you, God, and Callie will all forgive me for letting you find out like this that I'm not the woman who gave birth to you. Please don't be angry with Callie. I'm gonna beg her to do this for me (she ain't even here yet) even though it's wrong, but I think she'll do this terrible favor for me 'cause I'm dying. Just so you don't have any doubt how much I wanted you to be my little girl, here are the papers that I hope will prove just how much I wanted to be your Ma. I made it real official right away…when you were just a tiny baby. You need to know that, Frankie. I'm giving these to Callie Mason to give to you, 'cause I'd never want you to find them by mistake when you go sortin' through my stuff after I check out of this joint.

"Oh, Ma…" Frankie cried.

> I know how bad I fucked up your life, Frankie. It wasn't because I didn't love you. Your Pop had walked out on us and Paulie was out on his own by nineteen, and your selfish Ma didn't wanna be alone. Didn't know HOW to be alone. Maybe deep in my brain somewhere I had other stuff going on. Maybe I should have seen a headshrinker. I don't know. But I do know that I couldn't have asked for a better daughter, Frankie. And one last thing, I had a long talk with Callie Mason, and in all my life, I ain't never seen one friend care for another in such a sincere and loving way. And don't think your Ma didn't grill that girl to death. You know I can

read people well, Frankie, so you believe what I'm telling you. You hold on to that. And keep your brother in line. Oh, and for the record, he didn't know none of this either, so don't cop an attitude with him, okay? You two need each other. And you need your Pop, but not that bitch. Fuck her! Don't forget me, baby. I'll never forget you. Now get out into the world and live your dreams. Love always, Ma.

Frankie lay the papers in her lap and put her hand over her mouth to stop from crying. She stared vacantly ahead as Ruby's words began to sink in. As she picked up the adoption papers to take a second look, she noticed the letter from Callie lying underneath.

Dear Frankie: I hope you won't consider this typed letter impersonal. My hand was shaking too much to write. I'm still in shock over what happened between us yesterday. I <u>never</u> meant to hurt you, but to be completely truthful, I've been over and over this, and don't know if I'd have done anything differently had I been given a second chance. For me, there was no easy way to do what your mother had asked of me. I <u>can</u> assure you, however, that I had no intention of keeping this from you for any length of time whatsoever. I only wanted to give you a brief respite between your mother's death and this stunning news. I do wish you'd shared the news with <u>me</u> when you found out; maybe then this could have been avoided. But it was certainly your right to keep it to yourself for as long as you needed to, or forever, if that's what you wanted to do.

Frankie, I <u>can</u> get over the things you said to me because I know what a heavy toll life has taken on you all these years. Any weaker person would've lost it long ago, and that includes me. You've been amazing, and I have so much respect for you. I could never convince you just how much; you wouldn't believe me. What I <u>cannot</u> get over is the thought that our friendship has ended. My heart will never accept that, no matter what yours decides to do. You'll always be <u>my</u> best friend, whether or not I'm yours.

Jackson came back from Seattle last night. I'm so happy to have my husband again. Do I sound selfish for wanting my best friend, too? We're both so hopeful that you'll change your mind and come live in our home. And by the way, I've told Stephen and Molly about it, and they think it's great. 'I'm psyched for you, Mom,' is, I believe, a direct quote from my son. Please reconsider, Frankie. These words are from my heart. This is not a limited time offer for 'one best friend' or 'one sunny apartment.' There is no expiration date. You will always be welcome and wanted in my life. In our lives. Please get in touch with me. Maybe I can help you sort through some of this. I don't know what else to say that I haven't already said. Just one last reminder that you are much loved. Please come back into my life. Love, Mason.

She signed it "Mason," Frankie thought, overwhelmed with emotion. I can't believe she did that. I remember back when we were nine. We were sitting on my bed, making beaded necklaces, and I suddenly started callin' her "Mason Jar" 'cause I'd just learned from Ma what they were when I had asked for something to put our beads into. Guess I dropped the "jar" after the joke got old, but I never stopped calling her "Mason." She always told me that I could call her anything I wanted, but that she wasn't gonna refer to herself as that, not for all the tea in China. And she never did. Not until this letter.

Frankie ran her fingers over the handwritten signature. Maybe to Mason, I *am* worth more than all the tea in China. Wouldn't that be something?

Jackson had hoped that his afternoon frolic with Callie in their chlorinated wonderland would have been enough to boost her spirits for the rest of the day. But their bold lovemaking adventure had exhausted her, which only served to aggravate her unfailing depression.

For one wonderful hour, Callie had freed herself to find some treasure among the ruins. But when the hunt was over, all she could see was the destruction that surrounded her, knowing that with each passing day, the chance for any realization of her dreams was growing dimmer, just as the days of summer were growing shorter. At seven o'clock, Callie told Jackson she was going down for a nap. Sleep, for the time being, was her only method of escape.

Jackson felt helpless. There was only so much brazen adventure that he could offer her, and he became increasingly troubled as he saw his wife wrap herself in depression. Simultaneously, Callie was so deeply entrenched in her guilt over dragging Jackson through her dolor and dejection that she unwittingly intensified the pain for both of them.

By eight forty-five p.m., Callie's peaceful retreat had ended. Jackson was gently rubbing her back, coaxing her awake.

"Please, Jack," Callie mumbled, turning her head and sinking it into the pillow. "Just let me sleep."

"If you sleep like that, my little chickadee, thou shalt suffocate thyself."

"It would take me out of my misery," Callie said groggily.

"And it would put me in mine forever," Jackson said, his tone changing drastically. "Don't ever talk like that again, Callie."

"I'm sorry, sweetie," she said, dragging her words, her eyes still closed. "You know I didn't mean it. I swear, Jack. I really didn't."

"All is forgiven then," Jackson said cheerfully, shaking her more forcefully by her shoulders. "Now, you shall awake for someone has come to see you."

Callie awoke with a start. "Oh, God, Jack, please!" she said loudly. "Not Naked Matador again! He's ravished me enough for one day!"

"Naked Matador?" the voice in the hallway exclaimed.

"Oh my God!" Callie screamed. "Frankie!" She looked at Jackson excitedly. "Is she really here?"

"I'm here, Mason," Frankie said, entering the bedroom as Jackson motioned her to come in. "What's this Naked Matador stuff? Poor thing. I wish I had your problems. My heart bleeds for you."

Tears fell freely from Callie's eyes as she jumped out of bed to embrace her friend. "I'm so glad to see you that I'm not even embarrassed! Are you here to stay? To live in the apartment?"

Jackson smiled. "I think I'll go downstairs and help Paulie unload some things from the truck."

"Does that mean what I hope it means?" Callie said, barely able to control her exhilaration.

"If you'll still have me. My goodness, Mason, this house is a palace. It goes way beyond my expectations. It's beautiful and incredible. Just like you are. And I'm *so* sorry. I can't believe I was so horrible to you. It wasn't me talking, I swear."

"I understand," Callie said. "I told you that in my letter. Sit down, please."

Frankie hopped onto the bed and sat cross-legged. "I didn't get your letter until this afternoon. Can you believe that it was delivered to Reg's house by mistake and that she kept it for two damn weeks?"

"You're kidding!" Callie said. "How dare she?"

"Oh, she dared all right," Frankie said.

"Well, no sense in laboring on that now. It's done with. I just thank God she finally deigned to give it to you."

"Amen to that," Frankie said. "You know, Mason, even though Ma told me her secret before she died, I never got to ask her if she legally adopted me. I was so sure she hadn't, so sure she didn't really want me. Getting those papers was like getting a Ma all over again."

"Oh, Frankie, I'm so glad you feel that way. But why didn't you ask your father about it instead of assuming the worst?"

"I've been in a horrible place, Mason. No way could I have opened up this can of worms to my pop. Doing so would've given him a license to blubber about all the shit he's been holding inside since he left us. I couldn't deal with *me*; how in the world could I have dealt with *him*? But maybe someday soon, Pop and I will be able to have that talk."

"It'll be good for both of you. But only when you're ready."

"And another thing," Frankie told her, "I didn't think I could have taken finding out that Ma hadn't adopted me. It would've been a double whammy, you know? Not knowing, this way I could still hold on to the chance that she had."

"I understand," Callie said tenderly.

"Ma wrote me a beautiful letter," Frankie said as she looked around the bedroom in awe. "She told me how much she loved me and begged me to follow my dreams."

"Is that when you decided to come here?"

"I *wanted* to," Frankie said. "But I didn't think you'd want much to do with me after the horrible way I treated you. I thought you'd be scared to death of me, figuring I'd go ballistic like that any time I got upset. Then I found your letter, under the adoption papers. You know what convinced me you really cared about me?"

"No," Callie said, intrigued. "What?"

"You signed it 'Mason.' "

"Yeah," Callie said nostalgically. "I guess I did."

"You swore you'd never call yourself that."

"I know," Callie said. "I remember. And, listen you, don't think it was so easy for me to cave in and do it. And absolutely, positively do not expect it to ever happen again. Because it won't."

"Oh, I believe you, Mason," Frankie said. "But I'll always cherish the letter. Anyway, soon as I'd finishing reading it, I ran to the phone and called Paulie. Told him to borrow Pop's truck and bring it over to the house. You've never seen Paulie get anywhere so quickly. Seemed like he was on the doorstep in two seconds. We packed enough to hold me for a bit. I guess I'll be like you. I'll go back every day and do a bit more."

"And you know I'll help you," Callie said eagerly. "With the sales process too, but *only* if you want me to. I don't want to push."

"Sure, I'd *love* your help," Frankie said. "I just can't wait to put up the 'For Sale' sign. And I'm not telling any of those people where I'm going. Wouldn't want to deny them the pleasure of speculating for the rest of their lives."

Callie laughed. "We'll have to take a picture of the sign once we get it up. It'll be fun to see the looks we get while we're cleaning out the house."

"Oh, God, Mason. You've had enough of Rainytown. I can't ask you to help me clean out the house. You just finished cleaning out your—"

"Don't worry about it," Callie said. "You're right. I have had enough of Rainytown. But you've had even more of it. Way more. Besides, knowing I'm there to help you get out and move to a happier place, here with me, well, I can brave it. Might even enjoy it. I'm tough."

"You sure are," Frankie said. "You survived me."

"Barely," Callie said, then smiled. "C'mon. Let's go downstairs. Don't you want to see your new residence?"

"I'm dying to!" Frankie exclaimed. "Jackson wouldn't show it to me. He said that pleasure belonged strictly to you."

"There's no way this can be real!" Frankie said, after her tour of the apartment was over. "It's so big and bright and beautiful. And that marble in the bathroom. How elegant is that? Really, Mason, just seeing that kitchen with all those beautiful appliances makes me actually want to start cooking again. Oh, and those closets are enormous. And the bedroom…it's the size of Ma's room and mine put together. Even bigger, I think! And what a beautiful walkway to my own private entrance. I love the way it's lined with flowers on each side. Believe me, I'll use it. I swear, I'll never bust into your house from the other door if you don't know I'm coming."

"And I'll give you the same respect," Callie said. "You know that. After all, we are two adult women."

"Is that what we are?" Frankie said teasingly.

Callie laughed. "Well, now that you mention it…"

"Oh, and the view!" Frankie continued excitedly. "I never thought I'd see anything like that out any bedroom window of mine. I can't wait until daytime to really get a good look. Least you've got enough lights on your property for a proper sneak peek. Gee, Mason, if I'd known this place was *this* fabulous, I might not have been so quick to throw your ass out of my house."

Callie looked at her with mock indignation. "You may lose your mind at times," she said, laughing. "But you never lose your sense of humor."

As they exited the apartment through the foyer entrance, coming back into the main house, they met Jackson and Paulie on their way in. Callie gulped at the sight of seeing the two men together.

"Hey there, Step Sis," Paulie said immediately, giving her a brotherly hug.

There was a silent but collective breath of relief as Paulie's quick thinking momentarily settled everyone's nerves. In a heartbeat, Callie and Paulie exchanged glances — so meaningful, so rife in impropriety, yet so quick they were imperceptible to Jackson and Frankie.

"You and Jackson have an incredible place here. I'd give anything for Ma to see Frankie's new home. Her eyes would light up so bright..."

"Yeah, wouldn't they?" Frankie agreed, putting her arm around Paulie. "She'd be so happy for me."

"I'll bet she already is," Paulie said comfortingly, stealing another glance at Callie while there was still an acceptable reason to do so.

Callie's searching blue eyes looked back at him, but they quickly aborted their mission before Frankie could notice.

"Callie and I are going to the den to listen to some music," Jackson announced brightly. "Right down that hallway, first door on the right, if you need us. I think maybe you two might like a little time alone together in Frankie's new home."

"Thanks, Jack," Paulie said, with a pained yet growing respect the man who was Callie's husband.

"You're welcome," Jackson said, feeling more comfortable with his new brother-in-law.

"Come with me, my meadowlark," Jackson said, wrapping his arm around Callie, while the eyes in the back of her head saw Paulie wince and her heart felt his pain. "I'll even let you pick the CD." His voice trailed off as they walked down the hall. "We've got Fred, Wolfgang, Franz, Johann, Ludwig..."

"How about some John, Paul, George, and Ringo," Callie said at her playful best as they turned into the room.

Paulie stood in the foyer, waited until they were out of sight, and then smiled at his sister. This was her time; she was the star of the show.

"I've never been more happy for anyone in my life, Mary Frances. You sure had me scared. Real scared. I wasn't so sure you'd come around."

"I see *you* have," Frankie said cautiously, nodding her head toward the room where Callie and Jackson had just entered. "*Haven't you?*"

"Working on it," Paulie said. "That's the best I can do. Jack's a good guy. I actually really enjoy the lucky SOB's company. And although I hate to say it, those two look good together." Paulie brushed off the niceties like an unwanted suitor. "Well, shall we go take another look at your new place? Together this time?"

Paulie took his sister's hand as they entered the apartment. "It really is beautiful, Mary Frances. So spacious and tasteful. I love the built-in bookshelves in the alcove. But aside from all that — it's so *light* in here! You can actually see real colors in here. Look, there's blue, and green, and over there, damn, why if there isn't yellow! Colors! In the home! Now, isn't that a concept."

Frankie gave him a loving but dirty look.

"You're going to just shine living here, I know it." He took a seat on the window bench beneath the bay window, beckoning for Frankie to join him. "Yeah, I'm sure of it. Living here will make you glow, just like that moon out there."

Frankie glanced out the window wistfully. "You never knew this," she told him, "but I hung that moon."

"You did, huh?" Paulie said, his eyes gleaming. "All by yourself?"

"Sure did." Frankie paused to reflect. "You don't think it's crooked, do you?"

"All depends on how you look at it," Paulie said thoughtfully. "Looks perfect to me."

Frankie smiled and looked up into the sky. "That's what Ma said," Frankie told him. "That it's as the eyes see it…it's only crooked if I see it that way."

Paulie smiled tenderly. "Ma say anything else?"

"That when I look up into that sky I should be proud, because I've done a wonderful job of hanging the moon."

"Ma was right," Paulie said, giving her a loving squeeze as tears of unknown origin fell from his eyes. "In all my life, I've never seen a more beautiful moon than the one I'm looking at right now, and I couldn't be more proud of my big sister."

"This is really getting way mushy," Frankie said. "At least for us. But who gives a flying—"

"Yeah, who gives one of those?"

I love you, Paulie," she said, resting her head on his chest as she continued to admire her handiwork in the night sky.

"Right back atcha, Mary Frances, with every bit of my heart."

THE END

Printed in Great Britain
by Amazon